INTRODUCTION

In the course of my collaborative project with Richard L. Tierney in a Simon of Gitta novel (*The Gardens of Lucullus*), I had done a great deal of research into the personalities and history of the Roman Julio-Claudian dynasty. *Lucullus* deals with the conspiracy of Messalina in 48 AD and is concerned with the dramatic action encompassed over several days during the reign of Claudius.

While waiting for *Lucullus* to sell (that wouldn't happen until 2001), I felt ready to do another novel just one year later (1982). Because my original research had been so extensive, I had information enough for seeding more than a single novel. I therefore thought it would be sensible to write another adventure set in the Rome of the same period. Long before this, I had become interested in the life of Caligula, who had reigned during this period. Caligula had, in fact, been already featured twice in the Simon of Gitta stories. For almost two thousand years, the mad emperor has been held up as an example of how bad the head of a tyrannical government can be.

I wanted my novel to more fully flesh out the Caligula story. In "The Ring of Set" (set in 37 A.D.), Caligula becomes Tiberius' successor. Simon would not meet with Caligula again until the last days of the emperor's life, in the story "The Scroll of Thoth" (41 A.D.). That meant that the whole of Caligula's reign was left for me to explore. I was ready to fill in some of the events of this period. This time I would be going solo. Richard and I had only lately completed *Lucullus* and I felt it was much to soon to impose upon his time for another major work. He had his own busy life and the 80's was the period when most of his Simon stories were being written. He had, in fact, only lately completed his solo novel *The Drums of Chaos*.

So, my book stood in need of new heroes. I had introduced into *Lucullus* a good-natured, rollicking gladiator character named Rufus Hibernicus, who was a very rare specimen—an Irishman living in imperial Rome. (This was an echo of Robert E. Howard, with his consistently Irish heroes). I had liked working with Rufus very much, but instinct told me that he would best serve the plot of my new book in a supporting role.

So, who should be my main hero? I wanted a mover and a shaker. That meant warrior with gusto; that mean sorcery. I wanted a fresh point of view and the idea of a German barbarian hero seemed appealing. Having been interested in the lore of myths and legends since my high school days, I already knew the story of the Ring of the Nibelung. From my reading, I had taken away the impression that it was a powerful and very evil token of magic, destroying the lives of any who came into contract with it. What would happen, I wondered, if this magic ring was to arrive in ancient Rome just before the reign of Caligula?

Next question. What was the power of the ring? The main source material for the ring is modern. The four operas of Richard Wagner's Ring of the Nibelung are surprisingly vague on details pertinent to the ring. Oddly, too, the main source that Wagner presumably used, the 14th century *Nibelungenlied*, seems not to mention the ring at all and is even fuzzy on who or what are the Nibelungs. However, I had more and better information on the ring (called Andvaranaut) from a book reconstructing Northern lore, written by the 19th Century mythographer Viktor Rydberg of Sweden. For any reader or writer interested in Germanic lore, I would recommend consulting the pertinent books of Rydberg. While stodgy academic mythographers come, go, merely parroting safe and derivative ideas, Rydberg's work has stood the test of time and all of his mythological studies have been translated into English.

But all ancient lore tends to come across as vague to modern tastes, so I felt I had to clarify things. I present Advaranaut as an enhancer of a wizard's magical spells. Basically, it supplies the user with the magical *mana* he needed to successfully cast the spells that he already knows. But the ring was demonic in nature, created to be used by demons to bring about the end of the world. Short of that, it was capable of drawing ill fortune upon anyone who was reckless enough to use it. (Even the mighty dragon Fafnir was brought to his doom as a result of his obsession for hording the baleful token in his lair.)

Over all, the plot for my new book was taking shape. A German wizard would journey to Rome to try to retrieve the ring and prevent the resurgence of its ancient evil. But should this German be old or young? The saga of the ring is backed up by ancient lore, suggesting age. But a sword and sorcery tale is best presented in the context of deeds of daring. My solution was to feature both an old and a young wizard, the latter being the disciple of the former. The old wizard finds the general location of the ring and the young wizard is then forced to complete the task—made especially difficult because he is unseasoned, both as a warrior and as a wizard. The tale would shape up as a classical coming of age story.

So far, so good. But this was the world of Richard L. Tierney, and that meant that I needed to introduce into my pages the influences of Robert E. Howard and H.P. Lovecraft. The story by its very nature fits into the mode of Howard, i.e. a barbarian warrior coming up against a decadent civilization. Moreover, I was able to make use of Howard's version of the Dwarves, the evil Children of the Night. As for Lovecraft, I had particularly enjoyed those Mythos stories that draw in drawn elements of actual ancient lore

HEIR OF DARKNESS

by

GLENN RAHMAN

ISBN-10: 1-953215-63-7
ISBN-13: 978-1-953215-63-5

Published by Pickman's Press
Edgewood, NM, USA
www.pickmanspress.com

Table of Contents

and magic. To my knowledge, no other story had previously tried to unite Northern lore with the Cthulhu Mythos. Instinct told me that it should not be an especially difficult undertaking.

At this stage, I thought I had the grounding for a good story. Extrapolating on what I had, the tale would relate the adventures of a brave but inexperienced warrior who was trained in sorcery (i.e. a rune warrior). He arrives in Rome, a city so strange and complex that a barbarian from Germania has trouble understanding it. I decided to make him an Engle (i.e. an Angle, the ancestral stock of the English people.) And his quest is challenged by a powerful rival, a sorceress who has been sent by a coven of Northern witches to gain the Ring for their own people. This evil agent is aided by a lackey-helper who is a half-blooded Dwarf and a minor sorcerer in his own right.

Meanwhile, Caligula is just coming to the throne. The story of Caligula explicitly continues the story that Richard Tierney started in "Ring of Set." Caligula has used evil magic to curse Tiberius' luck, leading to his death. Unfortunately, that dark magic is hard to lay to rest, becoming a trap for Caligula, too. As *Heir of Darkness* unfolds, Caligula begins a years-long struggle to save his soul, which initiates a course of dire events that will take him from being a merely bad and ambitious young man to becoming the overtly mad and vicious character that we read about in the ancient histories. What can one say? Bad things happen when one gets involved with the dark power of the Old Ones.

Thus the story stands—with Romans, barbarians, sorcerers, witches, gladiators, manly men, and a good share of beautiful women, all getting into the action.

Though written later than *The Gardens of Lucullus*, *Heir of Darkness* was published first. Completed in 1985, it would be released in 1989 by New Infinities, a short-lived company founded by the *Dungeons and Dragons* creator Gary Gygax. How short lived? The company failed to last long enough for me to even collect so much as my first royalties check!

Well, life is hard—a maxim that Osricus the Engle will confront in the course of the book you are now holding.

— Glenn Rahman, 2023

FOREWORD

Although Germanic mythology is closely identified with the medieval Vikings, the author of this adventure accepts the persuasive arguments of those scholars who hold the view that the lore of the Northland was the common heritage of all Germania's far-flung tribal groups and that it developed contemporaneously with classical mythology.

THE DEMON

PROLOGUE

"Where is the wizard Loderod?" the tall Greek demanded as he twisted his fingers in his captive's hair.

The victimized woman winced, but a sudden scream sounded behind the Greek. An *optio* and several legionaries were manhandling a second group of captives up the weedy hill.

"Here are the additional Germans you wanted, Zenodotus," said the low-ranking officer of the raiding party, wiping his soot-stained face with his arm.

"Bind them and put them on their knees in a circle around that stone," commanded Zenodotus. He was pointing to a large, flat, and nearly-square stone slab some four yards wide which occupied the summit of the hill. Then he resumed his interrogation.

"Tell me, barbarian hag, where is Loderod?"

"Mercy, master," the village woman gasped. "He's gone; there is plague among the Cherusci tribe. They asked him for aid two days agone!"

Zenodotus pushed her away, looking satisfied. A plague—yes, one spun from sorcery, he had no doubt. The German witches whom he had won to his cause had taken his gold for promising to lure away the rune-wizard. The Southern mage did not care to confront the most feared magician of the Rhineland. Amongst the priestly mountebanks of Egypt and Syria he knew where he stood, but the famous power of this Teutonic sorcery made him cautious.

Aye! The latent wizardry he sensed upon this knoll hung so thickly, so oppressively dark, that it almost choked off his breath. Yet he had come a long way to please his emperor and was determined not to fail....

Zenodotus signaled to his apprentice. The Egyptian boy drew a burning splinter from the campfire that he'd been tending and passed it to his master. The wizard placed it an already-prepared brazier to light the incense, which spewed a cloud of pungent effluent above the hilltop.

The apprentice subsequently took a box of arborvitae from their gear and handed it to his master. Opening it, the Greek removed a silver ceremonial sickle, its ivory handle and curved blade inscribed with hieroglyphs. The Egyptian priest who had sold it to him claimed it came from a vanished land far older than their own, Stygios, where the darkest sorcery had been practiced.

Reaching down, Zenodotus forced the tribal woman up to her knees. Holding up her chin with one hand, the Greek raised his sickle high with the other. He spoke in low tones, but his final words boomed:

"List, ye gods, let the debt of life and blood be paid!
Let by magic be moved that which magic has laid!"

He deftly cut the captive's throat and threw her thrashing body aside. In the aftermath, the murderer went around the circle of prisoners, dealing out ritual death to each in turn. The legionnaires blanched to behold such casual slaughter, but none considered impeding a wizard who was so high in Caesar's favor.

With a scowl of distaste, Zenodotus snatched a rag from the benumbed fingers of the Egyptian boy, saying, "Now, back, all of you, except Khet." He paused to wipe the gore from his hands with the piece of sacking. "Back I say, or let your souls be blasted! Boy, bring me the ceramic jar!"

The wizard stepped to the edge of the basaltic slab and contemplated its surface while the optio led his squad farther down the hill. Zenodotus commenced walking around the stone, sprinkling a trail of red powder from the earthenware vessel that Khet had passed to him, not stopping until he had made an unbroken ring all around the stone. Finally, taking a stance behind the brazier and breathing deeply of the incense, he recited a chant in a tongue which none of his listeners understood:

"Shadab serdukeret heiwan!" he shouted. "Let it be done!"

His apprentice felt the ground tremble with vibrations, which rapidly grew stronger until the hill rumbled. As Khet watched, the stone slab stirred with a groan and slowly pivoted back to balance on one narrow edge. It teetered for only a moment before toppling backwards, breaking into many fragments upon the earth.

The frightened boy stared in expectation—but saw nothing within save for a square bed of ice.

From behind the brazier, Zenodotus bellowed: "Rise, demon, and heed my commands!"

A bluish vapor wound up through the ice and gathered into a cloud above it. The effluent quickly thickened, coalescing into a Cyclopean shape. The astonished Egyptian lad dropped to the ground and cringed; the Romans, who had been watching from the lower slope, saw enough of the tableau to rout in all directions.

The materializing figure was roughly manlike, but not even Rome's strongest gladiator had ever possessed such massive shoulders and arms. Though it loomed fifteen feet above the stone, fully half of its shape must still have remained beneath the ice. It resembled a barbarian warrior garbed in pelts and holding an ax of gigantic proportion. Its form was plastered over with hoarfrost and sharp icicles hung from its crude wrappings and brutish face.

"Your life is forfeit, mortal!" the demon declared, its exclamation like a wintry blast. "None of Heid's creatures may disturb the seal upon this spot and live! Your destruction is written into the runes which has called me forth from Jotunheim to ward this spot!"

"We do not serve Heid, ugly one!" Zenodotus answered with bravado. "You have no power over us here, but by the spell of the Chthonioi I command you to depart! Return to the netherworld from which Loderod raised you long ago!"

"I obey no weakling!" The troll vomited a numbing gust through its cavernous throat. The Greek shivered from the permeating cold, but the worst of the blast had been mystically contained behind the red-powder barrier.

"Your strength is nullified by my spells!" Zenodotus informed the puffing troll. "I bind you! Accept me as thy master!"

The hillock trembled with the intensity of the ice-demon's rage. It struck the ax against its invisible prison, and though the blows made dazzling flares as they met the magical barrier, the creature's might was much less than the strength of the wizard's conjuring.

"Enough!" bellowed Zenodotus, holding up a rod of green glass. "As I break this wand, the unnatural spells which maintain you in this sphere are sundered! Begone!" He shattered the rod against a basaltic fragment, chanting: *"Ptepihu ni Nyarlo!"*

The entity received the words of power like a mighty physical blow. Its density thinned and, a moment passing, it faded to a ghostly outline. When this, too, had vanished, Zenodotus could no longer sense the chilling presence of the troll.

Although weary, the conjurer staggered to the rim of the ice-bed and looked down. Its top portion had already thawed into slush. The Greek drew a symbol-cut, wooden rod from his garments and waved it above the pool of melt-water. It was a witching-wand, and its tug urged him to step into the water, no longer very cold. Zenodotus' wading came to a pause over the very center of the cavity.

Khet, at last uncovering his eyes, realized that the demon had been vanquished. He watched his master, uncertain about what it was he sought. He observed the wizard pressing the tip of his wand into the icy water and, with it, scooped up something, the sight of which transformed his face with triumph.

"Come here, boy," Zenodotus commanded, excitement making his tone waver.

As Khet edged closer to his mentor, he saw a heavy, masculine-looking ring dangling from the end of the wand—golden and bearing peculiar markings. What could the little device be good for, the youth wondered. Was it *this* that had enticed his master to risk life and limb in the barbarian wilderness? Why had he needed to claim it at such a terrifying risk?

"Put out your hand, Khet," the sorcerer instructed him. Obediently, the Egyptian extended his palm. When the cold ring slid from the wand and dropped into his hand, a shiver ran up the lad's arm to the very center of his breast. Startled, he looked askance at Zenodotus.

"You will have the supreme honor," the Greek told him, "of personally carrying our trophy to Emperor Tiberius himself."

The Ring of Sorcery

CHAPTER I

"Put that man in bonds!" commanded Tiberius Julius Caesar Augustus, second emperor of Rome.

A hush fell over Caesar's banquet guests. A moment before, Tiberius had casually busied himself reading the report concerning a prisoner's interrogation. Now finished, he glanced up, his ulcerous face showing no more emotion than a lizard's. He vaguely pointed to a section of the table and his cracked-voice gave out an arrest order to his Praetorian Prefect, Macro. All eyes turned in alarm toward the master of the world. An order of arrest issued by Tiberius Caesar was tantamount to a death sentence.

Doubt crawled across Naevivus Sutorius Macro's face. The tall, strong-looking soldier glanced uncertainly at the emperor's grandson Gaius and, next to him, Agrippa, the Jewish prince. Either of the pair might have been indicated by the emperor's sweeping gesture. Both princes had gone equally pale. Macro swallowed hard. If his patron Gaius fell now, all of their cunning plotting would come to naught. But he had to make some sort of reply immediately or risk the emperor's ire:

"Which man do you ask me to bind, O Princeps?"

Tiberius pointed a beringed finger at the diners. "*That* man! And I ask nothing. My words command!"

Macro stood up quickly. "Do you order me to bind Marcus Julius Agrippa, Imperial Majesty?" Macro did not care what befell the prince from Judea. In fact, he would have happily seen the man gone. Agrippa was his chief rival for the friendship of the emperor's grandson. But a single break in the web of Gaius' conspiracies could bring the young man tumbling down, and Macro with him.

"Yes, dolt! I mean Herod Agrippa!" the old man rasped, using the prince's nickname. The elegant, middle-aged wastrel was a grandson of Herod the Great, but in Rome only amounted to a court hanger-on of no real importance.

"It shall be done!" shouted Macro, saluting from his deep, massive chest. "Guards!"

"Augustus!" the Easterner blurted, but the malignant stare of the Roman emperor cut him short. Agrippa glanced to Gaius, the thin, blond young man whose good regards he had been cultivating for months. Alas, Tiberius' anger always terrified the youth—his grandson by adoption, but also his nephew by blood. Gaius would not meet the Jew's glance. Instead, he gazed down into his bowl of candied fruit, his lanky body shrinking into itself, as if to tell the Judean prince that he was on his own.

Agrippa sat, stunned, until the Praetor's guardsmen laid hands upon him. One snapped an iron cuff around his wrist and locked the other end of the manacles to his own left forearm.

"Take him outside!" the emperor said. "At my convenience, I will give orders concerning him to Macro."

The guards dragged the staggering Agrippa away. When they were out of sight, a sigh passed through the room. But Gaius' personal distress was not yet lifted. He stole a glance at his grandfather's face, and thought he saw an expression of disgust. But the old man at once shifted away from his wastrel heir and composed himself.

Tiberius, calming, said to Macro: "Clear the room, Prefect. I would interrogate the German prisoners now."

Senior servants urged the distinguished diners from the hall, and all of them were glad to leave. Gaius and Zenodotus exchanged hopeful looks. The Alexandrian scholar had grown very thick with the imperial prince of late.

"Zenodotus," Tiberius called after the man, "you will remain with me."

Gaius looked questioningly at the impeccably-dressed Greek, but Zenodotus only shrugged and then, bowing smoothly, approached his imperial master. Tiberius bade him to stand behind his dining couch chair, but said nothing to him just then.

As soon as the last dinner guests were gone from the hall, a half dozen Germanic barbarians under guard were ushered into it. They were dressed for travel in their native attire. Most sported bronze decorations and armlets, but the apparent leader of the group looked the most barbaric, simple though his costume was.

The later appeared to be seventy years old or more, his long, thin hair tumbling over his leather-cloaked shoulders. His modesty was safeguarded by no more than a woolen hip-wrap. He wore no ornaments other than a dark disk that dangled from a thong around his wizened neck. This bore the relief of a symbol which Zenodotus had seen occasionally during his travels along the Rhine. It was a stick-like figure that the barbarians regarded as a sacred symbol representing divine power.

Tiberius studied the barbarians from his couch. They had come to Tusculum demanding to see the emperor, but in a manner so aggressive that Macro had taught them imperial protocol by means of a thrashing and imprisonment. Interviewed in confinement, they turned out to be distinguished men from the Mattiaci, a friendly tribe dwelling on the right bank of the Rhine. But no business of the Mattiaci had brought them into Italy. They were merely guides for the man leading them—a person of no certain affiliations. This elder had come to demand the return of a certain sacred object taken, months before, from a German village by agents of Caesar.

It was not hard for Tiberius to guess which object was meant. Zenodotus had lately come from the North bearing what he claimed to be his supreme prize—a ring cut with strange foreign letters. The Greek had told him that the annulet represented the most potent of all the barbarian magicks, a source of strength, health, and long life. At first Tiberius had felt quite ill after donning it, but before his doctor could arrive he had arisen from his couch feeling like a new man, full of vigor and energy.

"I remember you, Tiberius Caesar," the old man spoke up in barbarous Latin. Tiberius, who had spent years campaigning across the Rhine, could understand the tribal patois without much trouble.

One guardsman lifted his rod, intending to silence the ancient, but the emperor stayed his hand with a gesture. "You surely are old enough to remember me, graybeard. Many were the tribes between the Rhine and the Elbe, the Danube and the Frisian coast, that I reduced to slavery. Many were the red-haired chieftains who arrived at my camp begging for alliance, lest they be utterly destroyed by our legions. Tell me true, what is said of Tiberius in Germania to this day?"

The old tribesman's eyes held weariness, but not fear. "My people say Tiberius Caesar became the savior of our land when he blunted the keen sword of his son. That one, allowed to wage war, would soon have undone the work of the chieftain Hermann and covered Germania with blood."

The Roman's brow thickened. The "son" the barbarian referred to was Tiberius' nephew Germanicus, a man whom he had resented for his popularity, but had been forced to adopt under orders from Emperor Augustus. Germanicus had been hand-picked by the late Emperor as the only one worthy to take the purple after Tiberius. Tiberius' own successes in Germany had come hard-won. But, contrariwise, the gods seemed to bless everything that Germanicus attempted in either politics or war with easy success. The young man's victories against the tribesmen had paled Tiberius' earlier ones. Tongues had started to wag that his "son" should become co-emperor, or even that Tiberius should retire early and let Germanicus reign in his own right. Hence, it had been necessary to withdraw him and his army from Germania before they won any decisive victory. Tiberius was willing to lose an entire province if it would prevent his rival's star from shining any brighter.

"I know the impudence of your race," Tiberius muttered, "or else that remark would have cost you your life. Is death what you seek, Old One?"

"Nay, Lord," the tribesman answered. "Least amongst men do I wish to die. For the greater portion of my life, my spirit has been foredoomed to Nifelhel, where the damned are tortured. Yet, do what you will with my body, Great One. Execution can shorten my time by very little. I have read the runes and know that the door for my passage out of Midgard is about to open.

"The powers which oppose us both have planned well, Mighty Caesar. Osric, my son, is as yet ill-prepared to succeed me. But still I have time to ask, nay, *demand* from Caesar that which threatens all the world. If the famed Tiberius is as wise a ruler as once he was a crafty chieftain of warriors, he will pay heed!"

"You, who can barely stand under the weight of your stinking cowhides, dare to make demands of *me?*" the emperor scoffed. Nonetheless, his temper held; barbarians talked like children, and children amused Tiberius Caesar. "I do not know whether to send you back to your cold swamps with no more than a scarred back, or to hand you over to my swordsmen. Your life hands in the balance, Ancient One. Do not weary me with threats of mythic doom."

Now the Roman leaned a little forward. "Tell me, is this the ring that you want so much?" He spread the fingers of his right hand before his nose. The old tribesman beheld the circlet with a fast-changing gamut of emotions: awe, pain, fear, need, resignation.

"It may be too late for you," the old man warned. "Your die must have been cast from the moment that you first fitted it upon your hand."

"Are you prophesying doom for your emperor?" Tiberius demanded with a scowl. "That is a capital crime!"

"My life runs like water from a clock. Wherefore should I fear to speak my mind? Heed my words and be made wise. Treat with me as one honorable chieftain to another."

Tiberius shook his lank, thin locks. What effrontery for a miserable forest chieftain to consider himself on the same level as Imperial Caesar! The Germans had not changed in the last forty years; they still talked in endless circles, all the while complimenting their own directness of speech.

"It was *you* who usurped the ring!" the old German accused suddenly, pointing a bony digit at Zenodotus, the dapper man standing behind his master. "You took it but live still. No doubt you have acted in cunning and foreknowledge to avoid its curse so far. Or does it have a purpose for you? Does it merely prefer to make your destruction come slowly and painfully, letting it unfold with the measured pace of a turtle? Tell me, thief, did your own hand bear the ring away from my village, or did you place its pollution into the hapless palm of an underling?"

Zenodotus flinched. Having studied the legends surrounding the ring, he had judged it prudent to impart it over to his apprentice to carry. The boy had broken both legs in the Montgenevre Pass. He had screamed for three days before the guard commander put him out of his misery.

"Have you nothing to say?" the old German chided Caesar. "I give you warning. If you have but passingly touched the evil token, it will remember and repay you. Once my arts might have purified and saved such a reckless one, but now… but now…." His head fell forward as if it had become very heavy.

"It is *I* who ask the questions," the emperor reminded him.

"He knows nothing, O Princeps," interrupted Zenodotus. "I have studied the German race. They live their lives guided by superstitious nonsense."

"Is *this* nonsense?" Tiberius demanded, shoving his ring into the soft, carefully-cut beard of the Greek. "What has become of your boast of having wrested from the barbarians their greatest magic for my glory?"

"I—I have done what I have said. But this man, who is he? A half-naked curmudgeon…."

"I am Loderod, who serves the god Loder," the old German declared firmly. "List, Tiberius Caesar. More than one hundred summers have I seen, and this by the power of the ring Andvaranaut, or in spite of it. Since days long past, since the times when these thin limbs rippled with sinew, when these hoary locks shone like dark copper, I have kept the ring away from those who created it for evil purposes in years gone by."

" 'From those whom created it,' old man?" echoed Zenodotus. "And you call *me* a thief?"

"Be silent, Zenodotus," growled Tiberius, foam at the corner of his lips. "You, Loderod, truly claim to have lived a hundred years and that this ring is responsible?"

"A small blessing, if such it may be called. Rather would I say it has done no more that subject me to a fatal burden, and the weight of it has been a torture to bear."

"What burden?" scoffed Tiberius. "A long and robust life, if I take your measure correctly?"

"Every life must end in death, Caesar of Rome! He who practices forbidden sorcery is lost, even if he has used its evil for the enactment of good. There is no escaping the penalty for sorcery. Woden himself once paid a harsh price for using dark magic to deliver the Golden Mead out of the maw of Jotunheim's monsters. Whosoever wields the ring forfeits hope, but if he has used it with wisdom, he gives hope to the world. That is my comfort now, as I die."

"You will not die until you have unlocked for me the secret of this ring's magic power. What ritual has given you longevity? How have you warded off the unavoidable curse that you claim it carries?"

"You will have no longevity, Caesar of Rome. The ring is not meant for you. You are not of the Magic Blood."

"Dog! My blood is finer than any! You will do as I demand."

"Nay, Caesar of Rome. I behold that shadows are crowding about you. Your life is already in ebb-tide, but if you do as I counsel, you may yet be spared the agonies of Nifelhel—a blessing that I cannot bestow upon myself."

The stubborn set of the old man's jaw told Tiberius that only prolonged torture could ever hope to break down such barbarian intransigence.

The emperor looked to his guards. "These common ones can go to the stone quarries of Libya. But turn the old one over to Macro. Take care not to slay him. He knows many things I wish to learn them."

"Yes, Imperial Caesar," saluted the attending centurion. At the latter's signal, the Praetorians ushered the Germans away.

When Tiberius and Zenodotus were alone, the emperor turned uncertainly to the Greek. "What do you make of the wizard's warning, Zenodotus?"

"I think he wants the power for himself and nothing more. But it is your right to hold the annulet. It is the greatest magic found in all Barbaria, Princeps. Do not doubt it!"

"I have lived so long as I have by trusting no one." Tiberius sighed. "I wish Thrasyllus was still alive," he mused. "I could trust him, and he was never wrong when he scried into the future. Now I am forced to depend on lesser wizards who court the favor of my worthless grandson Gaius." Suddenly the emperor twisted the circlet off his forefinger and pressed it into Zenodotus' palm.

Taken aback, the man near dropped the accursed thing. His features flickered with unhappiness, but he quickly regained his composure.

"You shall keep and study the ring until we are quite certain that it is safe for me to wear," the emperor ordered. "And don't seek to deceive me. I will find out." He sighed. "I think these questions may be easily answered if this Loderod could be made to speak."

"I will carry out your commands successfully, great Caesar!" the Greek declared.

Tiberius's expression darkened. "Did you know beforehand about the legend of the ring's curse?"

"No, Dominus! Of course not! There is no legend, no curse. The old man is a liar, a charlatan out for himself. Never would I endanger you!"

The emperor swung away from his chief magician. "I hope that is so—at least for your sake."

THE BARBARIANS

CHAPTER II

"A party of seven-odd German barbarians led by an old man?" repeated Appius Saurcus, the innkeeper. He stroked his tiny, pimply chin thoughtfully. Small eyes twinkled behind folds of greasy flesh while they studied the three men across from him.

The oldest of the strangers, he who had done all the talking, was undoubtedly Italian. Dressed in a sad brown tunic, he wore a broad-brimmed hat and a traveler's cloak. His hair had retreated to a thin gray frizzle between large, heavily-lobed ears. His browned face was wrinkled and weathered. Saurcus would have taken him for a bankrupt trader just back from the barbarian wilds. His accent was not typically Italian, though. It was as if he had been living away from his own kind for a long time.

"As a matter of fact, I think I can help you," Saurcus said, nodding. "Tusculum's a small place; most of the people hereabouts are senators or *equites* with their servants. People take notice of visitors who seem out of place. About five months ago, a band of barbarians came to town. It's unusual to have free barbarians visiting. If their sort comes at all, they're usually in tow to a master, like your two boys."

He gestured toward the young men, each nineteen or twenty years of age. Seated on either side of the Italian, one was fair-skinned, but dark of hair and eyes. A pretty young Adonis, Saurcus grinned privately. The innkeeper pegged him for the half-breed son of a barbarian woman and some Roman soldier or trader. Saurcus cocked one eye—yes, there *was* a resemblance betwixt the youth and the old man, particularly in the chin and nose.

"What befell the Germans?" asked the other slave boy, this one's voice being impatient and husky.

The innkeeper took the aggressive one for a full-blood German—red gold hair, dark gold skin, green gold eyes. In truth, there was so much gold about him that he might as well have been one of Midas' victims brought back to life. Saurcus squirmed under the young fellow's gaze. Something about this barbarian was intimidating—and it was something beyond his rangy musculature. He had good looks, but his handsomeness was of harder stamp than his companion's, being long of face with strong cheekbones and a jutting jaw. Women would have liked the fellow about as much as they would the other one, but they would be expecting a harder roll in the hay with the blond fellow.

"That was the month that the emperor Tiberius visited Tusculum," reminisced Saurcus, addressing the old man. "The barbarians wanted an imperial audience, I suppose. If so, they got more than they bargained for! The old goat flew off the handle over something or other and sent them to the rock quarries in Africa."

"Africa?" exclaimed the elderly trader. "*All* of them? Are you sure? One of them must have been an old man of… of very venerable years!"

"Well… a soldier told me that Tiberius tossed one fellow into the local prison, but didn't give any details. With equites and senators being executed every day at Tiberius' command, who worries about the fate of some tick-eaten barbarians?"

"We worry, fat man!" growled the blond barbarian, half rising. "And do not use that Roman scorn-word referring to my people. We are not barbarians!"

"Osric! Sit down!" the old man shouted. "You are in Rome now. Insolent slaves might be thrown to the wild beasts, or even nailed to a cross, for offending a free citizen!"

With a contemptuous snort, Osric checked himself and settled back on the bench

"Listen to your master!" Saurcus advised him with a scathing frown. "This is a civilized country! If you and your sort aren't barbarians, I don't know what the word means! With Jove to witness, I think that the term was *invented* for you Germans!"

Osric's knuckles were white, his teeth clenched, but he held his tongue. The old man gushed apologies which the innkeeper condescendingly accepted.

"If the man you're looking for was thrown into the prison, he might be there yet," Saurcus told them. "We don't have a bad prison, as far as such things go—not a pest hole like the Mamertine in Rome. Our jail is one Tiberius uses to keep people he thinks he might have a use for later…."

The innkeeper broke off suddenly. "*Venus' Tits!*" he cried, heaving to his feet and gaping at the window. The three men turned quickly but saw nothing untoward outdoors.

"He's… gone now," Saurcus muttered bemusedly.

"What did you see?" asked the trader.

"A face at the window—damned queer! A man, I guess—a tiny, hunched-over, brown-faced man who was watching us like a devil from the dark." His hand shaking, the Roman slopped more wine into his beaker and gulped the whole of it down without drawing a breath. "Forget it, friends," he gasped. "It must have been some freak from the Roman circus—a clownish dwarf full of dances and frolics—harmless. Come now, it grows dark. I'll show you and your servants to your quarters."

The old man had asked for the man's least expensive accommodations. Saurcus led them outside briefly, past a stable where not only horses and donkeys were kept, but also pigs, chickens, and geese, too. A row of humble sleeping rooms filled the rear of the building. Saurcus showed them into a vacant room, with a pile of manure just outside the door. The old man paid him and the innkeeper, bowing laboriously, turned away and left.

Besides horse apples, their room also smelled of dust, mildew, and mice. Cobwebs ran a tapestry of dirty filaments from one end of the ceiling to the other. The only furnishing was a bed with a leaking straw mattress. Two bags stuffed with grass lay on the floor, presumably deposited there for the repose of a traveler's servants or children. It was a strange inn to have a name like "The Equites' Palace."

"How can they call this place a 'palace,' Father?" rumbled the dark-haired youth. "From what you have said, palaces are stone halls and each is as large as a whole village. To touch these filthy bags will cover us with lice and fleas."

The old man shook his gray head. "This should warn you, Mar, about how the men of the cities use words. They commonly seek to boast and mislead. The innkeeper calls this a 'palace' not because it is a palace, but because he wishes people to come to it supposing that it is better than it is."

"If the man is a liar and a braggart, why has he not been challenged and slain by those who have seen his 'palace' and have been undeceived?"

"It is hard to explain, my son, but in a civilized land, men are seldom surprised when they are lied to. What the innkeeper does is not deemed something worthy of rebuke. Moreover, if you *do* feel like striking one who has offended you, take care! Men do not avenge their own wrongs here. One who is ill-treated must bring a complaint before a magistrate—a city leader. It is up to such men of status to punish the wrongdoer."

Mar puzzled over the idea. "What sort of people are these Romans? I would be ashamed to run to a city leader for every small problem like a child runs to his mother."

"Civilized life is far different from what you know. Should you dwell in Rome for a time, everything will eventually become clear."

"May Woden grant that I need not remain in such a land for long! As soon as Osric's quest is done, I will waste not a moment returning to the villages of the Chatti!"

The golden boy raised his chin and spoke up. "Calusod, these Romans have so much! Their houses resemble more the work of gods than of men. Fat and healthy are their animals; the mightiest *eorl* of the North does not possess a herd so large as do the simple farmers we've seen along our way.

Where we dwell, the weather is still sharp and frosty; the grass has not yet awakened, and the trees stand barren. But in this land the Roman gods have already spread warmth and greenness. All that sane men seek to win, Rome already owns. So why do its soldiers so often come to conquer our small, poor villages?"

Calusidius, whom the Chatti called Calusod, shrugged. "We Romans not only conquer for riches, but from fear, too. We feared the Greek kingdoms and so gave them no respite from war. We feared the cunning men of Carthage and the daring warriors of Gaul, and so attacked them endlessly until they knelt to the yoke. Since Marius' day, when the Cimbri and Teutones bested Roman armies, Rome has feared the Germans. Forty years ago, Rome conquered Germania to the Elba, robbing and punishing its people without justice or sense. Your people had no peace until they rose under Hermann and destroyed the Roman soldiers. But this humiliation has only made the Romans more fearful and gives them cause for even more wars."

"Strange men, to whom even conquest and a warrior's glory are acts of cowardice," frowned Osric. So much about Rome seemed to run against the grain of common sense. But he did not wish to think about the foolery of the Romans. So much else was crowding his thoughts.

He recalled the day when a host of Roman raiders had struck Loderod's village in the Chatti lands. The hoary sorcerer—or *helrun*, as Osric's people, the Engles, called one who was skilled in the magical arts—chanced to be absent. The Roman leader, a foreign helrun, came to steal a prize he knew was protected there. By means of a bloody sacrifice, this man, Zenodotus, had nullified the spells by which Loderod had warded the much-feared Ring of Sorcery, called Andvaranaut.

When Loderod returned and beheld the disaster, he swore to recover the stolen treasure. By means of his divining sticks and from the reports of German spies across the Rhine, he learned that the raiders were bound for the very house of Caesar himself. Accordingly, he appealed to his Mattiaci friends for aid, since some of them had already visited the empire and were on friendly terms with it.

When Osric returned from the mission that the helrun, his adopted father, had sent him on, the village held only two survivors—Calusidius and his son Mar.

Calusidius was a man who Loderod had held in confidence. The Roman exile had been asked by the helrun to await the youth's return and inform him of all that had happened. He had also agreed to guide Osric to the city of Rome as quickly as possible.

Osric, well disposed to Calusod and his son, wasted no time in commencing their journey. The old Roman had earlier taught him the Roman writing and speech. These lessons continued along the long road into the empire. Calusidius had spoken in detail about the Romans' ways and their strange laws.

Many times, the youths had supposed that the old man was waggishly exaggerating; they often reacted to his assertions with laughter, assuming he was teasing them as if they were children. Osric remembered one such story, to the effect that even if all the towns and villages along their way in Gaul and Italy were placed together side by side, the sum of them would not equal the size of just one city—Caesar's Rome. It had given them pause that some of Calusod's contentions had already been borne out as true as the journey progressed.

While Calusidius accepted the dirty inn room for what it was, Mar was glowering down at the ants and centipedes racing by his clogs. Osric heard from outside what sounded like the padding tread of a hunter. He went to the window to see, for a forest beast was out of place in a land that was given over to tillers, idlers, and vagabonds.

A tall, broadly-built man strode out of the inn-shadow. When the newcomer saw Osric, he smiled and approached unguardedly, like a friend.

Osric stepped warily from the inn room. This was no Roman, but a man of his own race—light-haired, big-boned, and fair-skinned. He wore a long German tunic and walked, Osric noticed, with some stiffness in his right leg.

"The prosperity of Frida be with you, friends," the big man hailed. "Loderod told me that his son Osric would soon arrive from the land of the Chatti. When I heard that men of our sort were seeking about the town to find an old man and a party of Mattiaci, I came as swiftly as I could." He met Osric's glance squarely. "Are you the son of Loderod?"

Calusidius and Mar, behind the Engle, would have spoken, but Osric hissed them to silence, asking: "Are you one of those who guided Loderod into Italy?"

"*Ja,*" grinned the man. "I am Heinwulf of the Mattiaci."

"I heard Loderod mention one that he called Heinwulf," volunteered Calusidius.

"I was away buying provisions when the Romans seized and imprisoned the others," Heinwulf explained. "I lurked about, seeking news of what happened to them. I learned that my countrymen were soon removed from the city, but I also heard that an old German was taken to the prison. There was no help for me to offer, but I have remained in Tusculum, trusting to the gods that I would find the means to bring Loderod succor. Only weeks ago, the Romans released the helrun, contemptuous of his age and helplessness. They had used him cruelly, I fear."

"Where is he now?" asked Osric.

"He lies near to death, asking for Osric hourly. Come, the hut I share with him is not far distant!"

The young Engle motioned Calusidius and Mar to arm themselves. "You bear no weapon yourself," he addressed Heinwulf.

"No… there is no danger," the German replied. "Besides, the law of the Romans forbids the brandishing of arms. While there are so many Romans hereabouts and we are few, it is cautious to observe their customs, ja?"

Osric frowned. What Heinwulf told him was true. The Romans treated those who went forth armed like outlaws, or so Calusidius had said. Because of that, they carried their blades, short swords taken in war from Roman dead, inside their bundles. "Lead on," Osric told their self-appointed guide.

They left the inn and followed Heinwulf along the dark, flagstoned streets of the town. The daylight bustle had fallen to quiet now that sunset's glow was fading. The buildings along the way, some marble, some made of rough-looking tufa blocks, loomed gray in the shadows. Though larger than any German village, Tusculum proper was only a few minutes' walk in breadth. Heinwulf had grown quiet and it was Osric who broke the silence:

"How did you provide for yourself and for Loderod in this strange land?"

"By doing what I could," replied Heinwulf. "I am a strong man and the Romans pay for labor. But it has been hard; I am thankful that Woden has sent friends of Loderod to share my burden."

At the dark mouth of an alleyway between warehouses, Osric moved suddenly, clubbing his fists and dealing his guide a staggering blow between the shoulders. Heinwulf pitched forward and struck the cobblestones with a grunt. Reflexively, the man groped for something under the hem of his tunic. Osric grabbed the fallen one's arm and drove a hard punch into his bearded face.

"Osric!" Mar cried, bewildered. "What are you doing?

"He gives no respect for Loderod, and also lies about being unarmed! See!" He dragged up the German's tunic and uncovered a *gladius,* sheathed in deerskin, strapped to the man's heavy thigh "This is why he limped." Wrenching the weapon free of its sheath, the Engle pressed the point against its owner's neck. "Who do you truly serve? Speak quickly, if you would not be freed of the burden of living!"

Heinwulf's eyes, fear-brimmed, rolled. "It is as I say! You wrong me! I did not conceal my blade from you, but from the Romans!"

"Why go armed? There is no danger! Bah! You lie as badly as you imitate the Mattiaci dialect. I think that the Bructeri speech might flow easier from your serpent tongue!"

"Bructeri?" muttered Mar. That tribe was infamous for its worship of the Jotuns and for making criminal sacrifices.

"I am not Bructeri!" the man protested. "You are young, untutored, and mistaken!"

"Did I mistake that you said Loderod has lain sick for weeks? That makes no sense, not unless he has lost his power over the runes! Loderod would heal himself swiftly, or die if he could not. Your tale is as full of errors as the weaving of a blind woman."

The German kept glancing expectantly into the darkness behind his captors.

"A trap!" cried Osric. "Free your blades!"

At that, the Engle shoved Mar and Calusidius behind himself, then slashed the Bructeri's throat—not the first enemy he had killed. Barely in time did he skip out of reach of the attackers storming up from the rear. Turning at bay, the youth bellowed "Heimdall!" in challenge.

"Heidr-geshod!" answered the attackers, accents that were clearly Bructeri, and their blades came swinging out of the dark. Slashing, dodging, and feinting, Osric fought to keep himself from being encircled as he withdrew down the black maw of the alley.

In another moment, Mar was up beside him, adding to the clatter of blades. Steel glanced off steel, sparking like fireflies as men cursed and vied.

Against the weight of numbers, the pair gave back but slowly, taking cuts and giving them. One of Osric's strokes found its way into a foeman's belly. Yowling, the barbarian went down, getting under his allies' feet, and their disarray allowed Mar to likewise strike true for blood.

"Boys!" came Calusidius' shout from the darkened alleyway. "This way!"

"Break off!" Osric told Mar. "Follow me!" Together, the youths dashed over uncertain ground, leaping over clutters of garbage, making for their elder's position at the throat of an alleyway.

Osric saw nothing in the dark, but heard a bestial grumble. The sound came as a surprise; animals usually fled when men made too much noise. His flesh pimpled from a sense of unseen danger. For an instant, he thought glowing eyes flashed balefully from behind a pile of refuse. Then he heard the pounding of feet behind him as the Bructeri came up to renew the fight. Momentarily, the Engle hesitated between threats.

Suddenly, the Bructeri stepped back for no reason. That was when a vaulting body struck Ostric at his midsection, knocking him head over heels. The attacking thing had not felt human, the force of the blow stronger than a man's could be. Before the warrior could scramble to his feet, something sprung upon him again and a raking pain slashed at his chest. He reflexively struck out with the hilt of his sword and hit something, but the blow felt cushioned by muscle and thick fur.

He heard the Bructeri babbling with surprise. Lights had suddenly appeared near the mouth of the alleyway and Osric heard snatches of Latin. Soldiers—*Roman* soldiers! But the beast-thing pressed the attack, pushing him against a tufa wall, his sword arm pinned between their bodies. Shifting his weight, he broke clear, allowing his freed blade to slash at the creature's underbelly.

The cry the beast gave out sounded almost human. It rolled away, but the lights were almost upon them, carried by armored men. Osric, suddenly, did not feel well. When he turned and sought to flee from the newcomers, he staggered with weakness. Out of the corner of one dazed eye he thought he saw a tiny, manlike shape disentangling itself from the melee and sprinting light-footedly away to be lost in the shadows.

Someone struck him down and the Romans with lanterns started to kick and club him. The pummeling was softened by stinking garbage, and so gave him less injury than it might have.

"Jove!" shouted one of the attackers. "A wolf!"

"A wolf is loose!" another Roman yelled. "You, you, and you! Get after it! Somebody bring up a net! The damned thing must have escaped from some circus!" Men in clattering armor rushed off on the beast's trail.

Feeling increasingly sick and weak, Osric lay there and let the remaining Romans take him in hand. He faintly scanned the lamp-lit alley for Mar and Calusidius. The old man was nowhere to be seen, but Mar was already down, struggling with two soldiers. The Bructeri enemy also seemed to be have been disarmed, held face-first against the walls by Roman who seemed to know how to do their jobs. The Engle wanted to fight free, but there was no more fight left in him. His head was swimming and his limbs had gone feeble.

"What's Tusculum coming to?" the Roman leader rumbled. "Wolves running wild, barbarians fighting one another in the dark of the night?" He prodded Osric with his boot, saying, "Get up and walk!" But a sick, hot darkness was taking over his body and the German was, a moment later, no longer aware of his surroundings.

ALIVE OR DEAD?

CHAPTER III

They had always called him *Caligula*, "Baby Boots." This was his day, his time had come. Not a man alive would ever again dare to be condescending to Gaius Caesar Augustus Germanicus.

Fifty-odd Roman dignitaries looked Gaius' way when he entered the garden.

Silently, the young man surveyed the crowd, immaculate men in purple-trimmed togas and tunics. Originally, having come to Misenum to flatter the ailing Tiberius with their well-wishing, they had stayed as he continued to weaken. Much was at stake. If death took the emperor, the state, the Principate, would doubtlessly fall upon Gaius, a youth of just twenty-four.

The prince they knew conveyed a passable presence. Though not heavily muscled, his color was good, his eyes intensely blue, and his blond hair thick. Macro was looming behind him—a powerful and deadly politician-soldier very protective of Gaius. His intimidating presence added import to whatever the prince intended to say.

"My grandfather, Tiberius Julius Caesar Augustus, is dead!" Gaius announced. At last, the fateful words had been spoken.

The gentlemen of Rome frowned, pursed their lips, and grimaced. Did they dare to believe what Gaius averred? Doubtful glances passed from one to the other, until one of the *eques* found the courage to declare: "Long live Emperor Gaius!" That bold declaration brought his companions to life and they gushed with a mutter of praise and congratulations.

"Rome is delivered from tyranny!" shouted one of them. "A new Germanicus reigns!"

"A new Augustus!" an old senator trumpeted.

While the acclaim went on, Gaius smiled, nodding regally. Macro carefully regarded these men of influence and authority, lowering thoughtfully.

The excitement showed no sign of abating. "To the Tiber with Tiberius!" yelled a high-born wastrel. Not to be outdone, some of the togaed flatters approached Gaius and kissed him—mostly at his gown hem or his hands, but some even put their lips to the young man's smooth-shaved cheeks.

"Let the tyrant's name be erased from all monuments, public and private," came another shout. "Let the world forget that Livia's son ever disgraced the seat of Augustus. A new, benevolent star has risen over the empire!"

"Loyal friends," Gaius proclaimed, raising his soft, white hands, "praise the gods of Rome who have delivered us from slavery to a despot and his foul crew of murderous favorites...."

Macro cleared his throat and Gaius, glancing back, changed his rhetoric hastily. "My so-called grandfather died a bad death, a fit ending to what was an unspeakable life. He lay in a delirium so profound that he could recognize no one, not even myself, his heir, and Macro—that faithful and dedicated mainstay of the Roman state."

"Hear me, leaders of Rome," Macro broke in, his tone being hard and devoid of rhetorical flourish. "For the safety of the state, Gaius Caesar must be proclaimed imperator immediately. That was the will of Tiberius and it is certainly the will of the people of Rome. Dispatch riders will be sent across the empire to spread the momentous news. Soon the sailors and soldiers in Misenum will assemble to hail Gaius emperor. The armies and governors of the empire shall be ordered to make the recognition of the new princeps universal."

The Praetorian Prefect drew his sword and knelt before the emperor-to-be, presenting its decorative hilt to Gaius. "Let me be the first, O Caesar, to offer my sword, my service, and my very life to that one who is the sole legitimate heir of Augustus."

"And I will be the next!" shouted one Equestrian sycophant who had, until lately, been one of Tiberius' most enthusiastic grovellers.

"And me! And me!" echoed other Romans present.

"I accept your homage, Prefect," acknowledged Gaius with heady glee, "and also the homage of all the noble gentlemen of Rome. Rise, friends. I am no Tiberius demanding bowing and fawning from proud, free men."

Suddenly a servant named Menedius burst into the peristyle, shouting: "Masters, the emperor is alive! He asks for his grandson. Please, go quickly, Dominus!"

Faces turned livid. In the few minutes since Tiberius' death announcement there had not been a man there who had not committed the fatal crime of *maiestas*—treason. Smaller offenses than theirs had heretofore cost even greater men their lives.

But of all of them, Gaius was most afraid. With fumbling fingers, he slipped the telltale signet from his treasonous finger and hid it under his girdle. If the youth could have sacrificed the guilty member as his proxy for the crimes committed by his whole being, Gaius would have sliced it off without an instant's hesitation.

As his well-wishers began to draw away, he became the axis of a hollow circle—as if he were a secret leper whose hood had just fallen away from a noseless face. Alone where he stood, Gaius reeled, ready to fall.

"The slave is addled!" Macro bawled toward the backs of the departing. "He saw the wind move the curtains or heard the creak of the bed frame. The emperor is dead! Gaius and I will go to Tiberius' room, reconfirm that fact, and put an end to this nonsense!" He took his patron by the arm to steady him. "Come, Prince—and you too, slave."

He seized Menedius by the scruff and shoved him ahead. Gaius followed them unsteadily. In his swirling thoughts, the imperial youth could almost hear the raw, cracked voice of Tiberius shrieking: *Take that treacherous offal to Capri and throw him into the sea!*

His mind reeling, Gaius imagined rude hands upon his body, felt himself pitched like rubbish into an abyss that had no bottom....

He flashed with anger. "That lying magician swore that Tiberius was cursed to die!" mewed Gaius. "Give me your dagger, Macro—I'll finish the tyrant myself!" Then he backed off. "No... *you* do it! I'll marry your wife Ennia. Your compensation will be the greatest ever seen! You will rule a kingdom of your own! Only kill Tiberius!"

"Speak not so freely!" Macro admonished, glowering at Menedius. The Greek slave, shielding his brown locks with lanky arms, shrank to the floor. "I didn't hear what he said, masters! I heard nothing—*nothing!*"

"No?" rumbled the praetorian. "Then your ears must be clogged. Let me clear them for you." He clamped his thick, calloused palms around Menedius' ears, gave a sudden, powerful wrench, and heard the satisfying snap of vertebrae. Disdainfully, the soldier threw the twitching body to the tiles and, exuding cold formality, said: "Come, my prince. Dead or alive, Tiberius waits."

The youth had by now regained some strength in his legs but still trailed behind Macro like a frightened child. The halls, stairs, and colonnades seemed to tilt and turn around him....

Crossing over the threshold of Tiberius' room, a chill stabbed at Gaius, penetrating his woolen toga.

Faint, mellow light diffused around the room through the variously colored pieces of glass in the windows, and a tiny brazier flame flickered next to the four-posted, silk-curtained bed, put there to warm the sick man. The shadowy figure was covered by costly sheets, and Gaius noted with relief that the emperor was not sitting up, not glowering his way.

Macro approached the wasted, wane body of the geriatric. Standing over the still lich, Macro pinched its cold cheek. "Fah! The old goat is as dead as the Republic!" he said. "That fool Menedius—except for his waking nightmares, he could have been living yet!"

"Are you positive?" Gaius asked with a gulp.

"See for yourself!"

Still lacking confidence, Gaius stepped around the bigger man and peered at the corpse of the man whom he had feared and hated his whole life long. He poked at the body through the coverlets, feeling its cold stiffness. *Tiberius was dead.* Giddy with relief, Gaius removed the signet ring from his girdle and twisted it back onto his finger. But no sooner had he done so than an icy claw shot out from the sheets and locked like an iron shackle around the young man's wrist. Gaius screamed and wrenched away, but the sculptured arm of Capri's bronze Hercules could have held him no more firmly.

In the clumsiness of panic, Gaius fell across the dead man, his face inches from his grandfather's glare. In it a corpse-light flickered that eerily simulated a kind of ghastly life. Gaius lay there, rigid and spellbound. Macro saw the light, too, and stood at a loss to understand it. Then the lich spoke in a sibilant whisper:

"For a life and death, a thing was promised, Gaius Caesar. Payment has come due. We are not patient."

The luminescence vanished from Tiberius' eyes and Gaius sought to pull away, but the clenched fist still held him fast. Macro sprang to his aid, seized the prince's wrist in one hand, the cadaver's in the other, and with his great strength he tore them apart.

Gaius tumbled to the thick carpeting, hysterically gasping.

The Praetorian commander regarded the corpse with one more baffled glance before hastily gathering Gaius up into his arms and retreating with him into the atrium. Two of his officers were already there, drawn by the shouting. They offered their assistance.

Macro waved them away. "The prince is overcome by grief," he jabbered. "Send for Doctor Charicles at once. And… and then tell the gentlemen on the grounds that Tiberius Caesar is dead.

"Most definitely dead.…"

THE OWL

CHAPTER IV

Osric the Engle sought to open his eyes. Something cold and wet was blinding him. He clawed away a sodden cloth with a hand that felt as heavy as a Yule log. The light pained his eyes, but gradually the blur resolved into a gray plaster ceiling marred by cracks and cobwebs. It was daylight; the night was gone. He discovered himself on a blanket on the floor of a modest-sized cubicle. Puzzled to be in an unknown place, he forced himself up on one elbow. That was when someone spoke from behind him:

"Ah, master, you are stronger."

Osric squinted at a plump dark man with a fringe of a beard. "W-Who, who…?" he tried to ask.

"I am called Stechus; I treated your wounds, remember? The master will be pleased to know that you are better." Osric rested his head back on a cushion, vexed to be helpless among strangers. How had he come to be here?

Osric strained to remember what had happened to him. Dimly, he recalled the fight in the alley, his capture by Roman soldiers. The mortification of captivity made him feel his illness even more keenly.

Osric remembered nothing from the lost hours except disconnected snatches of conversation, the movement of shadows, and flashes of strange faces. He thought about Mar and wondered where he was.

When the German next opened his eyes, it was at the touch of a hand. A stranger was above him. He realized that he must have been awakened from another blackout.

"Who… where…?"

"I am called Marcus Julius Agrippa," replied the stranger. "We are both confined in the prison at Tusculum. The night watch took your companions to Rome, but you were too sick to be moved. The centurion in charge here has permitted my personal physician to attend to you. That barbarian friend of yours informed me that your name is Osric, and your father is Loderod. Is that right?"

"Loderod… is he…?"

"Rest for a while and later we'll speak. Your wounds are not severe nor have they putrefied. Nonetheless, you seem to have little strength. Is it possible that your attackers were wielding poison blades?"

Again it became hard to think and a new flush made his face hot. His illness, Osric guessed, was the result of being wounded by the evil beast. The things of darkness could inflame the spirit as easily as they wounded the body. For too long had the necessary cleansing ritual been delayed, and of such things this civilized doctor would know nothing. Never would he be well unless he took a hand in his own healing.

"Bring me bark or a cloth… something to write upon…" he gasped, but the taxing effort caused the whole room to go dark.

"He's fainted again, Excellency," said Stechus.

"Stay by him. Have pen and papyrus ready for him. He cannot be an ordinary barbarian if he knows how to write."

"Yes, Master," the physician said.

The prince of Judea shrugged, stood up, and left the room. The rain-roof of the open porch kept the drizzle off his head. The prison commander, Paulus Didius Norbanus, came hurrying toward him through the rain. Norbanus had been bribed to make the prince's imprisonment as comfortable as possible. Such amenities for those well-off were so common that the law hardly considered the bribery involved in them to be corruption. But Agrippa did not disdain venality when it improved his lot. Besides, Norbanus had a cordial side. At least he wasn't always lapsing into brutality, like his superior Macro would do.

"How does the barbarian fare?" the Roman asked.

"The doctor can't find anything seriously wrong with him, and doesn't know why he isn't making better progress than he is."

"What sort of wound does he have?"

"It appears to have been an animal attack."

"Why are you bothering to help him?"

"Call it a good work. The god of my country honors such things. But, more importantly, something happened to me last September, right after my arrest. I think that the arrival of this young German represents a personal portent for me."

"What can a German vagabond have to do with a prince of Judea?"

"If I told you the truth, you'd probably think me insane or a fool."

"I already think that," the officer quipped, "so on with your tale."

Grinning ruefully, Agrippa began.

"When I was arrested, I was chained to a guard and made to wait outside in the heat for hours. Though it was October, the sun was oppressive. My guard had a bottle to drink from, but wouldn't so much as let me take a sip from the nearby fountain. If Tityus, one of Gaius' slaves, hadn't come carrying a full pitcher, I surely would have fainted."

"What has any of this have to do with the barbarian?" asked the warden.

"It presents a perfect set piece. Listen. After my refreshment, I felt better, but I still expected to have my head lopped off. The waiting was unendurable.

"Now as it happened, I was not the only newly-made prisoner that day. Several German barbarians were led out from Tiberius' villa in chains. Most kept to themselves, but one of them—this old man—approached, saying that he had words for me. Normally, that would not have been allowed, but his own guard was being strangely passive. My guard ordered the elder away, but his words suddenly choked off and he started acting like he was half asleep. I had seen sorcerers put such glamours on men before, and so I suspected that the old one might be a man to be reckoned with. 'What words do you have for me, venerable one?' I asked.

"The hoary German informed me that he possessed the gift of prophecy, and that he foresaw that my present misfortune would soon be happily resolved.

"I thanked him for giving me something to laugh about, but I unfortunately did not have so much as a *semis* to reward him.

"But the man insisted that his gods had bidden him to inform me of what he needed to say.

"So I let him speak. He divined that I would soon be delivered from my bonds and be set free. Even less credibly, he claimed that I would be promoted to the highest dignity and power, that my countrymen would remember me for thousands of years as 'the Great.' He also said that friends who were pitying me now would soon envy my happiness.

" 'In what stars do you read these wonders?' I put to him.

" 'In no stars,' he answered, 'but in that bird that the gods have sent to be an omen of things to come.' He gestured toward a tree and I saw an owl in its topmost branches. 'You will be happy and you will pass on your happiness to your heir. But beware! When you see this bird again, you will have but five days longer to live.'

"I thanked him and said that if what he predicted came to pass, he would not go lacking for a reward.

"In reply, he shook his head and said: 'Soon I shall be beyond reward, lord, except that which I have earned by doing forbidden conjuration with the Black Runes. But I foresee that my son shall pass before you in need and distress. If I have lent you any comfort this day, I bid you to return comfort to him.'

"I asked him how I should know his son, and he replied, 'Know him as Osric, son of Loderod.' "

The amused centurion was listening with skepticism, but Agrippa continued:

"When the Lady Antonia, Tiberius' sister-in-law, heard about my plight she interceded with Macro. I thought then that the German's prediction was coming true. But as the months passed and my imprisonment did not end, my hopes sank very low.

"Then yesterday, when I least expected it, I observed the guards bringing a party of German prisoners out of the magistrate's office. These were clearly wild Germans, neither slaves nor war prisoners. At once my curiosity was piqued.

"I inquired after their names but, except for one, they were a surly lot who would speak to no one. That one was unusual, in that he spoke Latin. His name was Mar, and he was tending to another prisoner, one who had been clawed by an animal of some sort. The stricken one's name, he told me, was Osric, whose father was Loderod!"

"I see!" whispered the warden. "Incredible!"

"I tried to speak to this Osric, but he could not be brought around. Nor could his dark-haired companion tell me more before your guards moved the Germans away. I later learned they had been transported to a gladiatorial school."

"Aye, that's so," nodded Norbanus. "I think our esteemed magistrate gets paid by the head for every poor devil he sends up for gladiator training."

"Well, you know the rest. Osric was too sick to go with them, and so I asked you to allow my physician to see to him."

"A strange story," murmured the officer, pensively stroking his long nose. "If you are to be soon elevated to power and riches, I have not done wrongly in being so patient with all those favors you've been asking for."

"I never forget a friend," Agrippa asserted, "that I promise." The Roman and the Jewish prince clasped hands and then the latter returned to his office and Agrippa withdrew into his cell.

Agrippa reached into his robe and took out a dark disk attached to a thong. It appeared to be composed of mere dross. "When you find my son," Loderod had told him, "and when your cup of happiness is full, pass this, his legacy, on to him."

The Easterner had wondered if the object were not a good luck token or a sorcerous talisman of some sort. The raised figure upon it was not dissimilar to symbols used by the mages of Parthia and India.

Agrippa shrugged. There would be no answers to the questions he had unless the young man recovered.

It had rained, on and off, most of the night, leaving the pre-dawn air clean, fresh, and chill. The young slave Cruptorix, a gardener's assistant, hardly felt the nip in the air as he nestled in the straw beside his mistress' wardrobe-maid, Astyoche. Cruptorix ran his fingertips over her goose bumped flank, causing her to stir in her sleep.

Cruptorix sighed. The Roman woman forbade all liaisons between her servants on pain of flogging. Life wasn't fair. The lady should confine herself to her own illicit liaisons.

Astyoche's eyes opened then and she smiled up into his face. He brought his mouth down to meet hers, kissing her hungrily. His hand went to her small, conical left breast and pinched the nipple sharply.

"D—Don't!" she gasped. "That hurts!"

"I won't, if you'll give me a big hug."

She surrendered to his teasing and rolled toward him, her body pressing softly against the whole length of his own. A clamorous barking of a dog pack broke their mood and she frowned. "Are those the master's hounds?"

"No," whispered Cruptorix throatily, his lips licking the woman's tiny earlobe, "it's not their sound…. Must be the *vigiles'* dogs… hunting some poor escaped slave, I suppose."

"Brrr," shivered Astyoche. "I'd hate to have dogs after me. It's not fair; some women have riches, titles, beautiful clothes, as well as suitors by the score—and what do I get? A strapping if I kiss a man, dogs on my heels if I try to run away."

"Where would you run to?"

"To Rome!"

"What for? To become a whore? You'd make a good one… mmmm."

She pushed him away. "You're so crude! Why don't you talk to me like you did last night? I was nice to you, and now you start calling me names."

"Then we'll both stop talking—it wastes time, and we've got to get back to our beds before the overseers start wondering where we are."

"Did you see that?" Astyoche asked nervously.

"See what?"

"Something slipped through the doors and went behind the hay mound. It looked like a dog."

"It might be one of the vigiles' hounds," conjectured Cruptorix. "Those things can be vicious. We'd better get back into the house. Come on."

Rising quickly, they slipped on their tunics. Cruptorix glanced at the haystack, saw nothing, and took Astyoche by the hand. He led her briskly toward the barn doors in the opposite direction. He pushed them open and stepped outside, only to be wrenched back by a powerful tug from Astyoche—a tug far in excess of the housemaid's natural strength.

He lost his hold on the girl and stumbled. The maid cried out from the shadows and some animal snarled. He saw a frenzy of movement; Astyoche and a gray beast were rolling over the horse droppings, the animal tearing at her.

Reflexively, Cruptorix seized a dung fork, rushed the animal, and stabbed with all his strength. The tines connected with fur and hard muscle.

The beast shrieked and, with a blur of movement, knocked the gardener's leg from under him, its claws cutting incisions into his thigh.

Afraid, Cruptorix scrambled outside, limping on his bleeding limb. "Help!" he bellowed to anyone who could hear. "Help! A wild dog is killing—somebody!"

The snarling of several hounds made the young man whirl. In his dismay, he supposed the brute was from the same pack, but then realized that they were leashed and held in groups of three by uniformed vigiles. An officer ran toward him, demanding: "What's happening?"

"In there—an attack—quick!"

The leader yelled: "Let them loose!" The dogs broke away and darted *en masse* into the stable, which erupted with yelps like Cruptorix had never heard before. In a couple minutes, a vigile came out.

"Wh-What was it?!" the youth moaned. "What attacked Astyoche?"

"An escaped wolf!" the vigil answered impatiently. "We've been after it for more than two days." He pushed the slave out of his way—to safety, perhaps—and shouted, "You men—bring that net up, quick! Some of you get around to the other side! Don't let that thing escape the barn!"

Belatedly, Cruptorix remembered his pain and touched his furrowed flesh, feeling warm rivulets of blood flowing from claw marks. Already distraught, dizzy, and weak, his breath was coming in short, rapid snatches.

The shouting and barking brought many more slaves pouring from the barracks. The slave boy tried to call out to them, but he suddenly lacked the strength.

After a few minutes, two peace officers emerged from the shed, carrying a slight shape between themselves. The crowding slaves gave back to let them through. The vigiles laid their burden down, and the slaves could see that it was the maid Astyoche. Blood covered her and viscera poked through deep wounds. She moaned faintly, but hardly any of the onlookers believed that a woman so mangled could survive for very long. The villa overseer took charge, directing a couple of the farm slaves to carry the dying servant into one of the buildings. Cruptorix tottered, nearly fainting. A moment ago Astyoche had been so beautiful, so full of life. Now she was mangled in a horrifying way, awaiting death. How could something so terrible happen so suddenly, he wondered.

The dogs were brought out, now leashed again, their work done. A moment later three more vigiles came from the barn, dragging something behind them, something ensnared in a net, a dark, furred shape, snarling and struggling. It was a filthy looking thing, though the mesh kept the gawkers from getting a good look at it.

"What do we do with the beast, sir?" one of the net-haulers asked his officer.

"It's a wild and smart killer," the squad-leader replied. "People would cheer to see something like that fighting *bestiarii* in the arena. It's in your hands, *Optio*. First, find out if it escaped from one of the amphitheaters in the area and give it back to them."

"What if it's a wild one from the Apennines, sir?"

"Then find an amphitheater that can use it, naturally! But get a receipt and a fair payment for it."

The optio sighed. Such a job could take a lot of his time, and require him to do the kind of paper work he hated.

THE SCHOOL OF JULIUS CAESAR

CHAPTER V

Ahead of Calusidius lay the object of his quest—the wide, high-walled compound of dark brown peperino stone, the Julius Caesar School for Gladiators. He sighed, despising himself for fleeing the fight and abandoning his son! He had panicked when the Bructeri attacked in Tusculum. The sudden appearance of the wild beast had added to his panic. The shouts, lamps, and swords of the vigiles had recalled for him the terrors of the Roman police. Instinctively, he had fled and left his precious son Mar to the mercies of the people whom he was most afraid of. His terrible failure had to be undone!

Calusidius had learned in Tusculum where local prisoners were confined. He went to the site in full darkness and slept in a grove of trees. In the morning, the prison clerk who received him said that their centurion didn't accept private petitions and he would have to take his problem to the magistrates. The old father had then withdrawn miserably, afraid that his name and crimes of old might still be remembered. What if he was recognized as a fugitive? How could he help Mar if in prison himself?

For the whole morning he watched from out of sight, hoping to learn some information of Mar and Osric from persons leaving the prison. But when the gates opened, a cart containing several German prisoners joggled out. Calusidius spotted Mar chained to one side of the vehicle, surrounded by his fellow captives, the Bructeri assassins. The grim demeanor of the guards warned the old Roman against hailing them. Instead, he dashed back to the gate sentries and begged one of them to tell him where the cart was taking the captives.

"To the Julius Caesar School in Rome," he was told. His heart trembled. *His* son, being sent to a gladiatorial school? That was a sentence of imminent death! Dismayed, he raced after the vehicle. But the capitol city was twenty-five Roman miles away, and about halfway along his journey, the old Roman fell down exhausted. Though he wished to rest for only an hour, he fell asleep on a grassy spot and lost more time than he intended.

He pressed on and, from time to time, managed to buy a little food at roadside farms. Upon reaching the second milestone before Rome, darkness was coming on. A row of tombs along the Via Tusculana offered the best nighttime sheltering available.

With first light, Calusidius again set forth, again walking the narrow, winding streets of Rome for the first time in so many years. The byways were just starting to fill with schoolboys, poor-looking men in old tunics, and shoppers patronizing the uncountable street-side vendor stalls available. The walk brought back many memories—the sweet ones as well as the bitter. In general, the city looked the same, but in detail it was all different. Fires and collapsing construction had always forced regular rebuilding across the length and breadth of the metropolis. As well as he had once known Rome, he frequently had to ask directions. At last, Calusidius managed to locate the forbidding walls of the gladiatorial school.

If his information was good, Mar would be in there.

Mar, my precious Mar, he thought, *this is not the way I wanted you to first see Rome.* Chained, probably beaten, what would he think of his father's city after this?

Calusidius had guided Osric south to help the youth and his worthy master, certainly—but he had also wished to do something for himself and for his son.

The barbarian Chatti had received him hospitably when he arrived in their domain, a fugitive in fear of his life. He would always be grateful to the tribesmen, but in late years, since the death of his wife, Germania was gray for him. The invisible cords that bound Calusidius to the land of his nativity were pulling ever stronger season by season now that he had attained old age. He wanted to close down his life in Rome, not continue in barbarous exile. And more than that, he wanted to give to Mar his birthright as a Roman citizen.

Ah, Mar, will you ever forgive Rome now?

Marshaling his courage, he stepped up to the guards at the school gate. They wore helms, breastplates, and greaves, but he knew that they were not real soldiers, only private hirelings. "My son is in there," he told them. "I wish to speak with someone in charge."

"Haw," laughed one of the sentries, a short, flat-nosed man with a broad, simian face. "Lots of peoples' sons are inside. I rank high enough to hear out the likes of you!"

"He's the son of a citizen!"

"What if he is? Look, gladiator slaves cost a lot of money. If you can pay the price of one, we'll see if Galvius Halotus cares to bargain. Otherwise, be on your way."

"I—I have almost no money."

"Well, then wait for your bastard outside the *spoliarium* of the Tauran Amphitheater." The guard smirked. "Most of the pupils inside end up in it sooner or later. *Haw!*"

Calusidius shuddered; the man was referring to the morgue of the arena, where bodies of slain animals, slaves, and gladiators were thrown awaiting burial in mass-grave trenches. He backed away from the guards. His only hope to get inside was to haunt the street outside in the chance that the owner or some personage with influence might happen by and yield to the entreaties of a miserable father. He withdrew to a wall sheltered from the cold drafts from the nearby sea. There he sat, waiting, ignoring the chill, ignoring his hunger, and fighting off the impulse to weep.

" 'Soon I shall be beyond reward,' Loderod told me," Agrippa was saying, " 'except that reward which I have earned by conjuring with the Black Runes. But I foresee that my son shall pass in need and distress before you. If I have lent you any comfort this day, I bid you to return comfort to him.'

"When I asked him how I should know his son, he told me: 'Know him as Osric, son of Loderod.' "

Osric, now resting on Agrippa's bed, could hold back his most important question no longer. *"Does Loderod still live?"*

The prince of Judea shook his head. "Shortly after we spoke, he collapsed. I think he knew that he was dying and had been using the last of his strength to prepare your way. The guards eventually ordered me along with the Germans into a cart and brought us all to this place. I learned later that the morning jailers discovered Loderod dead when they returned to his cell."

After a silent moment, Osric asked the fate of the Mattiaci.

"They were taken to Ostia and put aboard a ship to Africa. That's what they usually do with prisoners condemned to the mines of Libya."

The young Engle sagged forward and closed his eyes. "What sort of man is this Tiberius Caesar," he asked softly, "to treat an embassy of selfless men in such a way?"

"A hard man and a cruel one. The day he dies there shall not be a wet eye found in all the empire."

Osric sighed. All this time he had been hoping to find his aged mentor still living. To receive the report of Loderod's death while he still felt so unready to walk in the old man's shoes delivered him to a crossroads in his life, one that he had once believed still lay years away.

"Boy!" called Agrippa, loudly but gently.

When Osric looked up the Jew asked: "Are you well?"

"I am sorry, lord. You were asking…?"

"My man Stechus tells me that you are curing yourself with these signs you draw on papyrus. Is that true?" He held out several slips of paper, each marked with a series of runes.

"*Gese*," Osric replied in the affirmative. "Some are called the *limrunar*. They close wounds and restore strength. Those others are meant to dispel witchcraft and are known as *bjargrunar.*"

"Witchcraft? I thought you were wounded by an escaped wolf."

"Not a wolf, but a creature of Heid in the guise of a wolf."

"And Heid—that is a god?"

"A dark goddess—and such a one! The mother of all the world's monstrosities! She has many names—Angerboda, Gulveig, Shobnigerod— but her cultists prefer Heid. Legends say that the god Heimdall created the White Runes, but Heid came after him and taught the Black Runes to the wicked."

"And you are a sorcerer? Certainly Loderod was one—to be able to divine the future the way he did."

"I am not a sorcerer!" blurted Osric, stung. "What we think of as sorcery is the use of Black Runes, and he who writes the evil signs is called the *zauberer*. The White runes do not betoken sorcery!"

"Be at ease, young friend. I did not mean to offend. I have read some books of the magical arts and am aware that some terms will translate badly from race to race."

Osric bowed his head. "I should not be angry. You have honored your promise to Loderod, and I am grateful. In truth, I would be honored to be called a helrun one day, but I am still unworthy of a title so lofty."

Alas, Loderod had died before teaching his chosen disciple either to release the potential within his being or to draw power from Outside, from spirits both clean and foul. Osric's mastery of the runes was far from complete. Although he was one of the Magic Blood of King Scef, as Loderod had been, he felt like a fledgling with no parent bird to teach him to fly. Now that his mentor was dead, it fell to Osric to decide whether to take up the old helrun's quest to recover Andvaranaut, at the price of for- feiting his place in Valhalla, or else to let it remain in the hands of Caesar— or worse, allow the Cult of Heid to reclaim it.

"While I thank you for your help, even more succor do I need request of you. Do you know any means by which one may win free of this prison?"

Agrippa crossed his arms and leaned back on his stool. "I am a poor one to ask about escape; I am too good a prisoner. You might well be able to flee back to your wild forests, but of what use is escape to one like me? The whole world—or at least the livable parts of it—lies under the eagle claws of Rome. Living impoverished in foreign exile, afraid to hear my own name spoken aloud—that is not any life I care to live."

"I know a Roman who came to the territory of the Chatti when the anger of the Romans turned his way."

"He must have loved life, that one. But, for me, living would lose its savor without regular warm baths and kosher meals. Your friend must have been a barbarian at heart."

"Perhaps. Knowing him led me to expect that Romans were a fine race of men. In meeting Caesar's soldiers, I have found that assumption to be wrong."

Agrippa grinned ruefully. "Romans are like all men, everywhere—a confused jumble of good and evil."

"What did these good and evil men do with the body of Loderod?"

"He must have been burned on the common pyre in the field behind the prison. That is what the guards normally do with guests who leave unexpectedly."

"Good," said Osric with a nod.

"Good?"

"It is an honorable funeral for a Germanic lord."

"I'm glad to hear that."

"Agrippa," the Engle asked suddenly, "you have said that Mar was removed from this place two days ago. Where was he taken?"

"To a gladiatorial school in Rome. That's where men are trained to fight for the amusement of the crowds."

Osric's face took on a weary, troubled cast. "My friend Calusod spoke of such things...."

"Rest. You are by no means strong as yet," Agrippa observed, rising. "We shall speak again later and at greater length." He extended the pieces of papyrus. "Do you need these still?"

"Gese," Osric nodded, soul-tired, and received them from the prince's hands. Agrippa took a fresh robe and a towel from a chest, then went outside. The weight of Loderod's talisman that he still carried reminded the Jew that he had been less than honest with the young barbarian.

Loderod had given him the charm to pass on to Osric once his "cup of happiness is full." In his own superstitious mind, Agrippa hardly considered himself to be happy. If he should pass on the legacy of Loderod now, might not the barbarian's god judge him to be satisfied and in need of nothing more? No, it was better to wait for an even happier hour than this one.

Stechus met him on the portico outside the bathhouse. "Did he tell you what he told me, Master—that those marks he drew on papyrus are responsible for his returning strength?"

"He did. Do you doubt it?" Agrippa asked, amused.

"Barbarian nonsense! It has been my poultices and tonics that have sped his recovery so far—not that any savage would understand."

"You are too vain, my friend. Is not the healing of a patient all the recognition that a noble physician needs?"

"I am no philosopher," the freedman replied petulantly, "and clearly you are no doctor."

"True, I may be no more accused of medicine than you may be accused of philosophy. Well, excuse me—I intend to enjoy a bath."

Suddenly, Agrippa heard his name shouted and turned to see Marsyas, his freedman valet, bounding excitedly his way.

"What ails you?" the prince asked the black-bearded newcomer.

He was breathlessly puffing. "I—I rode all the way from the gates of Rome when—when I heard...."

"Heard what? From the looks of you, you must be carrying the warning of my imminent execution...."

"No, Master, no...." Marsyas said. "Good news. The... *the lion is dead.*"

The prince blinked, trying to grasp the meaning of the words. Then his face filled with understanding. "Thank you, good Marsyas. I think my cup of happiness is just beginning to fill."

Hours had passed outside school of Julius Caesar. Calusidius had seen no one going in or out whom he thought he might importune for help.

Despite all, the old Roman could not help but notice the many teenage boys passing by in their new, manly gowns. He had almost forgotten that this was the day of the Liberalia, when youths of fourteen to sixteen put off their juvenile togas and were from then on regarded as grown men. It reminded him, as most things did, of his son. Had the father's life turned out differently, the child would have been reared as a Roman—and this would have been the second or third anniversary of Mar's coming of age.

He had many times regretted having too strongly urged Germanicus to rebel against Tiberius and lead the army to Rome. It was not that such an idea would not have been good for Rome, but it was a petition that had failed and by it Calusidius had made himself an outlaw and an exile.

Suddenly, the clouds passing, the weak, ruddy glow of the evening sun revealed a man and woman approaching the guards in front of the Julius Caesar School.

"Ho!" shouted the male newcomer. "Tell your master, my good friend Cornelius Volcatius, that Rufus Hibernicus comes to call."

One of the sentries, the burly, apish one, sized up the tall, strong stranger and decided not to be coarse or flippant with him. Hibernicus carried not an ounce of wasted fat. His hair and mustache—worn in the old Gallic fashion—were coppery red. Thick arms dangled at his sides and they, like his legs, displayed a faint crisscross of cut and burn marks. Plainly, the man was a gladiator or an ex-gladiator.

Rufus Hibernicus. Aye, the name rang a bell within the sentry's dull mind. He had been one of Rome's top-ranked secutor swordsmen a few years back. After his fifteenth kill, the mob had compelled the Master of the Games to grant him freedom.

"Cornelius is away at his estates in Vulsinii," the armored man replied gruffly. "His assistant, Galvius Halotus, is in charge until he returns."

"Galvius—that hyena bait?" snorted the giant. "Oh, all right; I'll have to talk to him then. Open the gate."

At that instant Calusidius shook off his hesitancy and hurried up to accost the ex-gladiator. Grasping Rufus' huge arm, he said: "I appeal to you, Dominus…."

Surprised, the swordsman looked the elder over and replied, "If it's a handout you want, Citizen, you've caught me at a bad time…."

Calusidius dropped to his knees to clasp Hibernicus' boots. "Dominus, if you are a man of influence with the owner of this school, I implore you to help me. My son is imprisoned inside and they will not let me see him!"

"You whining dog!" the ugly guard cursed. "You were told that no visitors are allowed!" He lashed out with his foot, but before the leather could connect with flesh, Rufus deflected it with a deft movement of his leg. The guard, put into a spin, was toppled into the sand.

"The citizen was speaking to *me*, in case you misunderstood," Hibernicus rumbled. "He's… uh, a *client* of mine, and I'm persuaded to let the good fellow accompany me inside. Any objections?"

"None from me," the second guard answered, while the ruffian on the ground held his tongue. The ex-gladiator helped Calusidius to his feet. When the gate was unlatched, he guided the old wayfarer and the woman into the front court of the training camp.

Only now did Calusidius pause to take a good look at Hibernicus' female companion. She was a young, tall, and dark-complexioned—a barbarian, he thought, an Iberian or Aquitanian, probably. Her eyelashes were thick, and her glossy black hair fell as a heavy wave behind her head. She wore a short tunic displaying most of her shapely legs, which in Rome denoted a slave or prostitute. Both the gladiator and his companion appeared to be inadequately clad for the month of March.

As they crossed the compound, Hibernicus spoke up: "I'll get you in to see the boy if I can," he promised. "It's allowed sometimes, but Galvius is a devil for petty rules. Let me do the talking.

"And you, Tatia," he addressed the woman, "remember that I learned my craft here years ago and I want everyone to know that I've made good. So try to remember to call me 'Dominus,' won't you?"

Tatia answered, "Rufus—you can't be serious about giving yourself up to gladiator slavery again. You could get killed!"

"Tosh," the big man admonished, "I'm finished with that life for good, but the news going around town has given me an idea. If Tiberius is dead, there's going to be games staged to honor the new emperor. That means there'll be a demand for gladiators like there hasn't been in twenty years. I'm betting that the Julius Caesar School will be paying top wages to any good trainer. I can probably swing a large loan, too; that should take care of our temporary embarrassment. Our hard times won't last for long, love."

Doubt crossed Tatia's comely features, but she declined reply.

Just ahead was the school director's office. The secretaries tried to stall their approach, but Hibernicus shouldered right past them and barged up to the polished desk where the hollow-cheeked Galvius sat.

"*You!* What do you want this time?" the Syrian Greek demanded of the ex-secutor. After receiving Hibernicus' blunt explanation, he leaned back in his chair, scowling. "We have all the trainers we can use."

"Have you taken leave of your senses, man?" protested Rufus. "Everyone says that the emperor's heir Gaius loves a good sword-fight. The amphitheaters will soon be burning up men's lives like faggots in January."

"It doesn't matter what Gaius loves—Tiberius is emperor. Oh, sure, I've heard the talk of Caesar's death this morning—but I wasn't fool enough to believe it. If you ask me, Tiberius started the rumor himself— just to find our who's loyal and who's not."

"Alive, eh? If he is, may the Dagda bless our beloved emperor," Rufus muttered disappointedly.

"Stow the sarcasm. If someone reports your disloyalty, Rome will lose a fair gladiator."

" 'Fair'? The man insults me! If I wasn't here to do him a favor he can't refuse, I'd be out that door at a snap of my fingers."

"Quit bluffing, Hibernicus. I've heard that you've gone broke—that you invested everything you had in a shipment of wine and that all five of your ships were wrecked off Calabria. People say that you've been evicted from your *domus.* You'll be lucky if your girl isn't seized and sold against your debts. You might even be sent to a forced labor crew to pay off your creditors."

"The things people say behind a man's back!" the secutor grumbled.

"Well, I'm not one to throw a decent sword-fighter to the dogs. When you're willing to bind yourself over the school for at least a year, we can draw up a premium arrangement."

"For a *year?*" Hibernicus thundered. "Not on your life! I've been making my contracts for one show at a time."

"I have big plans!" Galvius informed him. "I want to build a traveling extravaganza around a few starring swordsmen, climaxing in an appearance at the amphitheater of Statilius Taurus. A one-fight contract isn't worth the papyrus it's written on."

"When's Cornelius due back?" asked Rufus. "That man knows an opportunity when it's offered him."

"In five or six weeks. Until he returns from Vulsinii, you deal with me."

"Well, in that case you'll see me in five or six weeks. In the meantime, I have a favor to ask on behalf of my client here."

"Your *client?*" Galvius looked sourly at Calusidius. "Does your 'client' have anything to do with that roughhousing at the gate?"

"I was only trying to keep your armored loafers on their toes. What's important is that this man's son has been sent here. The two of them didn't even get the chance to say 'goodbye.' It would be decent of you to give them a few minutes together right now."

"He came from the prison in Tusculum," Calusidius added hopefully.

"Get smart, Hibernicus—" said the school master "—we don't need a lot of bawling relatives coming in, tearing their hair and ruining the men's morale! A gladiator has no family. When a man understands that, he fights a better fight and lives a good deal longer."

"Come on, Galvius. You owe me one for the upset against Serapion four years ago. You collected forty thousand sestertii when I sent that animal to the spoliarium."

"You did that for *me*, eh? As if you wouldn't have tried to keep his trident out of your throat if you weren't thinking of me? Oh, all right. But tell your so-called client to talk fast. We can't give him a lot of time, or the rest of the men will be wanting the same treatment."

The Entertainer

CHAPTER VI

Galvius took a description of Mar from Calusidius and sent a servant to arrange for the visit. Another menial led Rufus and his companions to the edge of a barred enclosure which, the secutor knew, was a place where prospective buyers got a first—and safe—view of the school's human livestock. After a wait of a quarter hour, two guards appeared on the other side of the bars, leading a dark-haired youth between them.

"Mar!" Calusidius exclaimed, sticking his arms through the barrier.

The young man regarded his old sire. After moment's perturbation, he raised his chin, frowned, and stubbornly refused to respond to his father's hailing.

Unheeding, Calusidius babbled out the story of his recent adventures. Eventually, through his haze of excitement, the concerned parent sensed the coldness of the boy.

"Mar—what's wrong? Have they treated you badly?"

"No better nor worse than any Roman slave, I suppose," the youth answered stiffly. "You should not have come."

"Why on earth not? You are my son!"

"No, I am not!"

"Mar… I know I have erred. I curse myself a thousand times for not seeing through the ruse of that lying Bructeri. I would not have witnessed you being imprisoned for anything!"

"You witnessed nothing! When the fight began, you fled, thinking neither of me nor of Osric. If the father of any of the other Chatti had behaved so, that man would have hanged himself rather than return to his kinsmen in shame."

Rufus rubbed his chin. So *that* was what was eating on the boy. The ways of his own countrymen, the ways of Hibernia—Erin—were not much different. A man who broke ranks to save his own life was shamed unto death.

"You do not understand, Mar," said Calusidius softly. "I love the Chatti well, but sometimes it is not easy to live the way they live. You have never dwelt in a land like Rome, never dreaded having its overwhelming power turned against you. You do not know what fear the agents of the empire evoke in a man who has been reared under their harsh sway. I have spoken to you about such things. I have tried to rear you as a Roman…."

"I am no Roman!" Mar declared angrily. "I am Chatti! The Romans may kill me, but neither they nor you can make anything but what I am!"

Both father and son were talked out. The guards, sensing this, led the sullen Mar away. Calusidius, muted by sorrow, ground his forehead against the bars in front of him, seeking to turn his internal ache into an external one that he could more easily bear.

Rufus sighed. Stubborn kid; there never was a man so pure and certain of his ways as a half-breed. He drew Calusidius away from the bars before he skinned himself to no purpose. Already the ex-gladiator had taken a liking to the old Roman; it would be too bad if he was left on his own in such a state of mind.

"Do you have any place to stay tonight?" Rufus asked.

"N-No," Calusidius mumbled, his tone spiritless.

"Good! Tatia and I don't either. It's a lot cozier for three to sleep together under a bridge than for just two. Come with us."

The centurion Paulus Didius Norbanus had entertained Herod Agrippa many times inside his living quarters, but seldom had the prince appeared at his door in spirits so light and convivial. As it happened, the Jew was delivering the first news the Roman had heard of the emperor's fate.

"But, Prince," the officer asked, "can you be absolutely certain that Tiberius is dead?"

"All I know is what is being said in Rome. But Marsyas has always been careful about repeating mere nonsense to me."

Norbanus shrugged. "What is, is; what will be will be." He went to his wine shelf and poured a glass vessel full. "Who do you suppose will be the new emperor?" Norbanus asked. "Caligula or Gemellus?"

"Caligula—but if I were you, I would never use that name in front of our new imperator; he hates it."

"Cal... *Gaius*, I mean. Well, good! His father should have been emperor before him. I don't know much about young Gemellus, but the further one gets away from Tiberius' tainted bloodline, the better!"

"Some say Gemellus has nothing to do with Tiberius' linage," the Easterner quipped. "They have it that boy's mother was the mistress of the traitor Sejanus."

"Well, hail Sejanus, then," toasted Norbanus, "for putting an end to the dynasty of the Claudians!"

While they conversed, a dispatch rider came from the Prefect of Rome. The gleeful Norbanus invited him in and offered a toast to the late emperor's sufferings in Tartarus.

The messenger, a Praetorian whom Norbanus knew slightly, drew back. "Centurion, there were rumors, but they should not have been believed!

The word is now coming to the city that Emperor Tiberius has gotten much better and plans to visit Rome in just a few days."

Norbanus' face drained to whiteness. In a burst of anger, he turned on Agrippa.

"Damn your lying hide!" he growled.

Agrippa knew better than to add fuel to the fire by defending himself.

The officer roughly dragged the Easterner from his couch. "Did you think that lying about the emperor would go unpunished?"

Norbanus went to the door and called for his orderlies. These he ordered to cast Agrippa into the filthiest pit beneath the prison, chain him, and hold him under close guard. Despite his alarm, Agrippa let himself be manhandled away, silently cursing rumor-mongers and lying prophesies.

Gossip about Agrippa's fall traveled on falcon's wings into every part of the prison. Osric, hearing it, found himself wishing that he could help his benefactor, but lacked the means. Why, he wondered, did the servants of evil thrive so well, while problem after problem beset better men?

Suddenly, Osric heard the clump of men striding on the outer portico. The door was flung open and Roman soldiers barged in. Osric braced to defend himself, with his bare hands if need be.

"Save the dirty looks for your gladiator-trainer," growled Norbanus. "After what that Jewish charlatan has done to me, I'm not going to anger the magistrate by blocking your sentence any longer." He glanced to the men with him. "Take him to the Julius Caesar School and bring me back his price!"

More than a year had passed since Rufus Hibernicus had existed so abjectly. For three nights, he, Tatia, and Calusidius had been living amongst the homeless flotsam of the imperial metropolis.

Many thousands of Romans never worked but instead traded their grain dole to bakeries for bread or bartered it for wine. Then there were the unemployed freedmen, beggars, orphans, and foreigners who drew no dole but survived by begging, chance and wit. He regretted, and not for the first time, that he had not been manumitted by a citizen instead of by a Greek *lanista*. A Roman citizen's ex-slave received citizenship, albeit one of a poor kind. But even the worse sort of citizenship would have allowed him to qualify for the dole, a benefit which he and his companions very greatly needed just then.

The only bright spot was that the vagabonds huddled near to them were even more wretched. Some of these lived in the streets with their whole families. Others had not occupied a permanent address for months or years, but instead sought shelter from the rain at shadowy places such as the Aricine Bridge, a notorious colony of beggars. If their winter kill rate climbed high, no one cared; Rome would fill their empty spots with new dispossessed people soon enough.

Rufus had seen the city at both its best and worst; he knew the familiar shelters. On the first night with Calusidius—the coldest—the three had napped huddled together between the deep pilasters of the Temple of Hercules Musarum, only a modest walk from the Julius Caesar School. The next night, they bedded down on the hard stone portico of the Tabularium, until dispossessed by the archivists' men at daybreak. Finally, just the night before, the trio had enjoyed the scant amenities of the Porticus of Octavia.

Despite the harshness of Rome by night, daylight held its pleasures. Diverting things were going on continually in the forums and public districts—entertainment, speeches, readings, processions, and other events. There were even preachers who declaimed the glories of strange foreign religions. Rufus didn't care about those, but enjoyed joining in their hymn singing. There were many public parks, too, as well as warm, ornate bathhouses, whose offerings the poor could enjoy for free or at a very small cost.

Nonetheless, outdoor living was made considerably safer with a protector like Hibernicus. Rome had more than its share of roughnecks, tough kids, and illegal slave-traders. By day, food was their main concern. The first day had exhausted both Hibernicus' and Calusidius' last few coins. Non-citizens drew no dole and Calusidius was no recognized resident of Rome. He would need official documentation to establish his citizen rights, but the very suggestion of approaching men of authority sent a shudder through the man. Nevertheless, the elderly Roman was tough despite his age. The life he had lived in Germania had beaten civilization's weakness out of his system.

Tatia was otherwise. Although half-barbarian by rearing, she had been the daughter of an Iberian brigand chief. Captured by the Romans and purchased by Hibernicus, she had been well provided for as long as he could afford her upkeep. But hunger and cold sleeping made her grumpy, complaining, and sometimes—which was worse—passively sullen.

Tatia was, in fact, his main concern. As his slim week of grace melted away, his creditors would soon get around to the idea of seizing her toward his debts. Rufus had privately sworn to save the wench from that fate if he could. He liked her brassy spirit as it was and wouldn't like to see it broken by some lout of a master. He could not even free her legally beforehand, as there was a lien placed on all his property.

But food was of immediate concern. In Rome, one could beg his bread, steal it, work for it, or acquire a loan. The least objectionable option was the latter. Alas, he had already tried that with some people he knew, only to be told, "Not a *semis* for the likes of you; go away!"

Even the lady Marcia Priscina had let him down. A couple years earlier, she had kept him like a king. Now some Greek actor, Mnester by name, was cutting a dashing figure on the stage and also in her private chambers.

While enduring their hunger, they took care to stay informed of the daily news. Macro had lately written from Misenum officially informing the city leaders of Tiberius' death. The word of the day immediately became "Tiberius to the Tiber," but many citizens were happy in a more positive way. Soon, young Gaius would be riding into Rome at the head of the imperial party. No one spoke of Tiberius' other heir, his grandson, Gemellus. Both his father and grandfather had been unpopular. Besides, the boy was considered too young to rule.

Fortunately, the news of the emperor's death improved the material circumstances of the trio. For the next two days, they did not lack for food—it being the custom in Rome to set out lunch tables for the poor as a sacrifice offered in gratitude for divine blessings.

While savoring the noonday warmth in the Saepta Julia, Rufus encountered a worker from the city's largest arena, the amphitheater of Statilius Taurus. The man carried news that Decimus Coeranus, the procurator managing the amphitheater, had reacted to Tiberius' death notice by announcing a renovation project, confident that Gaius would be a better patron of the public games than Tiberius had been. The Hibernian considered carpentry to be no fit work for a fighting man, but Calusidius perked up with immediate interest. He had been, he explained, an optio in the engineering unit of his legion in Germany and later, among the Chatti, he had taught his barbarian neighbors better ways to build. Rufus offered to put in a good word for him with Coeranus, whom he knew. The three, their spirits buoyed, set out for the arena.

Passing under the gilded columns of the Temple of Neptune, they heard the laughter of a crowd around the temple steps. Taking Tatia by the arm, the giant elbowed his way through the mob to see what the excitement was all about.

"What is it?" Tatia asked Rufus. Unlike her towering master, she could see nothing but the shoulders and backs of those in front of her.

"A dwarf—a street entertainer!" replied the ex-gladiator. On impulse, he picked the young woman up and perched her on his bench-sized shoulder. Calusidius pushed up and also watched, standing on his toes.

The little man was putting on a frenetic show, keeping three red balls in the air while standing on one hand. A good trick, but what a repulsive freak! The gladiator had seen baboons just as human-looking.

The entertainer wore barbarian-type trousers and a child's ragged tunic. His bare feet were oddly deformed. Though his skin was dark, it was not so dark as an Ethiop's. His ears would have better suited a goat, as his brow would have dignified a chimpanzee. These Romans often sported mighty beaks, but the performer's put them all to shame. It was so large and hooking that it nearly touched his hard, jutting lips. Surely the dwarf could lick its tip with his tongue.

The little man's hands were large with fingers thin and exceedingly dexterous, as his juggling amply demonstrated. His limbs were long and spindly, though obviously very strong. But the acrobat's torso stood in contrast to them—being thick, short and solid. Rufus had encountered many queer sorts in his time, but was stumped by the question of what race could have spawned such a sport.

"Gold! Gold for Galar!" the performer whined thickly, his voice being high with an odd buzzing quality. As for the heavy accent, the secutor couldn't place it. The juggler's appeal for alms drew a sprinkling of coins—copper *asses* mostly, with some brass *dupondii*, silver denarii and Greek *didrachms* thrown in. But only one *aureus* answered the entertainer's call for gold.

Chuckling wickedly, Galar scooped up his bounty. He dropped all the coins into his scrip, except for the single aureus. This he showed off to all, holding it between his long-nailed thumb and forefinger. Then, sniffing the air like a hunting dog, the dwarf perused the faces of his audience. His yellow stare, following his nose, soon fixed on Calusidius, then rose up to the high-perched Tatia and, last of all, on Rufus who supported her.

With a facial twist that might have been a smile, Galar bounded toward the red giant.

"See how Galar makes money," he chirped, holding out the golden coin so close to Rufus' face that the ex-gladiator could make out the stamped features of Emperor Tiberius.

Flamboyantly, the dwarf placed the coin upon his brown palm and displayed for all his spectators to see. Then he blew on the coin and glided his other hand over it. Suddenly, two aurei rested in its place. The audience smiled with restraint; it was no great trick. Neither did the public response warm up appreciably when he rapidly turned the two into three, the three into four, and the four into five.

"My gold does not please anyone?" the creature mocked. "Then surely no Roman would wish to accept Galar's coins for his own!"

A laugh came from the spectators. "I'd take them!" called out one pleb, who was then echoed by several others of his ilk. But Galar shook his hideous head. "No, not you, nor you!" He thereupon leered at Tatia.

"The girl with pretty legs. She much pleases Galar. Will the pretty one take Galar's gold?" He extended his largess.

The creature's stare chilled Tatia, but the coins were a powerful entice-ment. She and the exgladiator might eat for weeks upon them. Tatia looked doubtfully down at Rufus.

"Go on, love. You have an admirer!" he reassured her. Accordingly, the slave girl reached out her slim, olive palm, though with a certain wariness. Galar's small yellow eyes glittering evilly, he poured the coins into the young woman's hand.

At that moment, with an awful laugh, the dwarf sprang into a series of somersaults that took him away from the temple steps. The spectators dodged to either side to let him through. The little fellow persevered with his acrobatics until he was out of sight.

Rufus set the girl down on the paving stones. Calusidius pressed up closer to stare at the aurei, asking, "Are they real?"

Rufus took the coins from Tatia's hands; they had the heft and feel of bullion. He bit one. "I'll be," he chortled, "they appear to be of the emperor's best minting. Win a few more admirers like that fool dwarf, my darling, and we'll be building a senator's fortune in no time." He placed them into his purse.

"Please, Rufus—let's just get something to eat!" Tatia urged.

The Hibernian returned a cheerful nod and looked around. Near the temple stood a hot food stand and from it the ex-gladiator ordered bread, sausages, and three bowls of stewed vegetables. The vendor quoted his prices and held out his hand.

"I hope you can make change," Rufus said in high-spirits, reaching for his scrip. But he grimaced perplexedly when the weight of the bag was all wrong. Looking inside, he saw only a few pebbles. Quickly, he scanned the pavement beneath his boots. "Well I'll be crucified!" he exclaimed.

Disgusted, the restaurateur snatched his wares from Tatia's grasp before she could taste a single crumb.

Decimus Coeranus was in an especially foul mood. To impress the new emperor, he needed to put his amphitheater into order and have hundreds of performances lined up for the accession celebration. But his staff, ruined by years of inactivity, were worse than useless when called for helping him with anything better than fetch-and-carry work. He felt like Atlas, holding up the weight of all the world's incompetence alone.

An arena servant scuffled up and started talking: "An optio of the vigiles is outside. He wants to leave off an animal."

"Tell him to go away!" growled the procurator. "Today I don't feel like seeing anyone under the rank of tribune!" The slave shrugged and withdrew.

But another intruding voice chimed, "Still a natural leader of men, I see!" The short, heavy-set bureaucrat raised his puffy, vein-traced face and looked over his shoulder. Rufus Hibernicus loomed in doorway.

"You! *Hrumph!* I thought you'd been killed in one of those backwoods arenas. What are you doing here when there's no show going on?" asked

Coeranus testily. *He probably needs another loan,* the administrator thought. *The no-account!*

"There's talk that you have work opening up for skilled carpenters. Is that right?"

"You consider yourself a carpenter? Just because you've taken apart a few taverns, it doesn't make you a carpenter!"

"You know what my tools are, Coeranus. But my client is a man that you can't do without." He stabbed a thumb in Calusidius' direction. "He has no local residence and can't get on the corn dole. In short, he has a good reason to work hard!"

"*Everyone* needs a favor," Coeranus declared disdainfully.

"Don't they though?" the Hibernian agreed. "Remember that time that some unsportsmanlike scoundrel drugged Milo the Gaul, allowing a few rascals betting on his long-shot opponent to make a fortune? The crowd rioted and started looking for a scapegoat. I didn't let them drag you to the crocodile pit, now did I?"

"As much as I like being reminded of all my most humiliating moments, I don't have time to spare. As for your *client*, being a friend of yours is about the worst credential a man could have!"

Good-naturedly, Rufus persisted in his persuasion. Coeranus covered his ears. "All right, all right! I'll give him a chance," he declared. "If I find out that he doesn't know one end of a mallet from other, he goes!"

"You won't be sorry!" Calusidius promised.

"Every time this big ox shows up I'm sorry!" the procurator answered. "Go and find my assistant Vibo; he'll tell you what to do." Calusidius nodded, thanked Hibernicus, and ran out the office door.

"I'll check in on you in a few days," the ex-gladiator called after his friend. He knew that the old man would be able to sleep safely inside the arena cubbyholes until he could afford an attic room somewhere.

The secutor looked back to Coeranus. "Now that that's taken care of, I want to brooch another subject. Finding myself temporarily embarrassed financially, it's fortunate that I had a good reason to drop by your office today...."

"*Out!*"

The Wooden Sword

CHAPTER VII

Gaius was gazing down upon Tiberius, who was wearing rags, surrounded by filth and flames. The former emperor stood glaring up at Gaius, his eyes baleful. Gaius began to laugh, pleased to see his grandfather's small and foul-smelling domain. "Stay there a thousand, thousand eternities, tyrant!" the prince jeered. "When you are tortured, think of me!"

Suddenly, the old man's arm shot out across the distance, seizing Gaius by the neck, choking him as he was pulled him down, down, down....

The prince awoke with a shriek. He fought the tangle of bedclothes. He felt the hands grasping him. When his mind cleared, he recognized the man with whom he struggled. "Charicles! Thank the gods it's you!"

"Peace, Divine Caesar," the elderly physician said. "You dream; you but dream."

Gaius had been bedridden for five days, plagued by nightmares, only occasionally half-lucid in bleary stupors.

"Is Tiberius dead?!"

Charicles sighed.

At each awakening, Gaius had asked that same question. The Greek again urged not to give way to immoderate grief.

"Where is Macro?" the prince gasped. "I need Macro!"

The doctor, having reason to hope Gaius' brain fever may have finally broken, assured his master that Macro would be summoned. Excusing himself, Charicles withdrew.

Soon, Macro was standing at the door, saluting with a strong sweep of a powerful arm. "Hail Caesar!"

"Macro, for the love of Jove, I must... I must...." Gaius babbled. Macro frowned and ordered the prince's attending slaves away. Then he strode up to the bedstead, helmet in hand.

Gaius shuddered. "Macro... did it happen, or did I dream it?"

The armored man frowned. "It happened. But Caesar, it was nothing! Tiberius revived briefly, but he died for certain while we stood by."

The prince looked away, unconvinced.

"You are to be congratulated, Caesar!" said the prefect with forced heartiness. "A ship is just back from Rome. After only two days, the Senate has proclaimed you emperor in absentia."

"I am officially emperor? Has Tiberius' will even been read?"

"Not yet, Imperial Majesty, but you are the choice of all the people of Rome, regardless of whether or not you are the choice of Tiberius."

Gaius fondled that thought. The people had always loved him for the sake of his warrior father Germanicus, and the way his mother Agrippina had so long defied the tyrant to his face. But what Gaius wanted was to be loved for *himself*, not because of his forebears.

"The people don't even know me!" he complained. "Not the man I really am. Tiberius hid me from the public since the day he murdered my mother."

"They will know you soon enough, Princeps," promised Macro. "By the way, I have been organizing your arrival into Rome. If it pleases you, the funeral train of Tiberius shall accompany us."

"Have him thrown into the Tiber, like our friends wanted!"

"Wouldn't I like to!" grinned the political soldier. "But, alas, the disrespect of a proceeding Caesar would work against you in days to come. People who do not honor a past master will not honor their present master either."

Gaius' contemplated that glumly.

"When you feel fit enough," Macro went on, "we can leave for the City. If possible, we should do that as early as tomorrow."

"Tomorrow? No. Impossible."

"Impossible, Caesar?"

"I need to speak to that fool of a sorcerer, Zenodotus. Where is he?"

"On Capri, at the Villa Jovis, I suppose," replied the Praetorian.

"Send for him. Bring him here!"

"Here? Should he not join us in Rome? Your presence in the capital is vital for establishing your position beyond challenge."

"Don't contradict me! I'm emperor now!"

Macro, who was used to mollifying the boy's tantrums, betrayed only a glimmer of annoyance. With a stiff salute, he declared, "I beg Caesar's pardon. Your order shall be obeyed!"

Osric the Engle lay on his back, the sole prisoner inside a small plaster-and-stone room. Soon dawn would bring another day of rigorous exercise at the school of Julius Caesar.

It had been during his transportation that he first laid eyes on the city of Rome, and nothing could have prepared him for what he saw. Since a child, the young man had supposed that Calusidius' tales of the marvels of Rome were wistfully exaggerations. Now he realized that the old man's stories paled in the face of the reality. Dozens of German villages might have fit within the precincts of this single great city. And the numbers that inhabited it! Everything he had seen and heard had overwhelmed his imagination.

If every able-bodied Roman had been reared to bear arms in the manner of the Germans, this population could go out and overcome the world with bloody war. Never again would the Engle marvel to see that the Roman frontier armies were so large, but rather would be grateful that the emperor was content to maintain war bands of only modest size.

In fact, it was hard to believe that men and not gods had built Rome. The stones of its great buildings displayed all the colors of the western sky at sunset. Its countless structures covered over every slope and crest of its hills. Surely, the tribe of Woden who feasted in Valhalla would readily trade their giant-fashioned hall for the palaces and temples over which mighty Caesar held sway.

On the contrary, no hand but man's had raised up the stark, ugly school of Julius Caesar. Once inside its gray barracks, his wounds were indifferently tended by one who was supposed to be a healer. He was allowed some days to rest and regain his strength, given plain but plentiful food. Finally, when judged fit for the "training," he was led out into the camp.

These Romans had to be mad! He already knew how to fight. They called him a slave, yet they put weapons into his hands, a risk that the Germans would never take. To be sure, Calusidius had explained what a gladiator was, but to grasp that concept was elusive.

For the first couple days, Osric had only been required to watch the men at training. The day before, he had been told that the time had come for him to handle arms himself. Mar, he knew, was already in "training." He had seen him in the yard several times. At their reunion, the young Chatti was acting strangely, wearing more of a look of chagrin than of gladness. For some reason, Mar was not welcoming Osric's arrival.

Presently, the cell door sounded with heavy pounding. That would be the attendant, rousing the inmates to take their predawn breakfast. Grudgingly, Osric drew on the coarse woolen training tunic provided him and joined the stream of trainees. They shuffled in lines outdoors to the roofed, open air eating shelter. Plentiful guards were standing by with whips to hurry along any sluggard.

Slave women were already inside, prepared to serve the gladiators water and bowls of porridge. The men swallowed their bland portions with speed and then the trainers ordered them to assemble before the arms shed.

Outside, the chief trainer, Cocceius, unexpectedly prodded him aside. Though at least twice the Engle's age, Cocceius was a man of immense musculature. His nose was badly scarred by an old slash wound and other scars, some greater, some lesser, scored much of his body.

"Step up. Quickly, barbarian." His voice was not loud, but with the confidence of command behind it.

The hint of defiance in the Engle's deportment brought a satisfied smile to Cocceius' lips. "Good, your spirit is high; let us hope it remains so. A broken man is only sword-meat in the arena!"

Osric stood there attentive, wary, and silent.

"From this day on, you'll answer to the name of Osricus; get used to it," the trainer said. Osric stood soberly, taking the man's measure.

Cocceius chuckled. "You're a German. I like Germans; they haven't lost their manhood, unlike the city thieves that the courts keep sending us. But you don't like *me* much, do you, barbarian?" Cocceius suddenly challenged. "If I put a sword in your hands, would you have the guts to express your hate?" The man's expression was ordering Osric to answer.

"Gese!" the younger man snarled.

"The answer must be 'Yes, Dominus,' but I'll let that pass *this time*." Cocceius signaled a guard, who brought over a wooden sword. The mock-weapon was notched and chipped from many a hard bout. Osric regarded the thing disdainfully. It was hardly suited for clubbing a man, much less for penetrating his rib-cage. It encouraged him somewhat to learn that these Romans would not risk facing a German warrior with honed steel in his hand.

Then, to the Engle's surprise, the trainer threw his gladius to Osric's feet and gave a nod, conveying permission for the youth to take it up. Then the Roman himself took a pose holding the wooden weapon.

"Take the sword and try to hit me. If I'm wounded or killed, you will not be punished. This is the *only* time you'll ever have the chance to assassinate me without losing your own life. Show me you have the guts to kill an enemy, or else I will treat you like the slave girl you are."

Seething at the insulting challenge, the barbarian snatched the sword from the ground, took a step backwards, and glared at chief trainer with angry eyes. He suspected that this odd offer might be only a trick to give the guards an excuse to overwhelm and slay him, but he hoped otherwise. Perhaps his guardian spirit, Heimdall, had driven the Roman to folly so that Osric could take some small measure of vengeance against the world of Rome.

But it was Cocceius who began the bout. The trainer moved with the swiftness of a striking snake. Osric could not block the oaken sword before it stung his left arm. After making that easy score, Cocceius sidestepped away and laughed. *Laughed!*

Enraged, the Engle pressed in, as he had done in deadly battles. The older man parried his lunges skillfully, riposted, and poked his blunt-tipped weapon into the Engle's breast. Osric staggered away; had it been an honest stab with a steel blade, he knew he would have been run through a lung.

His indignation renewed, the barbarian returned and laid on with a tempest of blows. To his consternation, none of his moves could win through the wicker basket of wood that Cocceius was weaving about himself. Frustration made Osric's attacks grow reckless. But his contempt for Cocceius' weapon gave the trainer the opportunity to deliver a punishing chop to his exposed thigh, hard enough to wrest a yell from the young man.

Now the chief trainer became the aggressor, testing his pupil to the limit, assailing him with a cunning series of slashes and thrusts that inflicted weals and bruises in rapid succession. Then, unexpectedly, Cocceius allowed Osric to retreat.

From a little way off, the Engle regarded his opponent with grudging respect. Never before had he encountered a fighter who made him feel so unskilled. As far as he knew, this mighty man had sung no runes, used no spells, and yet was playing with him like a novice whom he didn't fear. Osric was tempted to shout out a rune to reverse the issue magically, but he checked himself. He had acquired but small power over the runes thus far and could not overcome the mass of enemies ready to come to Cocceius' aid. If he hoped to escape, he needed to hide his special skills until a better opportunity was presented. For the moment, he fought down his anger in order to duel with care and cunning.

Cocceius, having granted his adversary a short respite, once more pressed in. Osric came on boldly but, after just a few passes, Cocceius' mastery reasserted itself. The bewildering rain of blows the man subjected him to sent Osric stumbling backwards.

Now the master swordsman pursued his foreign prey closely, forcing him to fight until the steel sword started feeling very heavy. Suddenly he was close enough to kick Osric's legs out from under him. His fall knocked the wind out of him and the next thing the German knew, the wooden blade was pressing into his panting throat. Controlling him with the pain of it, Cocceius used his heel to force the youth's hilt out of his grip.

"You're a dead man," Cocceius said.

"I'm tired of being hungry, tired of being cold, and tired of having only one dress to my name," Tatia scolded. Rufus' week of grace from his creditors was passing quickly; fear of the looming auction block had made Tatia into a veritable shrew as fear and uncertainly preyed upon her.

"Is that so? Why have you been so quiet up to now?" Rufus answered sarcastically.

"You're always claiming that your name is your fortune," she challenged, "so why don't you hold your hand out and ask a passerby for an *as* for the glory of Rufus Hibernicus, and see how many it get you?"

Being a man slow to anger, Hibernicus responded with a sigh. For certain, Tatia was his legal slave, but it wasn't his way to make a big issue out of a fact like that.

As the bickering couple descended the Viminal slope, they could see that the motley mob below was astir. Varlets in clean tunics were warning of the approach of some noble, shouting: "Make way! Make way for Her Magnificence Cassilla Felicia!" Rufus and Tatia judiciously stepped up onto the narrow walk that edged the street.

As the lady's party of bearers and attendants neared, Tatia stood on tiptoes, craning to see what the noblewoman was wearing. Her party was a rather large one, with some two dozen guardsmen doing an imitation of the military step. To the rear of the armored men, a gaggle of clients wearing white togas came on, not one of them showing a trace of gentlemanly purple. In their wake, flanked by slaves of both sexes, the luxuriant covered litter of Her Magnificence was borne into view.

Cassilla was a light-haired woman of about twenty-five. She leaned back upon cushions, affecting a pose of studied boredom. She seemed unaware that the whole street stood admiring her costly embroidered silk mantle, her sparkling diamond tiara, and her gold-sprinkled hair.

"Cassilla!" Rufus Hibernicus shouted. "When did you get back from Parma?"

The millionairess glanced in the direction of the greeting. At the sight of the giant, her face brightened with cheer and she cried, "Bearers! Stop!"

The twelve stout males knelt to lower the conveyance to the pavement. Rufus shook his head; Cassilla Felicia had always carried on in this ostentatious way. The ex-gladiator took her merry smile as an invitation for him to step up and meet her.

As he drew near, Cassilla put forward her cheek for a kiss—which, being gallant, he complied with.

"Rufus, darling," she exclaimed. "Such stubble! When was your last shave? Are you not prospering?"

The debtor briefly cited his recent indignities.

Tatia scowled as she beheld this reunion. This wealthy woman was far too pretty and was looking much too happy at seeing her master. The brunette slave stepped up to the litter and stood beside Rufus like a wary guard dog.

Cassilla looked the Iberian up and down. "Is this a trifle you picked up along the street, my love?"

"Aye, this is Tatia of the Lalerti; I bought her in Spain."

"How nice. Is she for sale? She has the hips to make a good breeder," the lady commented. Rufus shrugged noncommittally.

"Please, fall in with my clients," the millionairess urged. "You look in need a good supper and a soft bed." The secutor thanked her profusely and motioned Tatia to merge with the gaggle of sorry hangers-on behind them.

"Why did she want to buy me?" the Iberian asked indignantly.

"Think naught of it. I'm sure she was only teasing. She owns a slave-breeding farm."

"Rufus, we don't need to beg help from a senatorial bitch. We're doing well enough without her!"

"No, Lass, I can't stand the sight of seeing you languish in hardship. Anyway, Cassilla's not so high and mighty as she makes out. Her father and grandfather were business-savvy freedmen who started out poorer than fishermen in the Sahara. She wouldn't work so hard at looking rich on the outside if she didn't feel so humble on the inside."

The Pact

CHAPTER VIII

Gaius wrathfully paced the emperor's suite in Misenum. Not long before, a lookout had sighted Zenodotus' galley arriving from Capri. Soon, very soon, he would be wresting some needed answers out of the unctuous wizard, or else end his life. Perhaps both.

Macro's daily spy reports convinced Gaius that he had no effective opposition in Rome. There was hardly a murmur about restoring the Republic. The Senate had apparently gone passive, merely holding their peace and hoping for the best. That was wise of them, since ancient principles could not stand up against modern swords. Who, really, wanted Roman freedom anymore? The mob didn't care about it. The last real Roman patriots had died along with Brutus and Cassius at Philippi.

All that mattered to the present-day mob was the continuation of the dole and the restoration of the public games—the suspension of which had made Tiberius very unpopular. A philosopher had once written that the common man will weakly protest the execution of his father, but one who has the audacity to deny him a free meal or an amusement is creating a revolutionary.

No, Gaius need not fear the Senate nor the man in the street. The greatest danger any emperor faced was the all-powerful Praetorian Guard.

Those dangerous men had to be mollified and controlled. For now, Macro was his key for controlling the Guard.

Macro had married a beautiful woman of high birth and then had used her to charm and beguile Gaius. The ambitious youth had gone along with the farce to make Macro think that he was easily to control. He had even promised to make Ennia his empress and give Macro fair exchange for her. The Prefect loved no woman more than he loved power and privilege. A common lout like him could not aspire to the Principate himself, but he aimed at becoming the real power behind Gaius' throne.

The emperor put that out of his mind for now. His meeting with Zenodotus was the thing that mattered most to him.

The magician, escorted by Macro, found Gaius waiting for him in a sumptuous chamber. The Alexandrian sensed that the youth was in a dangerous mood and was taken aback. He had expected to be greeted with praise and rewards.

"How was the crossing, Zenodotus?" Gaius inquired coldly.

"We were borne in the cradling arms of the Nereids, O Princeps—a fitting auspice for this happy reunion."

Gaius seemed to rankle. "What infernal pact did you make with demons to bring about Tiberius' end?" he demanded.

Nonplussed, Zenodotus eyed him carefully. "A pact we agreed to, Caesar. You told me that you did not care to be told the details."

"I want to hear them now, you knave!"

Zenodotus shrugged. "As I said, Tiberius was fated to live for another ten years; his favorite wizard Thrasyllus foresaw this. What was worse, the same stars foretold that your own death would come by violence during this very year. To circumvent what was predestined, I had no choice but to appeal to the most ancient and formidable powers of the nether world.

"Bending the future to our mortal design took me to the limits of my power. Destiny cannot be sewn and shaped at whim. To cut off Tiberius before his time and give you added years, I had to offer much to the all-powerful Chthonioi, the gods who rule beyond the gates of death. Invoking them very nearly cost me my life!"

The Chthonioi! Gaius knew that name from his reading into arcane sorcery. They were the most ancient gods remembered in the legends of man. Even the Olympians were but late-comers by comparison. Old Ones were said to rule eternally in the underground and in realms so terrible that no other gods ever ventured there. Some said that the Chthonioi were imprisoned gods, perhaps even the Titans themselves, ever seeking to escape and reclaim the world. It infuriated Gaius that Zenodotus had involved him with such malignant forces.

"You idiot! You did not need to turn the whole world of darkness against me! Another sorcerer, one who I questioned myself, predicted accurately that Tiberius was already doomed to die for having donned an accursed ring of ancient power. He gave up his spirit very quickly after putting it on. It was nothing that you did!"

This surprised Zenodotus. Was the prince talking about Loderod's ring? Who had informed him?

"Where did this evil ring come from, Dominus?"

"It was the Ring of Set from Egypt! What does that matter?"

Egypt? Zenodotus was at a loss to understand what had been happening during his absence, but he did not want Caligula to learn about Loderod's ring. The heir of Tiberius was a dangerous man, and that ring could be a weapon against Gaius too, if he needed one. "The Chthonioi do not usually fell a man by striking him with the thunderbolts of Jove," said the Greek, "but they are more likely to bend their victim's path away from life and into a deadly trap. This seems to be precisely what happened. But believe me, Princeps, my spell-weaving is entirely responsible for your present happy condition!"

"Happy condition? Are you insane? What did you promise to those devils? Upon Tiberius' deathbed, a voice came from his corpse making demands upon *me!*"

"Aye, Princeps," Zenodotus admitted reluctantly. "Recall that I asked for a vial of your fresh blood when we last met? I was forced to burn your vital fluid to the Chthonioi in order to enable their blessing in your cause. It was absolutely necessary if you were to avoid the evil fate that I have already described."

"You dare!" fumed Gaius. "And what happens if the price of the Chthonioi is not met?"

"It must be met, Caesar! Unless payment is made, the years granted to you will not be forthcoming. Instead, the demons of the dark will be dispatched to drag you down to the bottom-most of all the hells."

Gaius looked to his Pretorian Prefect. "Kill him—slowly!" he told Macro.

"No, Imperial majesty!" Zenodotus babbled as the prefect seized him by his long hair and brutally dragged his head back. "The price is easily paid!" The Sicilian's dagger moved in a deliberate arc toward the Greek's exposed throat.

Gaius held up a hand to hold Macro back. "What is the price?" he rasped.

"You will certainly agree that it is but a small expenditure for which to gain both life and empire!"

"What is it?"

"A Rite of Abominations, Princeps—a sacrifice of the darkest kind, made when the stars are in their proper order. I warn—that is, I *caution* you, Dominus—no other magician in all Italy knows the rituals of the Chthonioi so completely as I do, nor could anyone begin learning them without years of searching. You *need* me, Caesar!"

"If a sacrifice is needed, the monsters may have your life with my blessings—"

"Imperial Majesty! My life will not suffice! A Rite of Abomination is an unnatural immolation, one so hateful to the natural order of the universe that it cheers the entire nether realm. In that moment, Chaos becomes disposed to grant very powerful favors. The most propitious time for the sacrifice will be the Kalends of May, the day which the Druids called Beltane."

"And what sacrifice is demanded?"

"The dark gods require the ritual death of one that is a personal treasure to you, Caesar—one whom you truly love."

A fire licked in Gaius' eyes, his cheeks trembled with relief. But was this testimony true, or was the wily magician lying to save his own life?

"Confine him, Macro," the prince said decisively, "until his talents are required. Allow him to have none of his paraphernalia, lest he invoke some means of escape. He will accompany us to Rome. It is high time that we journeyed to the capitol. How soon can the procession begin?"

"The organization of it is far along, but the Romans will need to have news of the date well in advance, so that they can fill the streets and welcome you properly. I would safely say that we should enter Rome for best effect in four or five days."

"Make it happen as swiftly as possible. Now, take this Greek fool away!"

The prefect bullied Zenodotus from the emperor's presence. Gaius, for his part, stepped up to a large window and stared into the sky.

So, I need to choose a victim, the prince thought. But whom did he love? Ennia? Certainly not! One of his parasites, his fawning clients? No, they all disgusted him. Did he love any of the women whom he'd seduced thus far? Hardly, unless lust satisfied and quickly forgotten amounted to love. What about family? He surely wouldn't miss his sister Agrippinilla—but that was the rub; he had to care for the victim—and care dearly.

Gaius scratched the short, golden stubble on his cheek. This was an unexpected complication. Was there anyone in all this empire whom he actually and truly loved?

Rising late and returning to his apartment in the house of Cassilla Felicia, Rufus Hibernicus found Tatia sitting in a curule chair, waiting for him.

"Look at what that monstrous woman is making me wear tonight at the supper!" Tatia complained. She stood up, held out her arms, and displayed a shapeless African garment that resembled a Bedouin tent.

"It should be warm enough, anyway," Rufus grinned. "Too bad you weren't dressed so well when we were sleeping on porches."

"And where were you sleeping just now?" she accused. "I've hardly seen you in two days! You're always arm-in-arm with that overdressed slut!"

The ex-gladiator yawned. "She continually draws me into long conversations. That lady can talk a blue streak. The prattle never fails to put me to sleep."

"I just bet you went to sleep!" the brunette scoffed. "Well, I'm not going to serve her supper as if she owned me, and certainly I'm not wearing a thing like this." She plucked hatefully at the robe.

"I'm positive Cassilla is only teasing you. The way you so easily lose your temper only encourages her to do so."

"Well, I'm not going to serve her or her rotten friends tonight while she fusses over you like the matron of some third-rate *lupinar!*"

"Yes, you are, lass," he said firmly. "We both owe the lady much. It won't trouble us to go along with a few of her whims. Without her support,

I wouldn't be able to pay the first installment on my debt tomorrow, and you'd be off to the auction block."

"So, you've been sleeping with her for money!" Tatia yelled. "You contemptible gigolo!" She looked around for something to throw.

"Tatia, I'm trying very hard to be patient with you," he began. When she picked up a molded flagon he declared, "Put that down, girl. If you throw that thing I swear—"

He ducked as the vessel sailed overhead and shattered against the wall, sheeting off a large patch of decorated plaster. Rufus marched sternly toward her and, belatedly frightened, Tatia darted for the rear door. With a few powerful strides, Hibernicus caught up with her and together they tumbled to the rug. Tatia scratched and kicked, but the man pinned her limbs easily. Then, turning her over on her belly, he delivered ten solid whacks across her buttocks. Her cries of anger changed to furious chagrin.

Rufus got up, dusted off his hands and pointedly reminded the girl to be dressed and ready in time for the evening meal.

"Stop sulking!" Cocceius had told Osric. "Not a half dozen recruits in the last year could have fought so well as you have. No barbarian knows how to use his blade intelligently, but you've shown the makings of a real swordsman."

The Engle remained silent and sullen.

"Toward the last, when most tyros would have been lost in an angry fog, you started using your head. That's what a fighter *should* do. Don't get puffed up, though—you've got a hell of a lot to learn, but you have less far to go than most men.

"Just remember this: You're a slave; I and a few others here have the power of life and death over you. We demand total and instant obedience. If you strike a trainer, if you attempt to escape, you will die by crucifixion. The other men can tell you what that is, if you don't already know. With the training you'll receive here, you'll survive many arena matches. Fight and live and you'll eventually be awarded freedom. That's the choice you have: life or death."

Two days had passed since his besting by Cocceius. The trainer's words, as much as they angered him, had also given Osric much to think about.

He'd had no choice but to fall in with the school's routine. The pupils, the Engle found, did not train every day. One day per week, after morning exercise, the trainees were put at leisure. For some, this meant time with a slave woman. Others—the veterans who had proved themselves in the arena and accepted discipline at the school—were permitted to leave the enclosure and visit the city. Osric, Mar, and the other tyros were at least allowed the liberty of the training yard. For the first time since his arrival,

Osric had been able to approach Mar and engage with him. The Chatti looked fit and well, but his peculiar humor had not abated.

"Call me 'Marcus,' " Mar had corrected his friend's greeting. "That is the battle name that Cocceius has imposed on me."

Osric regarded him with amazement. "Cocceius is a good swordsman, yet I would not grant him the right to take away the name with which my father gifted me."

"Oh? Have *you* not been answering to your new name?"

"A prisoner must endure much in the way of indignity, but this spirit of mine has not surrendered to him."

"That is the difference between us, then. I have ceased to value those things passed down to me from my father."

"Why do you speak so of Calusod? Are you bereft of wits, my friend? Your sire is an honorable man and has proven himself many times over."

"I—I cannot speak of this thing; too deeply am I ashamed. Calusod fled from the fight and thought neither of his companions nor his dignity until long afterwards."

"Is that what troubles you? Mar, he is an old man. It is our duty to protect the village elders. A father protects his child; a man protects his father."

"Older men than him have covered their hoary locks with glory."

"Not all men are the same. He is a Roman, and their ways are not our ways. One must learn the worth of each different breed. Think of the fearful Romans when they enter our forests, how they quake when the wind whispers, the shadow of the oak moves, or the raven cries out. How bravely will the legions strike at some unguarded village and call it a victory, but then will hurry back across their bridges, terrified by the shouting of our pursuing warriors. Sometimes Romans leave behind their wounded, whom we are able ransom for metal goods and bolts of cloth."

Mar maintained his obdurate silence. Osric still pressed him.

"It is the Roman way to draw strength from great numbers, each man glad to be only a small part of the whole. It is not in such men to stand alone and trade blow for blow with an equal, unless these 'gladiators' are the exception. But Calusod has always had more to offer the Chatti than martial prowess. The great Hermann himself sometimes discoursed with your sire on the matter of defeating Roman soldiers. Without his patient teaching, you and I would be like children in this land, uncomprehending of what we see and hear. No, Calusod is my friend; I will not renounce him. Will you, who are his son?"

Mar belatedly made answer. "You are not the first to remind me that Romans are cowards, Osric. From childhood I was mocked by the Chatti of my own age. By my coloring, it was plain that I was not one of them. They called me 'Enemy,' 'Invader,' 'Roman.'

"Calusod, too, preferred me to be a Roman and tried to teach me their ways. Whenever I failed at anything, or was deemed to have failed when I did not, I was told it was only because of my Roman blood. In truth, to this day I do not know whether I should be called a Chatti, a Roman, or neither. I can name but few friends that I had before you came to our village with Loderod. I think it is because we are both outsiders amid the Chatti, though I have known no other home."

"Fools make their accusations, Mar, but you hold yourself to blame more than any of them do. All the Chatti thought well of Calusod and also of your well-born mother, Berhga."

"Yet no Chatti would be surprised that the 'Invader' has been taken slave, beaten with a wooden sword, bested though he held steel in his hand...."

"I, too, was shamed by Cocceius. But however great a warrior is, there is always one who is greater still. At the least, every fight we lose teaches us something. As for being called a slave, it is something that a captive must endure. Remember what the elders say: a man is not made a slave; a slave makes himself. Our captivity need not continue—not if we act with care. Soon we shall find the means to escape this place and get on with the urgencies that brought us here."

"You are wiser than I, and well-versed in the runes. You quest is a dangerous one. The company of a poor companion like myself would only hinder you," Mar said moodily.

Without another word, the dark-haired youth shuffled away. Osric stood and watched him go, not knowing words wise enough to end his sorrow.

The hour being late, the streets on the Viminal slope were no longer crowded and Tatia could make her way swiftly. She had taken nothing from the house of her rival, except her newly-laundered chiton. The Iberian scorned to take anything that belonged to the hated Cassilla. Tears burned her eyes. What did Rufus see in such a shallow creature?

Not recognizing the landmarks and feeling lost, Tatia sat on the step of a doorway. She had left Cassilla's house without pondering her future. If she did not return to the secutor, where else might she go? Spain had been her home less than two years before, even though she knew that her own tribe had been subdued and scattered. But if she went to seek them, how did one reach Spain?

Walking so far would entail months of privation and constant danger. Though ships made the journey regularly, a merchant captain would demand payment. Furthermore, if the ship captain suspected that she was a runaway slave, he might turn her in to the authorities. Worse still, he might chain her and sell her in some remote port.

Tatia's anxiety grew with the lengthening of the evening's shadows. How different it was to walk the streets of benighted Rome when a strong, protective man walked beside her! The girl pressed her forehead against her drawn-up knees. How she wished that she could swallow her pride and return to Rufus. But that would be too humiliating. If she made a surrender of her heart, would it not be the same as declaring that she was nothing but a slave, both inside and out? But if she didn't go back, where could she find so much as a safe place to sleep?

All at once, Tatia leaped up. A sound had told her that something was lurking in the shadows. The Iberian scanned the lowering gloom, a chill of apprehension running through her sleek limbs. Suddenly, she glimpsed a pair of tiny, yellow lights blinking from the darkness. Giving a cry, the girl sped away.

Tatia ran with only one thought in mind—to get back to Rufus Hibernicus, no matter what the injury to her pride. Afraid, she frequently cast looks over her shoulder, sometimes believing that she saw the yellow orbs floating after her.

At last, already hurting from many trips and stumbles, Tatia found herself at the terminus of a blind alley. Unable to go ahead, afraid to go back, she sagged breathlessly to the cold stones. Possibly, she slept.

Something jabbed her and she woke. Above her were lumpish silhouettes against a moonlit sky. "It's a whore," judged a gravelly-voiced speaker.

Rude hands assailed her body. "She's smooth," the searcher declared, "she can't be very old. And she fights like a cat! Lentulus' might hand over a good price for her, if she has any looks at all."

Someone muttered agreement. Then one of the strangers grabbed Tatia by the locks. She shouted for help, only to be cuffed until she begged them to stop. Thrown down, hands turned her roughly onto her belly and pinned her arms behind her. Were they going to tie her, or do something much worse?

Suddenly the men above her yowled as if cut or stabbed. The one holding her let go. Around her, the enclosure sounded with noise and confusion. The next thing the girl knew, scuffling feet were fleeing toward the mouth of the alley.

Tatia straightened up despite her bruises, distraught and blinking into the surrounding blackness. But even now she was not alone. Before her glimmered *a pair of yellow orbs.*

She must have swooned, for her eyes opened to the gray light of dawn. "Lass, have you been hurt?" It was the voice of Rufus Hibernicus and she turned toward him frantically. The moment he put his arms around her, she broke down into a hysterical crying fit. Softly, he lifted and carried her back to the house of Cassilla Felicia.

The Father-in-Law

CHAPTER IX

As Macro had wished, the whole city turned out to hail the new emperor. Along the Sacred Way, from the Tiber to the Via Flaminia, altars smoked, sacrifices bled, and torches wavered.

The generous shopkeepers and residents filled tables with food to share with the needy on this happy day. On the rooftops, dealers in flowers threw crocuses, snowdrops, and other flowers of early spring down upon the triumphal route.

Gaius made his advent into the heart of the city standing in an elaborately decorated chariot. He wore clothes of mourning, but otherwise the festive parade resembled not at all a funerary procession.

"To the Tiber with the tyrant!" a stentorian pleb yelled and his sentiments were echoed by many bystanders.

"Long live Caligula!"

"Fortune and long life to the son of Germanicus!"

"Chicken!"

"Pet!"

"Star!"

"Baby!"

To capture for themselves the new emperor's reflected glory, dignitaries, military officers, and Praetorian Guardsmen accompanied the circuitous procession along the traditional route of past triumphs, passing the Forum and proceeding up the Clivus Sacer, the air filled with robust cheers and spinning blossoms. The train continued past the monuments commemorating Rome's long past, and approached the Temple of Jupiter atop the Capitoline Hill. It was there that sacrifices of the highest order would be held, but Gaius would not be attending them. He had instead appointed high-ranking office-holders to officiate in his place.

At the temple, Gaius and his favorites separated from the completed procession and made their way in sumptuous litters toward the Palatine Hill, where the palaces of Augustus and Tiberius awaited their new proprietor.

Somewhat behind Gaius rode the ungainly, inexpert horseman, Claudius, the young emperor's uncle, the dead emperor's nephew. In his mid-forties, Claudius was a man of strong, graceful features, but possessing of wandering, bovine eyes. Although of the highest-ranking males of the imperial family, he had lived a most undistinguished life. The equites, out of courtesy, had appointed him to their delegation.

At the House of Tiberius the wealthiest equites, the most dignified senators, and the personal friends of the imperial household broke out in cheers as the emperor was brought up. A tribune of the Praetorians helped Gaius arise from his litter with dignity before a crowd of city elders. Not in many years had so much in the way of senatorial and equestrian purple been gathered together at one place and at one time.

The hails and congratulations from the ranks of the great were deafening. It was Macro's job to move the process ahead and to keep order. "Peace, Elders of Rome! Let the emperor speak!"

The Heir of Tiberius took his place and addressed his audience confidently. His prepared speech was a string of platitudes, but the good response from his listeners moved him into grandiloquence: "You are the best sons of a great nation. You are the scions of heroes! You are a people chosen by the gods to rule the entire world! In my person, Providence has restored our Republic to its ancient state of freedom. I, its defender, shall never let liberty depart from our seven hills so long as I live!"

"Caligula!" a woman hailed him. That nickname would have been an insult, had he not recognized the voice. His searching glance soon picked out the face of his paternal grandmother, Antonia, and extended to her his welcoming hand. Claudius, her son, noticed the woman at the same time and clumsily tried to embrace her. She stepped up and took Gaius into her arms.

"Welcome, Grandson. Glory be to the salvation of Rome. Let me kiss you."

The youth grinned as the matron's lips touched his cheek. Except for the protocols, he would have led her aside at once and, like an excited boy, told her about the four-day journey from Misenum and of the people's love that he encountered everywhere. Antonia had always been the one person, other than his mother, who never sneered at him for his faults and misbehavior, or sought his favor in hope of gain.

Suddenly a thought fluttered through his mind like a bat on the wing.

"Gaius, that strange look on your face," Antonia remarked. "Are you not well?"

The emperor regained his poise. With wondering and troubled eyes he said: "I was just thinking about how much I love you, Grandmother.

"How much I truly love you."

A few days later, Lady Antonia dined with Senator Marcus Junius Silanus, father-in-law to the new emperor Gaius, at his home. They were joined by his cousin, Sextus Junius Gallio.

"Antonia," said Gallio, "no one knows Caligula better than you. Will he become the good emperor that the people were hoping to have before his father Germanicus died so young and tragically?"

Lady Antonia's expression became serious as she considered the question. Hers was an intelligent, grave face, a face like a judge. "I love Caligula very much," the lady sighed, "but of all Germanicus' male children, he was the one least like him. I can only pray to Venus that his new responsibilities will strengthen what has been a self-indulgent character."

"What disturbs me," Silanus broke in, "is what Lucius Arruntius said to me on his deathbed." Though somewhat older than his cousin—and he was virtually the Father of the Senate— Silanus had held up better physically, retaining a head of hair that was whiter than a well-laundered sheet. He was one who ever exuded thoughtfulness and genial sobriety.

"Arruntius?" murmured Junius Gallio. "That's the senator who committed suicide under a warrant from Tiberius. What did he say?"

"Arruntius told me he was tired of living in a world he had to share with the likes of Tiberius. But he feared that even worse days were coming. He told me: 'If a mature Tiberius, with all his experience and soldierly discipline, was morally ruined and mentally deranged by having attained absolute power, what can we expect from a boy who was reared by one criminal—Tiberius— and advised by another—Macro?' He said that he preferred to leave the world by his own hand, not so much to avoid the evils of the present day, but so he wouldn't have to see the even greater evils that are yet to come."

"That was harshly said," Antonia remarked.

"These are harsh times," Silanus asserted. "Gaius needs to be guided by sensible advice. It's a shame my blameless daughter, Junia Claudilla, died in childbirth. A prudent wife reinforced by the sobering responsibilities of fatherhood might have worked wonders on the boy."

"Too true," said Gallio. "Brutus and Cassius have been slandered by historians, but they were the finest Romans of their day. Who can fault any man who would stand up and fight against Caesarism? Alas, Caesarism defeated them and I am myself a living example what befalls any man who stands up against it. Now I'm tired. Rule by the descendants of a mighty general is an inescapable fact, and the best that Rome can hope for is that the gods will provide good and sane men to be its Caesars. They did well with Augustus, but not so well with Tiberius."

Antonia made no response, but Silanus nodded. "I cannot help but agree. Caesarism has destroyed all that our country once took most pride in. Rome used to be filled with hardworking, self-reliant men. Now slaves and freedmen do the work. Our plebes have interbred with ex-slaves and have adopted their outlook. Could the empire be worse if Pompey had won the civil war? Magnus ever sought to work with the fathers of the

Senate. But Augustus paved his way to personal rule by striking down the great names of our past."

"Take care, Silanus," cautioned Junius Gallio. "Remember that the lady is nobly descended from the house of Caesar?"

"Don't be shy on my account," Antonia told the cousins. "In my younger days, I admit, I believed in what Augustus established. But now having time's perspective, I can see the truth of history much more clearly."

"But can Gaius not be an improvement?" Junius Gallio asked hopefully. "He has known injustice himself."

"Yes," Antonia sighed wistfully, "if beating the puppy will rear a gentle dog."

The cousins let her assertion stand. Shortly thereafter, the Lady Antonia excused herself, averring that she was committed to visit another friend before nightfall.

The cousins walked with her to the portico. As Antonia's train departed, it crossed two people—a red giant and a dark, under-dressed girl—who stood watching. Antonia had noticed the pair in return and supposed that they represented a gladiator and his harlot. *Why were the likes of them standing on Silanus' portico?* she wondered. But on second thought, she didn't really want to know.

"The lady looked at us like we were trash," Tatia whispered unhappily.

"Don't begrudge the Lady Antonia for her mood, Love," Rufus recommended magnanimously. "Her surviving son is a fool, her grandsons want to kill each other, and three of her granddaughters are the most celebrated whores in Rome."

Tatia nodded forlornly. Rufus regarded her gloomy continence. He had done everything he could think of to help her forget about her bad experience on Rome's streets. But not even Gaius' parade had cheered her up to any great degree.

"Rufus!" exclaimed Silanus from his townhouse door. The dignitary motioned to his bodyguards to make way for the wayfarers. As his visitors ascended the marble steps, he said, "I had no idea you were still in Rome! Is this a social call?"

"No indeed, Dominus," Rufus replied respectfully. "I've come with a favor to ask."

"Come in! Come in!" the senator urged.

Rufus and Tatia accompanied Silanus and Gallio into the same entertaining room where Antonia had dined. Hibernicus had an unlikely friendship with the former consul. Silanus had been the editor of the games in which the Rufus had been awarded the wooden sword of freedom, the *rudis*. Later, the Irishman had been able to do the Senator a good turn of his own. Silanus was no fickle fan; everyone held him as a man of constancy and bounty. After brief amenities, Silanus coaxed Hibernicus' whole story from him. The latter described the failed business venture that had ruined him.

"Two hundred and fifty thousand sestertii lost?" echoed the Roman when Hibernicus had finished. "Well, think no more of it! I can help you restore your fortunes. And don't worry about any day-to-day expenses either. I'd be honored to have a man of wide fame for a client."

"Nothing would please me more, Silanus," Rufus replied sincerely, "but I'd be determined to pay back every *quadrans* you loan me—just as soon as I find employment."

"Hmmm," the old man mused. "My son-in-law Gaius is creating a new squad of bodyguards. He may have a place for you in his imperial household. No doubt he has heard all about your many victories in the arena."

Hibernicus thanked his patron with gusto. Encouraged, he presented his second request, that Tatia be allowed to serve in Silanus' house until he was able afford a place of his own.

Silanus replied that he would be pleased to entertain a woman so beautiful as his companion.

"Silanus," Rufus chuckled, "you're a patrician and gentleman."

"Beloved lady!" cried Herod Agrippa from his couch. "Of all the sights of Rome I've been deprived of, I have most missed your pleasant, smiling face."

"You speak the sweetest lies, dear Herod," the lady Antonia admonished.

The lady Antonia had become a second mother to the Jew. An orphan, his guardians had sent him to Rome to be educated. Antonia took him into her home, as a courtesy to the politically-vital Judean royal family. After his arrest, the lady had interceded with the warden to ensure he received far better than the ordinary treatment.

"Every reason I once had to smile has long since blown away with the dust," Antonia continued. "However, if anything can still make my heart feel light, it is listening to your gay nonsense. I'm certain that you have missed the chariot races at the Circus Maximus more than you have ever missed me."

The prince, not denying the observation, smiled.

Then the lady's tone became more serious. "Dear boy, your friend Silas told me something you did not—that you were badly treated in Tusculum."

Agrippa shrugged. "Silas exaggerates. The warden, Norbanus, believed that I lied about Tiberius' death and so threw me into a dark pit for one night. But the next day, when the truth became known, then he couldn't have been more solicitous. I think he feared the withering reproof of Rome's last virtuous woman."

"You flatter me too much, Herod, but I'm happy to see that prison hasn't changed you at all. Tell me, were you actually guilty of whatever it was that you were imprisoned for?"

The Jew grinned sheepishly. "I confess. Last spring, I was riding with Gaius when we stopped on a shaded lane to converse. That rogue of a servant Eutychus was sitting at our feet when I carelessly let slip a sentiment I nursed."

"What sentiment?"

"That I hoped old Tiberius would die soon so that Gaius would come into his inheritance, and that Gemellus need not be an obstacle."

"Herod—you didn't! How could you be so cold to poor, innocent Gemellus? He has as much right to his legacy as Gaius does—and he's never been such a bad boy as his cousin."

Agrippa shrugged. "Others have said much worse things about Gemellus. These are evil times we live in."

"I don't doubt that you mean Gaius himself! But you shouldn't encourage the wicked side of his nature. If only you were not such a rogue! Caligula listens to you to a degree that he listens to few others. Of his confidants, Macro only thinks of himself, while those wild youths, Lepidus and Aulus Vitellius, continually egg him on into further vice. Our Gaius needs good counsel. Is there any wisdom in you, Agrippa?"

"I would wisely advise him to keep his soldiers well paid and the arena well stocked with gladiators. That is the way of Rome. Its people never think about politics and its army thinks of nothing else."

Antonia shook her snowy head resignedly.

"Tell me, beloved lady, why has Caligula been keeping me confined? I'm allowed to leave the house under guard, but that is no substitute for true freedom. Have I become an embarrassment to my friend?"

"Far from it. He would have released you even before he left Misenum, but Macro was against it."

"The dog!"

"And he would have freed you immediately after his arrival in Rome, but *I* was against it."

"My lady!"

"Oh, Herod, impulsiveness is Gaius' cognomen. I asked him to delay a reasonable length of time before pardoning you—not because I bear you any ill, but as a nod to common decency. It must not look as though Caligula is impatient to undo the whole of his grandfather's works in their entirety.

"Be patient; your release will come very shortly. In just two or three weeks, people will be distracted by public games and chariot races and will not be paying heed to small acts of clemency."

Agrippa sank back and sighed. "I have waited six months; what is another two weeks?" Then he changed the subject: "What news from my homeland?" He knew that Antonia, unlike many women of rank, liked to keep abreast of public matters.

Antonia frowned. "The last I heard, Lucius Vitellius was posted on the Euphrates, lest the Parthians try to cross it. Have you heard about Pontius Pilate?"

"Pilate? No. What has that desert devil done now?"

"He's been recalled to Rome. Tiberius summoned him to face charges for massacring civilians in Samaria. He's been confined in a comfortable villa awaiting Gaius' convenience."

"That man was a plague on my country! His wild and angry actions kept the whole province on the edge of revolt. It is ironic that his downfall should come over something so unimportant as slaying Samaritans!"

"Are not the Samaritans your own people?"

"No, they were outsiders sent into the land as colonists by the Assyrians after they destroyed Israel. They were pagans, but God sent them so many tribulations that they accepted the faith of Abraham merely to appease Him. Even so, their adopted religion has been ignorantly practiced and is very corrupt."

"I will never understand the politics of your country, much less its religion."

"Would that we were blessed with the sane and loving ways of Rome, dear Antonia."

"It pleases me that your spirits have stayed high, despite all."

"As high as an owl, I think," Agrippa remarked, touching Loderod's medallion, which was hidden under his clothes.

"Do owls fly so very high?" Antonia inquired.

Agrippa shrugged. "Not particularly. But circumstances cause me to be very interested in owls of late."

THE WOLF

CHAPTER X

Finally, thought Optio Petillius Quintius, *I'm rid of that disgusting brute.* The Tusculum vigile was impatiently standing next to the procurator Decimus Coeranus while the amphitheater slaves wheeled the cage through the gate. Its occupant was a howling, teeth-gnashing monstrosity that the peace officer called a wolf for want of a better description. Many times before, Petillius had felt like running the repulsive creature through with a spear, except he didn't want to disappoint his superiors, who wanted a cash return for it.

It was bad luck for the old emperor to have died just then; every civil servant in the vicinity of Rome was so busy scrambling to protect his own job with the incoming administration that no one had time to spare for a lowly optio with one wild wolf to place. Inquiries had proven that no such animal was reported missing from any amphitheater. That left him free to approach any potential taker he could find. Petillius had managed to coax Decimus Coeranus' signature onto a papyrus, allowing him to wash his hands of the beast.

"That's an odd-looking wolf," Coeranus mused aloud. "I don't think I ever saw that species before!"

"Call it the Coeranus Wolf, for all I care," Petillius snorted. "Just being around the thing makes my skin crawl. An ordinary animal wants to eat you alive, but I'd almost believe that this monster would like to do something a lot worse!"

The bureaucrat sympathized. The wolf—and that is what it seemed to be, despite the fact that all of its proportions were oddly wrong—was not large, though it was yet ferocious and strong. Lean of body, its tail was short, its ears small and low-set. The hind legs seemed appreciably longer than the front pair. Its fangs were especially wicked-looking and its paws were—well, Coeranus got the impression that they were deformed without being able to put his finger on what, exactly, was wrong. Even the fur, lusterless and off-colored, came off as peculiar. But the eyes were the most disturbing. They seemed unnaturally cunning—diabolical even.

At that moment a pair of his carpenters came over to get a look at the animal: Calusidius and Menius, a Sicilian freedman.

"Brrr!" Coeranus said, holding his round, soft belly. "That thing will scare the bowels out of any gladiator who has to fight it in the arena, eh, Menius?"

"I'd say it would," replied the craftsman.

The other man, Calusidius, asked bemusedly, "Where did it come from, Dominus?"

"Tusculum," said the optio, answering for Coeranus. "We caught it wandering around and attacking people. It killed a slave girl and mauled a gardener. The last I heard, the man wasn't doing too well."

Calusidius' and the creature's blue eyes met and locked, like the eyes of old enemies.

At the command of Gaius, Zenodotus had converted a cell in the palace substructure into a magic chamber. The desired alterations had not been difficult to achieve, for in this very room Thrasyllus, Tiberius' late wizard, had often worked his incantations. One of the unseen changes that the Alexandrian had enacted was to consecrate its elements—the wood, the stone, and the soil—in the name of the all-powerful Chthonioi. A great circle had been drawn, its sectors inscribed with prayers and mighty invocations in Greek letters. Within the circle, upon a couch, Gaius lay in a trance.

The worried and frightened emperor had ordered Zenodotus to erect a strong barrier against the Chthonioi's baleful power and he had done so. Closely guarded by Praetorians, Zenodotus had made a foray into the slave markets and looked over the youngsters available there. He had selected, and purchased, a nine-year old virgin girl reared on a breeding farm in Parma.

Now, on an altar at one side of the room, the unlucky girl slept in death, runnels of her blood streaking her pale flesh, the powerful life force of her youth having been drunk away by the unseen forces that were invisibly crowded into the magic room.

Over the last weeks, Zenodotus had changed his attitude toward Gaius. Before he had been an employer whom he wished to please. Now he was one to resent and hate. The Greek would, if he dared, have manipulated the ceremony to send the ungrateful prince's soul hurtling down into the poisonous coils of the Chthonioi. But his vengeance would have to wait. Attendant sorcerers, loyal to Gaius, stood watchfully on either side. Macro and several Praetorian swordsmen waited just beyond the mystically-sealed portal. His rival wizards did not understand all he did, but he sized them up as being competent enough to discern any sign of chicanery that Zenodotus might try. Though now was not a good time to act, the wizard had to act soon. Gaius considered him a betrayer; as soon as the cruel youth managed to wrest all the services he need from Zenodotus, the wizard could expect to die.

The Alexandrian's mind had been sifting through many plans of escape but, so far, an infallible method eluded him. For now, to placate Gaius and buy time, Zenodotus had to do whatever he was commanded.

He prayed:

"Let no fell magicks assail this man,
Ye spirits of Chthonioi race.
Be mollified by prayer and gifts;
Accept another in his place."

Zenodotus took a blood-bathed talisman from the altar, a green jade head of Hecate. The emperor had told him that it had once belonged to his father Germanicus, who believed it could ward off the powers of evil. The magician crossed the chalk line into the circle and carefully cinctured the charm's golden chain around the young man's neck.

Already the wizard had placed strong warding spells about the emperor, but the amulet, hallowed by a virgin's lifeblood, would amplify these several-fold. Soon, the Greek knew, Gaius would awaken.

Being sensitive to psychic resonances, he surmised that the ceremony had gone well. The spirits of Chaos had let themselves be temporarily placated. They had accepted the sacrificial victim today, though very soon the dark gods would be renewing their demands for the specific soul that had been promised them.

The youthful sovereign blinked and awoke without bleariness, mystically charged in some way. "Is… is it done?" he gasped.

"The dark gods are satisfied, for now, Princeps. Still it would be wise to provide the special sacrifice promised them on the Kalends of May."

Gaius dropped his head back upon his pillow. For days he had prepared himself for this ceremony—with diet, prayer, meditation, and invocation. Between supernatural and mundane concerns, he had not had a moment's peace, not an hour of easy rest. Nightly, he dreamed of Tiberius rising from the smoke to fetch him down into the pits of Tartarus, there to be crushed by the Titans as they writhed in their bonds.

The Kalends. The date was little more than three weeks away. Before then, he had to choose a loved one to die in his stead. And not only must that one die, but was to be plunged into an eternity of terror and agony. Gaius, after much internal wrangling, had decided that he loved but two people sincerely—his grandmother Antonia and his sister Drusilla.

Drusilla. He could never give her up, never. Even though his other sisters, Lesbia and Agrippinilla, he would have given to the Chthonioi for the asking, they would not serve. Sour and overly proud as they were, he loved them little. Antonia would have to be his choice, though it made his stomach churn to think of damning her.

Gods above, he thought, *if this sword is not lifted from my throat I soon shall be driven mad!* He ground his teeth, knowing that he was inwardly a coward who would agree to pay any price demanded of him in the end. This was all Zenodotus's fault! He would pay for his bungling, for making Gaius learn things about himself that he didn't want to know. Oh, how he would pay!

On the Kalends of May!

By midday, Decimus Coeranus had already checked over scores of amphitheater accounts, as well as having inspected the extensive renovation of the spectator area. Thinking he had well-earned an hour's rest and a meal, he was about to head out to the street markets when, suddenly, the amphitheater shook with roars, trumpets, and bellows.

"Blessed Hermes!" the bureaucrat swore. "Those animals are going crazy *again!*"

Coeranus darted out his office door and scuttled into the darkness of the animal enclosure. In it, the din was so great that he had to clamp his hands over his ears.

"Demipho! Anthor!" he yelled. "Can't you keep this howling down? What's wrong with these stinking beasts? Are they all going rabid at once?"

The two attendants—one an old, hobbling Greek in a stained chiton, the other a bulky Italian peasant—hurried out from behind a bull pen.

"Well?" the director demanded. "What's all this racket? I can't hear myself think!"

"It's the wolf that the vigiles brought over from Tusculum," shouted Demipho. "It's driving the other beasts out of their minds—and it's killed every other wolf in its cage!"

"Killed every other wolf in its cage?" echoed Coeranus. "That's disastrous! Why didn't you stop it?"

At that instant, the silence of the tomb fell over their surroundings. The suddenness of the quietude had come on like something unnatural. The three men could actually hear the animals' breathing.

"This has been going on since that creature arrived," insisted Anthor. "One moment they're tearing their cages apart, and the next they're standing like stuffed trophies. I've had enough of it! Either we send the wolf to the spoliarium or you'll have to give me a new place to work. Otherwise, I'm taking the corn dole!"

"If Caesar wants to feed a lazy incompetent, he's welcome to you!"

Flustered, Anthor threw his iron-tipped prod down. "That's it! I quit! I hope Caesar throws you to your own wolf!"

As Anthor stomped from the enclosure, Coeranus turned peevishly toward old Demipho. "Are you quitting, too?"

The crane-necked Greek ducked his head between his bony shoulders. "Not me, Coeranus! I'm not a citizen, and eating is a hard habit to break!"

"Well," the procurator muttered, uncertain if he had won his point or not, "let's take another look at the wolf that's giving us so much trouble!"

The rumpled Roman eques followed the slow-moving freedman down an aisle of pens where leopards spit threateningly and wild African dogs, still held by the spell of silence, bared frothing jaws. At last, they arrived at a spacious iron cage roofed over with wooden poles. The fly-covered carcasses of three wolves bore out what Anthor had already told him. The sole occupant of the pen crouched with its head facing away from Coeranus.

"Oh, this is a dreadful!" complained the imperial agent. "Just when the emperor's special games require that we find hundreds of beasts, one crazy animal wipes out three perfectly good wolves. If I didn't need it for the arena, I'd have the guards bury their javelins in the freak's body!"

At his threat, the wolf turned sharply, its blazing stare overwhelming Coeranus' own. With a shudder, the man looked away.

"We won't have any peace until we destroy it," the Greek warned. "That is, if doing so pleases the dominus."

Nothing would have suited the eques better, but that went for most of the foul-smelling brutes he was responsible for. Alas, these animals were valuable imperial property. If it got out that Coeranus had destroyed a fascinating and loathsome freak, thereby cheating the crowd of its entertainment, the director would have a fat chance of landing a better job in the civil service.

Anyway, the harm was done and one wolf was better than no wolves. A bestiarius would undoubtedly put an end to the creature very soon—and good riddance. If its fight and death were exciting, the wolf's destruction would help Coeranus' career instead of hamstringing it.

"Do anything you have do to keep order! Drug the monster if necessary, but I want that wolf for the arena!"

"Aye, Dominus," Demipho responded glumly. "But we'll need a replacement for Anthor. One man alone can't tend to so many wild brutes!"

"All right, all right. I'll see who I can find," the procurator agreed, and turned toward the exit. On the threshold, he met the carpenter Calusidius. "Why are you coming down here?" the irascible Roman demanded.

"I—I met Anthor going out. He said he's quitting."

"What of it?"

"I'd like a chance to work with the animals, as he did—unless you have someone else in mind, Dominus."

"Why?"

"I've always been fond of animals."

"You'd like to exchange your hammer for a dung fork? You're crazy, old man, but I don't care! If you want the job, it's yours. Demipho will tell you what you have to do!"

As Coeranus bustled away, the carpenter heard the wolf's throaty rumble. At the source of the ominous sound stood Demipho, standing a safe distance from the beast's cage. "I'm taking Anthor's job," he told the freedman.

The old Greek looked him up and down. "Is that so? Not the smartest thing you ever did, Calusidius, my friend."

The wolf growled again, drawing the carpenter's attention. He kept his expression controlled, as if uninterested in what the beast did. Inside, he was very interested indeed.

Since Mar had no interest in an escape attempt, Osric the Engle had worked out a plan of his own. To succeed, he needed to increase his power over the White Runes. For that reason, while others slept, or on the day assigned to rest and leisure, Osric meditated upon his rune lore. Though the Roman guards had weapons and great numbers, the rune-warrior was heir to a precious legacy of the North that made him a better killer than any of his jailers were. So, while others took their ease, he labored harder at his songs than he ever had at his sword-training.

At this moment, shortly after the midday lunch, Osric stole a moment from his meditations and sought out the son of Calusidius. He and Mar had not spoken in three days and it was high time to inquire after the latter's state of mind.

Osric wandered to the edge of the fountain, whose water flowed out of a vessel that was held by a nude man of bronze. Though the Engle had many a reason to be angry with the Romans, he never ceased to wonder at the marvels created by their craftsmen. In their cunning, they could actually make a stream flow above men's heads!

Just then, from beyond the fountain, there came a blast of laughter along with Mar's shout: "*Degenerate swine!* The Chatti would drown such twisted villains in the bogs!"

Osric raced toward the sound of his voice. In the shade of a building were four men—a Bructeri, a Greek, an Italian, and a Nubian, in whose midst Mar struggled.

"He's not only is as pretty as a woman, he protests like one!" the Italian mocked.

"Get off his breech-clout and throw him across the bench," the Nubian snarled, already undoing the knot of his own girdle.

Mar twisted, kicked, and cursed, but they were many against one. The Greek pinned his arms, while others tore at his garments. An unexpected blow from behind sent the laughing Bructeri down into the dust.

The others dropped Mar and shifted toward their attacker. The Italian growled: "It's the lad's blond lover! Don't be jealous, Pretty Boy. Share a little and wait your turn!"

The Engle's fist crashed into the speaker's jaw, folding him up. The remaining three, including the recovering Bructeri, came at him all at once, driving Osric to his knees with their blows and kicks. But before they could get a good grip on him, one of his opponents was yanked away. Mar was back in the fight. The Bructeri seized the Chatti from the rear but Osric, regaining his footing, struck the German renegade across the side of the head, driving him back into the dirt.

"What's going on here?!" bawled Cocceius, running up flanked by three guards. It took only seconds for the trainer to nail down the cause of the fight. The rape of a new student was actually a common occurrence, but discipline had to be maintained.

"Five lashes for the boy Marcus," ordered Cocceius. "He caused the fight by not being able to handle himself. Ten lashes for each of these four needy lovers." Finally, he said, "Twelve stripes and eight days in the pit for Osricus. If we let everybody get involved in every fight, this place would fall into bloody chaos!"

This was the night Calusidius had been waiting for. He would be sitting out the dark watch alone. Privacy suited his plan well. He patted the vial of poison hidden under the folds of his old paenula. In Rome, even the tools of murder could be purchased.

"How was the wolf today?" he asked Demipho when the departing Greek came to get his cloak.

"It behaved itself," Demipho replied. "That roughhouser Anthor must have had a way of upsetting the thing. Some people make animals act crazy just by being around them. What a job! Hundreds of yapping, barking, roaring, screaming brutes, and every one a killer. Some entertainment! Give me a good play by Aristophanes any day." Demipho ambled out the door.

The Roman waited for several minutes, not moving from his spot until the attendant had time enough to walk a goodly distance.

How was it that things had fallen into place without any great effort on his own part? Had it been the stern but fair gods of Germania who had purposefully brought the wolf to this particular amphitheater at this particular time? Though he could think of no way to redeem his son from bondage, divine providence had at least provided him with the opportunity to earn back Mar's respect—by destroying the very enemy whom he had earlier fled from.

Calusidius went into a side room where animal provender was stored. This included a pen of live chickens for the carnivores. Snatching the feet of a rooster, the Roman dragged it out and trapped it between his knees. Then, squeezing the base of the bird's bill with the fingers of his left hand, he opened the beak slightly. Then the old man put the narrow spout of the poison-filled bladder inside its mouth with his right hand and sent a long squirt down the fowl's gullet.

With marvelous quickness, the bird stopped its rapid breathing, its struggles. Calusidius forced even more of the bane into what was already a carcass, then poured the rest over its feathers. It was then that Calusidius sensed rather than heard a movement behind him. He turned sharply, afraid of being seen by one of the night guards, but no one was there. *Jumpy old man*, he scolded himself. *This place is full of life and movement. Ignore it.* He got to his feet.

With nervousness but also determination, the old Roman approached the wolf cage. The lupine was fully awake and wary. He wondered if the thing had recognized him, just as he had recognized it. Calusidius did not doubt that the demon-beast possessed sentience, this fiend in animal form.

"Here, wolf," he said, forcing his faltering voice to be stronger. "It's time to eat." He pushed the dead rooster through the feeding slot and pulled his hands away swiftly. The wolf peered at the slack and dead bird. The predator's lips curled back over black gums and ivory fangs. *Eat it and perish*, ran the old man's thoughts, *eat it and go back to the hells of Heid!*

The brute sniffed the rooster, licked it tentatively, and then a buzzing shout rang out: "No, *Glaejord*, do not eat!"

Calusidius whirled toward the sound, but a numbing pain struck the back of his head. Lightning flashed and then came blackness.

As the old man fell groaning, a dwarfish shape stood above him, leering down. The stranger tittered approvingly. "Not dead! Not dead! Good, not dead!"

The wolf whined at the newcomer and tried to stand up on its hind legs. The dwarf sprang to the cage bars. "Galar did not forget. Galar sought! Glaejord is pleased?"

The wolf yowled and coughed, as if in imitation of speech. The dwarf nodded, undid the cage door's hooks and latches.

Just then, Calusidius came to and struggled up to a kneeling position, a sharp throbbing in his skull. He heard the clicks and clacks of loosening catches and with horror discerned what the dwarf was doing. He fought to rise, but at that moment the door swung open. The wolf leaped from the cage like a projectile from the cup of an onager.

"No!" shrilled Calusidius, getting up and beginning a run for the exit. As he touched the door that meant escape, a blow from the rear drove his head into the boards. He felt the weight of the thing now clawing at his back, forcing him down....

Galar scampered to the top of a stall rail to watch the wolf rip and gnaw into the chest of its dying victim. He observed what the beast sought—something red and glistening. Throwing its head back, the thing wolfed down the bleeding heart-meat. But the wolf suddenly seemed ill—very ill. With a whine of agony, it lost the strength of its legs and fell outstretched beside the corpse of Calusidius.

Galar watched the transformation of one who was chosen of Heid. The wolf's lanky body deformed. Some bones grew, some shrank; its tail atrophied. Jaws diminished and the muzzle blunted. Toes lengthened into fingers; the neck narrowed.

A moment later, a young naked woman lay across the dead-man, writhing and groaning. She turned a face of anguish toward Galar, her lips, teeth, and small chin stained crimson. "Galar," she cried, "help me! I'm poisoned!"

The dwarf sprang through the air and agilely landed at his mistress' side. Though she was larger than he was, the little man picked her up by the strength of his arms.

"Galar has promised to serve the Glaejord Frigerd," he told the blonde maid. "He shall make her well...."

THE GATE

CHAPTER XI

Punishment had initially filled Osric with fury. But what angered him most of all was that Cocceius, whom he respected, would flog a man for having been the victim of a shameful attack. And then, too, he would also flog a friend who had rightfully stood by him! The Engle decided that the whole race of Romans are insane.

Osric sang his *fimbul*-song to heal his lashes and by the second day he was feeling improved. His anger diminished and he realized that Cocceius had unwittingly done him a good turn. Solitary imprisonment merely provided the Engle with the privacy he needed to practice his arts, meditate upon the runes, and jar awake the power slumbering in his blood.

Rune magic, Osric became increasingly aware, took considerable power from the practitioner. The singing of fimbul-songs taxed him even more than the writing of runic spells. Restoring the expended power required rest and meditation. Nonetheless, if he were to recover the ring Andvaranaut, he must become proficient in all the sundry applications of the runes.

The chief trainer apparently wanted to keep him fit, for the food brought to him was good, and the energy he drew from it made it easier to attain deep trance states. Loderod had, in fact, taught him that all men are slaves to Fate and what they might do with evil intent, the gods may channel into good.

In the course of dedicated practice, Osric eventually discovered the pitch of intensity for his fimbul-song to magically unlock his iron shackles. Free to move about his small cell, he found relief from meditation by doing physical exercise.

Over the ensuing days, Osric expanded his command over the runes by opening his bonds time and time again. After that, he practiced at unlocking the door. Though escape had become a possibility, he was reluctant to quit the school without first inviting Mar to join in his stab for freedom.

After his time was up, Cocceius returned the Engle to the surface and hard training. Osric let a day and night go by, but on the second night, he carried out his and Mar's long-deferred escape.

Well after midnight, when sleep held sway over all except the guards of the night shift, Osric acted. He carefully painted the proper runes upon the door of his cubicle with pigment from a jar of cinnabar paint stolen from the training area. Instructors used it to mark the targets on a human body—such as the heart or throat—that gladiators should aim for. Osric gathered his willpower for a long moment, then whispered an incantation.

The bar on the outside of the door rattled. Again and again the bolt was fumbled, as if a clumsy paw manipulated it, and he would have to begin anew. After many tries, the latch released.

The Engle rose weakly, his body soaked with sweat. For a moment, he prayed silently to Heimdall for replenished strength.

Osric stole from his cubicle and with soft, padding steps he crept along the rows of prison doors. Soon he came to Mar's locked cell and pressed his ear to the wood to confirm that someone was within. Carefully, the Engle slid the bolt aside and slipped within. Mar, on his tick bed, sensed an intrusion and awoke with a lurch.

"Mar! Be still! It's me!" the rune-warrior hissed.

"Osric!" said Mar.

"I am sworn to leave this place, and I will go tonight, if you are with me or not!"

"Osric, you are too stubborn for your own good!" the Chatti complained.

"I have much to do without, and I cannot do it as a prisoner!"

"Very well," Mar said. "I am not afraid to die." The youth drew on his tunic and they slipped from the cell together. Running in a low crouch, they attained the wall separating the training yard from the outer court. Osric's plan called for leaving over the interior wall, since it would be less guarded than the walls facing the city streets. Crossing it would not lead to freedom, but the walls beyond that one had no direct access from the prisoner area, and hence might be less guarded. The audacity of such a route, the Engle hoped, could conceivably make up for the added difficulty in using it.

They crouched in the dense shadow of the wall while a guard shuffled past them, humming a tune. The Germans took him from behind and rendered him senseless as gladiators are trained to do. "We've earned death on the cross for certain now," warned Mar.

Osric, arming himself with the guard's gladius, whispered, "If we are doomed to die regardless, we may as well be bold."

To climb the wall, Osric made a sling of his hands and invited Mar to step into it. The latter, hoisted upwards, managed to gain a secure grip and swung his legs astraddle of the edge of the wall.

Osric threw the blanket taken from Mar's room to the Chatti. The latter let it dangle within reach of the Engle's powerful leap. Osric, climbing strongly, joined Mar on the coping.

Osric gathered in the blanket and dropped one end over the other side of the parapet. While Mar held it firmly, the Engle ambled down.

Osric surveyed the courtyard, listening for movement. Detecting naught, he whispered for Mar to come down. The boy lowered his legs and then let go. Osric, catching him by the waist, softened his fall.

"Narbo," a voice whispered from the other side of a buttress, "I think I heard something."

Guards, at least two. Osric and his companion dropped to their bellies, depending on the shadows to conceal them.

"It was along here," one of the sentinels insisted.

"Gladiators are murdering devils," said his partner. "Let's get a light and summon some help."

The Germans waited for them to draw away, then took them from behind. Osric beat his man senseless, but Mar's opponent managed to bawl *"Escape!"* in a loud voice.

A blow from the Engle's hilt quieted him, but too late.

"To the main gate, now!" Osric yelled. Already the shout had aroused excitement all around them. To the one side, the rune-warrior heard the yelping of a dog and the tramp of many boots.

Someone ran up in front of the gate with a lantern. Osric made straight for him. A face-blow staggered the sentry and his lamp broke up-on the ground, spreading a small puddle of flame.

Near him Mar, armed with a sword from the second sentry, was assailed by another guard springing out of the dark. The attacker was a poor fighter compared to the young Chatti, and the latter's heavy blows drove the Roman stumbling out of reach.

The yard continued to fill with torchlight and voices. Lacking the time to work the gate's mechanism, the young men started climbing. "Hold there!" commanded a guardsman from the observation ledge above. The fellow, when he thought he saw movement, didn't hesitate to stab at it with his spear, missing Osric's face by inches. Surprised, the Engle lost his grip and dropped down to the sandy courtyard.

Men piled on him there, cursing and kicking. The German rolled away and tried to spring to his feet, but a hard-driven baton between his shoulders knocked him down again.

He heard Mar shouting, and then the boy's voice fell off.

"Wait!" one of their attackers bawled. "Don't finish them off! Let Cocceius make a lesson of the pair! We've watched too few crucifixions lately."

"Spare me, Heid!" Galar had heard his mistress' shout and dashed to his mistress'—Frigerd's—aid.

The woman had awakened from her nightmare and was peering with alarm around the shadowy room, trying to comprehend where she was.

The witch felt hot, stifled, and so kicked the tattered woolen blanket away from herself.

She panted, trying to think. The bane that Calusidius had used to poison her must have been partly magical, the sorceress realized. For days, she had been lapsing and relapsing into delirium, tormented by Hel-visions. In lucid moments she had added her own healing arts to those of the dwarf. Alas, neither was skilled in the *limrunar* and she still felt weaker than an infant.

It was a pity, she now realized, that her teachers in sorcery had concentrated so intently upon the crafts of illusion and destruction. As a result, the use of the White Runes for healing didn't come naturally to her.

The rune-witch was not able to stretch comfortably on the short bed. An itch forced her to scratch her scalp. Fleas! The place was foul! The bed teemed with biting bugs and the walls were hung with moist, grimy cobwebs. The air smelled of mice. The poorest German thrall sleeping with his eorl's cattle was better off than any wretch housed in this attic cell beneath a leaking roof.

"The Glaejord feels better?" Galar whined, using the witch's Sitonian title. Frigerd started; she hadn't realized that the dwarf was with her just then. She saw him now squatting in the corner like a spider on its web. He resembled one of the *dvergar*, his father's race—called by some the Children of the Night. Others had called them the Worms of the Earth. She preferred the term "maggot."

The dvergar had been the only one of her escort to escape the fight in Tusculum. From the bits he'd told her during her brief waking moments, she'd pieced together what had happened. While she fled in wolf guise, pursued by men and dogs, Galar had followed the Roman soldiers to the prison-house where her Bructeri servants were confined. When they and one of Loderod's allies, a black-haired youth, were moved to Rome, Galar followed. He observed them imprisoned in a lodge complex where captives were trained to be warriors and, by keeping periodic watch over it, witnessed the young Osric's arrival.

Galar had subsequently worked tirelessly to locate his missing mistress, and also find word of Andvaranaut. He existed by stealing food and earning coins posing as an acrobat. That's how he'd discovered the third member of the Chatti party—the old Roman called Calusod. He, in the company of a red giant and a woman, had chanced upon one of Galar's street performances. He'd followed the three to a mighty circular structure called "the amphitheater." Thereafter, Galar maintained a close watch on the old man. On his last foray, he'd scented the Hel-wolf; he'd also smelled poison, comprehended what Calusidius intended, and moved decisively to thwart him.

Frigerd shivered. Once a witch assumed the wolf-guise, she was unable to shed it until she could drink the heart-blood of a human whom she'd slain herself. It was an odious experience being an animal for as long as she had. Whenever Frigerd closed her eyes, she could still hear echoes of the hounds howling over her spoor. She vowed not to take a lupine form again, except in the most dire situation.

For rescuing her from the cage and from her miserable metamorphosis, Frigerd had promised Galar the boon of his choosing. So far, he had not named his desire—but knowing the dvergar race, it would surely be something vile.

"What have you learned about the whereabouts of the ring?" the witch suddenly asked her diminutive helpmate.

"Nothing, Glaejord. Mayhap if the magician gave the ring to the old Caesar, he may have given it to his young heir with the whole of his legacy."

"Andvaranaut is *my* legacy!" Frigerd reminded him coldly. "From infancy, I was reared to attain the mastery of it."

Once, long ago, the cult of Heid had controlled the ring Andvaranaut and worked vast destruction upon the world. They sought to use its power to free the demonic race of Jotuns from the prisons which Woden and the Aesir had forged for them, and thus cause the world's ending—Gotterdammerung. The witches of Heid had *almost* succeeded…

But then the ring was stolen.

"We must find out if this young Caesar has the ring Andvaranaut. Have you found the means to spy on him?" she asked.

"That is very difficult. No man of Midgard is so well protected."

"Would he receive a chieftainess of the North and accede to her just demands?"

"I do not believe so, Glaejord. But there are more subtle ways to enter into the company of the young Caesar…."

Marcus Silanus sat pondering family matters while waiting in one of the high-vaulted atriums of Augustus' palace. Emperor Gaius had not yet risen. That boy! Junia Claudilla had many times mentioned to her father what a sleepyhead her husband was, loving the festivities of the night and scorning the morning.

Perhaps he should admonish Caligula for his careless ways. He dreaded to think what could happen to the affairs of state if the boy continued to be guided by a self-seeking lout like the praetorian Macro. If his son-in-law wasn't careful, he could be reduced to a mere puppet.

Macro's scheming had become clear when the prefect had read Tiberius' will before the Senate, the august fathers learning for the first time that Gaius and Gemellus had been named heirs in equal parts. In spite of that, Nonius Macer, a confidant of Macro, denounced the whole idea of sharing imperial power. He dared to say that the Senate could honorably ignore the will, since it showed every sign of having been written by a man who had taken leave of his senses. The Senate, to its disgrace, moved without discussion to award Gaius all the specific powers and titles of the Princeps. That left Gemellus' rights wholly ignored, and Silanus couldn't help but think that this reign had begun under a shadow of ill auspices.

Afterwards, Gaius addressed the Senate, refusing only one of the offered titles—"Father of his Country"—in respect of his tender years. Then he went on to promise that all of Tiberius' bequests to the soldiers, as well as to the commons, and individuals—except for Gemellus, apparently—would be paid out punctiliously. Moreover, the legacies of Livia, long hoarded by her avaricious son Tiberius, would at last be released from the imperial estate.

In the mood of the times, the current consuls, Proculus and Nigrinus, offered to resign in Gaius' favor, but he had declined. Instead, he named himself, along with his uncle Claudius, as replacement consuls, *suffecti*, to assume office when the elected officeholders followed the accepted custom of resigning at midterm.

Silanus looked up, hearing footfalls. "Arise!" sang a herald from some other hall. "Arise for Gaius Julius Caesar Augustus Germanicus, First Citizen of Rome!"

Gaius entered the vicinity, preceded by bodyguards, mainly well-armed German warriors, courtiers wearing snowy togas, and by slaves garbed in palace livery. Silanus rose laboriously and bowed:

"Imperial Caesar!" the statesman said.

"Dear father-in-law," the imperator averred, approaching the elder with outstretched hands. The old man embraced and kissed him. "I was pleased to receive your request for a visit, Caesar. I see too little of my kinsman!"

Silanus thought Gaius' smiling face was as impenetrable as a Greek mask. The statesman moved forthrightly to the point: "I did not wish to intrude on the crush of your duties, Princeps, but I have been waiting for the opportunity to seek from you an imperial appointment for a friend."

Gaius looked soulfully away. "You understand my burden so well." Then he perked up. "But friends and family shall always have my boon! I owe you much for the gift of your much-beloved and eternally-lamented daughter, Junia Claudilla."

Silanus nodded. "Your sympathy is much appreciated, Imperial Caesar." He glanced at the German bodyguards wearing brown leather armor. "I am aware that you are forming a bodyguard of handpicked men. There is a brave and honorable ex-gladiator of my acquaintance. I am moved to inquire whether or not he may offer his sword as one of your protectors."

"A gladiator?" grinned Gaius. "Fascinating fellows! Is he a Thracian?"

"Alas, no, Caesar. He is a secutor of wide fame—Rufus Hibernicus."

The young man's brow knitted. "I *have* heard of him. I'd assumed he'd be dead by now."

"He lives, O Princeps—a most remarkable and far-traveled man in all ways. He begs to be allowed to step into the light of Rome's new sun."

"Well, this is not a boon I can refuse! Tomorrow begins the first of the circus combats, as authorized by the Senate. They will be the best games that Rome has hosted in twenty years. Join me in the imperial box, Silanus, and bring this Hibernicus fellow with you."

"I shall be honored to," said Marcus Silanus.

Gaius clasped the senator's hand as a gesture of his leave-taking. "Now we hurry on to another appointment, father-in-law. A guest, scarcely less eminent than yourself, is awaiting my audience."

Silanus nodded in acceptance of his dismissal and bade the young man adieu. Watching his son-in-law leave, the old man was left with the impression that Gaius, despite his cheerful pose, had seemed preoccupied during their brief interview. Something was bothering the boy and he wondered what it could be.

Emperor Gaius

CHAPTER XII

Gaius left his father-in-law with a feeling of distaste. Silanus was too much like his daughter, Junia—whom Gaius had never liked—in other words, fussy, moralizing, and conventional. When the young profligate had wished to be sharing in the delights of Capri's pleasure houses, he was instead dragooned into the role of being a conscientious husband. It had amused Tiberius to police his grandson's morals rigorously, keeping him in political training and at study. His nights were wasted in the cold bed of a foolish and conventional girl. When she died, he only regretted losing the unborn child that had died with her.

A servant admitted the emperor's party to the apartment occupied by Marcus Julius Agrippa. The latter stood up hastily.

"Leave us!" Gaius commanded his attendants. Agrippa, cheerful but tense, similarly signaled for his own staff to depart. Both men had risked their lives by speaking too freely in front of slaves, and would not be so careless in the future.

Once alone, Agrippa clasped the shoulders of his younger friend and kissed his cheek. "I never believed that you would forget me!" he declared.

"Has everything been provided as I ordered it to be?" Gaius asked.

"This apartment, these clothes—they are beyond all my hopes!"

"Your prosperity need have no limit, if you are as much my friend as I need you to be."

The youth's serious tone gave Agrippa pause. "Something is amiss?"

"Do you remember that conversation that led to that slave's denunciation?"

Agrippa frowned. "We spoke of Tiberius. Was the deed accomplished in the manner we discussed?"

"Yes," said the young man through gritted teeth. "But the sorcery involved... certain hazards... which that fool Zenodotus never warned me of."

"How so, my friend?"

Gaius told the story. Agrippa shook his head commiseratively. "One whom you love must die and be damned? This is vile, truly." He made hand-passes to ward off malicious spirits.

"If Macro had simply poisoned the old goat as I'd asked him to, none of this would have happened!"

"Is there a reason that we are discussing this in view of its happy conclusion?"

"I would speak to you, though I have many great men surrounding me, but they are self-seeking sorts and not my true friends. I need a veritable Achates, one to whom I may speak without guile."

Now Agrippa thought he knew why Gaius provided for him so well in captivity. Despite many temptations, the Judean hadn't exposed his Roman friend as a dire threat to the old emperor, though he easily could have. He'd gambled that his chances would be better if he endured imprisonment and bided his time. "You certainly may speak from the heart, my friend," said the Jew. "My family well knows the troubles of kingship."

Gaius then told him the story of Zenodotus' mad plan, and how it had endangered him.

"The scoundrel! Have you chosen the one who must die in your stead?" Agrippa asked.

Here Gaius demurred, well knowing how much the Easterner loved Antonia. "I—have not decided. But… but if I should need your help, your advice, may I count upon you absolutely?"

"Always, Caesar!"

"Well and good. For now, Zenodotus has provided me with a talisman of protection—if I can believe the words of such a rogue." He showed Agrippa the green jade amulet he always wore. Then Gaius' mood changed abruptly: "Agrippa, if you could ask any boon of me, what would it be?"

"You overwhelm me, Caesar! Yet, if I dare to seek more than I have already been given, there is a small matter that is dear to my heart."

"Speak!"

"When I was placed in bonds in Tusculum, suffering from thirst under a hot sun, your slave Tityus gave me water. I beg you, grant that man his freedom that I may employ him. I would make him steward over my properties here in Italy."

"He's yours! And if there happens to be any man whom you would want punished—such as Paulus Didius Norbanus—say the word."

"Caesar, in my present joy, how can I bear grudges?"

"Well said! Let us be men of generous spirit on this happy occasion. *Rebilis!*" he shouted over his shoulder. A servant entered the chamber carrying a bejeweled box of ivory. Gaius accepted the container and from it removed a diamond-studded gold diadem. This he placed portentously upon his surprised friend's brow.

"With this crown I make you king of the territories of Gaulanitis, Auranitis, Batanaea, and Trachonitis, all of which your uncle Philip has held. And with it you are granted Abila, to make you even greater than he was." Subsequently, the princeps drew another object from the case—a golden chain. "This is equal in weight to the iron one you wore in prison. It comes with the title *amicus Caesaris,* which declares you to be one of the special friends of Caesar."

Herod Agrippa couldn't help but tremble. In Rome, fortunes changed at such a pace that so much rising and falling could make a man dizzy.

"Your appointments will be presented to the Senate this very day," Gaius told him.

"G-Glorious sovereign," Agrippa stammered. He bowed and kissed the emperor's beringed hand.

Gaius pridefully accepted the homage. *No wonder Tiberius wanted to live forever,* the young man thought. *To be emperor is like being a god among mere mortals.*

A single servant was all that Marcus Silanus required for his dressing. The senator of Cato-like austerity had no liking to be fussed over by a troop of slaves day in and day out, with each of them falling clumsily over one another.

His dressing being finished, Silanus sent his wardrobe man away. As soon as he was alone, he heard a scratching at the window shutter.

"Who's there?" he demanded irascibly as the sounds continued.

"Nifelhel!" sounded a strange, rasping voice.

"What child's game is this?" the old senator muttered. He went to the shutters and unfixed the latch. The dawn light's was not yet strong but, for all he could see, the area in front of the window was empty.

"Most peculiar," he murmured to himself. Suddenly, something fluttered over the man's head and, fearing it was a bat, he ducked to avoid it. Silanus glimpsed a black thing settling into the shadows, a thing too big to be a bat.

The entity suddenly sprang out of the shadows and alighted upon the bust of Sextus Junius, Silanus' hero ancestor of the Hannibalic War.

A raven.

Silanus chuckled. *"Corvus!* Such a fright you gave me! Whose pet might you be?"

"Nifelhel!"

"So that was *you* speaking?" Only then did the senator notice the small object carried in the claws of one foot. "Hold now! Don't steal anything from this room!"

The old man shuffled forward, but the creature kept out of reach by fluttering to the crumpled sheets of the bed. There it dropped its loot before escaping back outside again.

The senator might have taken the brief interlude to be a dream, except that he could still see the abandoned object on his coverlets. He went closer and discovered it to be a pretty little bottle, a vial such as might hold perfume. "Some young matron will be missing this." He picked it up and drew out the stopper.

When the mysterious fragrance drifted to his nostrils, a tremor passed through him. The odor was hard to describe; not sweet, but neither was it offensive. In fact, the scent somehow made him think of the mountains. Yes, it reminded him of the evergreen forests of the Rhaetian Alps. As a young officer, he had served in the north country. As Silanus stood in place, feeling transported back in time, his wardrobe servant returned and at once asked what was delaying his appearance in the atrium.

"Dominus!" the man reminded him, "your clients are assembled. Shall I tell them that you are indisposed?"

Silanus shook himself. "No! Don't do that. I'm on my way." With a somewhat shaky hand, he put the stopper into the vial again and set it down on a shelf next to his bed.

"But are the two German boys good fighters?" asked Galvius Halotus.

"They're both promising," Cocceius admitted, "but what you're asking is going to play hell with discipline."

"Emperor Gaius' games require more sword-fighters than the area schools can supply on such short notice. The procurators are grateful for every man we can supply with two hands and two legs."

"I know, Dominus," the trainer replied with a grimace, "but sparing the young hellions will come back and sting us like a bee. It's only the threat of the cross that keeps our gladiators in line. Everyone knows that those two boys assaulted five guards. The rest of the pupils need to be reminded that escape attempts will draw the maximum punishment."

"At least they killed no one."

"What they pulled off was more than bad enough."

"Yes, but these are difficult times. You know discipline, but you don't know business. If we meet our new emperor's demands, it will make good notice for our school. We may even win an imperial endowment! And in any case, the two Germans sent into the arena will earn us a thousand gold pieces each. Dead they're not even good for raven's meat."

"I just don't like it."

"I have a suggestion. You tell them that if they fight well, they will be forgiven. Then, if they survive, we'll simply crucify them according to the protocol. In that way, discipline is enforced and the school gains a positive benefit."

The trainer knew that the manager wasn't open to sensible argument. Halotus was an ambitious, rising man; Cocceius was himself only a freedman grown too old to rise higher. But he wasn't too old to fall very low. He could easily be replaced by a younger ex-gladiator if he became "troublesome." Cocceius didn't want to end his days making morning calls on some new-rich patron, hoping for a few sestertii in handouts with nothing to offer in return except a few amusing tales about his bygone days in the arena.

Wherever he looked, there was no honor to be found in this matter.

Arriving in Silanus' atrium that morning, Rufus Hibernicus found over twenty of the senator's clients waiting there, most of them modest-looking free men. As a group, they had more status than the everyday city mob—but this was relative. Among them numbered a couple of "bloods" who had lost their fortunes, an unsuccessful scholar or two, a washed-up actor, and an undernourished poet who was trying to convince his neighbors that he was another Hesiod.

Silanus soon arrived and greeted his visitors. Those who were sitting stood up as a token of respect. The words exchanged were mere formalities without much meaning. When the banter died away, the senator took his purse in hand and parceled out a few coins to each of his callers. Afterwards, his attending servant bade the clients to follow him out to the portico, save for Rufus, whom he invited to share breakfast with himself.

The Hibernian was aware of how much he owed to Silanus. While Rufus had remained with Cassilla, Tatia had been living and working in the senator's home. Over the repast, the elder proposed that the maid should attend upon Rufus at the day's games. The ex-gladiator was pleased to agree.

Only an hour later, Rufus Hibernicus and Tatia, both wearing fresh garments, were walking closely behind Marcus Silanus' litter, along with a score of his other clients. Different men looked at the pair differently. Some disdained Rufus for being a freedman and an ex-gladiator, while others frowned with envy that such a "lout" had been promised a meeting with Emperor Gaius inside the Imperial Box.

In Hibernicus' estimation, the train of Senator Silanus' was an impressive one, much like the lady Cassilla's, but not so large. A Roman of truly great ancestry, the nobleman didn't need ostentation. The two lictors who attended him this morning, carrying the *fasces*—the ax bound in rods—represented a level of dignity that Cassilla lacked.

As he was borne along, Silanus sat reading something, paying but small attention to the street people. But a sudden impulse caused the senator to look around, as if a whisper had called to him. He noticed a dwarf standing by the wayside, one whose strange aspect forced him to look twice. Further, beside the fellow, stood a girl—a very pretty blonde girl dressed in a plain woolen slave frock. Silanus glanced away at once, but frowned when he breathed in a strange scent. He heard himself calling "Halt!" to his bearers.

The litter-men set him down smoothly while the dignitary searched the faces of the crowd, wanting to take another look at the blonde girl. It embarrassed him to be acting like a lusty boy of sixteen, but this was something he wanted to do.

As the old man caught sight of the maid and stared, she dropped her gaze coyly—not shyly.

The smirking dwarf ambled up to the litter, passing through his mass of servants, who instinctively recoiled from his repulsive person. The swarthy creature took off his shapeless cap and bowed jauntily to the man in the litter.

"Noble *huyrner* likes Galar's slave?" he asked, using the address of a tribesman to a chieftain. "Frigerd she is called," he explained thickly. "Very warm, very soft, very fitting for the house of a one who leads many men."

"She is yours, black man?" the senator asked incredulously.

"Galar has turned gold to flesh, now he would turn flesh to gold. Shall the huyrner buy from Galar his pretty girl?"

Silanus squirmed, wanting to say, "Yes!" but holding back. He wished to maintain decorum in front of his clients.

"Frigerd is fine woman," the dwarf mewed. "No doubt, even Caesar would favor her as a valuable gift."

At the name of "Caesar" the old man stiffened. He nodded mechanically and summoned his steward nearer, telling him, "Pay whatever the little man asks, then send the maid back to my house. Bathe her, feed her, dress her well. She must be made fit for…."

For whom?

"It shall be done, Dominus…" his bemused servant responded.

The transaction finished, Silanus felt more like himself and gave the order to continue on to the Amphitheater of Statilius Taurus. Behind him, those who knew him looked askance at one another, wondering at their master's uncharacteristic behavior.

"Rufus," Tatia said hushedly, "that is the same dwarf that made fools of us with his gold trick!"

The big man grinned. "Well, wherever he's been, he seems to be doing all right."

"He frightens me! His eyes remind me of…" she trailed off. What she remembered of her night on the streets of Rome, she didn't want to remember.

Rufus wrapped an arm about her. "The wench with him doesn't look roughly used. Maybe he's not such a bad sort. Anyway, lass, the runt would have to grow a lot bigger to ever be a menace to a wildcat like you."

Unreassured, the Iberian avoided looking at Galar and soon the order came for the train to move on. Hibernicus' backward glance lingered on the clean-limbed, full-bosomed barbarian girl. As he drank in her beauty, he missed the leer and excitement that transformed Galar's ugly face watching Tatia scurry away.

Cocceius paused before the barred holding cell. Within were the trainees from the Julius Caesar School.

"You two!" he called sharply to Osric and Mar. "Hear me! Not many get an offer of clemency from Galvius Halotus. Be glad that these are not normal times. Fight well, win, and you'll be returned to the school as if nothing happened."

Cocceius' tone came across as hollow. He knew the boys would soon be dead, regardless of their actions. He wanted to say nothing more in the way of lies.

"My best pleasure would be spilling that man's guts into the sand," Mar growled after the trainer had departed.

Osric shook his head. "He's a fine warrior and a cunning leader. I doubt that I could take him in a fair fight."

Mar swung toward his friend. "Are you becoming modest, Osric?"

"If I could have been taught the craft of arms from this Cocceius as a free man, I would have been much improved." Then Osric shook his head. "But I could not have tarried to receive his teaching. We have no purpose to be here but to find Andvaranaut, or die trying."

"Hah!" chortled a Bructeri, seated on a nearby bench. "Andvaranaut belongs to Heid's cult and to no one else!"

"Fool of a giant-worshiper!" snarled the Engle. "Do you not realize how dangerous is that piece of gold?"

The big German sneered. "One day, the giants shall break their bonds and overwhelm Midgard and Asgard. The world's ending is fixed by Fate. When the world is made anew, there shall be a noble place in it for all who helped Heid win her victory." His expression was fanatical. Osric turned grudgingly away, knowing the futility of arguing with such a one.

Mar had been oblivious to the exchange, his mind being laden with heavy thoughts. Suddenly the Chatti saw a man swagger past the bars and he leaped to his feet crying: "You there!"

Rufus Hibernicus swung about. He was killing time before the emperor arrived by exploring the amphitheater, hoping to run into people he knew.

"Say, I recognize you," he said to Mar. "You shouldn't be at the arena so soon. Cocceius can hardly have taught you enough to last through your first bout. If he's decided to use you for sword bait, he must have a damned good reason."

"You were with my father at the school," stated Mar. "How does Calusod fare?"

Rufus grimaced sympathetically. "I'm sorry to be the one to tell you, boy, but Calusidius is dead. I'm sorry. He was a good man."

Mar's color drained. "Dead? How so?"

"He became an animal-keeper inside this very amphitheater. A wolf escaped from its cage. It seems to have finished him off quickly, at least."

"A wolf?" echoed Osric, pressing up to the bars.

The secutor regarded this second German with curiosity, but answered him frankly. "Aye. About a week ago I came by to call on Calusidius, and his co-worker told me the story. The beast got clean away somehow. It's a wonder that we haven't heard about more wolf killings around the city."

"Where did—the wolf—come from?" Osric asked slowly.

"From Tusculum. That's not exactly the wild woods. Don't ask me how it got there."

Osric frowned at the floorboards. His knuckles whitened as he squeezed the bars.

"I'm sorry, boy," the ex-gladiator addressed Mar. "I don't know how it happened, but I surely do know how much your father cared about you."

Mar backed away, stunned. Osric thanked Rufus and the latter bade the pair a grave farewell. The Engle, taking Mar's arm, helped his comrade back to the bench.

"He—he must have tracked the wolf-fiend into this great hall," Mar declared. "He must have been planning to kill it, but it all went wrong."

"His courage was Roman—but it was courage true," Osric offered in consolation.

"The last memory my father will carry of me to the grave was my reviling of him." The Chatti's voice broke. "Osric—my shame is more than I can bear. I do not want to live beyond this evil day."

Osric, making no reply, stepped away. He knew it brought very bad wyrd for a man to wish aloud to die. A yearning for doom could too easily be granted by any malicious spirit who overheard. And this house of death must have been home to many a malicious spirit....

The Arena

CHAPTER XIII

After a celebratory ovation to Emperor Gaius and a lavish circus march, the games commenced with the release of a pride of lions upon a common criminal.

Gaius stroked his smooth-shaved chin in anticipation of the first blood. The man, the notice said, had been kidnapping women and children for illegal sale abroad. The procurer, as it happened, did not die well, merely cowering in place until the first lion to arrive sent him to a place that was beyond fear—unless there really was a Tartarus.

The mob booed at the lame performance, until more beasts were let in—bears and additional lions—to engage with one another. But Gaius could watch only so much rending of animal flesh before his active mind began to wander.

Near the emperor sat Marcus Silanus. His gladiator client, Hibernicus, occupied a back bench of the imperial box. Gaius had arrived too late to interview him before the games, but was looking forward to conversing with such a well-remembered ex-gladiator.

In the best seats behind the emperor sat Gaius' kin and personal friends. In a place of particular honor was Herod Agrippa, and beside the new-made king was the emperor's ungainly uncle, Claudius. He and Agrippa were both raised in Lady Antonia's house and knew each other about as well as brothers.

Gaius' three sisters shared a bench to the king's right—Drusilla, Lesbia, and Agrippinilla—though the last named had been calling herself 'Agrippina' since their mother's death. Most of the girl's friends went along with her vanity, but not Gaius. The name Agrippina was too special to him to be wasted on a cold-hearted schemer like his sister.

The three sisters were very different sorts. Gaius loved Drusilla, was indifferent to Lesbia, and was often at odds with Agrippinilla. The latter, noticing his uncordial stare, shot him a scowl. Gaius sneered. A week before, he had tried to avert the doom that seemed to be closing in around Antonia by forcing himself to have a change of heart regarding Agrippinilla.

She had too-eagerly accepted his unexpected overtures, being jealous of Drusilla's influence over him. Instead of inspiring love, her eagerness only incited his repulsion. When he could stand her insincerity no longer, he flung her from the bed. The princess, taken aback, had abused him like an irate fishwife. They had not spoken since.

Lesbia was marginally better in attitude, perhaps, but Gaius found her conversation insipid. She completely lacked the liveliness that he prized in women.

What a pair, Lesbia and Agrippinilla! He had paid them many high honors, but that was only to cover for those honors that he wished to lavish upon Drusilla. He had seated the both of them next to the censorious Antonia. The girls' bawdy comments, their comparisons of recent lovers, their gruesome, laughing commentary on the bloody conflict below, would scandalize the sober old dame. Hence they would need to place themselves under unusual—and hopefully unbearable—restraint.

Behind Gaius sat many of his friends and close male relations—except Gemellus. Agrippa and Claudius, he noticed, were engaged in serious conversation. Agrippa had sometimes referred to Claudius' good mind, a quality he had never himself observed in his uncle. Casually, Gaius wondered what the two of them could possibly find to talk about.

"C-Congratulations, Herod," Claudius stammered. "K-King, th-think of it!"

"It was preordained, Claudius. A sage predicted it."

"One of your desert holy men?"

"Oh, no! The prophets of our God never speak of anything good, only of more scourging for my people's sins."

"An astrologer, p-perhaps?"

"He may have been," reflected Agrippa, drawing forth the talisman Loderod had entrusted to him. "I'm convinced he saw the future truly. I am under obligation to pay the man back; I hope I may. He was the father of a young German named Osric. He was condemned to a gladiatorial school. I promised his father to give him this token."

Claudius frowned at the token. "It c-can't be very valuable."

"Whatever its value, if I do not keep my word, might I not forfeit all the good fortune that the sage predicted? I have the daunting example of old King Saul to keep me sober."

Claudius nodded. It was like Herod to impute some selfish motive to every gracious act he performed. Unlike most men of rank, the desert prince chose to feign villainy, not virtue.

The animal slaughter passed blasé before the eyes of Rufus Hibernicus. The first real sport of the day would be a combat between gladiators and a much larger band of barbarian warriors.

Not many true barbarians existed in Rome at this time—other than the group he had lately seen in the arena's holding area. That, unfortunately, would mean Calusidius' son would fight and probably die. But the secutor had witnessed many such tragedies in his life. To enjoy gladiatorial displays, one had to concentrate on the sport and forget about the death.

He knew most of the barbarians would be fakes. Common criminals dressed in skins and carrying unfamiliar weapons would serve. Only during periods of warfare on the borders did Rome have a dependable supply of seasoned barbarian prisoners.

"Master—!" Tatia, standing just behind him, whispered uneasily. He looked back at her, pleased. It had taken him a year to cozen her into calling him "Master" when in public. But, oddly, since he had rescued her from the Roman street, she had been observing better manners.

"What is it, Love?"

"I feel something watching us—*me!*"

"Of course! Look at the men in those bleachers up there. Can you blame them? You're the most eye-catching wench ever seen, royal princesses not excepted!"

"Master! Please, don't let the emperor's sisters hear you! They'd probably order my nose cut off for jealousy!"

Hibernicus laughed. "You're getting saucy again. Good! Come down here!" He scooped her up and set her upon his knee. "Watch the fight from my lap!"

"Rufus—the emperor!"

"Let him get his own girl!"

Tatia settled down. She well knew that Rufus was like a charging bull when he pursued a whim. But even in the shelter of his strength, she still felt a foreboding, a sense that there was someone in the audience that she needed to fear.

Osric and his companions, as barbarian sword-meat, had been allowed no part in the parade. Only when their time came to fight were they released from their cells and conducted under guard into an arena filled with blood-speckled sand. Amphitheater slaves were preparing the fighting ground, hauling away dead animals and covering the gore with fresh white sand. The bleached quartz dazzled the barbarians' eyes, having been long-confined in half-light. Enough swords, shields and spears were laid out on spread canvases on either side of the exit doors to arm the whole score of them.

The true barbarians pounced eagerly upon the weapons. The Roman cut-purses dressed as Germans took their leavings, accepting the poorest shields and blades into inept, trembling hands. Osric had selected for himself a large target shield, a spear, and a gladius; the latter he shoved into the sheepskin belt provided by the school, along with his silly cowhide garments.

Mar, who was similarly armed, grumbled bitterly. "They could have given us something to eat if we have to fight."

"Cattle are not fed just before the butchery," Osric answered with a grim laugh. "If food has no time to become sinew, why waste the porridge, eh? Anyway, a wolf is most dangerous when it is hungry."

"Don't speak to me of wolves," he said.

Osric sat back, chagrined.

From another arena door, ten gladiators paraded into the sunlight with carefree pomp. The Engle saw that their costumes represented several of the main Roman fighting styles. "They seem to think they will make short work of us," he observed.

"We know how well gladiators can fight," said Mar, clasping the shoulder of his comrade, "so they're probably right! This may be our last farewell, Brother. If I am Chatti and not Roman, I will next see you in the halls of Woden."

"I have never known a Chatti who was more Chatti!" Osric said, grinning. "But before we part, give me your sword."

Puzzled, Mar handed him his gladius. Swiftly, with sharp piece of beef bone which he had saved for this purpose, Osric scratched his most powerful victory runes, first into Mar's wooden hilt, then into his own.

Finally, he held a sword in each of his hands and projected his will into them, saying: "Hail to the gods! Hail to the goddesses! Hail to the bounteous Earth! Strength and victory give to us; let our death-dealing blades feast while we live."

A lick of fire burned Osric's back, pitching him to the earth, face first. Some sand got into his mouth, and he spat it out forcefully. "Go to the center, sluggard," snarled a guard, standing over him and brandishing a metal-tipped scourge. "Give the citizens a show!"

Osric sprang up and made for the flogger, but the man took fright and bounded behind a hedgerow of spear-carriers. Denied vengeance, the Engle returned Mar's sword and followed the others of their group toward the center of the ring, where the gladiators had already deployed. The guards trailed up a short distance behind.

"Two savages to each gladiator!" the optio of the guards shouted. "Spread out! Let the citizens see your weapon play!" Prodded into place at spear point, Osric and Mar found themselves deployed against different opponents.

The Engle's partner turned out to be the very Bructeri with whom he had earlier debated. Their foe was a *myrmillo*, a gladiator type that was also called a "Gaul." But the man, dark and rough-featured, seemed to be no Gaul by birth. He wore a metal sleeve on his right arm and a high greave on his left leg. His helmet was broadly-brimmed and for a crest it supported a metal fish. A wide leather belt, cinctured around his waist, protected his belly and extended down to serve for a groin-guard. A short woolen kilt, a long spatha sword, and a legionary's tall shield filled out his equipment.

"Amusing," Osric whispered to the Bructeri. "Do you suppose that these Romans know that the two of us would rather slay each other than go at this school-trained butcher?"

"That we would, Warrior!" the German renegade agreed with a grin. "But for the nonce we need to bury our differences. It is strange—but here in a foreign land, beset by foreign foes, even a wretch of an Engle begins to look like a countryman and a comrade of the shield."

This statement surprised Osric, for the very same thought had just passed through his own mind.

He heard the crunch of feet striding over sand behind them. *Guards!*

"Fight!" the squad optio ordered the pair. The arena guards' duty was to strike, and even slay, any slave who performed poorly.

The gladiator opposing them took a bellicose stance. "Come swiftly, dogs!" he cried out. "Never was there a Gaul who could not whip his age in Germans!"

"By Heid's Thousand Spawn!" the Bructeri growled. "Your jackdaw words are as false as the race you lay claim to! Go to Hela!"

The giant-worshiping German opened the attack, stabbing at the man's middle. The Gaul turned the spear easily, leaped up, and made a bloody score on his assailant's upper leg. Osric sprang while the gladiator was out of his defensive mode, but his thrusting spear struck nothing but the unyielding iron and leather of the man's shield. The Gaul himself skipped nimbly away.

Behind him, Osric heard shouts, clatter, and the cheering crowd. But the rune-warrior dared not look away from his own foe, lest it cost him his life.

Out of the corner of his eyes, Osric saw the Bructeri's leg dyed with blood, but his face showed more indignation than pain. Satisfied that the man thirsted more for the Gaul's life than his own, Osric guardedly moved against the gladiator's flank.

The Gaul circled away from Osric, but showed a limp. The angry Bructeri, seeing what looked like a weakness, roared a war cry and lunged.

It was a trap. The myrmillo shifted skillfully, slamming the rim of his shield into the Bructeri's face, crushing the bridge of his nose. Senseless, the German spun about and tumbled face-first into the sand. The Gaul came up to deal the death blow.

Osric launched his spear through the air. The myrmillo's spatha came around, intending to knock it out of the air, but the gods didn't favor the man's ploy. The spear's keen edge struck his grip, shearing off his right thumb.

Grimacing, the Gaul darted away. Though thumbless, he smoothly shifted his blade into his left hand and his shield into his injured right.

Osric pressed in, hopeful, but watchful for a trick. He could expect the gladiator to act with greater haste than before, fearing that his pain and blood-loss would weaken him too much. With the Engle coming on, the dark man tried another sort of trick, a false stumble. The youth was not deceived and kept his guard up.

Under more urgency than his opponent, the gladiator lunged at him, dealing an explosion of blows, forcing Osric backwards as he desperately dodged and parried. The Gaul fought to create an opening, then suddenly made a surprise move, aiming his toe at the Engle's groin. Osric's shield chopped downward in time, striking the man's greave and sending him stumbling. Osric came on hard while the gladiator was off balance and they collided shield on shield. The myrmillo may have been more injured than he looked, for Osric kept his stance and the Gaul did not. Osric read the fallen man's mishap as genuine and came in slashing. He cut into the man's left arm, severing muscle and forcing the myrmillo to drop his blade.

Refusing to give up, the gladiator rolled away and got to his feet. In the same motion he threw his shield at the Engle, but his wounds made the throw clumsy and the youth dodged. But the distraction was enough to allow the Gaul to scoop up his fallen sword. But, wounded in both arms now, the gladiator could not handle his weapon well. He might have made a gesture of surrender and leave it to the mob to save his life. Perhaps because he thought they would call for his death, he gritted himself to go down fighting. Osric attacked and beat down the man's clumsy defense, remorselessly driving his gladius into the man's exposed throat—a quick-kill point. The Engle didn't doubt the school had made him a better swordsman.

The Engle was free at last to take in the whole scope of the area battle so far. His companion, the Bructeri, still lay where he fell, unmoving, possibly dead. Osric had been told that if a man could not at least climb to his knees by the time the fight ended, a man dressed as a god would come forth and break his skull with a heavy hammer.

Osric saw that three other gladiators were sprawled on the sand, but few barbarians were still on their feet. Mar, now up against a secutor, was one of them.

"You and you! Fight!" the optio bawled from the rear. Osric understood that he was now to face the survivor of another contest—a Thracian-style sort, armed more lightly than had been the Gaul, wearing a helmet that covered his face except for grated eye holes, metal sleeve, and greaves. He carried an iron buckler and a small, curved sword of the type that Cocceius had called a *sica*. At the school, Osric had learned that Thracian success in combat depended upon rapid maneuvers against a more weighted down opponent.

"Come nearer, barbarian," the man taunted. "Let me win this fight so I can take down a real swordsman. One never wins the rudis for having danced with a clown in cowhide."

Osric assumed a defensive stance. The Thracian would be tired from his earlier dueling, but no more than himself. And this time, the Engle lacked any other to stand at his side. He carefully sized up this new opponent.

There was a superficial cut on the Thracian's side; it probably wouldn't make much difference. If the fellow had any weakness at all, it would most probably flow from his disdain for barbarian fighters, two of which lay behind dead him. But, Osric wondered, had one or both of them been, in fact, a disguised thief?

Now he felt free to use rune-magic. *You are not just a warrior; you are a rune-warrior!* he told himself. *Your blood is the blood of Scef! Sing the power of that blood!* To prevent the bullying guards from forcing him to charge in before he was ready, he made a few belligerent steps forward. But he suddenly drew up short and bellowed the chant of his shield song, the same that Loderod had used to empower his confederated tribesmen before their destruction of three Roman legions in the Teutoberg Forest.

The alien recitation made the gladiator stare, but his surprise quickly changed to contempt: "Do you pray to your gods? I hear that one of the weakest of the Olympians, Mercury, is your supreme deity, more a whoremaster than a warrior! My shout is the battle cry of Mars!"

For all his bluster, the Thracian felt uneasy. Some barbarians, he knew, were sorcerers. The gladiator thought it best to attack before the chanter put a curse on his luck. The Roman fighter sprinted forward, his sica whirring. The Engle dodged the stroke at his head then slashed low, cutting the man's thigh above one of his lightweight greaves. With a yowl, the Thracian stumbled away. Osric commenced a second song reinforcing the first.

Some onlookers were watching the pair carefully. "That b-barbarian is not b-bad," observed Claudius to Herod Agrippa. "Do you think he w-will take out his man?"

"Shhh," said the Jew. "I'm watching that brown-maned one against the retiarius. *Oh, good stroke!*"

"Germans fight so badly," Gaius yawned, "it's a wonder that they still run free behind the Rhine."

"Your two grand-sires and your noble father nearly took that freedom away," said one of his toady friends. "If not for Tiberius' jealousy, the Elbe and not the Rhine would be our border today."

Gaius nodded. "Perhaps in my reign we shall avenge the inglory of the Teutoberg Forest. Obviously these barbarians have no tactics and any gladiator can out-fight twice his number."

"Rome waits upon Divine Caesar for its greatness," put in another flatterer.

The possibility of future military glory pleased Gaius; he imagined that the rest of the combat was a victorious battle between disciplined legions and the wild hordes from the tangled forests.

By now the Thracian's nerves were on edge. That damnable song! He could neither stop it nor ignore it. As he looked at his opponent, he felt a qualm. It seemed as though his courage was becoming a thin web. *By the blade of Mars*, his pride shouted in defiance, *I fear no barbarian alive!*

Impatient with the stratagems that he had been trained to use, the Thracian sprang forward and came in fast. He slashed at Osric's shoulder, but was foiled by the Engle's shield. But the attacker had left an opening and Osric stabbed at the Thracian's upper stomach. Yelling, the gladiator lurched backwards, clutching his wound.

A good hit, Osric guessed, *but a slow kill at best. I must end this.*

Among the cheering hosts, Galar hung like an ape from a post supporting the canvas sun-shade overhead. He was dividing his attention between the slender, olive beauty on Rufus Hibernicus' lap and the combat below. The bloodletting resonated pleasingly with Galar's inhuman nature, but his falcon eyes picked out two of the contenders especially—Loderod's foster son and the dark-haired Chatti.

Probably, he believed, they soon would die by the swords of the Roman slave-fighters. Yet, would it not be sad if they should somehow win free? If they did, they would continue their search for the magic ring that his mistress Frigerd craved. Motivated by the urgency of his mission, Galar extended a finger at the dark-haired one and spoke a Black Rune....

Mar's secutor was down, trying to crawl away on his side, unhurt, but encumbered by heavy armor while the Chatti pressed him doggedly. He just barely managed to ward off Mar's blade strokes by skillful use of his long, Celtic sword.

Visions of psychopomps flashed before the beleaguered gladiator's eyes, but amazingly the young German's attack broke off abruptly. The barbarian seemed not to know where to turn, wearing an astonished look on his face.

Seeing his chance, the secutor threw a handful of sand into the youth's wide-open eyes. As Mar yelled and staggered back, the gladiator heaved to his feet and thrust himself at the boy. Knocking the Chatti's shield out of the way with a sweep of his own, he ran his sword through Mar's breast. It penetrated clear through him and extended four inches out of his upper back.

"*Osric!*" Mar gulped faintly. He sank to his knees, slackly holding the sword which impaled him. *Who had done this?* he wondered. Not the secutor whom he'd been fighting—that one had suddenly vanished, leaving nothing but an untrimmed log of alder behind. *Strange thing*, he thought, knowing he was about to die. In another second, Mar had passed beyond thinking. He sank to his side and lay inert atop the amphitheater sand.

Just at that moment, Osric's blade found a hilt-deep resting place between the ribs of his Thracian opponent. With a braced foot and a hard pull, he drew his blade out. Then, wheeling, he sought to see Mar's situation. Horror stiffened him; the boy lay on his side and his killer was standing over him. Shocked and vengeful, he raced across the intervening distance, the stadium echoing with excitement.

The victorious swordsman spotted Osric's rush in time to go defensive, but the German's onslaught made him stagger backwards. Against the hurricane of the Engle's berserk blows, it wasn't possible for him to do anything except defend himself.

This was such a violation of the rules that the young secutor shouted "Not fair!" to the guards. They were supposed to pair the duelists, not let some blood-mad barbarian take the initiative. *Oh, Mithra*, he thought dismally, *I must have just killed his brother or lover or something!*

High in the stadium, Galar chuckled with satisfaction. The illusion that confused Mar's sight had allowed the Roman to rise and strike, destroying one enemy of Blessed Heid. But one more was left. He now launched a different sort of spell.

Suddenly, when Osric hurled another blow at his foe, it struck with a ringing impact and seemed to break him into *three* different bodies, the double of the other two. *What sorcery is this?* his mind shouted through the rage that still had him it its grip.

He flung himself at the center of the three images but, to his dismay, he struck empty air and plunged headfirst into the sand. A blow to the back of his head kept him from rising and darkened the sight from his eyes. Before oblivion took him, he felt a blade resting against his spine.

Strange warriors, these savages, the Roman secutor thought. *Twice they had me, twice they each lost their senses.* Looking over the arena, he saw that the last of the barbarians had been slaughtered by a couple other surviving gladiators. With the pressure off, he could take his time and offer the life of this final foeman to the emperor. He did not forget to mutter thanks to his god; perhaps he would yet live long enough to leave this mad sport behind. He even dared to hope that he could return to his home in Moesia, a free man.

"Death!" roared the crowd, sounding like the wind and waves breaking on Moesia's bleak coast.

"These Germans fight like animals," said Gaius to his companions, being less than impressed by the exhibition. He extended his thumb and slowly started to bring it in to his heart as if it were a spear point.

"Wait, Imperial Caesar!" Agrippa shouted, waving. "I recognize that German down there! We were in prison together. I owe him a debt."

"You owe a barbarian a debt?" the princeps asked wonderingly.

"Strange, but true, Caesar. I intended to purchase him from his school, but did not realize until now that he was down there fighting. Spare him, Gaius!"

The emperor shrugged. "As you wish. He is your slave."

Gaius extended his right hand and stabbed thumb down, the traditional signal for the Moesian secutor to drop his weapon and let the blond madman live to fight again.

Far below, the gladiator nodded and stepped away from Osric, relieved that the bloody business was finally over.

THE SLAVE GIRL

CHAPTER XIV

During a short recess in the games, Marcus Silanus approached the Imperial Box shadowed by a large, strong man. "Permit me to present Rufus Hibernicus, Princeps," said the senator. "He won his liberty after fifteen kills. That was almost six years ago, when I was praetor. He's a brave man, a loyal friend, and the best gladiator to grace our city since the great Flamma."

Gaius looked up at the giant, a coppery mountain of beef and sinew. Without rising, he pinched the Hibernian's bare thigh, probing its musculature. At the same time, Rufus sized up this new emperor of Rome.

Thin, lanky, not economically built, Gaius would never make a fighter. His light eyes betrayed much more than did his bland expression; a fever stewed in them. They suggested a distinct hardness in his nature. What Hibernicus sensed most strongly in Gaius was an angry streak. Pity the man who got on the wrong side of this imperator....

"You have kept in excellent shape, I see," said Gaius. "Have you served in a bodyguard before this?"

"That I have," responded Rufus, "in Spain and elsewhere."

"I think we can use you, Hibernicus. Report to Axilares, my Guard's tribune, for a uniform and training."

Then the emperor glanced toward Tatia. "I find your girl lovely, gladiator. She's as dark as my Persian dancer, Daya. Does your wench dance, too?"

When Hibernicus carefully replied in the negative, Gaius sighed. "Too bad; if she did, I would have made you an offer. Anyway, take this seat next to me. Silanus, you won't mind, will you? I'd like to hear the opinion of an expert on the important matches that are coming up next."

A short distance away, a servant entered at the rear of the imperial box and respectfully bowed before Herod Agrippa, saying, "The barbarian gladiator is resting in the infirmary, Dominus."

"How is he?"

"Bruised, a bad head knock, Great One. The amphitheater physician believed that he would be up and around in about a week."

Agrippa excused himself from the imperial party and followed the attendant to a quiet and dimly-lighted room. There on the floor Osric lay upon a stretcher, watched by two slaves. The Easterner was presented with a chair and sat above the barbarian, whose eyes were pained and glazed. "How do you fare?" Agrippa asked.

The Engle didn't reply, didn't even seem to hear. The Jew frowned concernedly. Then, impulsively, he removed the dark Germanic talisman from around his neck and slung it over Osric's head. "Fetch my steward," he told one of his men who had been following. Then, to the arena servants he said, "My people will take custody of him now."

Technically, Agrippa had now kept his word to Loderod. Still, it would be far from the spirit of his pledge to simply cast the injured man out into the street. He decided to let the young barbarian recover at his townhouse. Afterwards, he would manumit him and give him the choice to either return to Germania or accept a job in Agrippa's own entourage. Eventually, he must return to govern his tetrarchy in Judea. The youth might make a good bodyguard, knowing the sword and also, he suspected, a bit of magic, too.

Just then, Agrippa caught a glint of yellow on the Engle's breast. He looked closer and stared with no little amazement.

The medallion of Loderod, here and there, seemed to be changing *to the color of gold.*

Two days after attending the games, Tatia sat on her bed, looking into one of the polished metal mirrors used by Marcus Silanus' maids. The reflection she saw had not changed from how it looked in the days before her fright. Still, something felt different. Maybe that difference was deeper than her skin. Why else would she be feeling so often afraid?

A snatch of poetry came to her mind, the *Lay of Murias the Damned:*

> *I hear the hounds upon my track*
> *Their voices well I know*
> *I feel the hot breath of the pack*
> *Wherever I may go*
>
> *The hounds draw near,*
> *Behind me bay—*
> *My sins the spoor they smell.*
> *Have pity on their damned prey*
> *Who must be dragged to hell....*

Hearing a brush of movement against the door frame, Tatia looked up. Frigerd was standing there, the new German girl with whom she shared the little room. The blonde was dressed in the livery of Silanus' female slaves, a long, white, sleeveless chiton. Frigerd's tanned skin looked as dark as hers against the snowy linen, but was golden, not olive. Her hair was smooth-combed, set with a braided lock before each ear. How calm Frigerd seemed, even though she had spent some time with the ghastly little man who had sold her.

Across from Tatia, Frigerd reclined upon her own bed with an animal-like grace. "You seem distressed," she said in heavily-accented Latin. "Surely there is nothing to be afraid of in a great, strong house like this one."

"There is always something for a slave to be afraid of," muttered Tatia.

"I do not consider myself a slave," Frigerd replied, as if the whole idea were somewhat amusing.

"Hold on to that feeling as long as you are able," Tatia advised.

"I shall."

Tatia put her head to the pillow, looking away from her roommate. After a little bit, she heard the German girl rising and then she felt the touch of her hand. "You are sad; that should not be," cooed the blonde. "Let me comfort you."

Tatia didn't fully trust the stranger and made no reply. Suddenly the Iberian jerked to feel a small, sharp pain. She turned and looked at the northerner accusingly. But rapidly, so rapidly, a numbing torpor came upon her.

Frigerd removed the thorn from her flesh. "Be gay, maiden! This is the day that you find a new love," she said. She opened Tatia's garment, sliding it down the girl's dusky shoulders and baring her to the naval.

"Galar is mad," Frigerd said, shaking her head. "To fulfill my debt to him, I would have lain a Roman queen at his feet—but instead he asks for a useless creature like *you*."

From under her wool-stuffed mattress, the sorceress took a disk of gold with a raised surface, the relief of an arcane rune. She fitted it into the center of her left palm and pressed the medallion into the flesh beneath Tatia's left breast. The touch was cold, stinging, but she could neither move nor protest.

"In the name of Heid," Frigerd intoned, "I mark you with the delusion of joy, of beauty, of passion. You shall be the servant of Heid's servant. Let your eyes be enamored and your heart bear the heavy chains of passion." She took the emblem away, leaving the Black Rune of love's delusion creased lightly into her victim's skin. It started to fade very rapidly.

Next Frigerd passed a vial under Tatia's nose. The odor repulsed the witch; it smelled of damp stones, of grave soil, and of ancient tombs. "Remember this scent; remember it," the rune-witch commanded her. "Whenever you smell it, you will feel an intense need for love."

Now the sorceress put away her simple paraphernalia, closed Tatia's gown, and pushed her open lids shut with her thumbs. "Stay asleep for a while, poor trull; when you awaken you will remember nothing of this."

She pressed her lips against Tatia's own and, with a sealing kiss, the spell was fixed.

Frigerd stood up and addressed the room. "Galar? Are you lurking in this place? She is yours. Just remember that my obligation to you has now been settled."

The rune-witch picked up Tatia's mirror and took it back to her own bed. Studying her own reflection, Frigerd looked at her made-up face. The Romans used paints and powders to bring out the subtle charms of a woman's appearance. She touched the soft garment she wore which hugged her nubile figure. Clothing like this was simply not to be had in the Northland. *A chieftainess would be pleased to wear it*, she thought, *but here in Rome it was something that the Romans merely used to beautify their slaves!*

In thinking of this plan, of getting her close to the Roman High Chief in the disguise of a lowly slave, Galar had shown more cleverness than she'd credited him with. By following this black-haired girl about the city, he'd learned how one person connected to another, until the trail had led into the very palace of the emperor.

Frigerd felt excitement. The fulfillment of her destiny lay within her grasp.

She'd been born from the purest blood of Scef. Her father, a rune-speaker of the Suiones—the Swedes—had carefully sought out a mate of Heimdall's divine bloodline to wed. But their child Frigerd had been abducted by the priestesses of Heid, who planned a very specific future for her. She was taught the runes and the metamorphosis of the werewolf. Then, when she reached sixteen, her teachers sent her on a soul-voyage to Nifelhel, where the souls of sorcerers and great sinners were punished forever.

Half mad with terror, she was brought back. Her instructors told her she was foredoomed for her practice of sorcery. Only by a life of service to the Jotuns would she gain their favor and reign a queen of Nifelhel, not languish in tortures without ending.

When the stars came around, permitting a chance to liberate Andvaranaut, the Romans seized the ring instead, thwarting the attempts of the cult to regain it. Frigerd was chosen one of the nine to aspire to the ring's quest. Nine women began the contest, but after three months, only two remained.

Frigerd and another were rowed out to a lake isle and committed to a duel to the death. It took a week to prove who was mistress. The other woman was older, more learned in sorcery, but she depended on the charitable gift of power from evil spirits; Frigerd's power was in her blood, for was not the greatest part of her a grandchild of the god of light? At last, Frigerd had cast a mighty rune of warding, banishing all spirits from the precincts of the isle. Her rival, deprived of her source of power, was easily stalked and slain by the werewolf. Not long afterwards, accompanied by several dedicated Bructeri warriors and the dverg-son Galar, Frigerd was dispatched to the city of Rome.

Now only Osric remained, saved from death by the young Caesar, to compete with her to recover the ring first. She had to get next to the king of Romans—their "im-per-a-tor"—before Osric stole or wooed Andvaranaut from his possession.

This Osric—she had heard it said that King Scef's blood ran very pure in him also. But even if that were true, Osric was barely trained in rune-magic. She didn't deem him to be a serious obstacle to her designs yet, because he was the disciple of the great Loderod, she dared not underestimate the young man.

Just the day before, Frigerd had enchanted Marcus Silanus to prepare the way for her to meet the young Caesar. He'd sent a servant to beg an audience with the Roman king. But she was impatient to get on with the plan; time enough had been wasted.

Resolvedly, the Swede now took a vial from her bag of cosmetics, unstopped it, and blew its scent into the air, where it wafted undetected through all the rooms of the mansion. It was only a moment later that Silanus came hurrying into the maids' room on old, stiff legs.

"Lady...?" he gasped breathlessly.

"Old man, I would go now to the hall of the young Caesar," Frigerd informed him. She would tell him no more. She didn't have to.

The man's heavily-lined face brightened. Of course he would take her to Caesar! After all, hadn't that been his own idea?

Osric, his head aching, lay staring at his window, though he could see nothing through it but the sky.

Sorcery! The magic of Heid was in Rome, and strongly. That had been no ordinary combat. The gladiator whom Osric fought had been aided by jugglery—the mystical blinding of a man's eyes to reality. The gladiator could not have been privy to such an art. He had received help from some sorcerer of the North. Osric knew that there was at least one sorcerer of Heid in Rome—he who had attacked him, and also slain Calusidius, in the guise of a wolf.

Very likely, the two murders had to be laid at the same man's feet.

Or *her* feet. More women than men served Heid inside the highest degrees of her order. The witches of Heid had been a particularly dangerous adversary for Loderod—and *his* mentor before him.

Long ago one of the Cult of Heid, a man name Ingfrid, had learned many of its Black Runes without being corrupted by them. He slew the priestess who wielded the ring Andvaranaut and wore it himself. Though his act damned his spirit to Nifelhel, he used the ring to defend himself as he carried the evil token away.

Long did the cult of Heid seek for Andvaranaut and for Infrid's life, but he avoided them and lived to a great old age. When he sensed his time nearing its end, he found a disciple—a young man named Loderod. Like Ingfrid, Loderod boasted the purest blood of Scef in his veins, the blood of heroes and of sorcerers. In truth, the ancient King Scef had been the avatar of Heimdall, the giver of runes, the protector of Mankind. Rare was the man or woman who could master the power of the ring if he or she were not of the magic line. For almost eighty years, Loderod survived his master and carried on his trust before hiding the ring with spirit guardian to protect it. Finally, in time, Loderod selected his own successor—Osric, also descended from Scef's bloodline.

He glowered at the decorated bedroom around him. It was one of the rooms assigned to Agrippa's use at the palace. Since Osric had been moved here, the servant Stechus had been applying his arts to heal him. But when he was alone, the Engle had applied his own runes to hasten his recovery. Hopefully, tomorrow he would be able to walk about house without headache or weakness.

Now, once again, he thought about Mar's death and became angry. He owed his friend a death. Every fiber of his being wanted to repay that debt. But where was the sorcerer of Heid from whom the blood debt had to be exacted?

At that moment, Osric's hunter's ears detected footsteps.

"Well, my friend," said Herod Agrippa, "you seem to be rallying well! Rome has not been kind to you thus far; may my hospitality give you respite from the rough handling that you have endured."

The German nodded respectfully. The servants had told him that their master often attended on the young Caesar. Sometime in the weeks since they had been imprisoned together at Tusculum, Agrippa had been made a king, and kings were to be respected and to his own satisfaction, this king fitted the role of a king. The Easterner wore an embroidered tunic of purple cotton, over which was draped a robe of scarlet-dyed wool; his dark hair was bound by a fillet.

"I am told that you have achieved a domain to rule, my lord," said Osric, not trying to rise. German kings did not command servility from warriors and about the protocols of other nations he cared little. "Loderod divined true. You have proven yourself my friend, and I am pleased that you have prospered."

Agrippa, standing at the side of the bed, replied, "I never cease to wonder at the way you are able to throw off the effects of great injury by your magical arts. Should you wish to remain in Rome, you could gain great wealth as a physician."

"It seems I must indeed remain for a time. I have much to do that is of the utmost importance."

"Fine, then! After I move to lodgings of my own, you are welcome to join my household as a bodyguard—unless you have other prospects."

"Tell me. Is it true that the Romans have given me to you as a slave?"

"That is true, but tomorrow I shall take you before the magistrates and have you formally released from bondage."

Bondage. Slave. Osric disliked such words. "I thank you, generous lord. I would prove a poor slave if you thought to do otherwise."

The Easterner gave a faint smile. "I have many slaves already. What I sorely lack are loyal friends."

"I can be as good a friend to any man who is a friend to me."

Suddenly somber, Agrippa said, "Osric, though it grieves me to admit it, I have not been so mindful of your interests as I have pretended."

"Lord?"

"Your father bade me to give you this talisman when I should become happy with my lot in life." The king drew the medallion out of his tunic. "When Loderod handed this to me, it was all dross. Now the tinges of gold are unmistakable. It started to change as soon as I placed it around your neck while you lay unconscious. How is this strange alchemy worked?"

Osric regarded the object with a start. It was the same amulet that Loderod had always worn. It had been true gold when last Osric saw it. Had it changed to dross before his master died?

"I do not fault you for withholding it. It is a terrible burden to bear," said Osric grimly. "Had I been given a choice, I might have told my father to give it to another!"

"Is it cursed? I've worn it for weeks! I had no idea...."

"The rune upon it is called the *fylfot*. It symbolizes power unlimited, power to be harnessed for either good or ill—but, by its nature, it is bound to neither. Fear not; it has not cursed us, but having it within my reach shall make it easier for me to curse myself."

How true that was! The fylfot was a charm that could awaken the mystical blood of one of godly descent. As long as Loderod lived, the talisman had served him alone and was of no use to any other.

The fylfot, upon touching Osric, had quickened him, caused a stirring in his blood. The more he wore it, the stronger its influence would become. The gold in the talisman was fairy gold, a mystic transmogrification of the fiendish dvergar. It both stimulated the mystic power within him, and mirrored that power's degree of development. Its purpose was to help prepare him for the day in which he must master the ring Andvaranaut itself. By passing on the mighty amulet, Loderod had placed damnation within easy grasp of his son. Loderod had accepted damnation as a sacrifice for the good of his people, but he had never urged his adopted son to follow the same path. As long as he used only the White Runes, his spirit was safe from Nifelhel. Loderod himself had begun with that conviction, but because of his love for his people, he had fallen from his original plan.

Osric now took the device from Agrippa's hand and laid it respectfully down on the coverlet beside him.

"How is gold made from dross?" Agrippa asked, his glance avid.

Osric shook his head. "There exists no such secret in Germania, be assured. This talisman is not true gold; it is, instead, the mystical manifestation of the *idea* of gold."

The Jew gave him a doubtful look. Did he speak true? As a master, he was within his rights to torture a slave to make him reveal all, but he was one who had only tortured slaves occasionally, when he was very angry. In his earlier days Agrippa had actively sought out alchemical secrets and, in fact, had wasted much of his fortune on mystic pursuits. He had even learned that there was, indeed, a form of false gold, and bad luck too often followed it.

Fortunately, merciful Providence had provided him with a source of abundant gold, along with a kingdom in Judea. Anyway, should Gaius ever learn that anyone knew the secret of gold-making, that person would be tortured until he revealed it. It was knowledge that ought to be avoided. With some regret, the Jew said:

"If you say there is no secret of gold-making, I will accept your word and not ask again."

Osric, a man of the Engles who himself did not value gold highly, scarcely realized the scope of the victory that his patron had just won over himself. Instead he asked:

"Lord Agrippa, what became of the body of Mar, my friend, who died in the am… *amphitheater*."

A shadow crossed the Jew's face. "By now he will have been buried in a common trench in the Campus Martius, his location forgotten."

The Engle's hands clenched furiously at his blanket. Agrippa gave him a moment and then said: "When I return tomorrow, I shall put an end to your slavery. For now, I must attend guests who will be arriving soon."

"Are we in the palace where Caesar lives?"

"Yes. Would you like to see more of it?"

Osric tentatively touched the talisman lying on the blanket. "Gese, lord. That would please me greatly…."

PHAEDRA

CHAPTER XV

Marcus Silanus, accompanied by his slave girl, were conducted into a decorous waiting room. The elderly Roman wasted no time in occupying a padded bench, but Frigerd lagged in front of a glossy black marble slab that was part of the wall. What she saw reflected a woman fit for an emperor.

Her linen tunic left her arms and neck bare while displaying her figure gracefully. The gold-chain necklace and bejeweled armlets with which she was adorned were calculated to draw the attention of every male eye to the sensuous promise of her body. Her long, slit skirt displayed a flash of thigh with every second step she took. Knowing that any man would find her beautiful filled her with confidence.

"Dear Father-in-law," exclaimed a male voice. "The message you sent referred to a gift."

From where she stood, Frigerd saw the speaking man's mirrored image among his slaves and attendants. She assumed he must be Caesar.

"May I play the prophet and guess that this beautiful creature must be the gift that you meant?"

"I can keep nothing secret from you, Caesar, not even to surprise you! This is a slave girl from the pristine North." To Frigerd, Silanus said, "Present yourself, little one."

Remembering to lower her head, the girl turned about. "Ah, lovely," said the princeps, nodding.

"I saw her in passing," said the senator, "and something spoke to me about purchasing her for your palace."

"You surely heard the speaking of your worthy heart, good Silanus," Gaius conjectured, grinning wolfishly at the girl. "Here, wench," the youth said as he reached a hand out to her. When she was near, he took her wrist and ran his fingertips up her arm, culminating in a pinch to her satiny shoulder. Frigerd maintained a pleasant expression while taking in this ruler of the Roman world. She had expected a giant, but the new Caesar stood up as a poor figure compared to the hearty warriors of Germania.

Gaius laughed. "She has a brave look! You've done well, Father-in-law. I weary of slaves blanching with terror when confronted by our majesty. What is her name?"

When Silanus pronounced the name "Frigerd", the youth shook his head. "Ghastly! That is no fit name for a boreal goddess."

"I… I had not thought about renaming her," stammered the old man.

"*Frigerd, Frigerd…*" Gaius pondered. "That name is not too dissimilar from 'Phaedra.' Phaedra was a lusty wench, according to the Greeks. *Phaedra* it shall be!"

Frigerd, now Phaedra, smiled uneasily but inwardly bristled. She liked not at all having her name ripped away from her.

"I've been impressed with the manhood of her nation," the emperor informed his father-in-law, "but now I see that their women may also be outstanding for their own sex. They say the women of the South are like poplar wood; their passions are easy to ignite, but their fire soon dies out. Northern women, it is said, smolder a long while before taking to flame, but afterwards they blaze eternally, like an oaken log."

Gaius glanced toward an attending steward. "Take Phaedra to the women's quarters. You, Silanus, please walk with me."

The senator watched the departing woman whom he had known so briefly and then fell in beside his son-in-law. The latter led him across a miniature courtyard and soon paused in a peristyle open to the sky.

"Among all my many cares, I am strongly considering establishing certain honors for my parents," Gaius remarked offhandedly. "I would appreciate the advice of one of the Senate's most sage heads."

"I cannot think there is any honor that the Senate would deny to Germanicus, the hero of the Roman people, nor to his noble mother."

"I was hoping that would be true. I'm considering changing the name of September to 'Germanicus.' And my mother surely deserves to be honored by annual funeral sacrifices and circus games in her memory."

"Such a proposition will make the voices of the Senate cheer," the elder statesman conjectured.

Gaius nodded. "By the way, I am already organizing a voyage to Pontia and Pandateria to recover the bones of my mother and my brother Nero. Their proper resting place ought to be in the mausoleum of Augustus, don't you agree?"

"Without doubt, Caesar! And Drusus too. Have his bones been recovered?"

"My brother was cruelly starved to death in the palace dungeon. The jailers who served back then are not to be found and neither is his final resting place, but I've ordered a cenotaph erected. There is talk that Tiberius ordered his flesh to be thrown to a pack of the vigiles' hounds."

"Has ever a family so noble suffered such injustice?" commiserated Silanus.

"The people should know the late emperor for the wretch that he was," Gaius said forcefully. "So that his notorious life becomes public knowledge,

I intend to lift Tiberius' censorship restrictions over the chroniclers and any others who care to denounce him. History should know his every crime so that he can be execrated for centuries to come."

"That would be very just," the elderly senator replied.

"And I plan to do the esteemed Augustus a good turn," said the youth. "Tiberius never completed his temple out of fear of a prophecy. Thrasyllus foretold that before its work would be finished, my stepfather would die. Thus the project has laid in abeyance for twenty years. I shall recommence construction at once."

"A very excellent gesture," nodded Silanus.

Gaius led the old man to a northern portico that provided a clear view of the city. "Look," the emperor said. "Compare the grandeur of Augustus' house to Tiberius' tiny construction! As a home it is better suited to the gardener of an emperor, not an emperor himself! Something about Tiberius loved smallness, I think. But how could it be otherwise given his tiny, shriveled soul? And, consider! With all the empire spread out for his wanderings, he shut himself up on the island of Capri, one of the meanest parts of it. But I am of a different stamp! I am ordering plans drawn for a palace so grand that every emperor yet to come will choose to live there! I intend for it to extend all the way to the Temple of Castor and Pollux."

"Great Olympus!" Silanus blurted. "All the way to the Forum? That will close off the Via Nova!"

"Not at all," Gaius said dismissively. "That part of the street will become a great colonnade with the traffic passing through unobstructed. The new palace will be decorated with the rarest marbles from Asia and the doorknobs will be cast from gold."

"Will not so much building so soon cause the small-minded to say you are extravagant?" Silanus cautioned gently.

A pregnant pause delayed Gaius' answer. "I must take my leave of you, dear Father-in-law," he said. "The delegations I am receiving are simply inundating these small hilltop palaces. But before we part, do tell me what training our delightful Phaedra has already received."

"I know not, Caesar," said the old man, abashed. "I can only suppose that she was recently traded from Germania."

"How impulsive you are," Gaius jibed, "to ask so few questions of beauty. No matter, I shall permit her to keep no secrets from me. But I must be elsewhere now. A thousand matters require my consideration. Again, I thank you." He brushed his lips against the senator's cheek, then walked away without looking back. His attendants followed him out.

Silanus lingered on the sunlit portico, wondering if Gaius was piqued at his implied criticism of his building ambitions. He had sensed a coldness in his parting words. By Venus, the lad was as scornful of unwanted advice as ever Tiberius had been! Nonetheless, Silanus saw himself as the closest thing that the young man had to a living father. He would be negligent if he did not act in his proper role and impart earnest counsel to the princeps.

But at least his gift had been cordially received. Now that he was away from her enchanting presence, he felt oddly embarrassed. How impulsive he had been regarding her! Hopefully his lapse into caprice was not yet another sign of old age.

"Look at my condition!" complained Zenodotus to Herod Agrippa. "I have given him everything that he has today—empire, life even—and he shuts me away like the next goat awaiting slaughter!"

Agrippa had been listening quietly while the prisoner ranted. He nodded without much sympathy. The Greek was not a congenial man, but he could be a useful one. Ever since Agrippa discovered the emperor was being forced to sacrifice one of his intimates, he'd sought an opportunity to interview Zenodotus privately. If anyone knew who the emperor intended to sacrifice, it would be the Greek necromancer. The prince was actually worried that the princeps had grown so fond of him lately that Gauis might consider *him* as a candidate for sacrifice. Or, if Agrippa wasn't endangered, who was? Many of the people dearest to him were members of Gaius' family.

At last, a useful agent of his had managed to bribe the evening jailer of the high-security dungeons. Even then, the prince was forced to don a slave's tunic to mollify the jailer's obsessive fear of discovery.

"I sympathize, Zenodotus," he told the Greek, "but you have been evading my most important questions."

Zenodotus grimaced, being in no agreeable mood. The Greek's appearance had suffered from his confinement. His beard needed trimming and his robes were overdue for a fuller's attention. Formerly smug and self-important, the agitated wizard paced back and forth. "You are Caligula's friend," he charged bitterly, "his *best* friend! It would make as much sense for me to open my heart to you as to his trained ape Macro!"

"I swear by my God that nothing you say shall be passed on to anyone else, or used to harm you."

Zenodotus gave a derisive smile. "From what I know your god, I do not trust him."

"Then I will swear on the lives of *my* wife and heir."

The Greek frowned, still suspicious, but impressed nonetheless.

"Loosen up, man!" the Easterner declared. "Does Gaius intend to harm me or anyone I care about?"

"How badly do you want to know? What can you do for me in exchange for such valuable information?"

The Jew's brows knitted. How far did he dare go in obstructing Gaius' plans? His prosperity and even his life depended on the continued good will of the imperator. If reprisals were laid on him, they could even extend to his family. "I could plead for you," he offered at last, "appeal to his better nature."

"*Yaah!*" Zenodotus jeered. "Caligula *has* no better nature. I want to know if you can arrange my *escape!*"

Agrippa winced. Helping a prisoner of Caesar to escape would earn a death sentence. In the face of such a thing, their friendship would count for nothing. In fact, Agrippa himself could scarcely have faulted him for doing such a thing.

"I don't know," he equivocated.

"What *I* know is that your worst fears are realized," said Zenodotus. "One whom I know you cherish dearly will perish in a manner so pitiless that it defies description. And remember that such a death will not end the victim's suffering. Instead, the victim's soul will be carried off to an eternity of torture beyond the grave."

"Who is it? Drusilla? Lady Antonia? Claudius? Who?!"

"Whoever it is, you have only until the Kalends of May to do something about it. By the Kalends, Caligula and I have to be at Capri to prepare a chamber for the necessary invocations."

"I can't promise anything for certain," Agrippa said, "but if I do decide to risk all on your behalf, what do you require of me?"

"My sorcery, if I could tap into it, will handily win me my escape, but Caligula knows how formidable I am and has denied me my paraphernalia. You must bring certain things I need. Make a list of these things...."

By his third day in Emperor Gaius' Household Guard, Rufus was able to take his job's measure. The work load was light, not requiring much effort other than standing around next to doors or walking fully armed at his master's side. As a job, therefore, it was a good one, the sort of thing that a man of Erin would not blush to be doing. He sometimes wondered if Rome had always been full of such unmanly men as the plebs on the dole. No wonder the emperors needed to hire foreigners. Could the Romans of today have stood up to the likes of Hannibal and his campaign-tested army? He doubted it.

The Household Guard of which he was a member numbered almost five-score men, mostly Germans, and it was growing every day. The core of the recruits were hired adventurers far from home. They were organized into squads according to their status and assigned duties on that basis. The band's officers held titular ranks in the Praetorian Guard, but were almost to the man foreign-born ex-Thracian gladiators. Unfortunately, the emperor was more enthusiastic about Thracians than he was in secutors like himself.

Augustus had also maintained a German bodyguard, up until the Teutoberg Forest defeat. After that, the Romans were in such a panic about German warriors that the special guard had to be quietly dismissed. Tiberius loosened up on this prejudice in his later years due to his growing fear of Sejanus and his Praetorians. The short memory of the Roman people allowed for a German unit to be reestablished.

Yet, all in all, guarding an emperor was hardly a diverting job, except for the bodyguards who were chosen to accompany the princeps to the circus games. Still, if a man had to join the guard, Rufus couldn't have picked a better time for it. The imperial paymaster had called on him right after he'd joined and had counted out a thousand sestertii into his helmet toward the donative paid by the emperor to his troops. Enriched, Rufus had gone domus-hunting and located a serviceable flat on the Aventine Hill, a fresh one built after the fire of the previous year.

A feminine cry of fear echoed through the door behind him. That meant Caesar was up and feeling playful. Rufus scowled at the memory of the prior night's screaming. Some men had a compulsion to inflict pain with their pleasure; Baby Boots was one of that kind. Already, the Hibernian had seen more than one imperial concubine run weeping from Gaius' chambers. Oftentimes, their tender skin bore scratches, bruises, even whip weals. Hibernicus hadn't been impressed with his new employer at first sight; getting to know Gaius's ways better was not improving his estimation.

At last, the arrival of his relief told Rufus that his day was over. Leading the squad was Einer the Frisian.

On his own now, Rufus went down to the guard room to leave off his arms and armor. This was a brown leather cuirass reinforced with metal scales, a battle-skirt of copper-edged metal straps, and a pointed helmet. Rufus disliked the red plumes topping the latter. They broke off easily and kept the servants busy replacing them, lest a man be raked over the coals for being in dishabille. Wearing his street clothes, he took the most convenient route leading out of Tiberius' palace.

Inside the intervening peristyle, he caught a glimpse of a golden-tressed wench barely dressed in a diaphanous green silk thing. She was sitting down on a fountain's edge, resting her chin on her clenched fists. Rufus grinned, recognizing Silanus' new girl—the same who had been sharing a room with Tatia. He had suspected from the start that the senator intended to make a gift of her to the emperor.

The German girl noticed him too, answering his admiring stare with a withering frown. *By Lugh, the wench has a bad attitude!* Rufus thought. Under other circumstances, he might have accepted her saucy challenge, aiming to tame her with a bath of kisses, but only a fool would lay hands on one of the emperor's playthings.

Still, her Germanic charms were hard to ignore. He forced himself to think about Tatia. He decided to make straight for Silanus' house and get the Spanish girl over to his new domus.

For a moment, it had seemed to Phadra that the big, red-mustached guard was about to approach her loutishly. When he went on his way, she was disappointed. Evading him with illusion and then punishing him with, say, lifelong impotence, would have given her a little something to smile about.

And she needed some cheering up.

This was the Swede's third day in the palace. She had expected the young Caesar to summon her as early as the first night. The problem was that the imperator owned too many women—and more arrived daily as gifts from the great ones of the empire. Though he had called for multiple concubines since then, he had not called for her. Being alone with him was important to her mission, and she found it mortifying to be judged as less than the best in the women's quarters!

Galar's plan had turned out to be not so cunning as she had at first supposed. Well, what could she expect from that ugly, stunted hybrid of a captive woman's rape by one of the earth's maggots? The time had come for Phaedra to take matters into her own hands.

Suddenly the *Suion* girl realized that someone was lurking behind her. Who? Another gaping servant? She glanced down into the still water and discerned his reflection. He was handsome, she realized with a tiny smile. She thought she had seen that face from afar before....

With a gasp, Phaedra leaped up. In turning, she lost her footing and tripped. Instantly, strong arms gripped her, arresting her fall.

Firmly held by her accoster, she found herself looking into the golden-tanned face of Osric, the son of Loderod....

A Night for Love

CHAPTER XVI

The day following their interview, Agrippa removed Osric's stigma of slavery.

The legal requirements were performed before a Roman city leader, one who was called a "praetor." The king placed a foolish-looking cap upon the Engle's head and declared him "free" before the witness, and a papyrus certification was drawn up. Afterwards, Agrippa informed the young man that he had become a citizen of the empire—though he had to bear in mind that his status would have certain restrictions in respect of his former servile status.

Romans! the Engle thought with exasperation. Over a free man's protests, they enslave him; then, having been liberated, they scorn him in respect of that enslavement!

According to Agrippa, a new citizen was required to take a Roman name or, more specifically, three Roman names. For the first of these, the personal name, Osric chose the name "Marcus," to honor his friend Mar as well as his patron, Marcus Julius Agrippa. For his second name, representing his family name, his royal advisor suggested he use a Latinized version of his tribe's name—Anglius.

The third name, his cognomen, would be what acquaintances would respectfully address him by. For this the youth chose his own given name, altered in the manner that Cocceius had altered it: Osricus.

Worse than the name was the supposedly dignified garment of a free man, a plain white toga, given to him by Agrippa. Never was more unwieldy attire ever fashioned! As soon as "Osricus" returned to his patron's suite, he exchanged the unappealing woolen wrap for a short-sleeved, mid-thigh-length tunic, two of which were provided by his host.

To commemorate the day, Agrippa assigned a servant to show Osricus the environs of the Palantine Hill. Most of what he saw was all new to him. Of special interest was the Temple of Mercury on the Aventine Hill. He was especially interested in Mercury because the Romans believed him to be the Roman version of Woden. Because of a recent fire, it was stained by smoke and scorching. But the smallness of the god's shrine surprised him, as did the effeminacy of the artistic representation of the god. In no way did Rome's Mercury evoke the powerful, white-bearded patriarch that German elders described to their eager listeners.

During his excursion, Osricus made various street-side purchases. When the pair returned to Caesar's house, Agrippa personally guided him in a tour of Caesar's palace. The immensity, the richness of it astonished him. This, he was told, had been the house where Augustus had held court. Oddly, the second Caesar had preferred to live nearby in a much smaller domicile that was named for him, the House of Tiberius.

The king was not averse to talking about the late emperor. Interestingly, Augustus would not accept Tiberius as his heir unless he first divorced his wife and remarried Julia, the princep's daughter. Unfortunately, Tiberius had truly loved his wife while holding Julia in scorn. But because of his ambition, he accepted the match. But Tiberius' dislike of this new marriage made his and Julia's relationship poisonous. Unable to abide the sight of his unwanted mate, Tiberius took himself away into exile alone. Agrippa only lamented that the man had not contracted some foreign disease while away and had been shipped back dead.

The failed marriage brought on much trouble. Julia found the chaste life of a cast off wife intolerable and became very adulterous. For that, her father sent her to a prison island and summoned Tiberius back to Rome. When Augusts died a few years later, the vindictive successor saw to it that Julia would die slowly of starvation in prison. Liking this type of execution, Tiberius used it to kill his own sister-in-law and nephew, and also to take vengeance on his first wife's widower, out of jealousy for the fellow having enjoyed the wife who had been torn away from him. Agrippa was of the opinion that the forced divorce had caused the emperor to renounce the love of women and to satisfy his lust by molesting children, notoriously keeping dozens of them captive at his Capri palaces.

One particular story about an abused child strongly moved Osricus. Wanting to destroy an enemy's entire family, Tiberius ordered the man's young daughter to be executed. But his advisers protested that the law did not allow for the execution of a virgin. So the Master of the World obligingly ordered his jailer to rape the child, thereby satisfying the letter of the law.

When Osricus returned to Agrippa's suite, he was firm in the conviction that the late emperor must have been one of the most evil men who had ever lived.

Osricus did not go out the next day, but sat alone in the room with the fylfot medallion hanging around his neck. With it, he found that his ability to meditate was stronger. The dross object's gold color continued to spread over it and he felt as though it was feeding him power. But the process was causing his body to ache, as if he were a leather bottle filled to bursting. So considerable did his discomfort become that he removed the talisman and concealed it in the vase atop his bedstand. The day was late when he left the apartment to walk the halls of the outer palace.

Eventually, in one of the small interior gardens, he spied a fair-haired slave girl admiring herself in a still fountain. The young man felt transfixed by the sight of her. It wasn't love at first sight, but it certainly was fascination. Impulsively, he stepped closer, ready to speak to her if she smiled at him. The youth was not at all prepared for her to lurch to her feet in alarm. He grabbed her as she stumbled, preventing the maid's fall into the cold water.

With the touching of their flesh, Osricus experienced a sudden electricity which was very like what he felt when he touched the talisman, only this touch was distinctly pleasant. Bemused, he let her go and the blonde girl staggered away from him.

"Did I frighten you?" he asked quickly. "I didn't wish you to fall into the water."

The Swedish girl's eyes, at first mistrustful, quickly glanced downward. "Many pardons… Warrior…." she said. "You surprised me. I have become afraid of being touched in this strange place."

Osricus thought she possessed the accent of a Scandian race. Lombard? Goth? He'd had little to do with Scandians before this, but here, in Rome, alone among his kind, he felt a kinship with all the peoples of the North.

"From what tribe do you come, *hlaefdige?*" he asked, using a respectful address, though she was obviously no more than a thrall. "I did not expect to meet a German in Caesar's palace."

Still she demurred from looking at him. "I was stolen by pirates… Master. Speak to me not about my homeland. If they knew of my fate, they would be ashamed of me."

Osricus nodded. Having only recently regained his own dignity, he readily sympathized with her lament.

"Will you at least tell me *your* name?" he asked with a reassuring smile.

"Emperor Gaius calls me 'Phaedra,' " she answered.

"Surely that is no name from Scandia."

"It serves, Warrior. The woman from Scandia has already perished." Then her expression turned severe. "Do you find my grief inappropriate?"

"Oh, not at all. I smile because I have met one who must certainly be the emperor's favorite."

"He has many bed-thralls," she whispered. "I have dreaded the hour when he deigns to beckon me. Forgive me, lord. You surely do not wish to be belabored with a stranger's tale of woe."

"I am not a lord," Osric corrected her, "just a man. The Romans prefer to call me Marcus Anglius Osricus. But I, too, have been enslaved. Only yesterday was I pronounced free under the laws of these strange people."

Phaedra looked up at him tentatively and asked: "Are you one of Caesar's guardsmen? Many of those come from the North."

The youth shifted. The girl's beauty and scant garment put him ill-at-ease, being used to the modest garb of German village women. "No, maiden. The emperor gave me as a gift to a king. The king became my friend and restored my freedom. Now, I serve with his war band."

Phaedra's stare held firm. "Were you captured in battle?"

"It was more of a brawl," he replied. "But I would ask a question of you, hlaefdige."

"What is that, warrior?"

"When I held you, a strange feeling came over me. Did you feel any such thing?"

"I must go," Phaedra said suddenly. "Perchance we may see one another again."

"If there is any way that I may help you...."

"If that is p-possible, I will seek you out, Warrior," she stammered over her shoulder.

Osricus stood staring after the girl's retreat.

The next morning, several of the emperor's concubines wakened with a gastric complaint and the air of their sleeping alcoves smelled foul. When the matrons saw that only Phaedra remained fit, they put her elsewhere, so she would not contract the illness from the others.

Doctors were called and they guessed that the trouble came from tainted food. Phaedra, who knew the truth, tried not to smile. From a peristyle garden she had gathered broad leaves—and upon each had written certain Black Runes of sickness. Once alone, she had hidden one of these between the layers of each woman's sleeping mat.

She had been moved to these desperate measures by the appearance of Loderod's son in the palace. When the rune-witch realized that he did not know her for what she really was, she refrained from attacking him. He might be skilled enough to resist her first rune-song and alert the palace to the presence of a sorceress. Moreover, the current she'd experienced at his touch intrigued her. The witch was reminded by it of how valuably one of the Blood of Scef could serve another.

In the afternoon, the Swede was informed that the emperor had asked for a German girl, and that she was the only one available. Just before twilight, Phaedra was prepared for her first meeting with Gaius.

When the time drew nigh, the matrons dressed Phaedra in a surprising way.

Her costume was more like a shield-maid's than a bed-thrall's. Her tunic was made of bearskin and belted by strip of lynx pelt. Her boots were of fur and cross-gartered, while she was crowned with a leather helmet with metal horns. No jewelry was provided, other than simple beaded wrist and arm straps. Likewise, no scent had been dabbed upon her flesh.

While being escorted to the imperial chamber, the witch reasoned that the young Caesar might wish to pretend that he was an *Einherjar*, one of the chosen heroes of Woden. As such, he would of course expect to be attended by a Valkyrie in Valhalla. Oh, the foolish games of men!

A plump, gray-haired matron met Phaedra outside the emperor's suite and handed her a buckler and a spear with a blunt wooden blade. "You'll serve the emperor," she told the Swede, "but do not let your play get out of hand. If you harm the master, you will die by prolonged torture."

Having delivered the obligatory threat, the senior slave ushered her charge within the suite and shut the door behind her.

The room she entered was an odd simulation of a German chieftain's hall. Various furs and pelts were strewn about, as were screens of wickerwork, rude wooden furniture, and potted evergreens. The chamber was lit by braziers that released piney incense. Painted wood panels decorated the walls displaying woodland scenes, of beasts, satyrs, and nymphs engaged in frenetic chase.

The rasp of swinging hinges brought Phaedra's face about. She beheld Gaius wearing a gleaming, gilded helm and a breastplate embossed with martial scenes. He wore a dark scarlet tunic, a heavy, elaborate cloak, and carried a legionary's shield on one arm and a pilum-type spear in his right hand.

"Rome conveys to Germania her ultimatum!" he shouted. "Lay down your arms, Savage Barbaria, surrender your towns, give hostages, and send your kings to kneel down before their conqueror!"

Phaedra blinked bemusedly. Had she been brought here to fight? Or did he really desire that she lay down her arms? In truth, these weapons were an impedance to her intentions. They prevented her from touching the man, a thing which she wished to do as soon as possible. Accordingly, the rune-witch dropped her spear and laid the shield down at her feet.

"Don't give up so easily, you stupid bitch!" Gaius scolded. "Fight to keep your land from despoliation, your children from slavery, your women from violation! Fight and find out how powerless is your barbarian ferocity against the might of Eternal Rome!"

Stung, Phaedra retrieved the lance and buckler.

"So, Germania stands defiant!" he observed. "What reckless arrogance! Do you think Gaius is the coward Varus, or that this battlefield is like the fatal Teutoberg Forest? You face now the herculean son of Germanicus! I am sworn to return to Germania the state of meek bondage that the treacherous Arminus so briefly cast off."

He strode her way and Phaedra gave back a step, the round wooden buckler automatically rising to ward her middle body. The Swede had received some instruction in arms, as did all the fit women of the warlike

Sitones. Even so, she realized that she was not prepared to combat a fully-equipped man, not unless her arms were lightened by means of magic.

"Ah, Germania, your stubborn bravado shall make you a conquest worthy of the Senate and the Roman people! What a triumph you will provide when your chieftains are led in mortifying chains behind the imperial chariot! Already I have vanquished the haughty Parthians, the black-as-jet warriors of Ethiopia, and even the trousered Dacians beyond the Danube. But I am not only a great man but a compassionate one. Before useless blood is spilled, will you not succumb to your fear and acknowledge Caesar as you master?"

Hesitantly, Phaedra lowered her spear.

The young man shook his head. "No, of course you will not, little idiot! Do not suppose that you will be allowed to cheat the lord of Rome of a glorious battle by means of an effeminate capitulation!"

Oh, the madman! Phaedra's declared silently. If he wanted to play at war, she would play it as a sorceress played it!

She shouted out a fimbul-song, one that sent unmanning fear against a foe.

Perplexedly, Gaius only laughed. "Well done, Germania! My father spoke of the bewitching songs of the northern hordes! But beware! The gods of Rome are greater than those of Germania. Let the battle begin!"

He jabbed at the middle of her shield; the iron pilum striking its wooden center with a hollow sound. The witch sensed the mystical vibrations in the room were all wrong; the spell was having no effect! Gaius displayed no sign of fear.

The youthful Caesar pressed his assault, making short jabs, purposely not going for blood. Meanwhile, he tossed insults at her, seeking to incite her, trying to make her strike back in anger. Unsure of herself, Phaedra gave ground easily, only occasionally stabbing back at the mock general.

Suddenly Gaius lurched forward, slamming his shield into hers, sending her staggering rearward. She caught her heel on a black bearskin throw and fell on her back upon it. Gaius scrambled forward, snatched her spear away, and drew the knife out of his belt. This he pressed against the girl's soft throat, saying, "Does Germania yield unconditionally to the sovereign mastery of Rome?"

"I yield, my eorl!" she gasped.

"It is a wise general who knows when he is beaten," Gaius said and triumphantly threw the knife away. "Now, as consequence of our victory, Rome lays claim to the spoils of Germania."

His mouth assailed hers, his tongue stabbing between her teeth while his eager hands made play all over her body.

Here was a passion as Phaedra understood passion. If Gaius did in fact intend to use her as a woman, it would provide her with the opportunity she craved.

Phaedra plucked a carefully-prepared enchanter's thorn from her garment. With her attacker engrossed in groping her, she stabbed it into his naked thigh.

"Ouch!" Gaius yelled and rolled away.

"Now, you miming fool," she snarled in her own language, "I am mistress here!"

But to her surprise, he was not paralyzed. Instead, scowling, the young man felt for what was hurting him and soon pulled the thorn from his flesh. Phaedra held back, dismayed that her spells and devices were failing. Suddenly, Gaius's arm shot out, seized her shoulder, and slapped her hard across the mouth....

Rufus Hibernicus kissed the woman sleeping beside him so softly that she did not awaken.

The room they shared was pitch black, its shutters being closed against the night's chill breeze. The rented apartment at least fit his guardsman's income and was definitely better than some of the slum-dwellings he had occupied in the past. Even better, its location allowed for an easy commute to and from the imperial palaces.

Drifting off to sleep, Rufus failed to notice the faint deep-earth scent that was now seeping through the room.

The Iberian girl opened her eyes, awakened by the odor. She was hardly aware of her protector's large body next to her. He might as well have been part of the furnishings.

Tatia slipped from the bed; Hibernicus shifted uneasily with the loss of warmth, but continued to slumber. Not conscious of any need to dress, the girl tiptoed to the shutters, opened them, and made the easy drop to the narrow walk outside. There, the earth-odor became stronger; it led her on like a dog on a leash. She hurriedly padded into a dark alcove with moon shadows around it.

"Tatia!" came a whisper like two stones grating.

"I'm here!"

Galar sidled from the darkness and stared at her intently.

The dvergson's fearful aspect had not altered, but to Tatia's ensorceled glance the dwarf appeared handsome. She smiled, but Galar returned no smile of his own.

"Master?" she inquired, puzzled.

He took her around the waist, his nails hurting her. "The gladiator has taken Tatia to his house! She comes to Galar still reeking of his lust—and her own!"

Tatia dropped to her knees and seized him unexpectedly, wrapping her arms around his hard knots of bone and muscle. "I cannot help myself! By daylight, I am bewitched. You, my beloved, fade from my mind like a spirit flying from the dawn. Forgive me, my Galar, I am not myself when the sun is high."

The dark one thrust her away. By Frigerd's spell, Tatia's love would arise to his call, but when away from him, she lost her memories of it, save as a creature in a nightmare of foul violation. Galar had heard her cries, seen her tears of terror, when she awoke, as if waking from a nightmare. He knew very well that her love was an illusionary thing not worth having. Surely Frigerd could have done better had she wished to—that selfish witch!

Galar rebuked himself. He should have been satisfied with working for the glory of Heid, instead of involving himself with a human woman. Her daily terror only reminded him all the more that he was a monster. He had no place in all the world. The Children of the Night had no use for a hybrid. Neither did his mother's kind—the mother whom he had never known, the mother who had fled from her abductor only to be pursued and punished with death months later.

"Galar, I am yours!" Tatia insisted. "We can leave Rome together!"

"You cannot be truly Galar's so long as the swordsman lives. You love him!"

"No!" she insisted. "Give me the order, and I will kill the gladiator while he sleeps!"

Galar grimaced, her words taking away some of his fury. He settled down into a squat on the curbstones. "No, Galar fights his enemies alone," he said. "To battle my rival is not a task I would set for Tatia."

"*You* kill him then, my darling! If he is keeping us apart, he must die!"

"These words come from bewitchment, not from Tatia's heart," he sighed.

"If this is bewitchment, I am happy to be bewitched. On my life I am!"

"No," he murmured sadly, "that is not so. But clutch Galar to yourself and speak all the words again, all the pleasing words."

"Tatia!" a voice boomed. "Where in the name of Lugh are you?!"

The gladiator was coming! Frustrated, the dwarf withdrew into the shadows. It was his wyrd to fight the gladiator to the death, but this was not the right time for the great battle.

Rounding a corner, the Hibernian saw Tatia faint onto the cold pavement. He rushed to her, touched her, and she began to scream.

He slapped the girl, bringing her out of her night terrors. When her gasping settled into a breathless quiet, he picked her up. Once more he had to carry her home from out of the night. While doing so, he did not sense the pair of golden, death-filled eyes following him….

REVENGE

CHAPTER XVII

The rune-warrior berated himself. *Fool, Osric, think less of the girl and more upon Andvaranaut!* He pressed his talisman between his palms; as it warmed, it began to send prickles of energy through his flesh. Its golden transformation had continued to spread slowly across its surface and it seemed to parallel the awakening divinity of his blood. But, even yet, the fairy-metal still comprised less than half of the whole. Periods of meditation, Osricus observed, accelerated the transmutation, but always a Scandian girl's face would materialize at the wrong moment, distracting him, slowing the expansion of his power.

He had spoken to the girl only briefly; why should he have fixated upon her? True, a child of the Vans could scarcely be more beautiful, but Osricus had never been one to exaggerate qualities that were merely physical. In appearance, she seemed only to be a mild and troubled village girl, like many another he had met in Germania. But why had he felt such strange stimulation at her touch?

If only he could....

Dolt! he scolded himself. *Concentrate on the fylfot—then you will have the power to help her, not before!*

Incredible! He was doing it again! Rune magic was intended for purposes that infinitely transcended the salvation of a woman whom he hadn't known existed a day before.

With a will, the rune-warrior banished the specter of Phaedra's young form. He forced his spirit to search the Nether Realm.

Where was Andvaranaut hidden? In this city of emperors? Elsewhere within the vast empire? Who would know? Tiberius, certainly; he had received the ring from Zenodotus—but Tiberius was dead. Questioning the dead was a perversion of Heimdall's edicts of magic. Legend recalled how the good and noble shield-maid Hardgrep had caused a shade to speak its wisdom for the assistance of the hero Hadding. She did not live out the night, but was snatched away by a demon hand from Nifelhel.

For the moment, Agrippa and most of his servants were away. Osricus cleared the center of his room of its rugs and furniture and then made chalk marks upon the floor. He divided the circle into sections and wrote potent runes upon them.

During his excursions about the city, he and Agrippa's servant had visited the Forum Boarium, the livestock market below the Aventine Hill, between the Bridge of Aemilius and the Circus Maximus. There Osricus had purchased a black lamb. Earlier this day, he had retrieved the animal from the pen of Agrippa's butcher. Now the rune-warrior took the lamb from its box and clutched it against his breast.

Osricus grasped a rune-covered blade, purified by ceremony, and held it to the creature's throat, saying: *"In the name of Ing, Lord of Fruitfulness; in the name Njord, Lord of the Winds, Sea, and Storm; in the name Woden, Guardian and Lord of the Fallen Good; in the name of Loder, Lord of Fire; in the name of Heimdall, guardian of the Gate, Far-hearing, Far-seeing One, I call. Give truth to my divining runes."*

He slit the creature's throat, held fast during its brief convulsions, and then let its blood pour into a silver bowl.

When the flow had stanched, Osricus laid aside the carcass and dropped the herbal offerings and mead into the blood-filled vessel. Then he touched a lighted twig to the floating matter and it lit with a faint curl of smoke. As the effluent rose, he sang a song of rune-words, using not his native tongue, but the secret cant of Nordic wizards:

"Reynir er osi stemma bjorg Donar; brottnigr skogar i vta sinni, fra Ing; fryrikri hronnjardar…."

Osricus took a white, folded sheet and spread it out on the floor tiles. From a bag, he took a handful of wood chips from the sacred ash tree and cut and marked each carved with a rune-sign. Casting his glance up toward heaven, Osricus blindly threw these across the cloth. Then the Engle spread his fingers over them, trying to find the ones filled with power, all the while concentrating upon the question: "Where is Andvaranaut?" When a chip seemed to vibrate to his touch, he set it aside without looking at it.

After drawing only a few chips, Osricus felt no more vibrations. Hoping that meant the message was complete, he opened his eyes and read the rune symbols in the order in which they were drawn. What the mystic alphabet spelled out produced two ambiguous sounds: "Kah-Prah".

He cast lots again, but this time changed the question. He wanted to know who was the keeper of Andvaranaut?

The answer came, SANODOTR.

"Sanodotr?" Aye. This was not the first time that the rune warrior had heard such a name. Loderod had imparted to Calusidius the identity of the thief of Andvaranaut, Zenodotus. According to the runes, this foreign magician was more than a thief; he continued to be the ring's keeper. But where could one find Zenodotus?

*　　　*　　　*

"Away from me, thrall," Phaedra hissed. "I don't want your balm!"

The matron, ignoring her, rolled the Swede over on her belly perforce. From an earthen jar, she spread a scoop of vile-smelling grease across the girl's bare back. This the severe and strong woman proceeded to rub vigorously into Phaedra's flesh.

"I said go away!" cried the girl, throwing her weight left and right.

"What an ill-tempered child you are!" the matron remarked. "The balm has done good work, healing you almost overnight. Be warned; I may use the scourge as freely as the emperor already has if you continue to hone your sharp tongue against me!"

Phaedra thought it best to play meek. It had been her runes, not the foul medicine, that had cured her so quickly. Mortified, it took all of the witch's self-control not to fling a curse of boils upon the imperious palace servant. She held back because it would be a waste of her power; moreover, she did not want people to notice that strange things frequently happened around her.

Rising, the matron cautioned, "Don't lie on your back until it soaks in." The Swede obeyed that order, not wanting to smear the sheets that she had to sleep on.

As Phaedra lay prone, the memory of Emperor Gaius haunted her. The prince had held her down, shouting: "Conquered Germania rebels, does she? Then prepare for the scorched-earth rebuke by which Julius Caesar tamed recalcitrant Gaul!"

Her magic foiled, she had been helpless. He had scourged her relentlessly with the whip, then raped her in every perverse and brutal way he knew, continuing the assault as long as his vigor lasted.

Now, as she recuperated in the women's quarters, she blamed herself for misunderstanding the resistance to her power. The imperator had been well-charmed against magic such as hers. Why had she not anticipated that a ruler so powerful would have taken every precaution against enemy sorcery!

"Glaejord!" came a thin whisper from nowhere.

"Galar!" Phaedra snapped. She was used to the dvergson coming and going more like a shadow than a being of flesh. "You maggot! Why are you here? I didn't summon you."

The tiny man was squatting out of view of the others occupying the women's quarter, on a pillow in the adjacent alcove. "Galar begs leave to destroy a man."

"What man? Some private vendetta?"

"The woman Tatia loves the red giant, not Galar. The glaejord's spell is too weak to banish the giant from her heart!"

"There is nothing wrong with my spell," Phaedra replied irascibly. "It's the sort of suitor you are! What woman alive could bear the touch of such a black worm?"

"Then make Galar a man! Slay the earth-maggot in him!"

She looked at him incredulously. "That would take a mighty spell! I need all my strength for purposes more important than aiding your pathetic love affair. You have accomplished very little to advance our mission. I know now why you sought to put me into Silanus' house. It was to make it easy for me to seduce that black-haired trull that obsesses you! I'm more in the mood to take vengeance for your presumption, not grant boons!"

"Galar's plan was good!"

"Impudent bug! Go, kill your red giant, but do not expect me to lend aid to your petty ambitions, not until I win Andvaranaut—and then only if you have served me meaningfully in attaining that end!"

Galar's golden eyes flamed with injury.

"Poor fool, you are far more useful to Heid as you are than as a human male. Your dverg-descended gifts give you the worth of ten men, but you have not the sense to comprehend it. You do not realize how blessed you are. You have no soul which one day could fall into Nifelhel! You should be rejoicing, but you lack any ambition beyond sporting with a worthless thrall. Begone!"

Seething, Galar leaped like a monkey to the sill of the alcove window and shinnied down a trellis, whereby he gained access to the portico roof. The ice-hearted witch! Descended from magnificent Heimdall, Phaedra's beauty could melt the heart of any man in Germania, in Rome, even. Yet never had a suitor warmed her to love. How he wished he could write a passion-rune against her, make her feel loneliness as he felt it, let her desire what she could not have, to always be scorned.

But Phaedra was far more powerful than Galar. If he were to have his way, he needed her help and consent to achieve it. His fury would have to be sated on some other enemy—such as the red giant.

For an hour subsequent to Galar's departure, Phaedra brooded upon her problems. Her session with Gaius had weakened her. One of the Blood of Scef should not let herself be served by any of the common stock. Even with ritual purification, it would take three days before her magical blood was shriven. To hasten the process, she would do well to lie with a man whose blood was worthy of her own.

Someone like Osricus. Loderod would not have chosen a disciple who was anything other than the Blood of Scef. And he was young—little older than Phaedra herself—so he might easily be beguiled. She smiled, remembering how easily he accepted her tale of pretended woe. To gain what she needed from him should be very easy.

Phaedra laughed.

*   *   *

As soon as he entered his palace apartment, Herod Agrippa dropped onto a couch, weighed down by melancholy. He had been too cautious. It was time to take some risks to learn which loved one was menaced by Gaius.

Suddenly, he sensed someone standing behind him. He looked over his shoulder. "Osricus. What is it?"

"I am sorry to disturb your rest, Lord Agrippa, but I need your help."

"What help?"

"Do you know of a wizard named Zenodotus?"

For a long while, Osricus had resisted involving any outsider in his deadly quest, but the urgency of it required that he get some help. He had found no reason thus far to mistrust Agrippa, and it was the way of the Northmen to speak truth to friends.

"Zenodotus?" Agrippa echoed, rising to an upright position. "Where did you learn that name? From palace gossip?"

The youth shook his head. "No one has spoken the name of Zenodotus within my hearing—not since I left Germania."

"You heard that name while still inside Germania?" the king asked.

"Gese!" Osricus affirmed.

Agrippa's brow furrowed. "I know that Zenodotus passed last summer along the *limes*, supposedly to learn the lore of the Germans. But if he is so well remembered after that brief visit, I suspect that he must have done more than he has admitted to."

"Gese, my lord."

With a serious tone, Agrippa said, "I have not wished to pry into your affairs, Osricus, but now I am forced to ask this: Who are you, and what do you know of the sorcery that seems to have taken a stranglehold on this city and the people I care for?"

"My own story is a simple one," replied the Engle. "My line descends from the god-king Scef. My father served a king whose was poor in comparison to my sire, and for that he was hated. Fearing that my family would one day supplant his own, the king sent men to destroy us in the night. My parents and brothers were slaughtered, and my sisters captured to be forcibly wed a pair of his brutish princes, in hope that their debased linage might be improved.

"I was away with my father's warriors when the foul blow fell. I returned and took blood vengeance upon the king's sons, but failed to free my sisters. These the tyrant sold to a pirate ship in retribution.

"I lived in exile, until Loderod found me and made me his son and successor." Then the Engle spoke of the legends of the ring Andvaranaut and how Zenodotus had wrested it from its hiding place.

"This ring of power, where did it originally come from?" asked Agrippa.

Osricus told the story as Loderod had often related it to him.

"The Jotuns ever sought escape from their confinement in Jotunheim and Nifelhel," Osricus explained, "but the means of their release could only be created and used in Midgard, from whence they were barred.

"Unfortunately, the Jotuns had dark allies within Midgard. These were the dvergar, creatures almost as old as the world, spawned as maggots in the rotting flesh of the first giant, Ymir—a monster slain by the three brothers, Woden, Loder, and Honer.

"Then," Osricus continued, "from across the gulfs of chaos, the Dark Goddess commanded her servants the dvergar to forge the Ring of Sorcery. They constructed it of fairy gold, an evilly-aspected metal of supernatural creation. With the ring, and by sacrifices that all but destroyed their underground realm, the Worms of the Earth summoned an avatar of the Dark Goddess, one who called herself Heid, to Midgard.

"Heid placed the ring into the keeping of the powerful dvergar prince Andvar, who set the demon-dragon Fafnir to guarding it. Then, in mortal guise, the queen of witches spread the corrupt worship of the Jotuns, teaching the Black Runes to mortals and also showing the greedy and corrupt how to use Heimdall's White Runes for wickedness. She intended to have her evil servants in Midgard destroy the world of men.

"The Aesir at length drove Heid from the world, but her cult and the Ring remained. But the witches could not claim the Ring from the mighty dragon Fafnir. Protected by sorcery, neither god nor an enchanted servant might wrest the Ring from its hiding place. But Woden chose to send a mortal hero, Sigurd, to slay Fafnir and claim Andvaranaut for the men of Midgard.

This was an error. The Ring brought naught but woe to Sigurd, but before he died, he gave it to his beloved, Brunhild, a goddess made mortal to aid Woden's plan, with instructions to hide it so well it might never be found. As doom befell Brunhild, she cast the Ring to the spirits of the Rhine, who safeguarded Andvaranaut until the witches of Heid conjured it away from them in Ingfrid's time. Ingfrid kept the Ring safe until the time came to pass Andvaranaut on to his own protégé, Loderod."

"I see!" said Herod Agrippa….

Galar, in hiding amid the marble gods and goddesses of a portico rooftop, picked out the swaggering figure of his rival. Rufus Hibernicus' unsuspected enemy had observed his movements of late and knew the route whereby he customarily approached the palace.

The ex-gladiator entered and gave a bluff greeting to the guardsmen on watch, then disappeared into the portico, out of Galar's sight. The dvergson abandoned his vantage point and darted inside through a barrel-arched window. From there he shambled unobserved along a series of service halls and back stairways. He had planned his revenge well and craved to observe its consummation.

Meanwhile, Rufus' thoughts were preoccupied with Tatia. Her state of mind continued to concern him. She kept having nightmares about being ravished by the dark dwarf, the very one that they had seen only twice about streets of Rome. How this obsession had laid claim to the usually strong-minded wench was beyond the Hibernian's guess, but her sleepwalking subjected her to potential danger.

It worried Tatia too. She had been begging him to lock her inside the domus, lest she unknowingly go prowling the midnight alleys on nights when Rufus could not be there to watch her. The secutor had complied, though he certainly didn't like doing so, not with fires being so common about the city.

Tonight Rufus was doing another night shift. After donning his armor, he went into the guardroom to report to the shift commander, Wulfgang, who had a detail of the guard with him. They were seated around a table, attended by a slave girl who kept their terracotta *potoria* brimming with wine. The girl greeted Rufus and urged some wine upon him.

"Just the one *poculum*," the Hibernian remarked. Then he heartily addressed his mates. "Old Tiberius once found a guardsman drunk and had him filled so full of wine that his innards burst!"

"Ah, Rufus!" exclaimed Wulfgang, in his thickly-accented Latin. A Langobard, Wulfgang sported the longest, blondest mustache in the palace. "We were dicing for the apportionment of stations," he informed Hibernicus. "Would you wish to try for the women's quarters?"

"Not on your life, you swamp boar!" the secutor boomed. "Not with the concubines all sick on their backs and fouling their linens!"

"Too bad," laughed Wulfgang. "That's the only post that is left." The laughing Langobard then scooped up his dice and put them away. "Drink up, drink up! If we are late to our posts, the young Caesar may kick us all the way back to Germania—and you, Rufus, back to your storm-beaten isle!"

As the Germans lifted their clay cups, the Hibernian noticed an odd series of scratches on the bottom of each. He wondered at them briefly, but saw no reason to ask about it. "Don't talk, Wulf," he replied. "Even the Romans didn't want that giant bog you crawled out of after they got a good look at it!"

His jibe fell coldly across the table. The camaraderie of a moment before had fallen so silent that the Hibernian could hear nothing except the whispered singing of some tiny, thin voice in some unknown language. But the looks he was drawing from his comrades were scorching. He had not seen such enraged faces since his last match with Phlegon—the retiarius he'd accidentally gelded in their previous bout.

"What's ailing everybody?" he asked.

Wulfgang's clenched jaw trembled with fury; the rest of the guards looked as if they'd discovered the man who'd raped their mothers.

"Was it something I said?" he asked with forced cheeriness. But Verner's thick hands were gliding to the sword worn upon his belt; the others were ominously rising.

"Fellows, this is no way to act just because of a little jape against Germania...."

Verner was now armed and Ragstan was inching forward, his blade drawn, also. *This is daft,* Rufus thought, but these men weren't counterfeiting anger. He saw real rage projecting from every angle of their bodies.

As quick as Mercury, Rufus snatched a Spanish sword and a buckler from the adjacent rack on the wall, then fell back toward the door. "We have no quarrel," he warned, "but that won't stop me from separating your bleached heads from your thick necks if you don't put your steel away!"

They didn't seem to hear him. *This is going to be bad,* thought Rufus. The slave girl, shrinking back, looked confused, as if she couldn't explain the flareup any better than the Hibernian could.

With the five Germans pressing in on him menacingly, Rufus warned them off, brandishing his shield and blade. His gesture made his foes hesitate, but their expressions still resembled those of rabid wolves.

Hader struck first, going for the Hibernian's breast. The Irishman used his shield to knock the blade aside and stabbed into Hader's unarmored lower arm. As Hader drew back with a yelp, Donargil and Ragstan shoved the man aside and double-teamed against Hibernicus. With four swords going for his guts and four shields battering at him at once, only the narrowness of the passage made standing his ground possible.

When Wulfgang's arm reached out too far from the tangled knot of attackers, the secutor maimed it, sending his decurion chastened to the rear. The unwounded three, undaunted, came on all the harder. Rufus could no longer keep command of the doorway.

Darting out into the hall, he took over a deep alcove and defended himself like a wild man. Gunnar, a Mattiaci, had been a skilled gladiator and scored a cut on the Hibernian's forearm. With a curse, Rufus' drove his sword into his assailant's thigh, but his forward strike left an opening in his defenses, and Verner's next thrust touched the man of Erin through a gap in his armor.

Dismayed, Rufus leaped back. The size of the alcove restricted him and the two swordsmen were drawing the secutor's blood from a dozen cuts. Only his arena training, instincts, and the armor he wore spared him a maiming or even a fatal wound. He couldn't avoid a killing blow for much longer; he needed a breakout.

Rufus thrust at Verner's breast, but struck only armor. Ragstan leaped in and slammed his shield into the ex-gladiator's helm. Stunned, the Hibernian slashed blindly.

Suddenly, a German voice shouted from out in the hall, behind the assassins. The unwounded men up against Hibernicus went into disarray, seemingly fighting with someone new on the outside.

Rufus rallied with hope and stabbed at the closest shape in front of him; he felt his weapon penetrate flesh and grate on bone.

But someone's shield crashed into him. Rufus's staggered back, struck his head against the alcove wall behind him, and slid to the floor in an ungainly sprawl.

The last thing the Hibernian remembered was one armed man still fit and standing over him....

Scef's Blood

CHAPTER XVIII

The Engle's intervention had been impulsive. Drawn to the fight by the clamor, he had no idea who was in the right in this fight between guardsmen, but thought it very wrong when one man had to be matched against so many. Moreover, he recognized the red-mustached giant, a friend of Calusidius. Something foul was ongoing and he could not stand aloof.

The three wounded men backed off into the guard room when he charged up, but the rune-warrior was only interested in saving the Hibernian's life. A blow taught to him by Loderod took down one of the determined assassins without killing him. He took the fellow's sword from the floor just in time because the other active fighter spun about to face him. The bodyguard stumbled over his sprawling cohort, allowing Osricus to wound his sword arm. Another blow disarmed the fellow and the youth stunned him with a left fist to the face. The Engle glanced back toward the guard room, but the injured warriors did not seem to be threatening him.

Judging the fight over, Osricus dragged the downed Hibernicus from the alcove and took him away.

Upon reaching the door of Agrippa's suite, a woman whispered, "Warrior! What has happened?" to the German from a shadowy corridor.

Osricus turned; the slave girl Phaedra had stepped into the lamp light. She was not so painted as before and her hair was uncombed. Her tunic was wrinkled and carelessly arranged.

"Phaedra, what are you doing here?"

"I—I was waiting for you to return...."

"You come at a bad time. I must attend to this man's injuries."

"Let me help, then," she said.

"Knock on the door," he told her.

The portal was opened by one of the tetrarch's servants. Another menial ran up behind the first. "Put this man on my bed," he instructed the pair. They took Hibernicus, who proved to be a daunting load for the two ordinary men. "I will need a basin of clean water and a towel... and quill and ink!" he called after them. Then Osricus felt a touch on his shoulder.

"How was your friend hurt?" Phaedra asked.

"There was a fight. Though he is a bodyguard himself, five other bodyguards attacked him. I cannot say why."

"Will it make trouble for you with the soldiers?"

"I think it was a private brawl." Now he noted her dishabille. "But you—why did you come here now? Has the emperor harmed you?"

Her cheeks flushed. From her disheveled appearance, Osricus suspected she was distraught over something. "Let us see to your friend first," she said.

Avoiding his questioning look, Phaedra followed along the path the servants, who had taken the big man into the Engle's bedroom. The Swede went to the shutters and opened them to admit the evening air. The serving men withdrew to fetch what Agrippa's guest had asked for. Osricus commenced to remove Rufus' bloody armor and tunic. Phaedra watched from aside.

"He fought well," the Engle told her as he worked. "He had beaten three men of the five before he needed aid from me."

"I have seen the man about the palace," said the girl. "Is he a friend of yours?"

"He was the friend of a good friend of mine," Osricus said.

Soon the servants returned with the requested water, towel, pen and ink, and put them down on a stand near to the bed.

"Wet the cloth and hand it to me," Osricus told Phaedra as the menials looked on.

Phaedra complied and the warrior applied the cloth to the Hibernian's wounds, alternately mopping and wiping them.

"The life burns hot in him," the Scandian judged. "His blood seeps, it does not flow. I think he was felled by the bruise to his forehead. Shall I fetch a medicine man?"

"No," replied Osricus. "I am a healer. Hand me the pen and ink."

He took the quill, tore off a dry end of the sizable cloth and, using his own blood from a dagger prick, he painted several rune-signs upon it. Finally, he slipped the scripted rag beneath the wool-stuffed mattress under the ex-gladiator's weight.

The busy work being done, the Engle struck up a rune-chant of healing. After some little time, the Hibernian began to snore peacefully.

Osricus backed away from the bed, tired and light-headed from the transfer of magical power. Suddenly, he felt Phaedra's arms around him, steadying him.

"You are a rune-wizard!" she exclaimed. "I never expected! Why has a great one of our people come to Rome?"

"It is better if I do not tell you."

"Then do not," she said, looking crestfallen. "The secrets of the wizards are not for one like me."

She followed him to a couch in the triclinium where he wearily sat down. In restless repose, Osricus regarded Phaedra closely, noting her reddened eyes and pursed lips.

"I have been thinking about you… occasionally… since I saw you in the garden," he said.

"I—I am pleased," she admitted shyly. "Why so, Warrior?"

"It is something we can speak of later," he said. Loderod had warned him he could never marry one of the common strain, for such intimacy would dampen his power over the runes. Only if the maid were of Scef's pure blood would the union of flesh enhance the magic instead of dissipating it. Loderod had always discouraged Osric from taking casual pleasure.

"I understand," she said. "I am one of Caesar's women, and you would be endangered if anyone knew we visited in private. Your master's servants may even now be gossiping. It is better I go, before you are blamed unjustly."

She started to back away, but Osricus caught her wrist. Again he felt a pleasant flow of power from her into himself. He tried to ignore it.

"Why did you come?" he asked. "You seem troubled."

Phaedra sat beside the warrior, not caring if their bodies touched. "The emperor called me to him two nights ago." From there, in low tones, she described the flogging and the ill way she had been used afterward.

"These civilized swine!" the Engle growled, infuriated by her tale of unnatural abuse.

To his discomfiture, Phaedra wrapped her arms around him and sobbed against his breast. Osricus' anger softened into pity and he stroked her hair.

"Once you asked if there was anything you could do," she said when her breath came back.

"Gese. What may I do, hlaefdige?"

"I am violated," she mewed, "I dread that I may be with child by a hated slave master."

He nodded, thinking almost any German woman would feel the same.

"Even if it is true, I do not wish to know… for certain… that I am shamed." She covered her face in her hands; such a request seemed to come very hard from her, and with great mortification.

Osricus had worried she was about to ask him for a cantrip to purge her womb of any unwanted life. Could he deny her if she did? It would be a damning sin for both of them, but…. For the first time he realized how easily evil could be mistaken for good.

"From the moment I saw you, I sensed there was a fate between us. I beg you—let me lie beside you tonight."

That was *not* the request he expected, and it caught him off guard. "Are—are you sure that would not hurt you more than you have already been hurt?"

She raised her eyes to meet his. Her expression became determined and brave. "No. It will heal me!" she said. "Then, in my heart, I will know any child I bear is the son of a rune-warrior of my own race, not a mad slavemaster."

Now Osricus understood. He drew her close and gazed down into Phaedra's tear-streaked face. Should he love this woman? He'd desired her from the moment he laid eyes on her, and ever since she'd been crowding at the edges of his mind. He dared not diminish his power at this crucial juncture in his quest. Yet he was also a man—one subject to the heart, and moved by the pleading of the helpless. If only she were one of the Blood, his choice would be much easier. But how could he be sure?

"It would please me to know more about you. Where do you come from, Maid? Who were your sires? Or do you still prefer not to tell?"

She sighed. "I was reared with the Swedes, but my foster parents told me that I was not theirs, that they had found me as an infant, hidden in the weeds at a village raided by the Goths. I know nothing about my true parents. I was told that it was a Siton village, however."

Osricus wondered. Could the strange current of power that passed between them be evidence that she—like himself—was descended of Scef? If it were true, it hardly could be an accident that they had found each other in this strange way in this strange land. The gods themselves might have been moving them like pieces upon a board.

It was then that the maid Phaedra brought her lips near to his, and it no longer mattered what her blood might be....

Tatia lay in a room with a bolted door and bolted windows, and she was glad of it. The door and the shutters were padlocked, and she did not have the key. Rufus had gone to the palace and his shift there would last until dawn. She wanted to be nowhere else except beside him. The streets of Rome had turned her into a coward. The Spaniard knew that everyone preyed upon everyone else out there. It was better to be a dog in such a city than a woman.

Tatia thought she must have napped, for a rattle at the door seemed to arouse her from slumber. Startled, she sat up, her breath bated. Someone was trying the latch.

The rattling stopped, but immediately afterward, a high-pitched voice rose up in a wavering song from a tongue she'd never heard before. Was it only some drunken barbarian wayfarer, confusing her door with another's?

The padlock outside was reinforced within by three bolts that she had thrown herself after Rufus' departure.

She looked with trepidation at the shutters; they looked well-made, but could not be so strong that they could sustain a determined attack by a husky man. Romans did not make helpful neighbors and there was never a vigil around when a serious crime was in the making.

She thought she would almost prefer an assault on the door than the continuation of that song. Its rhythms were unsettling; its mood was not like any merrymaker's strain that she had ever heard. Trembling, Tatia reached for the dagger on the night stand. Her Lalerti cousin had taught her how to fight with a knife if she had to....

Why doesn't he stop singing and go home? she demanded of herself.

Now the latch and bolts were rattling again. She gasped at the realization that they were not being shaken by any force from outside; they were moving of their own accord. Tatia rolled out of bed and made desperately for the door to reinforce it.

She seized a bolt grip, one already half out its niche, and held it in both hands. She stopped its withdrawal, but it could not be shoved back into place. Dismayed, she let it go and grasped another which was fully open.

The moment Tatia removed her fingers off the first bolt, it leaped open. The second bolt held frozen against all her effort slide it.

Now the latch itself lifted tentatively. With a frightened cry, Tatia braced her bare heels against the floor and pressed her shoulders against the door boards. Force answered force and the inward swing of the portal threw the Iberian into the center of the room.

She stood facing the door, her dagger clenched in her tight, sweating right fist. A dark shape lurched from the outer darkness into the light of the room's single candle and she screamed.

Tatia's wailing died in her throat as she recognized the invader.

Galar approached her slowly. The Spaniard, shocked, couldn't decide if the intruder was real or if she had lapsed into nightmare.

"Tatia belongs to Galar; she cannot kill him," the small cowled figured said in a small, rough voice. "Do not hate his ugliness. Mayhap he will become a man soon, large, strong, and pretty. Tatia…"

The whining voice broke the spell of inaction upon the girl. She dashed for the shutters. She had forgotten they were bolted and she beat futilely at them. Like a cornered cat, she whirled wild-eyed. Her dagger was poised as high as her jawbone.

The dwarf came no nearer, but sat down on the edge of the bed. He stared across at her with a sad, yellow-eyed intensity.

"Let me go!" Tatia shouted, her barbarian ferocity surfacing.

Galar shook his head. He had hoped to destroy his gigantic rival tonight by drawing Back Runes of enmity upon the guardsmen's cups to incite them against him—but Osricus had intervened. Disappointed, Galar now sought solace.

"Tatia has no reason to hate Galar. Never would he harm her. When evil men came upon her from the dark, Galar drove them away, and he watched Tatia sleep until the red giant came."

While speaking, he waved a small vial in the air. The scent issuing from it reminded Tatia of the cavernous underworld.

"If Tatia hates the look of Galar, he can cloak himself with illusion. He can be handsome, as handsome as the red giant...."

Fear fell away from Tatia; she suddenly could not remember what it was she feared. The rented room had vanished and she was in a cave beautiful with rock crystals. The dwarf had vanished, too, but on a stone bench warmly covered with a white bearskin a mighty blond warrior was sitting.

A fire gave a ruddy light and blazed warmly in a rock pit. The stone underfoot chilled Tatia's bare feet. When the man beckoned her way with an open hand, smiling, she ran to him, leaped upon the snowy bearskin next to him and savored the heat of his body against hers.

The stoking fingers of the warrior upon her cheek were indescribably pleasant....

She *was* of the Magic Blood; the fires of Heimdall burned within Osricus. He made love to Phaedra like one bewitched. He was intoxicated by her beauty as he knelt behind her; the way she moved, her golden hair, the hourglass curves of her hips, her waist, her back...

...her smooth, flawless back...

Reason suddenly returned to him. He froze mid-motion. "Why did you lie to me, wench?" Osricus suddenly demanded. "There are no marks of the whip on your back! I was a fool not to notice!"

Phaedra looked over her shoulder at him, and her face shone with a strange light. "I did not lie; I had weals, but they are healed already." She reached a hand back to caress his leg. "Even a chieftainess of Heid may use a white rune—"

"*You!*" Osricus blurted, but then winced as a sharp object stabbed into his thigh. With the quickness of thought he lost command of his body's movements and collapsed onto his back.

Phaedra turned around and knelt over him, shaking her head. "I would have thought that Loderod's disciple would be more formidable. Men are so sentimental and so vain! If ill-considered kindness did not undo so many of them, their mastery would be hard for a woman to manage. But they are so easily beguiled. There is not one of their breed who cannot be made to believe a woman who tells him that she prefers his goodly embrace over an emperor's."

Osricus' eyes smoldered but, below those eyes, he was no better off than a dead man.

"Oh, do not glare so! Have you never made a woman your spear-captive?" Phaedra took the Engle's dagger and drew a spot of blood from her wrist. "The Sitones, whom I was reared among, often keep virile males for their pleasure. The priestesses of Heid do likewise—but when we tire of them, we hang them by the neck in the sacred groves of the goddess."

With the drawn blood, her finger painted a Black Rune upon his breast. "Would that I dared to place a rune of amity upon you, to make you devotedly mine. It is like we are the two halves of one being. Alas, one of the Blood cannot be trusted. Some night when I am raping you, you might cast off my spell and slay me." She sang a rune-song to complete the incantation, then said, "Now I think you will be a more manageable foe."

She dabbed more blood on her finger. "You interrupted our lovemaking too soon. I burn with power, but *will* have more. Tonight I must be the most potent sorceress in all Midgard." She smeared a Black Rune of passion upon his brow and stared to sing a sweetly dark rune song. At once a flood of desire coursed through his veins; she laughed at the unwilling expression his body gave of it.

"For now, I require your embrace," she said as she straddled him, "but later I shall have Andvaranaut!"

Emperor Gaius tossed restlessly. Every time he closed his eyes, a pack of rabid hounds burst into his dreams to pursue him through a nightmare forest. Now, again, he snapped awake, his fright becoming bitter resentment. Had he known a single moment's peace since becoming Caesar?

Caesar! It was a word of power and glory. It should mean something!

He tried not to think of his unsatisfactory life. He called to mind instead the ships that would soon carry him to the islands. Many personages had accepted his invitations to sail with him to reclaim the ashes of his dead mother and brother.

But he was, in fact, little interested in old bones. He wondered how his family could have handled their affairs so badly. If they had done as he had the wits to do—flattering his grandfather and punctiliously complying with his every whim—they might still have been alive today. If they had wanted to remove him from power so much, they why did they choose to go to men of honor wielding the law? Did none of them know that the law was a dead letter in Rome? Instead, they should have sought out modern versions of Brutus, Cassius, and Casca—men of action who depended on nothing except dissembling and the length of their knives. Sometimes, his mother and brothers had played their game too quickly, sometimes too slowly. By being only an ineffective threat, they gave Sejanus plenty of time to make Tiberius hate and fear them. The manipulated emperor ordered them all arrested, treating them so vindictively that they had all died miserably in prison.

No, what mattered to Gaius was that these islands lay near to Capri. A single ship might steal away from the main fleet on any pretext and secretly arrive at Tiberius' main palace in time to conduct the fateful ceremony. After he had looted the accursed island, he would be done with it. Gaius preferred to display his greatness upon a more grandiose stage, such as the city of Rome itself.

But then the image of his grandmother Antonia flitted across his mind.

He clutched at the silken sheets of his bed, hating what he must do. Gladly would he have traded a hundred others—friends, servants, acquaintances—rather than send Antonia's soul unto damnation. But events had trapped him. More than he could love any living creature, he loved his own life more. There was absolutely nothing he would not do to prevent his damnation into the torture pits of Tartarus.

Disgruntled, the young man got out of bed. If only he could meet someone else whom he was capable of loving more than his grandmother. He had been trying to give his heart to some lesser woman, even to that Germanic slut Phaedra. But that night had been a useless waste of time.

He called to his servant in the next room and had him order up a pitcher of wine. While waiting, he wandered to the window overlooking the ground across which his new palace would be built. He would call it the House of Gaius and make it the crowning achievement of his reign. He was determined that no seat of the Ptolemide kings, no hall in fabled Persepolis, would ever exceed its grandeur.

That old fool Marcus Silanus had called his intentions extravagant. By the gods, what did that decrepit wreck know about anything? Did he think that just because his dimwitted daughter was no longer able to nag and badger him that he had inherited the privilege to do so? The presumption of it! Sometime, soon, he would have to make his displeasure known in a way that would make the old man feel it most keenly.

As the minutes passed, Gaius grew impatient. What was holding back his wine? He needed to drink very heavily if he intended to sleep and stay asleep.

As if in answer to his mental demand, the porter admitted a menial, one of the hundreds of nameless men serving in the palace. This fellow was short and slight, displaying strong classical features. His effeminate eyes were oddly fair for one with skin so swarthy.

"Dominus," the young Greek said, bowing. He was holding both a pitcher and a drinking cup. The latter he placed on the bedroom table, filled it, and offered the vessel to Gaius' hand.

The princeps took the *calix* irascibly. The serving man lacked style in the way he presented himself and prepared the cup. Some ignoramus from the farm, probably, not fit to serve in Caesar's house. If his ineptitude went any farther, Gaius was inclined to order him some stripes—and twice the number for the steward who'd placed him into personal service to the emperor without sufficient training.

As the imperator slurped at his drink, the Greek stood waiting expectantly. Gaius disliked having the man lingering, and especially disliked those impertinent eyes! "Drop your glance, Clodhopper," he said, "or I may have you blinded!"

Instead of looking away and cringing, the man commenced a song of gibberish. The barbarian words sounded like the tongue used by his German guardsmen. "What are you doing?" Gaius snarled; then his knees felt weak.

Rocked by a wave of dizziness, he reached out to the servant for support. The young man dutifully helped him to his bed. When his senses cleared, the servant was gone. Someone else was sitting at the edge of his bed.

"Phaedra," he mumbled in recognition.

The Black Rune

CHAPTER XIX

Herod Agrippa had spent an anxious evening. Messengers went out. Delivery slaves came in. They carried arcane items and preparations found only in those shops specializing in the needs of alchemists. All had been going well, but the king could not cast off a feeling of apprehension. Treason was never easy on the stomach.

Now, returning to his apartment with a freedman companion, he walked into the triclinium and beheld Osricus stretched out naked upon a couch, in a condition most incongruous with his aspect. As the man of the East beheld him perplexedly, Osricus' eyes had shifted his way, but the rest of the youth's body remained as still as if in sleep. There was drawn on the youth's brow a symbol in blood, and a different glyph decorated his breast. Agrippa at once suspected that these marks betokened sorcery, only he didn't know if they had been placed on his servant's body by Osricus himself or by an enemy. He called for his servants.

"What happened?" he demanded.

The two entering slaves looked disconcertedly at the Engle and one said, "He was well when we saw him last. He was in the company of a maid."

"What maid?"

"A concubine of Caesar, Majesty. We thought it prudent not to question a free man."

Agrippa doffed his cloak and threw it over the rune-warrior. Had the barbarian been poisoned by a minx using a dangerous philter? Or did Osricus have some secret enemy who could reach him even inside the house of Caesar? The Jew sent his serving men to fetch his physician, Stechus.

Then his freedman, Silas, called alarmedly, "Master, there is an intruder!"

The king hurried to join the man and saw by lamplight Rufus Hibernicus drowsing on the Engle's bed. "I know that man," Agrippa said. "He accompanied Marcus Silanus to the games. Wake him up!"

Silas roughly shook the ex-gladiator. Rufus' bleary eyes opened and looked around. "Who? Eh! You're the king of the Jews! What am I doing here?"

"That's what *we* want to know," replied the desert prince.

The groggy Hibernicus now remembered the guardroom fight and groped at his remembered wounds. They didn't hurt and were already scabbed over. "By Lugh! How long have I lain here?"

"It couldn't have been more than several hours," said Agrippa.

"A man can't heal so much in a few hours!" Rufus exclaimed.

The easterner frowned, knowing well how Osricus could heal by magic. "How badly were you hurt?" asked his host.

"I'm not sure. A man slammed my head with a shield." Then another image came to mind. "Where's that young German?"

"Osricus was hurt, too," Agrippa answered. "We want to know who's responsible."

"Hurt? I don't know anything about that…." The big man swung his legs to the floor and wobbled to his feet. Standing up, he didn't feel half as badly as he expected to. "Let's see the boy," he rumbled. Agrippa bade two servants to help the giant out into the triclinium.

Mostly covered by Agrippa's cloak, the Hibernian saw the youth lying stiffly on his back. Up close, Rufus realized that this was the youth whom he had spoken to in the amphitheater, the friend of Calusidius' son Mar.

Stechus now hurried into the room holding a pack of implements and medicines. Seeing the rune-marked man, the physician queried, "He's hurt again? Accident prone, isn't he?"

"Spare us, Stechus," Agrippa told him. "Just see what you can do."

"Those marks…" said Rufus, "I've seen like symbols near the German limites. They are marks of sorcery. Wash it off him and see what happens!"

"I'm the doctor here," Stechus reminded those present. "Slave, get a damp cloth and wipe away those marks of Satan!"

The forehead rune mopped off readily, releasing him from his unnatural state of sexual excitement. But, to everyone's consternation, the stain on his breast proved indelible.

"Look here," observed Stechus, "he has a thorn in his thigh. Such a thing could have introduced some paralyzing poison into his system." He plucked out Phaedra's thorn and Osricus at once moaned, stirring slightly, but again fell still.

"What can we try next?" asked Agrippa.

"I haven't the faintest idea," replied the physician….

"Where did you come from?" asked Gaius drowsily.

"You sent for me, Lord," said Phaedra. "Do you not remember?"

"No… I don't feel well…." Though ill, the sight of the woman absolutely fascinated him. "Speak to me," he murmured. "Your voice is like the strumming of a lyre."

"What shall I say, great king, except that your summons is a joy to my heart?"

To Gaius' own amazement, he felt drawn to the slave more powerfully than ever he had to his sister Drusilla. "Take off your tunic," he croaked, "and lie beside me."

"Not now, my lord."

Instead of anger, Gaius gasped with alarm. "You're angry with me! Is it because I used you ill? Forgive me!" He sat up and reached his heavy hands toward her. "I used you too harshly! I'll give you a fortune for restitution, a crown even!"

Phaedra shook her head. "Yes, if such would please you. But seeing to your pleasure pleases me most of all."

"Touch me, hold me."

"You are not well; you do not need more strain. It would perhaps make you even more ill."

True, his dizziness was returning. Gaius sank back into the pillow. "Stay…" he murmured.

"Do not fear, Lord, I will remain." She kissed him lightly. With a silly-happy smile, the young emperor dozed off like a contented child.

Phaedra had succeeded, but in a limited way. His earlier pollution of her had reduced her potency and, though her session with Osricus had more than made up for it, she still lacked the power to shatter the protective web around the Roman emperor.

She rose and started to loosen his clothes. She suspected that he was wearing a protective rune or else a physical talisman. Opening his tunic, she espied a green jade amulet with the face of a goddess carved into it, proud and cruel. Phaedra sensed great power emanating from it and wondered if she had discovered a charm of Heid herself, or the Roman concept of her. Her elders had informed her that southern people knew Heid under many different names. As an idea of overwhelming power, they called her... what was it...? *Shupnikkurat.* As a symbol of the procreative drive, they evoked her as Astarte. As a patroness of sorcery, they knew her as Hecate.

The witch removed the adornment and dropped it on the floor; charged with hostile spells, she did not want to keep it for herself. Almost at once, she felt a diminishing of the aura of protection around the young Roman.

Phaedra gave a tired sigh and rested against a canopy pole of Gaius' bed. Her spell upon the emperor was fragile, for all that she had used a harsh, dangerous series of runes incised into the bottom of his cup. For a moment, she'd thought that she'd be forced to return to Osricus, whom she'd left helplessly paralyzed in his patron's apartment, to restore her strength. But now, without his amulet, she would be able to nurse her enchantment on Gaius along with songs and rune-signs while he slept.

It had been fortunate that the sleepless young man had called for wine while she had lurked near enough to hear. Having intercepted the servant, all she had needed to do was to cloak her shape behind an illusion and put him to sleep. When Gaius awakened, she would demand from him the return of the ring Andvaranaut. With the Ring, could she conquer him completely? And to conquer the emperor was the same as conquering the empire....

After an hour's wait, Osricus moaned and a tremor passed through his frozen limbs. He lurched and cried out: *"Witch!"* Agrippa shook him out of his nightmare and he suddenly knew where he was. He glanced about the room.

"Of what witch do you speak?" Agrippa asked.

"Phaedra—a creature of Heid hidden amongst the emperor's concubines. By Heimdall's Sword! I will slay her! I swear it!"

Osricus sat up but, doing so, he blanched. Automatically, his right hand groped for the place he felt soreness. Under the breast symbol he still wore was a raw patch of skin. His face went pale.

"What is it?" asked Agrippa.

"My ruin, I think. Where has the witch gone?"

"The servants found you here alone," the king replied.

Osricus craned his neck and saw the ex-gladiator standing behind him. "You, warrior, are on your feet already," he muttered.

"Aye, thanks to your sorcery, they tell me," the man of Erin replied.

"I am no sorcerer—and now it seems I will be spared the evil fate of becoming one," he replied ruefully.

"What do you mean?" asked Agrippa.

"This mark is a rune crafted to deprive a sorcerer of the means of drawing upon mystical energies His anguish showed on his pale, perspiring face.

"Whatever is going on here, I need to thank you for saving my life," Rufus said. "If ever you need help, call on me. But for the moment, I have to go back and settle with those men who attacked me."

"You will heal faster if you return to my bed," Osricus said. "I enchanted it to speed your recovery."

"Thanks, but no. I've seen more than my share of sorcery and prefer to have as little to do with it as possible."

"Please friends," Agrippa said, "afford Osricus and myself some privacy. We have matters to discuss!"

At the request of the king, the servants retired to their rooms. The secutor bade them all adieu and followed them out.

"My impetuous friend, you have picked a mad hour to get yourself seduced by a witch. All evening I have been hard at work arranging for the escape of Zenodotus. Are you strong enough to carry out your portion of it?" From the look of him, Agrippa doubted it.

Behind dazed eyes, Osricus's mind smoldered. The rune-witch had used him long and well, draining off the built-up power of their love-making to weave it into her spells. With this rune on his chest, he would be no match for her. Suddenly, he perked up and rose. On wobbling legs he went into his bedroom and seized the vase next to the bed. Out of it slid his fylfot medallion.

"Will that magic amulet do you any good?" asked Agrippa.

"A moment, King Agrippa," murmured Osricus, pressing the symbol against his afflicting rune. He was hoping that if he had sufficient power within himself, he could banish the Black Rune from his heart.

The talisman felt hot when pressed to his flesh. When it had cooled greatly, Osricus removed it and looked anxiously at Phaedra's mark. The stain had lightened perceptibly but then, even as the young man stared, the dark rusty color returned.

He sighed grimly; the mark was a very stubborn one.

When confronted at the palace, Wulfgang and the other guardsmen had tearfully admitted to their superiors that their rage had been inexplicable and unprovoked. The woman slave had given her perspective on the brawl and Hibernicus, having added whatever he could, was released and allowed to go home.

When the secutor reached his domus, he found the padlock gone and the bolts still fixed within. He shouted Tatia's name, and was answered by the Iberian's scream.

Muttering a curse, he ran around to the nearest window and broke the shutters open. Ready for anything, he clambered inside, to discover Tatia lying on the floor, entangled in a mass of bedclothes.

Hibernicus lifted her and felt for a pulse, which was beating strongly. When the girl came out of her daze and realized who he was, she clung to him wildly. Tatia sobbed out a story of intrusion and violation by the dwarf Galar. The secutor listened quietly, not sure if any of it could be believed. When she realized his attitude, Tatia drew back shivering. "You don't believe me! *You don't believe me!*"

He carried her to the bed and held her, insisting that he *did* believe her, until she fell asleep. In the morning, he decided to confront the little man, hoping to find out if there could be any reason to think that Tatia's story was anything more than a nightmare.

But before quitting Tatia's company, he had to turn his girl over to someone who could keep a closer watch on her than he could. The girl's jealous dislike of Cassilla ruled out her house as a refuge. He could instead take the Iberian back to the house of Marcus Silanus, even though she hadn't been happy there, either. What was a man to do?

"Sure, Agrippa sent me word to expect you," drawled Servius Vitus, the Praetorian jailer. "But since when has the king become so thick with the princeps' German bodyguard? I like the gold, but I also want to know who and what I'm dealing with."

Osricus did not explain that his armor was only a borrowed disguise. Nor could he reveal to the jailer that Agrippa wanted Zenodotus freed; doubtlessly, he would not have permitted it. The Engle tried an impatient bluff. "I think the king has told what you need to know. He trusts you as little as you trust him."

The barbarian's surliness irritated the jailer, so he again shook the bag of gold. It was hefty and he decided he didn't want to give it up. "All right," he grumbled, "but make it snappy! My shift ends at sunrise. Be out of here by then, or neither of us will be in any condition to spend the Jew's money."

The jail-keeper ushered the mock-guardsman along an underground corridor. They passed watch points manned by bored Praetorians. Two more guardsmen stood on watch at the mouth of the blind corridor in which Zenodotus' cell was located, but there were none posted directly outside his door. "He's in there," Servius rumbled while unlocking the portal. "Remember, you don't have much time."

"I am more aware of that than you. Leave us so our business can be concluded," Osricus replied sharply.

The praetorian, still beset by misgivings, decided against making a request to stand in on the conversation. They might talk treason, and treason made him nervous. Then, too, just by letting an unauthorized person into the prison for a bribe, he had already earned a death sentence. Whatever else happened from this point could not make his position much worse. So, his metallic accouterments rattling, he withdrew in ill grace.

"Who's there!" Zenodotus asked warily at the sight of the Engle entering his cell.

"Agrippa sent me!"

The Greek mumbled a few foreign words, and a vibrant flame sprang to life upon the wick of the candle he held. It was unusually bright and Osricus looked away and shaded his eyes. Zenodotus perplexedly declared, "A barbarian!"

"I am here to help you, wizard. Do not provoke me by use of that insulting term."

"Who are you?"

"I am Agrippa's bodyguard. Did not the king inform you that I was coming?"

"He said that *someone* was coming. I did not expect a German."

"Our help is not a gift. Both of us expect much from you."

"I know Agrippa's price. But what would one like you seek from me?"

"Do you remember the name of my father, Loderod?" Osricus asked.

"Ah, the son of Loderod! I think I can guess the thing you want."

The young German nodded. "The ring Andvaranaut!"

"It's not here, of course. But I have it safely hidden. You could not hazard to retrieve it alone. Anyway, I would be well rid of the thing! It has cursed my luck!"

Osricus did not like this Zenodotus, beyond the fact that he was a murderer. His glance was too crafty, his cooperation too eager. Still, he was right about the ring cursing a man's luck. Loderod had said that it couldn't kill directly, but diverted a man's fate down evil channels.

"I have brought the gear demanded by you," the rune-warrior said. "Where is the Ring of Sorcery?!"

"On the isle of Capri," answered Zenodotus.

Capri? Kah-Prah?

The runes had not failed him.

Even so, Osricus only mistrustfully unslung his pack.

"I must at once speak to Emperor Gaius!" insisted Herod Agrippa.

The fleshy Samothracian steward shook his ringleted head. "The master would slice off my ears if I roused him from his sleep. I would have to have a very good reason to place myself at risk." Agrippa, used to court ways, knew that the man was soliciting a bribe. He pressed a bag containing a hundred denarii into the fellow's pudgy hand.

He smiled oleaginously. "Wait here," the servant said before disappearing behind the door. Two minutes later, he returned.

"The emperor is with a woman, and he is in a very heavy sleep."

"Too heavy to be awakened from?"

"You surely don't expect me to give the master of the world a hard shaking, do you, Majesty?"

"Never mind. What woman was he with?"

"I am no gossip, Dominus."

That meant the man required another bribe. Impatiently, Agrippa yielded up several aurei.

The steward shrugged. "The woman is that golden Northerner, Phaedra. Our emperor has excellent tastes, do you not agree?"

Agrippa glanced away in consternation. This was exactly what he had come to warn Gaius against. Osricus had cautioned him that Gaius had a northern witch in his women's quarters, and that she knew how to subject a man to her will. His mind raced. Did he dare try to raise the house against the sorceress? What if it was already too late? What if the emperor was already under her power?

He decided to leave quietly and make no scene. Now everything depended upon Osricus. Meanwhile, Agrippa would wait for a chance to speak to Gaius and observe whether there was a perceptible change in him. The sacrificial victim would be safe if the Engle succeeded in freeing Zenodotus. Moreover, if Osricus secured the magic ring he had come to Rome seeking, the witch would then be forced to follow him back to Germania, leaving Rome in peace.

Yet he'd had enough experience in both life and politics to know that no plan, no matter how well laid, ever operated smoothly.

Satan take all sorcerers!

Zenodotus had worked with feverish haste, laying out the herbs, animal parts, drugs, and apparatuses with which Osricus had provided him. He knelt above the large chalk circle he had drawn on the floor, inscribing rote-learned formulae. Osricus assisted in his preparations by stoking a small flame within the cell's brazier, feeding it with the odd ingredients that Zenodotus prescribed.

"Step into the circle, German, if you would not share the fate of all the others in this prison," Zenodotus warned suddenly.

"What fate?"

"Death."

The Engle felt appalled by the wantonness of the Greek's plan. Sorcery was a foul way to kill a man; warriors—even Roman ones— deserved to be vanquished honorably. More than ever, Osricus was beginning to disdain the world of magic. If he did not quit its practice soon, he would be left without a shred of honor.

Was it the lure of Andvaranaut that was leading him down a dark path? Could the evil device, even from distant Capri, debase, corrupt, and destroy all who sought for it?

The moment that Osricus crossed into the circle, Zenodotus sprinkled some additional ingredients into the flame. As they curled and blackened, he recited: *"Iä Rebathothos! Iä Typhonos! Iä Dagonos!"* he cried. *"Wagi nagi fthagn!"*

He prayed and chanted for five minutes. Finally, the brazier smoke began to resemble a hot gray mist. Rising in a tight, twisting funnel, it crawled from the bowl and seeped away like an intelligent thing, through the crack under the cell door.

At this moment, a nervous Servius Vitus was just outside Zenodotus' cell. Before too long, the relief shift would arrive and catch an unauthorized visitor with the Greek! Servius would be lucky if he wasn't crucified right beside the German whom he had so recklessly allowed to bribe him.

"Great Neptune!" the man blurted at the sight of a veil of fog snaking under the door. Fire? No, it didn't look like smoke…

No sooner had the first lick of mist wrapped its ethereal tongue around the optio than he felt the cut of an icy dagger. He struggled against his paralysis, but the ghostly mist strands tugged at his soul, drawing out his ghost to become part of itself. With a last, whimpering thought of terror, the Praetorian's spirit slipped free of its fleshy encasement and dissolved into the coiling cloud.

From there, the mist traveled on, penetrating the flanking cells to steal the souls of the sleeping prisoners within. The main body of it followed the corridors to each of the guard-points, where the soldiers watched it come with bewilderment until it was too late.

In only another moment, it had it reached the guard rooms, where the armored men were amusing themselves at a dicing table. With no smoke-smell to alert them, it enveloped them without warning. These distracted fellows were caught off-guard and perished before they could issue a single shout.

Zenodotus waited in his circle, giving his demonic ally time enough to do its work thoroughly. Then he quelled the flame by which he had summoned it. The mist faded into nothingness even more swiftly than it had arisen.

"Now we will leave this place, Warrior," the sorcerer said. "Let us hope that Herod Agrippa has planned his part properly." The Greek's tone was light, his spirit buoyed with the pride of a job well done.…

THE BOAT

CHAPTER XX

"Do you possess the ring of power?" Phaedra leaned over the lightly-sleeping emperor. She had written the *malrunar* upon his cheek to force from his slumbering mind the secrets that she craved to know. "Speak! Where lies the ring of power?" Again she described it. "You must know that Tiberius received it from Zenodotus!"

"Tiberius owned many rings…" Gaius murmured sleepily. "There was the one that the Samaritan wizard called 'the Ring of Set….'"

Always that name Zenodotus! Could it be that Zenodotus had not passed the ring on to Tiberius? Or that Gaius had not received it from his grandfather, who apparently despised him?

"Where is Zenodotus?" she asked.

"Prison… in the old palace… traitor…."

She questioned him closely and drew out the story of the conspiracy. The Greek had slain Gaius' grandsire by cursing his luck with the ring Andvaranaut. She also learned the tale of how Zenodotus had recklessly imperiled the young Caesar's soul while ostensibly serving his interests.

She let Gaius slip back into a deepened slumber. She would have to be careful. The wily Greek was more clever than she had surmised.

When a party of priestesses from the cult of Heid had first met him in Upper Germania, they had pretended to be selling information about a powerful device of magic, a ring, in exchange for gold. But in truth, they had sought—successfully—to use the power of Rome to wrest Andvaranaut from Loderod, who had for many years thwarted every effort of the cult to regain what they considered their own.

But Zenodotus had been a sly plotter. He had second-guessed their ruse and met them with a reception of swords and spells when the priestesses of Heid came to raid his encampment and seize the Ring. Heid's surviving witches barely escaped with their lives.

Doubtlessly, Zenodotus had believed that the victory had so chastened the cult that no one would dare to follow him as far as the dreaded city of Rome. Well, the Greek would soon know his mistake.

Gaius moaned in his sleep; Phaedra turned toward the youth. "Awaken," said the witch.

Gaius' slack, sleepy features tightened with bemusement. The golden beauty lay beside him, propped up on a pillow. Smiling at his memory of the night's pleasure, he reached out to capture one of her round, firm breasts.

"Dominus!" Phaedra declared. "You must rise. You spoke much about having urgent business with a man named Zenodotus."

Gaius' hands, woodenly, fell away from the Swede. *Yes, Zenodotus.* He must send for Zenodotus.

Reluctantly quitting his agreeable situation, the emperor called for his dressing slaves. While they tended to him, Phaedra reclaimed her garment from the foot of the bed and donned it.

In the hall outside the suite, Herod Agrippa was waiting on a bench when he heard a mutter of voices. He glanced toward the sound and saw Gaius and his attendants exiting the imperial chamber.

Rising from his seat, Agrippa hailed his friend. "Princeps!"

The young Caesar noticed him and nodded vacantly. Then he looked toward an attending guard. "Tell Macro I want Zenodotus brought to me within the hour!" The soldier saluted smartly and departed.

Agrippa winced. The escape—if it had been carried out—was about to be found out. It was then that the Jew noticed the young blonde standing behind Gaius. By the garb she wore, she was plainly a concubine. But was she also the one called Phaedra?

With feigned cheerfulness, Agrippa approached and waited for the imperator's nod to begin speaking. "Who is this magnificent child of the north, Gaius? I thought I had seen most of your best treasures."

The younger man smiled pridefully. "This is Phaedra, a gift from Marcus Silanus. Phaedra, dear one, this is Agrippa, the king of the Jews." The Swede sent the Easterner a frown. She already knew that he was Osricus' patron.

"Is she for sale?" asked Agrippa with a false grin. "I would trade a year's income from the city of Trachonitis for one like her."

Gaius flashed a mad look. "No! Impossible! Do not suggest such a thing! Not even in jest!"

Taken aback, the king looked again at the girl. He saw satisfaction writ large on her face. From every sign, it was too late to ask Gaius to arrest her.

"I have pressing matters at the moment," the princeps said, tone strained. "If you would speak with me, wait for me in my chambers; I will return when I can do so conveniently."

Agrippa bowed as Gaius and his entourage bustled away. Taking the emperor's suggestion, Agrippa withdrew into the imperial apartment accompanied by a servant. The emperors had created a tradition of suspicion, fearing what mischief persons alone in their chambers might create.

But the serving man only watched as he wandered about the rooms. Seeing the bed, he grasped the irony that in the most closely-guarded chamber in the Empire, the emperor had not been properly protected from being made captive to a foreign-born schemer.

Of a sudden, as the king surveyed the opulent room, the morning sunlight cast a green glint into the corner of his eye. Understanding what he was looking at, he was inspired to ask his unwelcome attendant to provide him with a good cup of wine....

"In the name of Immortal Isis," Gaius stormed at Macro, "what are you babbling about?"

The Pretorian prefect told his story quickly. He had been crossing over to the old palace to take custody of Zenodotus when he was accosted by a messenger sent by the optio of the incoming morning guard. Everyone in the prison quarter, the night optio, the guards and the prisoners alike, had been found dead in the morning. The valuable prisoner, Zenodotus, could not be found. Macro continued on to the prison, needing to confirm the report himself. He found it to be true, all too true.

"The physician who was already there cannot say what killed them all," Macro informed his imperial master. "The look in their faces...."

"Get a hold of yourself!" Gaius snarled. "Was it poison? Sorcery?"

"I know nothing of magic, Caesar, but we discovered many items in Zenodotus' cell that you had ordered be forbidden to him...."

"Has someone helped the Greek to escape? That man will pay!"

"He must have had a confederate, Princeps. They probably left the prison together. But neither of them can get far!" swore Macro.

"They'd better not!" Phaedra put in. Macro looked askance the slave, and then at his liege. The prefect expected his young master to rebuke or strike the impudent woman, but Gaius only pressed her hand and urged her to calm—a calm that he himself was clearly not feeling.

"I've already ordered guards dispatched to every gate and bridge on the perimeter of the city," the prefect said.

"Search inside Rome, too. He may stay hidden until our guard is down. And send riders along the roads in case he got out of the city before your men were posted. And be certain to send a troop to Ostia. If the Greek knows what's good for him, he'll be eager to leave Italy as soon as possible."

"That has already been attended to, Great Caesar."

As they left the Palatine Hill, Osricus and Zenodotus had been met by Agrippa's man Marsyas. He told them that they had to cross the Aemilian Bridge before any of Macro's Praetorians arrived to close it. On the opposite side of the Tiber, they found another friend of the Judean king standing by with horses. The trio rode slowly along the Ostian Road to avoid drawing attention.

They reached Ostia by mid-morning and Marsyas led them to the house of David the oil seller. The merchant received them at a rendezvous point and took them to one of his warehouses. There, waiting for them, was a confederate of the merchant's—a sailor named Samuel.

The fugitives were given packs of food for their journey. This was the point at which Marsyas demanded of Zenodotus the name of Gaius' secret victim. Zenodotus scoffed at the question. "If I am safe, the secret is irrelevant," replied the Greek. "Or does Agrippa plan that I should fall back into the hands of the emperor after I have given up my leverage?"

"The king is not so treacherous as you are," Marsyas informed him. "He has kept faith with you, and you will be wise to do likewise—if you stand in hope of leaving this town alive! As you say, your death would be another way of solving the problem."

Zenodotus glanced uncomfortably toward the grim, patriarchal David and guessed that this would not be good circumstances to break his word to Agrippa.

"Tell His Majesty that Lady Antonia is Caligula's chosen sacrifice. Gaius' safety depends upon her being slain by demonic attack between the fifth and seventh hours of the Kalends of May."

Marsyas didn't smile, disliking the fact that he couldn't verify Zenodotus' avowal, but he decided he had little choice but to accept the information. Without smiling, he said his goodbyes in a hurry, to take what he had learned back to Rome. Men who served David would ride the fugitive's horses away, lest soldiers guarding the Roman road grow suspicious of one man leading along two unridden saddled horses on a morning such as this one.

The German and the Greek had now been left in the care of the dark-bearded, muscular, and potbellied Samuel. He told them that he had a boat prepared to take them to the place they desired.

With their packs of gear, the three men hurried to the docks. Osricus saw that the activity about the port of Ostia was, if anything, even more hectic than at Rome's marketplaces. Its harbor teemed with ships and barges; the beaches and quays swarmed with sailors and longshoremen. Also, there were so many foreign transients about that a Jew, German, and Greek walking together would not cut a particularly conspicuous figure.

Samuel led the pair to a quay where several small skiffs were moored. "Where are we bound for?" the sailor inquired.

"The isle of Capri," said Osricus. "I am told it is well known."

"By God's holy Temple," Samuel remarked sourly, "it is that! It is also known as a place of unspeakable sin and torturous death! It is well-watched and well-guarded! It is madness to go there without an imperial invitation!"

"That was before," countered Zenodotus. "The parasites who once dwelt in Tiberius' villas have either followed Gaius to the mainland or have gone hither to attach themselves to new patrons. Many of the guards will doubtlessly have been recalled to their units back in Rome. Soon those palaces will stand almost empty."

Samuel shook his head. "It is said that the unquiet souls of those murdered still walk its gardens and rocky cliffs, craving revenge on the House of Caesar."

"Too much 'is said!' " Zenodotus growled. "I hope you can operate a boat with all the vigor that you are wasting on idle gossip."

Miffed, the Jew led them to a small skiff, one about the size and shape of an Egyptian dongola.

"Are we supposed to risk our lives in that small, unwieldy thing?" the Greek demanded peevishly.

"Aye—if you're not too high and mighty to help with the rowing that we'll need to take us to the island!"

At that moment, the not-too-distant rumble of hoof-beats drew Osricus' attention to the Roman Road. "Look!" he exclaimed.

A dozen mounted Praetorians were riding hard towards the beach, forcing the passersby in their way to dodge for safety. Theirs was no mere passing patrol; they were hellbent for the boatyard.

"Let's get launched!" the Engle shouted to Samuel, and the three sprang into the waiting boat. The Praetorians, a brass trumpet blaring, won free of the crowd and were coming on with increased speed. Osricus tore his gladius out of its scabbard and severed the boat's two mooring ropes with a single slash each.

"Shove her out!" Samuel was yelling to his passengers. Zenodotus, no friend of physical labor, leaped inexpertly into water at the prow and seized the gunnel to drag out the boat into the deeper brine. When the water was up to their breasts, the three men clambered back on board.

"You men, stop! Identify yourselves!" bawled the Roman decurion, now drawing up at the water's edge. When they ignored him, he waved his cavalry sword over his head and shouted: "After them!"

The riders plunged their mounts into the choppy swell, their *spathas* held high. The horses, wetting their fetlocks, balked and got skittish. By use of their heels and whips, the Romans did all they could to force the beasts to wade in.

The boatmen had been using their oars to help the vessel get beyond the drag of the sand, but now the mounted swordsmen were drawing up on either side of the vessel. With a war cry of "Woden!" Osricus struck at the nearest Praetorian. Samuel and Zenodotus followed his lead, jabbing with their own oars, hoping to panic the horses and get them to throw their riders.

Samuel toppled one rider into the sea, and Zenodotus held his own briefly, but then the soldier gabbed his oar and jerked it toward himself. Caught off-balance, the Greek tumbled over the low gunnel, head-first into the sea. Osricus darted to his aid, but the Roman cavalryman acted even faster, seizing the hem of Zenodotus' cloak and backing his horse away, before Osricus could intervene.

Another rider forced his mount up to the boat, but the gelding blundered into the prow and only managed to push it out into even deeper water. Taking advantage of the mishap, the two men still onboard dug their oars into the sand and propelled the craft further out from shore. The stubborn Praetorians were still game to make their animals swim, but their harried creatures stalled in defiance of all the blows they were given, or actually reared to shake off their insistent riders. In another moment, the skiff had slipped well out of range of any possible capture attempt.

Osricus and Samuel unfurled the sail. The determined soldiers tried to commandeer a couple of the other skiffs, but wasted time trying to understand the sails that they were unfamiliar with. Then they attempted to push out from shore with paddles, but they were inept oarsmen and fell farther and farther behind Samuel's well-operated boat.

The land breeze being fresh, they soon left their pursuers well behind.

"I shall steer us across some shoals near here," said the Jew. "If they switch to a larger vessel, they may have problems." Then Samuel added: "You handle that sail fairly well. I'd almost say that you know what you're doing."

"The Engle are fishing people," Osricus responded, winded. "Show me the use of this particular craft, and if this 'Mediterranean' sea is no more turbulent than our northern waters, we shall fare well enough."

"And where shall we fare to, now that the Greek is gone?"

"As before, to this island of Capri!"

Samuel groaned, but refrained from arguing. The German seemed determined and looked like he could fight, so he grudgingly steered for the south. Osricus, meanwhile, plied his oar with a determination that did justice to his smoldering anger.

The witch had bested him at every turn. And it also had occurred to him that she had probably been the werewolf slayer of Calusidius. It must have been her spell, too, that had cost Mar his life. He knew how easily her sorcery had won control even of himself; if she had bewitched the emperor, she would by now have almost endless imperial resources. Should Zenodotus fall into her hands, she would soon know the exact location of Andvaranaut, and could use Roman ships and Roman soldiers to help her seize it.

*　　*　　*

"Were there others in the boat with you?" demanded Gaius.

Zenodotus stood tight-lipped. The Praetorians had taken him directly to the emperor, who interviewed him in a private apartment, attended only by Marco and a few guardsmen—and one more who the Greek was astonished to meet again: a Germanic witch from the Cult of Heid whom he'd bargained with months ago.

"You can be *made* to speak."

"Perhaps, Princeps, but after I do, will I be fit to conduct the needed rite of Beltane afterwards?" Zenodotus replied. He had steadfastly refused to betray Agrippa. He would withhold the name of his confederate unless the man proved to be too slow in making another rescue attempt.

"There was a young German, Osricus," interrupted Phaedra. "We believe that he helped you to escape. Confess it!"

Gaius looked bemusedly at his concubine. "Osricus? Do you mean the gladiator I freed from the arena? The one you asked me to arrest for insulting you? What does he have to do with anything?"

"Nothing, my lord. I should not have spoken."

Phaedra remained certain that Osricus had been behind the escape attempt and Herod Agrippa had probably helped him manage it. But she thought that she should keep that likelihood to herself, at least until she could use it for the maximum impact. Fortunately, the witch knew where Andvaranaut was hidden, since Zenodotus had already given up that piece of information. Osric would be seeking it at Capri, too, and so that was where she needed to go. She had impressed that idea strongly into Gaius' mind.

"We have wasted enough time," said the princeps. "Tomorrow we sail for the prison islands and Capri. Zenodotus, when you have carried out your work at the Villa Jovis, I shall be in a better mood to speak of clemency."

Phaedra sensed time was running out. The emperor had admitted to her that he would put Zenodotus to death as soon as he had placated the "Chthonioi"—a word which seemed to be Greek for those beings whom the Scandians knew as "Jotuns." She had to interview Zenodotus privately….

"Master," cooed Phaedra. "Let me interview this man alone. A woman can often be more persuasive than even a king."

"Don't talk foolishness, girl!" snapped Gaius. "Macro, take the Alexandrian dolt to the dungeons and make sure he's uncomfortable. Maintain two guards outside his cell at all times. And take a couple of those hired wizards along to watch him, just in case."

Gaius' rebuff had warned Phaedra. When distraught, his powerful emotions weakened her influence over him. Because he was so warded against dark magic, he represented a subject that she had to manage very carefully.

"Dipytos!" the emperor called to one of his stewards.

The fleshy Samothracian came speedily to his master. "See that all the guests accompanying Macro and myself on our voyage assemble here at the palace at dawn tomorrow," said Gaius. "Carriages will be waiting across the river to convey us to Ostia."

"Of course, gracious master," the servant responded. "Alas, Prince Gemellus is saying that he is too ill to make the voyage. His physician affirms that he suffers from a chill involving his chest."

The imperator shrugged off this unimportant development. "Dipytos, is Herod Agrippa still waiting in my chambers?"

"Yes. When I took him lunch, he was still very desirous of a consultation."

"Send him to me now," Gaius said.

The servant did obeisance and hurried away.

To his concubine, the young Caesar said, "Phaedra dearest, you needn't wait around if you are growing tired."

"I'm not at all tired, Lord." She did not want the distrusted Easterner to meet with Gaius alone.

Soon, the doorkeepers admitted Herod Agrippa into the room. His expression wavered briefly at seeing Phaedra. Instead of a bed tunic, she was now garbed in a dignified stola. Gaius was insulting every free woman in the Empire by allowing a barbarian concubine to don the raiment of womanly rank. Usually, Gaius himself was a stickler when it came to the outward show of social dignity. This was more evidence that the princeps was not himself.

"I regret that I could not sooner summon you, Agrippa," remarked the princeps. "But I have been continually engaged with pressing matters. Zenodotus temporarily escaped confinement and I was preoccupied with his recapture. Now, what did you wish to confer with me about?"

Fortunately, Agrippa had already been warned by a spy that Zenodotus had been recaptured, and he was able to receive the news blandly. He gave an apologetic smile, saying, "I want to express my regrets that I shall not be able to leave Rome for the next three days; hence any voyage that takes place before then will be impossible."

"Why so?"

"A religious observance, Caesar, one particularly vital to Judean kings. It would be most inauspicious for me to omit it so soon after my ascension. My predecessor was careless about his sacred duties and the people used it as an excuse for their discontent. I think it would be appropriate not to provoke them and make a bad and lasting first impression."

"I see," sighed Gaius. "If each of our Roman gods had as many holy days as your single Jewish one, the year would be one continuous holiday! Very well, you are excused, but your company will be missed."

Gaius now rose from his chair and, arm-in-arm with his favorite concubine, withdrew. Agrippa was left alone with a feeling of dejection. He had wanted to speak with the emperor on a more pressing matter, but the presence of the witch had made that inadvisable. Now that it was impossible to stop the sacrifice at Capri, he had to depend on an alternate plan, one that he dreaded.

Poor Antonia.

Phaedra remained with Gaius for but a quarter hour before she left him alone in his chamber bespelled and slumbering. She removed herself to a small room and locked herself in. She had brought with her a basin of water, which she set down on a small table.

Phaedra realized now that she'd made a mistake by allowing Osricus to live, especially when she'd had the perfect chance to kill him. Yet at the time, she'd hesitated to slay him, anticipating that she might again have use for his captive blood. Once she had the Ring, could she not conquer him completely, make him a slave who would rejoice in being possessed by her? Owning a paramour whose blood was not unworthy of her own would be a rare distinction, even for a Sitone witch.

Oh, why hadn't she used stronger means to hold him? He could not have made a nuisance of himself if hamstrung or blinded. But she hadn't anticipated the Ring being so far away from the Emperor or taking so long to retrieve, nor Osricus escaping—at least, not so quickly and so completely—before Gaius could imprison him. Now Phaedra scolded herself for her oversight as she prepared to destroy Osricus once and for all.

Dipping the index finger of each hand into the water, the witch began an ancient invocation:

"Hear me, Kraken, great priest of the mighty Jotuns; hear me, god of the Deep-dwelling Ones, Dreaming God, Lord of the Gulfs, Master of Sunken Raelyeg. I call upon your power over the wind and the sea. Let your tentacles stir these placid Roman waters, Great One. Let the tumult of your wrath roil the sea, drowning all who are caught sailing before the tempest.

"Kraken of the many names, heed your servant. She serves your will and also the will of Heid, of Loge, and the mindless chaos Ginnungagap. Destroy my enemy and I shall send to you countless sacrifices of blood! Hear now my prayer! *Fungloui muglu'naf Kraken Raelyeg Iaga'nagel phatagen!*"

Phaedra continued her chanting for a long while, the sweat of intense concentration rolling down her face. The room seemed to sway about her and, finally, the water in the basin darkened. It seemed to reflect a nightmare shape, and then it grew so turbulent that the images displayed could no longer be discerned.

*   *   *

"I've never seen the sky turn so dark so quickly," cried Samuel, shouting over the whistling and wailing of the wind.

Without answering, Osricus brought down the sail, lest it be torn if the gale waxed. The black clouds swirled like a tumbling knot of serpents. Even without the sail, the gusts continued to drive the vessel swiftly before them. Suddenly, the Engle thought he could discern a gigantic form in the sky. Was it only a storm cloud—or was it an articulated being that was darker than the darkness of the roiling heavens?

A titanic lightning bolt separated the shape from the churning clouds, making its edges blaze with fire. He saw a beaked face and a ragged suggestion of tentacles and wings.

"Samuel!" the German cried. "Look! Do you see it?"

The Jew glanced up at the thunderheads. "See what?" He could make out nothing amid the clouds.

Osricus realized that the vision of the demon had been meant only for him, and now it passed from his sight, too—when a wave higher than the mast of their vessel broke over them....

Capri

CHAPTER XXI

The late afternoon's lightening crashed and Rufus Hibernicus felt like calling it a day.

Though he usually enjoyed four-horse chariot racing, the sport wasn't doing much for him today. After watching for a couple hours, he got up and left the Circus Maximus.

He'd been talking to doctors about Tatia's nightmares, but everyone had told him something different. One wanted to put more grain in her diet, another recommended that she be immersed in ice water regularly. A third suggested "giving her something even worse to be afraid of," such as by hanging a large snake above her bed. The man of Erin was ignoring them all. He was desperate, not stupid.

Tatia kept claiming that the dwarf Galar had enchanted her, filling her dreams with strange words and thoughts. When he suggested that such was hard to believe, that only made her insist all the more that it was true. Mostly to humor the girl, Rufus had traced Galar to an old insula to see for himself if the pathetic creature seemed in any way sinister, only to be told that the dwarf had already moved away. The ex-gladiator had shrugged the matter off; the quest had seemed be a fool's errand anyway.

Finally, Hibernicus had returned Tatia to Silanus' house, the best of many unsatisfactory remedies. At least she'd be constantly watched, distracted by work and kept company by friends whom she had already made.

The wind rose and the rain fell harder. The guardsman raised the hood of his paenula and paused at a sheltered pastry stand to get a bite to eat. While he contemplated the offerings, someone tapped him on the shoulder, saying: "Do you have a moment, friend?"

The Syrian accoster looked familiar. It was Silas, a follower of the Jewish prince. "My lord Agrippa bids me bring you to him for an audience," said the freedman. "Please follow me."

"What's this about?" the Irishman asked.

"I cannot say, but you will be well paid."

The idea of being paid always sounded good. "All right," the ex-gladiator agreed, moved more by curiosity than by cupidity. It was not often that he got a royal summons. Rufus had to admire the man ahead of him; the storm was beating down hard and Silas still continued on his way through the driving rain. They climbed the Palatine Hill and entered, sopping wet, into to Augustus' Palace.

At Agrippa's suite, Hibernicus was offered the use of a room and a dry change of clothes.

By the time the secutor was dressed, a Syrian maid hailed him with a chalice of Massicum wine. He barely finished it before Agrippa entered and motioned the slaves and Silas to leave. "I recall that you offered to help my bodyguard, Osricus," he said to the red giant, his tone grave.

"I suppose I did," Rufus replied with a twisted grin. "If he needs help so soon, the lad must be a lodestone for trouble. Well, I'm as good as my word. What's happened to him?"

Agrippa told him the story in some detail. The guardsman had already heard of Zenodotus' escape, but the way the Easterner told the tale, it almost sounded like he had played some role in it. The Jew must have some urgent business in mind, the secutor thought, for not choosing his words more carefully.

According to his host, dark magic was bedeviling the great ones of Rome.

"The emperor's bewitched?" Rufus muttered.

"Don't you believe it?"

The giant shrugged. "The older I get, the less skeptical about some things I become. But what do you need *me* for? I don't know anything about sorcery."

"If you help Gaius, you will be helping Osricus, too. Also, the information I have heard suggests that you are the sort of man that men of substance occasionally turn to."

"I'm listening."

Agrippa drew a green jade amulet from beneath his silken sash, the same object that he had discovered glinting in the sun on the floor of the emperor's bed chamber. "Gaius has told me that this talisman has been bewitched to protect him from sorcery. The witch Phaedra must have taken it away from him to impose a spell. I may be grasping at straws, but I hope that if this bauble is returned to the princeps, it may break the unnatural hold she has on him. Once that's done, he might listen to denunciations against her."

"Why haven't you returned it yourself?"

"I had hoped to, but the witch has always been at his side. I think she could foil me if she realized what I was attempting."

Hibernicus listened quietly, not being very eager to get involved with a sorceress.

"Gaius invited me on his voyage," the king continued. "But I dare not leave Rome at such a time. There are grave things afoot in the city, so that I must be here to head off a disaster."

"I see," remarked the ex-gladiator. "When you say 'voyage,' I suppose you're referring to the emperor's expedition out among the prison islands."

"Yes, but I'm convinced that his real goal is Capri. As an imperial guardsman, will you not be attending him during the sail?"

"I haven't been told that I will, but don't worry about it. If I need to, I'll be able to pull a few strings to get the assignment. But, by the gods, wouldn't it be easier to simply run this witch through the bowels?"

"If you are a reckless man, you may attempt it."

Just then, the Jew looked over his shoulder. *"Marsyas!"* he called. The freedman entered holding a small chest. "I will pay for your services," Agrippa assured his guest. He motioned to the valet, who opened the case. Hibernicus gave a whistle. It brimmed with gold enough to settle all his debts and still leave something extra for amenities.

A crash of lightning shook the windows. Under such a storm, Hibernicus pitied any men out sailing a small boat. Fate would have to decide whether Osricus would live long enough to benefit from any aid offered by mortal hands.

After the tempest passed, the waves outside of Ostia were still flinging themselves high up the beach as the imperial party arrived. In fear of seasickness, Marcus Silanus and a few others had begged the emperor to be excused from the voyage.

Gaius let them go indifferently, though he, too, had his misgivings. But time did not allow for any delay. He had to be upon Capri no later than midday of the Kalends, Zenodotus having emphasized that the ritual needed to be performed at the precise time.

So the emperor told his admiral put his guests into the shelters and to raise anchor. Even before that was done, the rocking of his flagship brought a wretched illness upon Gaius.

Miserable on his bunk, the princeps lay cursing the Alexandrian. All his recent griefs had sprung from that man's doings. He was looking forward to Zenodotus' death with nearly the same intensity that he had longed for Tiberius'.

After a mere hour at sea, Gaius had already vomited himself empty. In the gloom of his cabin, he lay with his eyes shut. He heard the door creak and opened his eyes to see Phaedra looking in, apparently checking on him. He attempted a sickly smile.

She came forward and ran her fingers over his cheek. "Sleep, sleep," she said, "in the name of Freya, sleep in the name of Eir the healer."

Gaius' lids closed again and his breathing fell into the deep, slow rhythms of slumber. The sorceress left him, being now free to do what must be done.

*   *   *

The German guard heard the cabin door open and stood up respectfully as young Caesar entered from his adjacent cabin. "My lady Phaedra is resting," the imperator informed the warrior. "See that no one disturbs her. Understood?"

"*Ja*, Princeps!" the man saluted. The emperor returned to the sloshing deck, crossed it, brushed past the guards and descended by ladder to one of the tiny cabins below. He bade the additional guards posted there to open the prison-cabin, then go above and give him privacy during the interview to come.

As the Roman prince entered, Zenodotus sat upright. "To what do I owe the honor of this…" he began, then stared with incredulity. "No, you're not Gaius. Your eyes are wrong. You're that witch!"

The denunciation of one while under an illusionary disguise always interrupted the spell. The white-stolaed woman now stood before him. "You are clever, Wizard," she conceded grudgingly.

"Not so clever. I'm sure you can sense magic in the air as well as I can. Also, a magician's eyes do not disguise well and can give away certain types of illusion."

"You are knowledgeable, Zenodotus. I am gaining more respect for the magicians of this southern clime."

"Speak, Witch. You did not come to flatter me."

"So true. Where is the ring?" demanded the Swede.

"Why should I tell you?"

"I can cause you very great suffering if you do not."

"With your magic? Do you suppose that I would not place about myself safeguards that are every bit as powerful as those I wove around Caligula?"

"I scarcely need sorcery. I doubt you would have great endurance against flames and blades."

"Torture will scarcely be necessary. Why should I not strike a bargain with you?"

"Treacherous Greek! We already attempted to bargain with you for little profit!"

"Ah, my beauty, *your* tribe's treachery ruined that agreement, not mine. Did I not pay all the gold demanded of me for knowledge of the ring's hiding place? I'm sure I would have been murdered and robbed had I not withdrawn from Germania quickly as I could, and with the strongest precautions."

"That is old business. The pieces of the game have been rearranged. What do you demand for your help in allowing me to attain the ring?"

"I would have my freedom!" said the Greek. "But for me to be truly safe afterwards, Gaius must die."

"That is a dangerous assassination. You ask a very great deal."

"He is dangerous to us both. And how else will you find the ring's location if I do not reveal it?"

"I know that it is on the isle of Capri," she bluffed.

"Capri is a small island, but not so small that it cannot hide a single ring. And remember, another besides yourself seeks it. What happens if he finds it before you do?"

"Osricus? He is drowned! I stirred the waters myself."

The wizard shrugged. "Whether he is alive or dead only the gods know."

"I will consider your demands," she replied annoyedly. "In the meantime, it is not in the interest of either of us that you should betray me to the guards."

Zenodotus nodded, his mood having become both sly and confident. Phaedra stood there singing the runes for a moment and once again cloaked herself with the imperator's gangling shape....

As promised, Rufus Hibernicus had finagled an assignment with the guard unit on the imperial voyage. Even so, he maintained doubts about the story told to him by the desert prince.

After calling at the isle of Pandateria, the bones of the emperor's mother were gathered. But the call to make ready to leave was not given. Instead, the fleet was told to stay moored beneath the cliffs of the island while the emperor took his flagship out for a peaceful sail to calm his grief and woe. It had shocked him, he claimed, to have taken his mother from what amounted to a felon's grave.

Rufus had seen to it that he was assigned to the flagship, along with almost thirty other barbarian warriors. The prestige passengers beside Gaius were his right hand man Macro, the magician Zenodotus, and two pasty-faced scholars whom Rufus didn't know. In addition, Gaius' favorite, the slave girl Phaedra, accompanied her ostensible master. The man of Erin winced. Wherever there was a witch, there would always be trouble.

The captain was not informed of any specific destination until the flagship was away from Pandateria. The imperator informed the crew that Capri was their destination.

In due course, the looming cliffs of Capri were seen. From the northern harbor, Gaius sent men ashore to perform various looting tasks. Then, disguised as a Praetorian tribune to avoid recognition, the emperor went ashore with his bodyguards. Also with him was Phaedra, garbed as an officer's lady.

Rufus confirmed that the sorceress was the same wench who had been purchased off the street by Marcus Silanus, the one who had shared a room with Tatia. He now began to wonder whether the latter's strange mood had been caused by a hex. If so, he would have all the excuse he needed to put his service dagger, his *pugio*, between her ribs.

Gaius and the woman were carried up the grade on a litter, but the Via Tiberio was a climb that everyone else hated. Zenodotus, also on foot, was well guarded by Macro and Axidares, the ex-Thracian bodyguard commander. Behind him trailed about twenty German bodyguards.

The island, away from the work of the emperor's gardeners, was a bare one. It presented a good view of the sea, but the growth went little beyond scrubs and rank grass. The climbers periodically scared up coveys of quail, and some semi-feral goats. It was this species, the *caper*, that had given the isle its name. Amusingly, it had also given Tiberius one of his nicknames. From the moment that he retired to Capri, the lord of "Goat Island" was spoken of as "the old goat."

The circuitous uphill track doubled the distance that a crow would have to fly. Even the sturdy Rufus Hibernicus was glad enough to reach the high ground of Tiberius' estate. The Villa Jovis was just one of twelve houses that the late emperor had owned on Capri. Nor was the Villa Jovis the only building upon the height; many pavilions, shrines, barracks, and guest houses dotted the promontory. The "Old Goat" was a miser when it came to entertaining the Romans, but guzzled their riches like wine when he was indulging his own extravagance.

No common man could have failed to be awe-struck by Caesar's high retreat. It had a vast frontage and the *horti*—pleasure gardens—were already abloom with early spring flowers. Pampered trees—ilexes, yews, cypresses, and other species—stood tall in the gardens and along the cliff edges.

Tiberius had even equipped himself with a private stadium. People said he had enjoyed driving a chariot around the track, and also watching serious races between professionals. And this was the man who had done so little to support the public games at the Circus Maximus.

Gaius had his litter taken into the villa and commanded Macro to follow along.

Going first into a vaulted hall of marble and porphyry, he ordered the guard captain on station at the villa to evacuate his men and the house servants and spend the night at the village below. The prefect needed to provide Gaius with the privacy the emperor required to keep his nefarious doings secret.

The emperor himself had occupied Tiberius' finest suite. "It's time," he told Axidares. "Have your Germans posted on the periphery of the villa.

Allow no one to enter or leave." He pivoted toward Zenodotus. "Now, wizard, the fateful hour is near at hand. Serve me well!"

"I will need a dram of your blood, O Caesar. I did not trouble to ask for it earlier because the potency of drawn blood lasts for no more than an hour."

"Have Polymnos take it," Gaius instructed his guard captain while nodding toward one of the two sorcerers. "I don't want that treasonous devil touching me."

"And also, Dominus," the wizard pressed, "I shall need a token from Lady Antonia's person, as I mentioned before."

"Kritolaos," said the emperor to the second wizard. "Give it to him." The hatchet-faced Pontian drew an antique ivory box from his pack and handed it to Zenodotus. "Before this voyage, I asked Grandmother for a lock of her hair," Gaius explained.

Zenodotus nodded; it would serve.

Just then Macro joined his liege.

"Prefect," commanded Gaius, "take two men and post them outside the magic room. Kritolaos and Polymnos are to assist Zenodotus. If they should shout for assistance within, your men will enter and slay the Alexandrian immediately. Is that understood?"

"Completely," answered the brawny Italian.

A little later, his blood having been drawn, Gaius dismissed the wizards and Zenodotus and told them to get the work done. They departed under guard.

When the young imperator and Phaedra were left alone, the rune-witch regarded him, realizing she could slay Gaius very easily. However, she thought it wiser to keep him as a bargaining chip. When he was dead, her power here would be considerably reduced. She would instead wait upon events, sensing that Zenodotus was less fearful of Gaius than he pretended. Moreover, the witch did not trust the daring and desperate man. What if he was angling to keep Andvaranaut for himself? If the rogue did claim it, it would doom his soul, of course, but he was probably too irreligious and cynical to believe in the might of Nifelhel's dark gods.

"You are tired from the journey, Lord," she suggested to Gaius. "Let us rest until Zenodotus' work is done. Let me massage your tense body."

"Yes, yes," Gaius responded, "anything to get my mind off this infernal waiting." He allowed his mistress to lead him into Tiberius' bedroom, which was garishly and erotically decorated to suite the late emperor's bad taste.

Phaedra helped the youth doff his military disguise and bade him to stretch prone upon the wide, silk-sheeted bed. She applied her skilled fingers to his taut muscles, making him sigh with pleasure. While she worked, the

German woman sang a fimbul-song, using sweet, enchanting tones. A moment later, Gaius was sleeping soundly.

The Swede got to her feet, weary from the trip and weary from the use of magic. Maintaining her power over Gaius was taxing her. How she wished that it was not Gaius, but Osricus who was here at her mercy. Merging with that one's god-descended flesh would have trebled her power very easily....

Phaedra, however, bore down and moved ahead on her plan. She had brought a small bag from Rome that contained several useful items. She took the tiara from her hair and cast her scarlet mantle over a chair. Next, the witch stepped out of her gold-dusted shoes and removed the extravagant brooch from her shoulder. This permitted her white stola to slide down her youthful curves, to mound at her ankles. She kicked the garment away; contact with unsanctified garments when weaving a spell would diffuse and inhibit her enchantments. Finally, the Siton witch withdrew a jar of blue pigment from her bag.

With an index finger, Phaedra painted several runic designs over her arms, legs, and belly. Last of all, and with painstaking care, she stood before a mirror and drew a potent Black Rune across her forehead.

She picked up the mouse skin that she had already set aside on the table and seated herself on the mosaic floor, assuming a lotus-type position. Her fingers, clutching the mouse skin, were locked together. Now, holding the skin close to her heart, she sang to it softly and commanded her spirit to enter into a deep trance state.

The enchantress soon felt herself rising and drifting away from her mortal shell.

When Phaedra's senses next cleared, everything around looked very strange. The room had become gigantic, large enough to house a host of Jotunheim giants. The floor tiles had grown immensely, but she was ready for this effect. Each of these tiles was naught but a tiny mosaic square. Like all else in view, they had lost their color to her eyes. She saw them as either white, black, or some shade of gray.

Phaedra steeled herself and gazed at her own hands. Not for the first time, the sight of hideous black paws dismayed her. The witch steadfastly refused to look at the rest of her present body. She occupied the vile body of a villa mouse—a disagreeable if necessary thing. By comparison, occupying the body of a raven while enchanting Marcus Silanus had been almost pleasant. Nonetheless, in rodent-guise she would be able to explore the mansion stealthily and spy upon whomsoever she desired.

As the transmigrated witch raced along the baseboards of the deserted villa, she sought to find the basement chamber where Zenodotus had for years been carrying out his self-damning work.

THE MAGIC ROOM

CHAPTER XXII

Lady Antonia was found waiting in the garden of her town house for her caller. She accepted Herod Agrippa's kisses readily, but wondered at his seemingly cheerless mood.

"Come, Herod!" she coaxed, "Sit beside me. Have you ever seen such large almond blossoms as those above you?" When he didn't glance up, she continued in good spirits. "Your namesake, General Agrippa, brought the original seedlings from Greece."

The Jewish prince forced a smile, but the effort died on his lips. He followed his foster mother to an ornate bench in silence.

"What is bothering you, my son? You do not look well."

"It is nothing, Lady. I am not in the best spirits today."

"That is plain! But why? Have you quarreled with Gaius?"

"By no means! And I trust that he has been cordial with you as well."

"I have no complaint. He has been more cheerful than I ever remember him being, but I don't think his good mood can last, not if he doesn't curb his spending. Popularity that rests upon the giving of gifts, especially to strangers, never lasts for long. Might you be able to urge him to be more prudent?"

Herod smiled wanly. "I, council thrift?"

She smiled again. "It would be a change for you, for certain, but you at least have good taste in your purchasing. Have you seen the plans for the new palace Gaius is building? It's grotesque beyond description."

"I think it will suit him."

She regarded him curiously. "Is that a cat I hear hissing? Are you truly getting along so very well with Gaius? Tell me, has something he's said or done put you into such a dour state?"

"Lady," Agrippa asked suddenly, "do you believe that the remedy for evil must always be good, or is it acceptable if it is a lesser evil?"

Antonia frowned. "What a strange thought! Forgive me, Herod, but you have never shown interest in philosophy before. If you are suddenly interested in ethics, you must have some practical reason for it. There is something you are not telling me, dear boy."

"Do not ask. My peace of mind ends today. Can a man be damned if he is given no choice in what he has to do?"

" 'Damned'? I cannot remember you ever talking this way before, Herod. Whatever is the burden you are carrying?"

When she said that, the king glanced down on the small wooden box he had brought with him.

"Please, forget this passing gloom of mine," he urged. "Let us speak of happier things."

"As you wish. But do not forget that you may talk to me about any subject at all. I am an old woman who has seen too much of life to be shocked by anything that a favorite child may tell me. But for now, let us have lunch. You shall see that I still remember most of those strange dietary prohibitions that your people are sworn to live by."

Her visitor forced a grin. "I almost forgot! I have brought something dear to your own tastes, Madame."

Agrippa picked up the cherry wood box from beside him and opened it before his foster mother. "I know how much you enjoy my country's dates. One of my friends recently brought a stock of them back on his first spring voyage. I think these are the best I have ever tasted." He plucked the largest fruit from the top of the stock and placed it into his own mouth.

Antonia smiled. "Thank you, Herod. I suppose two or three will not unduly spoil our appetite for lunch."

The windowless conjuring room was dark, save for a circle around the brazier standing at the center of a well-laid out magical circle. The walls were of granite rubble, concealed by wide, fading charts and horoscopes drawn on large parchments. All about was a clutter of scrolls, bottles, vials, jars, and even a scrying basin. The largest furnishing was an altar with mystical symbols chisled into it.

As Zenodotus prayed to his dark gods, he ignored both the Pontian wizard, Kritolaos, and the rough-complexioned Polymnos of Argos. They had crowded into the powdered circle with him, allowing the man no freedom of action, no possibility of self-defense. Every apparatus he asked for, every scroll he read from, everything he burned in invocation of the demons of the Other World, they carefully inspected first, permitting the Alexandrian no latitude at all to play Gaius false. Resigned, he prayed:

"Tolle capra sine cornibus, ReBaThoth, insatiabilis accipientis sacrificium, et supplex petere non alia anima vivens."

"Take the hornless goat, Re-Ba-Thoth, insatiable receiver of sacrifice, and crave to claim no other living soul."

Though his language was Latin, the prayer was one passed down from the almost forgotten days when Egypt's ancestors had lived along a haunted river in a land named for it—Stygos. Its priests of Set had long prospered, pleasing the gods by means of the young hearts they ripped from the bloody casings of transient life.

He was crumbling into the fire a few strands of Antonia's gray hair at a time.

"Fiat!"

Zenodotus peered into the scrying basin, hoping to see the swirl of blackness that indicated that the Chthonioi had sucked old Antonia's soul away from the material Earth and taken it into their own hateful abode, Harag-Kolathos. The change did not come. Instead, he saw manifested a pale image beneath the ripples of the water.

It was a polished, grinning skull.

The magician drew back dismayed and the gathering forces of darkness quickly fell away. The Rite of Abominations had failed utterly.

There was only one thing that could be responsible for such a happening!

The lady Antonia was already dead....

Alone in the corridor of the villa, Herod Agrippa could hear the wails of Antonia's servants and the lady's gathered kin—Claudius, her son; Antonia, her granddaughter; her great niece Valeria Messalina, and Julia, the sister of the unfortunate Gemellus.

Beset by the sickness of regret, Agrippa trembled; he leaned back against the wall, lest he fall. Antonia was dead, but had she died in time to save her soul?

Would he ever know for certain?

Agrippa knew a witch knowledgeable in the art of poisoning, and had demanded from her a painless drug that would simulate a failure of the heart. The smaller dates that he had offered Antonia had been laden with the bane; he himself had eaten only the safe, larger ones. It had taken only a moment for the old woman to complain of dizziness and then to faint against him. He had immediately called the servants to attend her and they had carried her to bed. There, after a few minutes, they told him she had fallen comatose. By the time a doctor could be brought in, she had ceased to breathe.

"Go to Heaven, Antonia," he murmured. "Or to Elysium, if your people's reward is different from mine." Who and what was he? he wondered. Was he a murderer or a rescuer? How did the God of Israel see such a nuanced thing? Had he only traded Antonia's damnation for his own? Was it possible for him to claw back from the pit's edge after such a sin?

Suddenly feeling the hollow sensation of being a criminal. As soon as Antonia had been taken to her bed, he had gone to the family privy and, in the privacy of the tiny room, he'd refilled the empty box from a bag of untainted fruit he had brought concealed within his garments.

Hopefully, no man would find the proof that the law required to condemn him.

But this, he knew, was a matter that went beyond the jurisprudence of mankind. There was one judge who saw everything and it was His judgment that Herod Agrippa feared to an infinitely greater degree.

To survive in the arena, a man had to live by instinct—the instinct that told him when to act and also told him when to stand pat. His every instinct was warning Rufus Hibernicus that this was the moment for action. Something was going on inside the Villa Jovis—something as deadly as a cold stab in the guts.

But what should he do?

He had asked Axidares for the guard station outside a large window of the emperor's suite. Because the ex-Thracian trusted Hibernicus, and knew that Caesar favored the ex-gladiator, he'd seen no reason not to give the red-maned giant the requested posting.

From the terrace, Rufus had observed a bit of what had transpired within through the crack of the shutters. He had seen the witch strip and paint herself like a clown, then squat in the middle of the room, seemingly putting herself into a trance. A trance? Good, if the trance were deep enough, he could go in and assassinate her. Rufus unlatched the hook on the shutters with his knife blade. The light flooding indoors did not cause the woman to stir. Encouraged, he hoisted himself over the sill.

He paused behind the seated Phaedra, wondering whether the uncannily beautiful girl could be as dangerous as he'd been told.

He hated killing beauty. If Phaedra had been awake and in a rage, hurling threats, or trying to ensorcell him, he would have struck off her lovely head as a mere reflex. But to murder a girl in her sleep? That was a nasty thing. And how could he explain it? The emperor would surely throw him over Tiberius' cliff. That was what the old emperor had reputedly done with hundreds of annoying people at Villa Jovis.

The ex-gladiator did not strike. If the golden minx was fated to perish, let her blood be on Gaius' hands.

Rufus found the emperor abed, as if sleeping off a heavy drunk. He paused to take the green jade talisman from his scrip. Holding its neck chain open, he slipped it over the emperor's head. Gaius lurched from his sleep and Rufus reflexively flung a handful of bedclothes over the young man's head. Then he dodged from the room and went out the window again, before the bleary, disorientated Gaius managed to fight himself clear of the clinging wool and silk.

Gaius, now fully awake, looked around and saw he was alone. Had someone tried to smother him, or had he only tangled himself in his own bedclothes? He got up and looked for Phaedra.

When he saw her in her room of retreat, it was like he was looking at her with newly-made eyes. He still loved her, but couldn't understand why he had been so indulgent with such a forward wench. Oh, she was beautiful; to see her was to want to embrace her, but—by Pluto—no woman could be permitted to lead Gaius Caesar around by the nose!

Only then did he feel the weight of the Hecate amulet at his neck. When he saw it, he was surprised that he was wearing it. But, then, why should he *not* wear it? It was his best defense against the malign forces of the underworld, forces that were even now reaching out to drag him away.

What had been happening as he slept? Had Zenodotus done his job? Was Antonia dead?

"Phaedra! What are you doing there?" He looked again at Phaedra, still sitting silently in place like an image made of clay. "You will answer when I speak to you!" he shouted, annoyed, and then kicked at her haunch.

The girl screamed and crumpled unconscious to the tiles. Gaius wondered at her reaction—but not so much as he was wondering at the odd symbols drawn across her flesh.

He heard the suite door fly open and the sound of heavily-shod feet approaching. Gaius picked up Phaedra's discarded stola to maintain his modesty as the portal flew inward.

"Macro! Is this any way…?"

"Divine Caesar!" panted the prefect. "Z-Zeno—dah…."

"Stop mumbling! What are you trying to say?"

"Zenodotus says the ritual has failed! The lady Antonia—according to the Greek—is already dead and the magic cannot reach her!"

Gaius went livid. Shock made his legs like wood; he reeled. Was the Alexandrian lying, or had the gods cheated him of salvation?

The political soldier helped his imperator back to bed. Gaius was stammering: "Zenodotus… bring him! I'll *kill* him… I'll suck the blood from his veins!"

The Praetorian hurriedly saluted and turned his master over to the guards who were now entering from behind. Very shortly afterwards, he was ushering the failed wizard into the imperial chamber and throwing him down on the rug-covered floor. The Greek gaped fearfully at the princeps. The latter glowered down at him with shoulders rigid with fury.

"Savor this moment, Greek," he pronounced with a trembling voice, "it is the last moment you will enjoy without pain. You will be days in dying. Macro! Disembowel him!"

The bodyguards held the sorcerer's arms and tugged his head back by his long hair. With almost no emotion, Macro drew his dagger.

"No, Caesar, wait!" cried the Alexandrian. "There is *still* hope! We have lost one victim, but another can be found. Think of another whom you truly love. But we must hurry; the window now open to the spheres will soon close."

"Whom would you have me offer?" cried Gaius. "My sister? You crawling wad of slime! Before I gave her to the infernal gods, I'd...."

Zenodotus smiled ingratiatingly. "Caesar, Drusilla is a princess and her life needs be preserved at all costs. But, Dominus, have you forgotten how dearly you have come to love another, one who is a worthless slave who will never be missed? Her only worth to you is the fact that she has lately found great favor in your eyes."

Gaius stared at his henchman. "Phaedra?" he mumbled hoarsely.

"Perhaps the gods sent you the worthless creature so that you may be saved," Zenodotus suggested.

Gaius hesitated. He loved the woman, true, wanted her, also true, but....

The Greek's words carried the weight of good sense. It appalled him to think of his favorite dying, knowing that she would be damned....

But the very intensity of his feelings proved to himself that he did, indeed, love her.

Well, Gaius thought, *Caesar has to be capable of making sacrifices, no matter how painful.* His late-blooming love for the barbarian girl had been heaven-sent, truly. Zenodotus was right. It had probably been a gift from Aphrodite to save him. He could be saved and he would not even have to immolate the joy of his heart, Drusilla.

"Do what you must with the wench," Gaius decreed gravely, "but this time, *do not fail.*" He gave orders to his guards.

The German guards dragged away the manhandled magician and took away the unconscious northern woman.

The slave felt very light in their powerful hands. Both guards regretted that such a Fraulein was to be sent to her death.

The great ones of Rome were wasteful.

"Tie her down on that altar—and gag her," Zenodotus directed his untrustworthy assistants, Polymnos and Kritolaos. "She is a witch, knowledgeable in the words of power." He glanced surreptitiously at the now-closed magic chamber door.

Behind it, he knew, two guardsmen and perhaps Macro himself stood, waiting for the call of his helpmates if they should grow suspicious of him. That call could mean his death, should the prefect follow Gaius' standing orders literally.

He noticed that the lesser wizards were affixing bonds on Phaedra's wrists and ankles to the rough-chiseled basalt altar, and finding that man-handling such a lovely naked woman was very agreeable work. Their distraction gave Zenodotus his chance to act—very possibly his last and only.

He sidled to a wall, lifted a corner of a horoscope diagram and pressed a stone behind it. This stone released the opening of a secret hiding place. His nimble fingers quickly plucked from it something metallic and cold; a thrill ran along the length of his arm, like it had before on the only other occasion that he had held it. That alarmed him, but he could not expect help from Phaedra any longer, and he had no faith in Gaius' unforgiving nature.

"What do you have, Alexandrian?" the watchful Kritolaos asked. Zenodotus put his hands behind his back and slipped the ring on his finger. The assistant crossed toward the Greek, scowling. "Let me see what you have or I'll shout for the guards."

With reluctance, Zenodotus extended his right hand with a golden ring gleaming upon his middle finger. "It is harmless, a personal possession only—see for yourself."

Kritolaos reached out. A light came from nowhere and shadows suddenly flared as the Pontian was flung to the stone floor by a hissing web of blue, forking energy. It was like he had been critically injured by a Herculean boxer. He was dying, as Zenodotus had intended.

Polymnos turned sharply. He beheld Kritolaos crumpled underfoot. His hair had whitened and stood straight out from his scalp, his robes smoldered, and the air smelled of burnt cloth and flesh. The frightened wizard made to shout for the guards, but his first breath was never drawn. A pressure had tightened around his chest like a torturer's band of iron.

"Meryamut djesrkhot Set-Itnutay..." the Alexandrian muttered in the tongue of ancient Stygos. By a spell of Set, he had placed the death of serpentine constriction upon his jailer. With Polymnos silent and slowly dying, Zenodotus could only marvel at the ease with which he was performing these difficult cantrips. While wearing the ring, he felt that he could accomplish anything!

Black blood vomited over the doomed wizard's tunic and his legs buckled, sinking to the stones. Zenodotus continued watching until the Argosian's losing struggle reached its inevitable conclusion.

Zenodotus' soul felt pleasantly warmed. Untrained in sorcery, Tiberius had been able to do nothing with the ring, but it was different for the Hellenic wizard. He was practiced in many spells and felt eager to use them to destroy his enemies.

Phaedra awoke to a pounding headache. The flickering shadows confused her while she tried to remember how she came to be lying on her back. A moment earlier, she had been occupying the body of a rodent, observing Zenodotus and his two assistants in the magic room, reacting as if they were in some sort of a crisis—then a sudden searing pain had turned her blood to fire. Her entranced mortal body must have been disturbed.

The room, lighted by Zenodotus' brazier, seemed familiar, but the proportions were somehow wrong. In a flash, she realized that her *human* form was now in the magic room, and that Zenodotus was standing across the chamber. To her alarm, she realized she was gagged.

The Swede attempted to get up, but could not. For an instant, she supposed herself paralyzed, but quickly realized that she lay bound and gagged across a hard surface.

Phaedra looked right and left, but saw no one to appeal to.

"You are awake," said Zenodotus.

She regarded him with apprehension.

"The emperor has given you to me—to be sacrificed to the chaotic gods, for payment of a debt that he incurred some weeks ago. It's very fortunate that you had placed a love spell upon him."

The Swede understood her situation only too well and started to fight against her bonds.

When Zenodotus held up his right hand, she ceased her struggles. How bright was the golden band upon his finger in the firelight! She realized that it had to be Andvaranaut. Never before had the girl beheld the ring. It was by the incredible power that it radiated that she knew what it was.

"Your people know more about this ring than almost any other. Is it true that the ring damns the soul of any who wears it?"

Unable to speak, she nodded.

"Then you would not have sought it unless you knew how to avoid the curse!"

No, that wasn't true. All the true witches of Heid were damned from spell-casting with Black Runes. They only wanted the ring to make their spells irresistible.

She shook her head in negative to his question.

"I do not believe you. If you yield the secret of mastering the ring," he promised, "I would gladly spare you."

She felt her doom at hand. Zenodotus had been doomed from the instant that he had used Andvaranaut to cast a single spell. She had no pleasing truth to impart to him, no matter how severely he made her suffer.

Liking her expression of fear, Zenodotus smiled. "No, do not doubt my good will! Armed with the Andvaranaut, why should I fear the survival of one like you—especially after I take care to wipe your memory clean? I can be merciful."

She moaned under her gag.

If he killed her, her eternal fate in Nifelhel would begin this very day.

Three Heirs in Darkness

CHAPTER XXIII

The storm raised by Phaedra had nearly accomplished its murderous objective. The sailor Samuel had given up, bellowing out prayers to his nameless god, leaving his steering oar abandoned. Osricus maintained the fight, however; many a time he had vied with the maelstroms off Jutland. Taking the oar, he ran the small boat for the Italian coast.

The boiling waves raised and dropped the skiff repeatedly, and were beginning to break the craft into kindling. Finally, the sea hurled the men alive upon the cobbly beach.

For the rest of the day and the night, they hid from the lash of the tempest behind a line of rock outcroppings. With the morning, Samuel and Osricus got up stiffly and explored the lonely strand all the way to a small fishing village. Above it loomed a mass of barren rock which Samuel called Mount Circeo. He remembered the story that it had once been the home of an evil witch named Circe, and had been visited by one of Greece's mightiest heroes. But Osricus barely listened to the Jew's prattling. Dead heroes and dead witches seemed unimportant in the midst of such pressing events.

With some of the gold that Samuel still retained, the men bought a good fishing boat from a local family. Once the sea settled down, they set out over the choppy surface.

A brisk north wind bore them south-southeastward as they stayed close to the mainland. Samuel, increasingly unhappy with the voyage, could not be persuaded to go farther than the Bay of Napoli. At a small port town named Herculaneum, he disembarked after imparting to Osric his careful directions for crossing over to the isle of Capri.

The German returned to sea, but an adverse shifting of the winds tied him up for many hours along a promontory, frustratingly close to Capri, which Samuel had said he would find just a little beyond the horizon.

With a favorable change of the winds by the next dawning, Osricus cast off for the open sea. The sails, made firm by a fresh breeze, brought him into sight of the high and rocky island. Heeding the Jew's advice, the Engle steered south and west, watchful of a landing point on the isle's south side, near to the ridge-village of Capri. It was not yet noon.

After a hurried meal on the beach, he climbed a series of trails up to the central ridge of the island. From there, Osricus could see the imperial galley in the harbor at the islet's north side. The first local passerby he queried confirmed his worst fears. A party of imperial soldiers had landed that morning and ascended to the Villa Jovis.

Osricus continued on his way, joining with a track called the Via Tiberio. Along it, he encountered a host of soldiers and servants descending from the upper promontory and hid behind a mass of rocks. He lost time there because they were moving at a deliberate pace, but as they passed by he saw neither Zenodotus nor any high-ranking officer amongst them. When they passed, he pressed on toward the mountain height.

With the sun beyond the vertical, he reached the summit and left the road. There were gardens and woodlots enough to give him cover, and by these he avoided the palace sentries. When the Engle arrived at a point out of sight of any guard but one, Osricus crept in close and then rushed at the man's back, his sword drawn.

The wary guard heard him coming and brought his lance around. The attempted assassination turned into a desperate wrestling match, which the rune-warrior brought to a close with a hard right to the man's bearded chin.

Having appropriated the sentry's useful equipment, Osricus shook the German bodyguard enough to bring him around. "Where is the emperor?" he demanded of his captive. "Is a blonde woman with him?"

"The lord Gaius waits within a bedroom," the guard babbled quickly, his native language understandable to the Engle. "The woman Phaedra has been given over to the sorcerer, Zenodotus."

Osricus thanked the German for his information by knocking him unconscious without taking his life. Then he entered the immense house to commence his search.

"Guards!" someone shouted from inside the magic chamber. The sentries without, a German and an Illyrian, leaped from their benches and burst into the room. They stumbled and fell over a long, low shelf propped there to trip them.

As they floundered on the stone-block floor, Zenodotus shouted: *"Itht'lti t'ctmatfem Ihlhtotoa Io Saboth!"*

The bodyguards yowled in pain as stomach cramps, like hot knives through their bowels, coursed them. They uttered appeals to the gods, but the agony grew so intense that they very quickly could utter no sound other than screams. These carried down the cellar corridors and could be faintly heard in the service rooms of the main floor.

Blood and bile started to pour out from under their leather cuirasses, along with the worming tendrils that were their intestines. These resembled a nest of serpents emerging from hibernation.

Another figure appeared at the door to behold the guardsmen's anguish with astonishment and disbelief. He looked from one side of the room to the other, from Kritolaos' corpse to Polymnos', and then met Zenodotus' stare with horror.

"Many are the ways for a man to die, Macro," the Greek laughed. "Take your choice, Prefect; I am willing to oblige you!"

With a yelp of dismay, the soldier wheeled away and raced up the limestone steps. He continued to run on the upper floor, until he got the presence of mind to shout for additional guards.

Zenodotus stayed where he was, wanting his enemy to feel all the terror of Tartarus until the time came to send Macro there in reality. He stood admiring the circlet of gold on his hand. The experiment had gone exceedingly well. The more power required to work his sorcery, the more power the ring supplied him. No longer would he have to praise and propitiate the niggardly demons who lurked beyond the veil; this gleaming band was in itself all that he would ever require.

The Greek looked back at Phaedra, still well bound. He thought she would lay safely ensconced here until he got back to question her more about the ring.

The wizard took leave of the magic chamber and climbed up to the kitchen area of the Villa Jovis. He exited the mansion by a rear door, at which place a German bodyguard challenged him, but a spark flew from Zenodotus' finger and set the warrior's hair ablaze. The guard dropped his sword and raced for the nearest fish pond with the wizard's laughter pursuing him.

Then the world's mightiest wizard had an idea, which became his motive to go on to the Cliff of Tiberius....

As Macro had feared, Gaius did not take the account of Zenodotus' escape and newly-acquired powers gently.

"Go after him, fool! Slay him on sight! I'll find some better means to safeguard my soul. The Greek is too dangerous to live! Take every man, but put an end to him!"

Macro blanched at the prospect of getting close to the berserk sorcerer, but he had to either obey the man whom he still thought of as "Caligula" or else kill him. Though the emperor was vulnerable and the Prefect extremely ambitious, this did not seem like a good time for intrigue—especially since the German guards were loyal to the princeps and not to himself.

He ran to the atrium and barked at the few men deployed there, ordering them to follow him. When they could not find Zenodotus in the cellars, he decided to search outside.

Elsewhere in the palace, Gaius realized that in his haste he had left himself unguarded. He accordingly fled upstairs, there to barricade himself inside one of the servants' cubicles.

Osricus was hiding behind a pilaster while the prefect and his squad stampeded by. Realizing that they were leaving the villa, he pressed on, deciding to explore the cellars first. After vainly probing several of the dark cells, he caught the scent of pungent incense. The rune-warrior pursued what he recognized as a sorcerous odor until he entered an open room. There, in the shadows, a naked woman lay bound and gagged upon a raised platform, struggling against the cords binding her wrists and ankles. With satisfaction, he recognized Phaedra.

"When I left Rome," he said, "it seemed like you had become the mistress of emperors. Now I find you as helpless as one of those kidnapped virgins on the altar of your own bloody goddess."

Phaedra released a strangled, startled sound. From her perspective, Osricus' eyes must have looked as hot as two windows into Nifelhel.

The warrior gritted his teeth in fury at the sight of her. Osricus, who had never done violence to a captive woman before, had dreamed of a hundred different ways of ending the vermin-like existence of this one. He was almost certain that she was the werewolf! She had murdered two of his friends. She had manipulated his sympathies as if he were just a green boy; she had left him shamefully conquered in the sight of his friends.

The Engle drew his dagger. Phaedra, wide-eyed, wished that she could shrink away into the stone when he pressed the blade's point to the soft skin of her neck. "Whisper one spell, say one word displeasing to me, and you die," he threatened. When she nodded, he took the gag from her mouth.

"*Where is it!*" he demanded, his expression intense. To Phaedra he may not have looked wholly sane.

"I don't have it! Zenodotus took it! He's demanding that I teach him the runes of its mastery!"

"What did you tell him?"

"Nothing! There are no such runes. He intends to kill Caesar before he comes back! Spare me. We need not be enemies; we are of one descent."

"You are a murderer. You owe me blood vengeance!"

The witch knew enough about honest men to know that the best way to placate them was to tell the truth. "Yes, I killed the old man, but only after he poisoned me. As for the other one, I did him no harm! My servant Galar, a misbegotten spawn of dverg and woman, ensorceled him, just as he tried to do to you, also. I had given him no such order. In the name of your god Heimdall, our joint ancestor, have pity. A woman's blood pollutes a warrior's steel!"

"On one hand you dishonor every virtue of your sex, and on the other you claim it for a shield. You are well aware that our people do not hesitate to destroy sorcerers, male or female!"

"I can take the Black Rune from your flesh," she promised desperately. "Cut my bonds and take me into your embrace. Our union shall grant me all the power I need to erase the spell!"

"Loderod taught me the means to do that myself," he said as he worked the gag back into her mouth. "And to plunder you of the power of Scef's blood that I need—the blood which you *disgrace*—I see no reason why you need to be set free."

She saw in his face what he intended to do, and tried to prepare herself for the inevitable. At least the rune-warrior was delaying his decision to kill her.

That did not make what followed easy for her.

Nor did he try to make it so.

From around the villa, Macro had gathered up most of the remaining bodyguards, including Rufus Hibernicus. The man sounded slightly unhinged, but the secutor construed that they had to pursue a wizard gone wild and slay him on sight. Beyond this, Rufus knew that one of his comrades, Gruder, had had his hair burned away and his scalp scorched, apparently by Zenodotus' magical gesture. It sounded like Macro was probably on the right side this time.

One group of German searchers heard the chant of the magician before they saw him. Coming through the foliage, they stumbled to an astonished halt.

Zenodotus stood not on the cliff's rim, but *over* it, levitating with his loose garments aflutter in the sea breeze. The sorcerer was staring down at the Tyrrhenian Sea hundreds of feet below. The unnaturalness of the sight would have routed the superstitious guardsmen, if not for the steadiness of their leader, Axidares.

The ex-Thracian cursed them for cowardice and hurled a stone at the robed shape, but Zenodotus raised his arm and sent it awry, like a fly shooed away.

In reply, Zenodotus shouted to the waves:

"Ye lost and wandering souls who suffer from Caesarian tyranny, heed my call. Rise, walk, be avenged on the murderous Macro and the cruel Caligula, your destroyer's unworthy heir! Slay any who call them their masters. Let the sea and rocks release you to work your revenge!"

A heavy mist came welling up from the sea foam to overflow the lip of the promontory. The outline of the magician vanished behind its murky veil.

Osricus, having filled his spirit with the power of Heimdall's blood, now abandoned the witch in her bonds and cupped his fylfot talisman between his palms. Its dross had been metamorphosed into the brightest of fairy gold. Its flawless appearance was the symbol of his fully awakened potential. His blood seemed to run in a lava torrent through his arteries. But it meant nothing as long as he bore the Black Rune.

Drawing a nervous breath, the Engle pressed the raised surface of the medallion against the dark, runic blemish upon his chest as he had at Agrippa's suite. He cried out as energy seemed to overwhelm him. The touch of the fairy gold sent searing pain into his spot of tainted flesh, but not the hand that held it.

When the burning sensation ceased, he took the emblem away. The Black Rune had been banished from his breast, but the reversed brand of the fylfot was left behind, not as a burn, but a red-brown discoloration. More importantly, within his being, he felt a strange release. He sensed the freeing of some inner faculty....

He heard Phaedra moan from the room behind him and he looked back. She had served her purpose, he judged. Slaying her now would do something toward avenging Mar and Calusidius. Further, it would be a warning to the witches who might be sent after her from this point on. The girl met his angry stare with eyes inflamed by dread. She knew that if she died now, death would be only the beginning of an eternity of torture. She had never worshiped the kind of gods who would respond to appeals for mercy. Such gods would never waste pity on a mortal who had failed them.

Osricus drew his sheathed dagger and advanced on his captive. Her narrow throat beckoned the keen edge, like a sacrificial goat on a stone altar.

He wondered how a child of Scef's Blood could have become so degraded while still so young. His problem was that he could guess—and that guess undermined the perfection if his anger.

He turned away; there was so much of far greater urgency happening now. The fate of one witch could be decided later on. The ring's use by one as weak and untutored as Zenodotus would surely place him under its chaotic domination.

Osric left the magic chamber, knowing that he faced a battle unlike any he had faced before. He stepped outside into a heavy fog.

Axidares kept his men in order as they groped through the mist with *gladioli* drawn. The dense mist disallowed coordination between his five-man search squads. The ex-Thracian was advancing with his men in a line with no more than three paces more separating him from his fellows. So far they had not accomplished more than the scaring up of a few ornamental roe deer.

Suddenly, a man gave a shriek from out of the fog. The searchers with Axidares froze. He slugged the man nearest him. "Are you idiots, men, or just garden statues? Move!"

Move they did, but the guardsmen betrayed their jumpiness with every step. A moment later, they came to the original area of the shout, the cliff-edge behind the villa complex.

"Here!" yelled a guard. Rufus and the others came up to gather around the discovery. Gruder, the burned man, lay face-up on the grass, a gory piece missing from his throat.

"Witchcraft!" cried a man.

"Demons!" yelled another.

Axidares silenced them with a shout. Just then, a shadowy form wobbled out of the heavy mist. The ex-Thracian motioned his men to form up against the stranger and then shouted: "Who's there? Identify yourself or die!"

The intruder said nothing, but didn't have to. A clearer sight of him made the soldiers stare. It was not a man but a man's *corpse*, bloated, rotted, and partially-devoured by time and by the things in the sea.

Suddenly, an unseen Germanic voice yelped, but the cry was quelled as suddenly as it began. Axidares told Rufus to check out the problem, but to watch himself. Hibernicus stalked forward carefully and came face to face with another animated lich—a skull-faced horror almost devoid of flesh. The guard who had shouted would shout no more; the abomination held his slack corpse in a skeletal grip.

Rufus hurried back to his team leader with his report. "Fall back, men!" Axidares bellowed. The Germans could see several more of the impossible creatures stepping like insects into view. Hibernicus swung his blade at the monster nearest him and burst its head like a rotten melon. The released matter sprayed his face and arms and the stench was incredible, so offensive that he was sent stumbling away, retching. The other guards were disappearing, Axidares unable to control them....

The clamor of his returning soldiers brought Gaius down from his hiding place. "Caesar!" shouted Macro, running breathlessly to the foot of the staircase where his imperator stood.

"What has happened?" the younger man demanded. "Where is Zenodotus? If you've let him escape alive..."

"No, Caesar," the prefect began, but a cry made them all turn. There, staggering down the corridor, was a small lich with ragged gray skin, worms feeding where eyes should have been, wearing a few gold and silver bangles like a dancing girl might carry.

"Hold it back!" Gaius shrieked.

Suddenly, someone rushed the creature from a side hall and hacked it down. His first stroke cut its spine; the next few slices removed its rotted, barnacle-encrusted limbs, taking away its mobility, if not its unnatural animation. Gaius recognized the guard standing over it.

"Hibernicus! B-Bless you, warrior!" jabbered the emperor. "From here on, you are my friend."

The secutor had lost his own squad in the fog and had fallen back to the villa as his next best choice—as, he now saw, had Axidares and a dozen others.

"Caesar!" exclaimed Macro. "We must see to your safety. Let us evacuate this accursed island before it's too late."

"From where are they coming?" asked Gaius.

"I saw scores of them climbing the sea cliff like spiders," volunteered Rufus.

"Then the road to the landing might still be clear!" said the princeps. "Axidares, you must protect your emperor's retreat at all costs! They must not reach the village! Macro and I will send back help—from the mainland."

The two of them jogged away, leaving Axidares and his surviving men behind in fear and chagrin.

Rufus scowled after the fainthearts. He wondered if he would live long enough to find out what, exactly, the friendship of Gaius Caesar was worth!

Down a side corridor, oblivious to the commotion from the main atrium, a goat ran with silent stride. It paused at a dark, descending stair, sniffed the air, and skipped nimbly down the steps. The dimness at the bottom was no impediment to its golden, glowing orbs. The beast moved as if it knew exactly what it sought. If there had been human eyes about, they would have seen the creature's shaggy outline blur and alter. The humanoid shape that it took on halted at the entrance to Zenodotus' magic room and looked inside.

The bound woman inside stared back. *Galar!* Phaedra mewed urgently through the gag. Thank Heid it was him! Where had the earthworm been?

"Glaejord has not done well," a thin voice whined mockingly. But he made no move to free her. It was always hard for anyone to find a friendly look behind his luminous eyes, but just now it was impossible.

"Galar is less than an animal to Frigerd. Yet he must save the Glaejord yet again. Should he?"

Phaedra sank back against the stone altar. His rebellious tone promised trouble. Galar had been ordered to hide on the emperor's fleet under an illusionary disguise, but the dvergson had been sulky for the entire trip and had not shown himself usefully until now.

"Galar hurt the red giant. Frigerd might have slain him in the room of the black-bearded king in Caesar's house, but did not. Frigerd does not help Galar."

The witch shook her head, part in exasperation, part in fear. She wondered how violently he hated her—and how he might act out that hatred.

"The sorcerer Zenodotus calls *draugar* from the sea," the dwarf told her. "Caesar's soldiers shall not keep them away from this room for long."

Phaedra stared into his face—worried, but unwilling to plead.

"Galar shall go...."

Death Walks

Chapter XXIV

The Engle had been assailed by a mob of the undead shortly after exiting the house. Osricus struck an attacker's worm-bored skull. It collapsed into a soft mash of rotted bone and maggoty flesh. He darted through the door of the Villa Jovis, slamming it shut and throwing the bolt.

Draugar! Such creatures of chaos never rose by themselves, nor was it easy to raise them. Here, so far away from the northland, the ring Andvaranaut *had* to be responsible.

Had Zenodotus no sense at all? In Germania, no creation of the sorcerer's craft was more feared than the draug. Did he not realize that any man dying from a draug's wound would rise from the grave as a draug himself? Why did the man wish that? The undead were driven by a lust for flesh and blood. In a day, Capri could be left with no other inhabitants than a host of mindless, cannibalistic dead.

From afar, Osricus heard the clash of arms and hurried for the sound of the fighting. To fight draugar effectively, a warrior had to know their ways and their weaknesses—a type of knowledge that must be very scarce this far south.

In a nearby room, two bodyguards were shoulder to shoulder against a mob of clawing, jaw-snapping draugar. Some appeared not long dead—others were nothing more than partial skeletons, lurching spasmodically like giant beetles. Many severed hands and arms littered the floor around them, and these detached appendages were still grasping at the defenders' boots.

One large draug lunged through an open window. A spatha point pierced its cold, still heart and did no harm. The creature hooked an arm around the head of its assailant and pulled him over the sill, his bony limb being much stronger than should have been. The second man sought to seize his comrade's kicking feet, but his strength was nothing against the combined might of several liches intent upon dragging their victim away.

Osricus sprang into the room, hailed the remaining soldier from behind and urged him to retreat. The bodyguard didn't know him, but liked his advice. Two rooms away they found several other living men engaged with the dead. "Swords are useless," the rune-warrior shouted. "A blunt blow can kill them!" Picking up a hefty, iron-plated chest, the Engle hurled it into the faces of the draugar horde, crushing several and giving the embattled bodyguards respite.

One soldier, taking the newcomer's advice, grabbed a tripod and folded the legs to use as an iron club. Osricus' attention shifted to a wide staircase that flowed down into the chamber from above, where there were the sounds of fighting. Three guardsmen were backing down the stairs, fighting for every step. Several liches from upstairs were pressing them hard.

Osricus lifted a bronze-framed chair and ran up the stairs yelling to the fighters to make way. They dodged from his path and he hurled the chair into the face of a draug, smashing its skull and banishing its animating force. He shouted to the men to use blunt weapons, as he had before.

Another draug, craftier than most of its kind—or maybe only clumsier—toppled over the buffed-wood stair rail, landed unhurt, and placed itself behind the defenders. A growth of seaweed draped the small thing, a thing that had died still a child, dropped from the cliff for some petty offense done an aged tyrant.

While Osricus contested with a huge lich in the now-oversized armor of a wasted and long-dead Praetorian, one German bodyguard broke out of the melee, armed himself with a free-standing candle-holder, ran a few steps toward the draug child and delivered a blow with all his might. The impact broke the creature off at the spine. Its wavering legs and hips balanced themselves upright for just a moment, then fell over sideways, its unnatural life snuffed out like a candle-flame.

"That's it!" Osricus shouted. "Go about the house and show the others how to destroy these demons!"

As the guardsman nodded and stomped off, Osricus got in a good blow that at last quelled his armored adversary. Then he snatched a silver tray from a table and hastily scratched some runes into its rubbed surface with his dagger. Finally, holding it before his body like a buckler, the rune-warrior sang a chant for the banishing of unquiet spirits. It was a mighty enchantment, one learned by rote at Loderod's feet; attempting it expended the last of the power which he still retained from his encounter with Phaedra.

The draugar slowed, partially shackled by the runic spell, but did not perish. Osricus cursed in disappointment and backed away. Andvaranaut's spell upon the living dead was too strongly fixed for any lesser magic to undo.

At that moment, a half-dozen dazed, ashen-faced bodyguards stumbled into the chamber, their expressions betraying near-panic. Of them all, only Rufus Hibernicus seemed able to still speak intelligibly:

"So you finally turn up!"

"Have the portals been held?" Osricus demanded anxiously.

"We'd need five hundred men to close off a house this big. While we were busy defending the doors and windows, they entered by the upper floors. They got our tribune, Axidares; we're all that's left."

"I know another way to fight them," said the rune-warrior. "Fire! We need fresh wooden poles. Is there a garden?"

"Listen!" Hibernicus bawled to the men up ahead. "This man is a wizard. Let's do what he says. We need wooden poles! Come on!"

The soldiers who were still engaged broke off, and the nine remaining warriors followed the Engle and the Hibernian along alabaster corridors into an as-yet unviolated peristyle. They barricaded the doors behind them, but they were of light construction and would not hold for long. The indoor garden contained pots holding growing saplings, and Osricus directed the bodyguards to make trimmed staffs for themselves. Mostly ex-woodsmen, they worked quickly using their service knives.

"Now put your lances into this urn!" the Engle directed. They did so and the rune-warrior proceeded to circle his arms around the upright staves while droning a chant of the *brimrunar*, making the elements subject to his directing will.

Suddenly, there was a flash of blue sparks. In the next few seconds, the whole bundle was hotly aflame at their top ends. Unnaturally, the wood was only hosting the blue spirit-fire, not being consumed by it.

"Arm yourselves!" the Engle commanded. "Now we leave this accursed mountain top!"

Every man carrying his own magical torch, the band rushed for the nearest outside door and yanked it open. The draugar on the other side staggered through it to attack. The first of these was dressed like an Egyptian mage, an ankh talisman dangling from his putrid neck.

The German bodyguards plunged ahead, bellowing a cry of "Woden!" and striking at the ghouls with their jets of living flame. The undead swarms burned like sawdust under the purifying heat. But the sheer number of living dead was appalling due to Tiberius's sadistic passion for watching executions.

After the initial surprise, the draugar stiffened their resistance, burning, bursting, but refusing to yield a foot of ground. A guard cried out, then another. Filthy arms were wresting them to the earth. Another German man screamed as a hastily-swung torch sliced across his belly, roasting his bowels.

Hibernicus pummeled his way through the ghouls wielding the leg of a bench. The other survivors, despairing of aiding their savaged or burned companions, followed through the gap he made, fending off the draugar with flame. Out on open ground, they were at last able to outrun the stumbling dead men. As they spread out, they became invisible to one another in the supernatural fog.

Osricus and Hibernicus let the others go on. The flaming torches they still held had been fading for the last few minutes and now they extinguished themselves entirely.

"My power is spent," Osricus gasped. "I can maintain them no longer."

"Well, this is a fine time for burning out," the Hibernian grumbled.

"Flee if you must, friend," the Engle panted. "But I cannot go. Too much evil will be set loose in the world so long as Zenodotus holds that ring!"

Hibernicus frowned, not sure what to do now that he was not immediately fighting for his life.

As Galar backed away from Phaedra, she moaned, shook her head, and looked imploringly at one who should have been her servant.

"So, does Frigerd understand that Galar is important, too?"

She closed her eyes tightly and nodded.

"If Galar takes away the gag, will Frigerd swear on her soul that she will grant him three boons?"

Again she nodded.

"Galar shall permit Frigerd to speak. Do not try to bespell him."

He took the soaked sash out from between the witch's jaws. She swallowed down great mouthfuls of air.

"Frigerd must promise to make Galar a great, handsome man," said the dwarf. "She must use her best runes to conquer Tatia's heart for Galar. Give her not only lust, but also love. And Frigerd must never try to harm Galar or Tatia."

The witch hissed through clenched teeth: "I swear!"

"Now bind your words with magic!"

"I so bind them," the Swede promised reluctantly.

"Galar is satisfied. Know this. I will help you to claim Andvaranaut for Heid, but after that Galar shall be free."

"Be free, be dead, be anything you want to be, but be *gone!*" Phaedra snarled. Concentrating her will against her bonds, she hoarsely whispered unlocking runes and the ropes fell away. The witch, sitting up quickly, rubbed the circulation back into her hands and feet.

"Glaejord!" Galar yelped.

The Scandian looked to the doorway and saw a shriveled, blue-skinned draug wavering there. A rune leaped to her lips, but when the draug stepped into the magic room, it collapsed face-down, inert. The witch did not know why.

Of course! Zenodotus had warded the room for her protection, still intending to wrest her secrets from her. She flashed angry that the Greek feared her so little that he was deigning to protect her. Yet she realized that she had only herself to blame. She had done too little to make her enemy fear her. Throughout all history, only *fear* had been the proven way to wrest respect from a foe. That was the good lesson, along with so many others, that the Siton witches had taught her.

She steeled herself, knowing that the cause was lost unless she took the ring from Zenodotus. Nothing else mattered as much.

Phaedra wailed a spell of black runes and the physical change she wanted came over her with terrible swiftness.

The Swedish girl cried out as agonizing cramps curled her up like a fetus. Bristling hair erupted from her fair skin and her darkening face stretched and changed like clay worked by a sculptor's fingers. Her ears, lengthening, became pointed. When the convulsions at last stilled, a powerful beast rolled over onto its belly, panting.

The freakish wolf-thing walked from the room, growing stronger as the power of Nifelhel flowed into her.

Zenodotus stood overlooking the sea from the Cliff of Tiberius, grinning with childlike exuberance at the gleaming band of rune-cut gold on his right hand. Through his experiments, he had discovered that his limited knowledge of useful spells posed more of an obstacle to his desired undertakings than did any limitation on his ability to use spells. Powerful spells that he had previously failed to perform successfully he could now invoke with great ease.

Raising an army from the dead had been a good example of that. His previous necromantic experiments had never accomplished more than causing the fingers of an executed criminal to move a little.

Zenodotus gloried in the idea of raising every uncremated corpse entombed along the Appian Way, from Capua to Rome itself. In his mind's eye, he could already envision a host of ghouls marching on Rome, performing with a ferocity that even Hannibal himself could not equal.

Another wonderful thing was how his senses now extended beyond his own body. By means of an internal third eye, he watched Gaius and Macro flee from the villa, saw them run down the Via Tiberio. He could have slain the both of them with a concentrated thought, but it amused him to prolong their unmanning terror. He laughingly sent ghostly wails in their wake, driving them babbling like madmen all the way to the village of Capri.

Gaius and his loyal dog Macro would find no safety out on the water. Dark things plied the sea, and these Zenodotus might call upon to serve his bidding—tentacled monsters for dragging down the greatest of ships, races older than Man which infested submarine cities that were expert at inflicting torture. The souls of both emperor and prefect soon would be bleating with despair in the exitless darkness of Harag-Kolathos.

While enjoying his fantasies, Zenodotus paid scant attention to the battle inside the villa, or the bodyguards trying to flee from it. It was only an afterthought that made him scan the scene by clairvoyance. He saw that most were dead and that little trace was left of them; the ghouls were still feeding on the bodyguards' carcasses, poking warm entrails into their decayed jaws with skeletal fingers.

But the wizard frowned to observe that two men still strode the ground alive and fit. One was a guardsman—a common lout; the other....

The Engle!

That man was a threat that he could not ignore.

Zenodotus sent his undead minions a mental command, ordering them to slack their pursuit. This called for his *personal* attention.

When the omnipresent sounds of staggering, dragging and limping feet faded, the Hibernian and the Engle paused for breath in the shade of a grape arbor. "I think we've lost the dead men," Rufus suggested hopefully.

"They may be seeking easier pray. Very soon, I fear, they will shamble down to the village below."

"Well, you're the sorcerer! What can anyone do about it?"

"I am *not* a sorcerer!" Osricus snarled. "But even if I were, no power less than Andvaranaut's can put down what the Ring of Sorcery has itself raised."

"You talk as if that thing is alive...."

"There is less difference between the dead and the living than one might suppose." Just then, the Engle heard a rustle overhead.

Too swift to be evaded, a mass of grapevines dropped like netting from the boughs overhead, ensnaring them both swifter than an African python.

Rufus fought their grip like a wild aurochs roped by a *laqueurius*. Flexible vines simultaneously bound Osricus' hands against his body, so tightly that he could not reach his blade. Tendrils as supple as a noose started to strangle him, preventing the Engle to shout out even the weakest rune spell of self-defense.

As they stood entrapped, a lean shape emerged from the fog.

"We meet again, German," Zenodotus said. Now well dressed, the Alexandrian scarcely resembled the wretch whom Osricus had rescued from a prison cellar. But no part of his wardrobe interested Osricus except for the annulet on his slender second finger.

"Now I know why so many crave to possess this ring," the Greek said. "Had I donned it when I first found it in Germania, I would be ruler of the empire by now." He held Andvaranaut so close to Osricus' straight-chiseled nose that the youth could have bent his head and touched it, taunting him with its nearness. On impulse, Zenodotus mentally commanded the Engle's neck vines to loosen, just enough to enable his speech.

"Fool!" the German choked. "Don't you see that the ring is possessing *you?*"

"I do feel something, and the sensation is very pleasant."

"You can never be master of Andvaranaut. You lack inner strength and are but a thrall to its evil influence."

"How can I be a slave if I can do anything I want to do? If some of its influence is baleful, I will take measures to banish it."

"Do you speak of measures involving the witch Phaedra?"

"Aye, Phaedra. As long as she may usefully school me, I can permit her to live. I make you the same offer, too, Osricus. Your father knew more about the ring than anyone. How much did he teach you? Having your testimony to compare to the witch's should prove useful."

The power-besotted fool was doomed, Osricus knew, but before Andvaranaut claimed his evil life, what additional harm did he intend to do? To gain time, the German feigned interest:

"I prefer living to dying," he began, then broke off, as if staring in astonishment at something over Zenodotus' shoulder. Automatically, the magician turned his head. When he did so, the Engle shouted out a rune of terror.

The fear that came upon Zenodotus broke the Greek's mental control over the vines and Osricus felt them slacken. But the sorcerer shook off the terror and barked: "Close!"

The vines tightened like slipknots, shutting off the blood from both men's hands and feet and commencing their slow strangulation.

"Fool!" the Greek sorcerer said. "Do you prefer death to cooperation?"

The rune-warrior's eyes flashed with defiance.

"I see. You've made your choice. You will die very slowly. So far I've held my foul-smelling servants at bay. Now they shall have my leave to feast. Pray that you are throttled before the ghouls come to feed."

Suddenly, a gray blur struck the magician like a shot fired by an onager. Both he and it rolled across the grass, their outlines softened by the fog's density. But through it, Osricus made out a brief wrestle, heard a growl, and then came the loud report of flashing lightning. In unison, both man and beast screamed—one like a man and one like a brute.

Osricus, still watching, made out the brutish outlines of a wolf hunching over the outstretched form of Zenodotus. The creature tore at the Greek's chest and began gulping down chunks of gore, and doing so with frantic haste.

Then the creature attacked the arm of Zenodotus that bore Andvaranaut, its powerful jaws worried it violently. With a tearing sound, the limb came free at the elbow. That prize between its fangs, the werewolf loped away into the mist.

Andvaranaut

CHAPTER XXV

Without Zenodotus to control them, the grapevines fell flaccid about the limbs of the trapped men. Alas, by the time it took them to disentangle themselves, the wolf was long gone the misty air was filled with the rustling, drag-footed steps of prey-seeking draugar.

Rufus's booted foot doubled up the first one as it appeared out of the fog. Then, arming himself with the statuette-club that Osricus had been using, he laid about like a Scandian berserker.

"Get that damned ring back!" Rufus bawled at Osricus. "I'll keep this garbage off your track as long as I can!"

The Engle hesitated to abandon a friend, but knew the guardsman was right. "Until we meet in Valhalla!" he exclaimed and resumed his run sped away past the torn body of Zenodotus.

The fog, hanging thickly over the cliff-side grove, put Osricus' tracking skill to the limit, forcing him to proceed slowly—though every emotion was impelling him to greater haste.

He spied a dark stain on the grass and knelt there. When he touched, it left his fingers scarlet-dyed. Its smell was unmistakable.

The bleeding arm of Zenodotus was leaving a trail behind the fleeing werewolf. He guessed that Phaedra couldn't use the ring in werewolf form, so she would be eager to revert—and that would give him his chance to spring from the mist and slay her. He scarcely had a plan; he was simply allowing the gods to be his guide, opening his mind and spirit so that they might use him as best they could. He felt himself prodded to rise and continue the search.

Then, long before he expected it, his quest was concluded.

Out of the fog materialized a structure that looked like a small Roman-style stone house. Coming closer, he realized it was a house not for men but gods, a large shrine. Halfway up its front steps, sprawling across them unconscious, was Phaedra. She was wearing a woman's shape once again, and next to her rested the gory trophy wrested from the dead body of Zenodotus.

With his gladius ready, Osricus cautiously advanced. Standing over the girl, he saw her own bloody hand clutching her belly, holding a wound resembling both a tear and a burn. The blood that he had been following, it now appeared, had not been solely that of the slain magician. The meaning of the lightening flash that preceded Zenodotus' death was now made clear—a sorcerous blast that had mortally wounded the wolf-witch.

He pressed an index finger to her jaw and touched a pulse still faintly beating. Ironic, he thought, that the object of her long quest now lay within her reach with all the power she needed to save her life, but she was too weak to use it. The witch had no chance without the healing of the *limrunar*. But far worse than mere physical death would be that which would come upon her beyond the gates of life.

The creature of Heid next opened her eyes, she would find herself barefoot and naked on a path of thorns stretching out as far as her eyes could see. There would be a steep descent lit by volcanic fires, leading nowhere except into the torture pits ruled by the goddess Hel, whose trolls inflicted unending torture.

With an effort of will, he turned away from the doomed girl and with loathing picked up the severed arm of Zenodotus.

It still wore the Ring. Finally, here it was, the prize that Osricus had sought. So many had to die for him to possess this ring. But for the good of his own soul he dared not so much as touch it—and using it would absolutely destroy him.

He needed to return it to Germania and find a hiding place for it there. Mere concealment would not be enough. It needed to be sealed away using the strongest magic possible.

Warned by an instinct, he whirled suddenly.

They came out of the mist in a solid mass, a score of draugar or more, cutting off any retreat to the front or flanks. He scrambled up the remaining marble steps and crossed the platform-like floor of the shrine's interior, passing a bronze statue of Hercules.

He stopped short at the misty rear of the shrine—above a precipitous drop into the Tyrrhenian Sea.

Osricus spun around the face the draugar. If he fought, he would die. The ring would lie where it was dropped, to work its evil later upon the slave or soldier who casually picked it up. After the draugar had devoured his flesh, they would climb down from the mountain and slay everyone on the Isle of Capri. The broken remains of half-eaten wretches would then also become draugar. If all the island were draugar, would that confine the danger?

No. He knew many stories of the draugar, including that the undead could not drown and did not fear the sea. A draug who could find no human food might throw himself into the sea and be carried by the wind and wave to another land. Then the killing would begin again. The more that draug attacked, the more of his accursed kind he could create.

Could the Roman Empire deal with the danger? Osricus doubted it. These southerners knew nothing of this monster of the North; panic would keep them from acting together in time.

If the draugar advanced beyond Italy, they would cover the lands in a tide of such numbers that not even the Germans with all their tribes mustered could stand up to such an infestation.

Against the end of all life, what was the fate of one man's soul?

Now, Osricus realized, he was standing where Loderod had stood many, many decades earlier.

His master had also sworn never to wear the ring. But the world was not an ideal place. Loderod could not hide his eyes from the suffering all around him. That was his dilemma. He had the power to help many within his grasp, but if he did so, he himself would be lost.

He had accepted that price and used the ring against Germania's many mighty enemies for a span of over a hundred years. He had learned how to evade the will of the ring to slay him, but he could not evade it forever.

It had taken Loderod years before he felt forced to don the ring.

Osric was feeling forced to do this, on the first hour of his first day.

He was letting himself be guided by the gods, and he thought he was hearing the urgings of the gods plainly. Fate had chosen him to be the master of Andvaranaut. Götterdämmerung would not begin today.

Osricus tore the ring Andvaranaut from Zenodotus' bloody hand and donned it. He shrieked aloud as the astonishing energies of the golden band fed into him. He dropped to his knees and clutched at the little altar to Hercules inside the shrine, fighting down the turbulence in his mind and spirit. So hotly did the circlet's power burn his soul that he feared he was being consumed utterly.

There was a cry from the murk. Had the draugar found one last living human being to kill? He thought about the guardsman Rufus Hibernicus.

For just a moment, Osricus got the better of his mighty golden adversary and stood to face the host of undead executioners. Earlier he had recited the runes to shatter the spell which animated the draugar—and had failed. But that was before when Osricus had not ben wearing the Ring of Sorcery....

"Hlaoj naujur k'var njatra vaela vatta Lod!" he yelled in a voice like the storm-driven surf. *"Deren og bindelser!"*

The flood of Andvaranaut's power rushing through his soul staggered him and took his breath away. Finally the pain slowed and stopped, like water emptied from a vessel.

Osricus stumbled to the front of the shrine. There he saw the draugar, wavering weakly on spindly, wasted legs, dropping to the grassy sward in groups, like dry weeds of autumn under a gardener's scythe.

With the triumph of the *bjargrunar*, the fog thinned—like a series of gauzy curtains lifted one by one. The stage those curtains revealed was a field of putrid death.

Involuntarily, his glance shifted to the body of the woman.

The woman, like him, a *sorcerer.*

A woman, like him, already damned.

Damned!

He tried not to think about the day he would die, not to think about the tortures that lay ahead when that death inevitably came.

It amazed him how doggedly her young body clung to life, like a spider holding fast to a finger that would shake it off into a fire. Why should this witch *not* die and be damned? Had Phaedra ever done even one worthwhile thing in all her life? But yet he knew the story of how witches were made. She must have been taken from her family as a child and taught to do only evil. And had not the life of that misled child been lived as a crime against both the law of the gods and the law of men? Was not every Siton witch a blight upon the world? Was it not the right thing to actually hasten her departure? In Phaedra's helpless state, he would not even need a killing spell for justice to be served.

He drew his sword....

Unbidden, old angers, old wrongs were kindled in Osricus' breast. He beheld a vision of Heremod, the murderer of his parents and brothers, the enslaver of his sisters. He saw himself smite the king with a lance of fire, heard Heremod's screams of pain. Time after time he slew his enemy, but at each death, Andvaranaut called his soul back into his tortured shell, to die yet again.

Osricus saw Rome trampled into the earth by the red-haired hosts of Germania. One man led the northern throngs—himself. The treasures of Rome filled the carts or the conquerors; its women, fatherless, husbandless thralls in throat tethers, stumbled along behind the victorious van.

He saw....

No!

Osricus knew the Ring warped and corrupted those who wore it, but had underestimated how seductive, how subtle was its call. He must master it, as Loderod had, before it made him a mad and violent creature who lived for vengence. He recalled his mentor's black rune song for the taming of Andvaranaut; there was no white rune that had any power over the terrible ring.

Osricus knelt and dipped his fingers into Phaedra's blood, the sacred blood of Scef, which had almost ceased to flow. The blood of the dead was useless. He needed her blood before it ceased to be the blood of the living.

Rising, he once again felt the pressure of the ring's will against his own. The rune-warrior climbed back up into the shrine and knelt above the floor. With quaking hands he drew a series of runes which he had hoped he would never need to use—Black Runes, which had no power to harm a soul already lost.

"Olmoth!" he cried in anguish to the air and to the earth. *"Reibathod! Erana hjorvarth blokk! Zatho gagnradmthsognir!"*

Osricus struggled to repeatedly speak the runes which would grant him mastery over the ring of Heid while the band of dverg-gold fought to twist the man's fatigued will to its own design.

"Asathod! Njarl-Ahoteg!" he wailed in defiance.

Osricus' voice fell off as he felt the Black Rune of Heid subside. The sense of an alien will at war with his own vanished like the anger of a leashed dog deciding to break off its struggle.

The warm energy which had been suffusing his body ebbed, as if Andvaranaut, too, had been momentarily sapped by the battle of wills. Osricus' head swam; by overcoming the power that had sought to make him its slave, he had dissipated both its strength and his own.

Osricus rested a moment, recovering from the ordeal, then wearily got to his feet. He glanced down at the wounded priestess of Heid. Part of him still wanted to kill her… but the rest of him knew it would be the first step down the dark path Andvaranaut wanted him to tread. He sighed, shook his head, then knelt and heaved the unconscious witch onto his shoulders.

Osricus stood on unsteady legs, stumbled down the temple stairs, and staggered out into the garden beyond, heading back to the Villa Jovis. He hadn't gone more than thirty feet when he thought he heard Rufus Hibernicus calling his name. The Engle was about to answer his friend's shout—

—when pain exploded in the back of his head. His vision filled with black stars as he crumpled to his knees, then his sight dissolved into darkness and oblivion.

Rufus had drawn the liches away from Osricus, but they still followed him. Gaining a little on them, he paused to catch his breath. Suddenly, his closest pursuer collapsed. And as soon as that one had fallen to earth, the infernal mist itself started to dissolve. It was now possible to see other fallen corpses behind the first one. Warily, he stepped among the inert corpses, detecting not a spark of animation in any of them.

From there he went looking for Osricus, passing many of the rotting dead along the way. He soon found the blood trail that Osricus had followed and guessed that it might lead him to the wolf that he must kill. Up against the sea cliff he came to a small sheltered shrine that looked to be dedicated to the Roman man-god, Hercules.

The man of Erin gave a grim smile. That was the Roman god that he liked best. What a gladiator the fellow would have made!

Rufus thought he caught a brief glimpse of Osricus stepping between bushes in the garden, and called out his name. The big man expected a response, or for the German to come back into view a couple seconds later, but neither happened.

Some inner instinct was beating a gong inside his heart. He should have felt a lot better after the collapse of the walking dead, but he was far from at ease. There was still the killer wolf to be found, for one thing.

Rufus now ran to the spot where he thought he'd sighted the young German. There lay not only Osricus, but Phaedra as well. Collapsed together in a tangled heap, the pair looked either dead or dead to the world.

From behind him came a thin, whining laugh.

Rufus, turning, saw Galar amble out from hiding behind a pillar in the shrine. The sun was glinting off his finger. The little man was wearing a very shiny golden ring.

"You!" the Hibernian muttered. "This business gets madder by the minute!"

"Frigerd is fallen; Galar is free," the tiny creature cackled. "From this day forward, Galar serves Galar!"

"What's your portion in this lunacy, shorty?" asked the bemused ex-gladiator.

"Galar's portion is this!" He displayed Andvaranaut triumphantly. "Galar has no soul, and one who has no soul cannot be locked in Nifelhel. I shall wear the ring, be great and powerful and never die!"

"Easy now," the secutor coaxed. He didn't know how, but this dwarf had to be part of all of the magical monkey business that had been going on. Was he another sorcerer? Where did this ugly little shard fit into the broken pot?

"Put that thing away," the guardsman whispered mildly. "It doesn't belong to you and it's dangerous."

The dvergson backed off, his brow knitting. "It is right for Galar to take Andvaranaut. His father's people made the Ring. With the ring, Galar becomes king, and Tatia shall be his queen!"

Tatia?

Rufus was jarred. By Lugh's Hammer! The wench had been telling the truth! Galar *had* actually been the one following her, had been the one terrorizing her. He had even…. *Gods alive!* That was all he needed to know to want to kill the man—if the ugly freak could rightly be called a man.

"Frigerd promised Galar to make him the lover that Tatia's heart seeks. But because I have the Ring, Galar does not need help from Frigerd. From today, Galar will be denied nothing he wishes to have!"

"I've got a few questions," the Hibernian said sternly. "If I don't like your answers, this will be the day you die."

"No," said Galar. "This is the day that Rufus dies. A fight to the death will decide who Tatia belongs to!

"Gujuki-varthossonar-Fafnir!" the little man shouted from the steps of the shrine.

At Galar's rune-spell, a swift change came over the diminutive creature. The Hibernian's amazement held him rooted to the spot.

Galar was rapidly getting bigger and his rough skin growing rougher, even scaly. His loose homespuns filled up, stretched to the limit, and then split open, uncovering a belly like a Nile crocodile's. The dwarf's bone structure expanded, warped, distorted. His skull grew larger too, his jaws enlarged and pushed out from his face, becoming filled with long, spike-like teeth. He looked like he was turning into some sort of reptile!

Any man who had seen fewer wonders in his life than Rufus Hibernicus would have stood dumbfounded until it was too late. But the battle-hardened secutor shook off his momentary bafflement and leapt forward with his gladius at the ready.

The alert creature dodged, but the warrior's soiled blade nicked one of its scaly arms. The metal rasped against scales like steel honing sandstone, but the wound inflicted was not disabling. It bled a mere drip of something resembling greenish bile.

The monster, having been stung, backed off a few steps, still regarding the Hibernian with murderous determination. The mutant's long blue tongue shot out, its forks rapidly vibrating. Galar was still growing and now stood as tall as Hibernicus. Its girth was expanding, too, and hide thickened to form living armor. It was even developing a tail at the end of its spine.

Damn it! Hibernicus thought. A dragon was being born.

A dragon!

Hibernicus went in for a fast kill, but he might as well have been stabbing at a rock, so adamantine was the dragon's scales. Galar repeatedly slashed at the swordsman's head with his forefeet where, behind one claw, the Ring of Sorcery gleamed.

But the dragon's movements could not be those of an instinctual predator. Rufus doubted that the dwarf had ever assumed such an outlandish shape before. The proportions and coordination of his expanding body would still feel strange to him. Hibernicus, determined not to give the beast time to grow in skill, flailed at it. His wild blows were doing little harm, but they took the initiative away from Galar and kept him reacting to his attacker's moves.

Unexpectedly, the creature slashed with a clawed foot. Hibernicus swerved in time to avoid serious injury, but a clawed toe raked a red furrow across his right thigh.

Vengefully, the secutor hacked at the dragon's face, now towering a foot above his own. When the metamorphosed dwarf flinched and staggering backwards, the swordsman decided to blind the powerful monster. He concentrated his attacks against the monster's slit-pupiled eyes, but hit Galar's clawed hands, which he was using to protect his face.

The dragon spun suddenly, its tail brought to bear as a flail. Hibernicus tried to over-leap it, but was too slow. The scaled appendage hit his left-leg greave with an audible clang.

The blow gave him a bruising injury, but the wounded man kept his footing and stumbled away, taking shelter inside the shrine behind the bronze monument to Hercules. Rufus gave the abomination due credit; its tail trick had been a crafty one. Galar was swiftly learning the use of his unfamiliar armaments. The Hibernian had to get in a killing attack very soon or else he would be outclassed and very, very dead.

With a roar like a brass trumpet, the monster lunged at him, throwing its weight against the statue. The bronze tottered and then plummeted backwards. Rufus sprang away just in time, but the effort sent fiery pain through his injured leg. He limped away, down the steps of the shrine to the lawn, leaving the initiative with Galar.

The dragon followed after Hibernicus, cornering him against a thick hedge of rose thorns. Roaring like the dragon he resembled, Galar pressed his advantage, leading his attack with claws like flying daggers.

Rufus ran painfully back inside the shrine again, guessing its small interior would disadvantage his larger attacker. He limped to the shrine's low-ceilinged far end—but now the ex-gladiator was hemmed in, as the temple on that side overlooked the sea cliff.

Rufus heard a thud behind him, along with an animalistic cry of pain. Galar had lurched at him, but unused to his great stature, had banged his head—hard—against the shrine's architrave. With the dragon reeling stunned, he saw his last and fleeting chance to execute a meaningful attack.

Holding his sword like a javelin, he made a cast, hoping that the dragon's throat was less armored than his breast. But a chance stagger by Galar, obviously dazed by the blow to his skull, caused the blade to glance off the side of his neck instead. Rufus was now disarmed, but with the dragon stumbling his way, he ducked under Galar's arm and lay hold of it. Blocking one scaled ankle with his own leg, he gave a sharp tug and shifted all his weight forward, utilizing a throw taught to him by a Greek wrestler.

The badly-coordinated dragon crashed to the marble floor, its own momemtum keeping its unwieldly bulk rolling—right over the platform's edge and into the empty air.

A mournful roar followed Galar's plunge all the way down, to strike and bounce off the sea-washed rocks at the base of Tiberius' Cliff.

Hibernicus could see its broken body far below, sliding off the boulders and disappearing under the waves and foam.

THE DAMNED

EPILOGUE

"Why so glum?" Rufus Hibernicus asked his friend, Marcus Anglius Osricus. "The world is better off with the Ring—and Galar—at the bottom of the Tyrrhenian Sea, isn't it?"

The two men, both of similar barbarian stamp, found much in common. They had pushed aside the simple furnishings of Hibernicus' domus and now sat cross-legged upon rugs. Within their reach was a wholesome repast of vegetables and meat. This would be their last meal together before the German began his long trek north.

"One would hope so," Osricus answered gloomily. "Did the emperor reward you well?" he asked, changing the subject. The ex-gladiator had reported a rather embellished tale of how he alone had survived the fight and had cinched the defeat of the magician.

"Caligula took a bad scare on Capri," replied Rufus. "I actually couldn't tell whether he was glad that Zenodotus was dead or not. Anyway, out of 'gratitude,' he gave me a paltry few thousand sestertii and promoted me to optio. If I had known he was going to be so stingy, I would have filled another sack with loot from the Villa Jovis. Not that I could have handled any more weight on a banged up leg, before that magic of yours cured it." Rufus regarded his bare leg, marked with those strange glyphs that the Engle claimed he had used to heal his wound.

Though Rufus could grin, he had the uneasy feeling that Rome was in a bad way with such an emperor. Gaius had managed to hold himself together and made a big show out of interring the ashes of his mother and brother in Augustus' mausoleum, but a strange depression had prevented him from attending Antonia's funeral. Rome, misunderstanding his mood, had set its tongues wagging about how he had watched her pyre burn from a high window while dining without concern.

From the kitchen, there came a clatter of disturbed furniture, of dropping pots and pans, all accompanied by feminine snarls. A moment later, Tatia entered, balancing a pitcher of wine with one hand and dragging Phaedra by a twist of her golden curls in the other. The Iberian forced the Swedish girl down to her knees and said, "She will do nothing she is told; she ought to be whipped!"

Osricus addressed his captive severely. "Girl, are you unaware of how much mercy you have already been shown?"

Phaedra stood up and glowered at the Engle. Tatia, kneeling beside Hibernicus, poured him a cup of Caeubum wine. Unlike Phaedra's, her motions were graceful. Behind her, the Swede looked away from the man who called her his "spear captive," seething with indignation.

The ex-gladiator turned an appreciating glance toward Phaedra, and not for the first time. She was wearing a briefly-cut serving girl's tunic, her tresses left unbound and carelessly combed. Hibernicus noticed that she frequently tugged the hem of her skirt down to cover her left hip—mortified, no doubt, by the mark on it. Rufus had found the Engle passed out not far from the shrine of Hercules, and the unconscious blonde girl lying with him where he fell. Apparently, Osricus had been carrying the wench toward the villa when he was waylaid by Galar, who had knocked him senseless and stolen the ring from his finger. After Rufus had revived the German with a few sharp slaps, Osricus had somewhat impulsively saved Phaedra's life by applying the healing *limrunar*—then immediately affixed another rune upon her thigh while she still lay senseless. He'd said it was a Black Rune, like the one that Phaedra had placed upon his breast days earlier. Apparently, it had put a stop to her magical nonsense.

Hibernicus, as he savored his wine, noticed Tatia looking at him strangely. "What are you thinking about, love?" he asked.

"Nothing, Master," she answered. "I am only grateful that Galar is finally gone."

Unexpectedly, the secutor reached out and pulled the Iberian against himself. He pressed his drink cup to her mouth, and then licked the sweet beverage from her upraised lips. The girl found his roughhousing exciting and locked her arms around his thick neck, covering his mouth with hers.

Yet Hibernicus sensed there was a trace of pain in her kisses. He would have liked to know her thoughts, but he was no better at reading a woman's mind than was any other man.

In fact, Tatia was thinking that she belonged to one who never, truly, would let himself belong to her or to any other woman. She knew him well enough to know that loving Rufus Hibernicus meant accepting that fact.

Tatia had been working very hard to do that. But would it continue to be possible to go on that way forever, or even go on as long as the day after tomorrow?

"Why did you spare me, Engle?" Phaedra demanded. "To humiliate me daily? To display me to all Germania as a trophy of battle? To be condemned and publicly stoned as a sorceress? *Ha!* You are as much a sorcerer as I ever was!"

In truth, the Engle was not at all certain about what his answer should be. His decision not to kill this woman had been emotional with no rational plan behind it. All he knew was that some inner voice had warned him not to strike.

Now, days having passed, he realized that the two of them had some common ground. She was the only woman alive who could understand his own anguish, because she shared it with him. But he worried that the *real* reason was that she was the most beautiful woman he had ever met. He didn't like showing weakness, and uxoriousness had brought many a man to ruin. He would have to be very careful not to walk in their shoes. He decided to speak from his mind, not his heart.

"My reason for sparing you is simple," he said. "I'm unable to deny the fact of my sorcery. As I cannot repudiate it, I must use it well while I live, and need to understand it completely. Alive, you shall be able to teach me what you know about the Black Runes and, also, their fashioning."

"Why does a man like you need, or desire, to command dark power?" she asked with a suspicious frown.

"Too long has the Cult of Heid and its allies been allowed to attack the gods' order in Midgard. Too often Loderod carried on the war with them defensively. I cannot but think that the initiative should not be left with them. Your knowledge of their ways is the weapon I need most to defeat them."

Phaedra raised her chin defiantly. Did the man think she would serve him against her own people?

But then, as his words sank in, she reflected. How much did she owe her former teachers? They had killed her parents, made her their tool, taught her to be bold in using the Black Runes, and had taken all hope from her. Even if she could escape from her present captivity, what use would they have for her in her present condition? And what could possibly take the debilitating rune from her flesh except the power of the lost Andvaranaut itself?

She laughed bitterly. The witches did not indulge failure and helplessness. What use did they have for her except, perhaps, the breeding of as many children of the Blood as possible? A miserable fate! She was probably better off with the Engle.

Phaedra's eyes strayed to the lighted window. Everyone whom she had ever depended on had sooner or later betrayed her. She never had lived a life that was her own. She had always been used as a wooden chip in a game of gods and men. And it was a terrible game. One day it must avalanche both heaven and earth down into a common doom.

A doom called Gotterdammerung.

Listening to Phaedra and Osricus bantering reminded Rufus of just how young the both of them really were. He sensed something between the pair—a fate, perhaps. It was obvious to everyone, except—as it appeared—themselves.

On one hand there was Osricus, speaking logical reasons as to why he had no choice but to keep the wench of his passion continually beside himself. On the other was Phaedra, protesting her wretched lot and her ill treatment, but speaking in a tone of voice that didn't ring true. They both were damaged people, and both were in need of healing. Could they ever be kind to one another, growing out of such parched soil? Or would their pain just be added together? Hibernicus couldn't give good odds for a happy outcome, but stranger things had happened.

And the man of Erin had a few strange stories of his own to tell. If there was ever a good reason to spawn a mess of grandchildren, it would be for the opportunity to tell them how he had fought and slain a dragon. Even the heroes of old couldn't steal a march on Rufus Hibernicus.

He heard Osricus call for a cup of wine. Phaedra, with a resigned sigh, picked up a pitcher and refilled his vessel. As she offered it to his browned hands, her glance searched his face—for what? Approval? And, meanwhile, his eyes were fixed on her, drinking in her beauty and grace, while hoping to find... something more. These subtle looks were not things that the Hibernian could miss.

To the man of Erin, love was a simple thing, really. One didn't have to over-think it. Like the sun and the breeze, it came when it wanted to come, and while one had it, it couldn't be controlled, only enjoyed. He hoped for both of the pair that they found that simple secret out before they killed each other.

About the Author

Glenn A. Rahman, in the '70s and '80s, was a frequent per-computer era contributor to the semi-pro scene, such as *Fantasy Crosswinds*, *Eldritch Tales*, and *Crypt of Cthulhu*. His first professional publication came with the release of the fantasy board game *Divine Right*, published by TSR, Inc. in 1979. This was followed by *Knights of Camelot* (1980, TSR), the *Trojan War* (1980, Metagaming), and *Down with the King* (1980, Avalon Hill). During this time, Glenn Rahman and his brother Philip (founder of the still-extant Fedogan and Bremer book company, specializing in Cthulhu Mythos and supernaturally-themed literature) created a two-part article for *Sorcerer's Apprentice*, the *Lovecraft Variant* and the *Monsters of the Cthulhu Mythos* which amounted to the first successful transference of H.P. Lovecraft's style of supernatural literature into a modern role-playing format. In addition, Mr. Rahman has continued to publish board gaming and fantasy role-playing articles and supplements widely. His first book-length fictional work was serialized in *Dragon Magazine* (beginning in 1980), entitled *The Minarian Legends*, which keyed off his original *Divine Right* universe. In 2001, Sidecar Books of Minneapolis, MN published his *Gardens of Lucullus*, a Cthulhu Mythos novel in collaboration with Richard L. Tierney.

MORE BOOKS FROM PICKMAN'S PRESS

SORCERY AGAINST CAESAR

Simon of Gitta, escaped slave turned magician, roves the Roman Empire battling dark magic and demons, all while pursued by Caesar's soldiers in sixteen stories by Richard L. Tierney and others that combine historical fiction, sword & sorcery, and Lovecraftian Horror.

THE DRUMS OF CHAOS

In the Holy Lands, Simon become entangled in an occult plot call down a monstrous alien entity to herald a new aeon on Earth. Simon and his allies race against time to prevent the extinction of all life on Earth—but can they really thwart a covert scheme backed by the power of the Roman Empire?

REASSURING TALES

Creatures sinister but unseen. Madmen who may not be so mad. Realities that twist into astonishing patterns. Insidious new technologies beyond our understanding or control. Welcome to the existential weird fiction of master storyteller T.E.D. Klein, author of bestselling novel *The Ceremonies* and award-winning collection *Dark Gods*.

THE AVEROIGNE ARCHIVES

All of Clark Ashton Smith's weird tales of Averoigne—the sinister, monster-haunted province of medieval France—are collected into one volume. Werewolves and satyrs stalk dark forests, witches and necromancers lurk in swamps, and giants terrorize the cathedral city of Vyônes in the heart of Averoigne.

THE AVEROIGNE LEGACY

Over two dozen tribute tales and poems set in Clark Ashton Smith's world of Averoigne. Revisit Vyônes and Périgon, meet Luc le Chaudronnier and Azédarac once again, as tales of harpies and vampires, ogres and giants, changelings and cockatrices await you!

CORPORATE CTHULHU

Just like the Great Old Ones, corporations are powerful but unseen entities we have no control over, yet subtly manipulate our lives and our world—and we don't even realize it. Endure twenty-five Mythos tales of bureaucratic nightmare, but remember: it's nothing personal—just business.